Praise for the novels

Someone Saw Something

"A taut, harrowing read, with explosive twists and turns combining with genuine, heartfelt moments of one family confronting their worst nightmare and fighting back."

—Lisa Gardner, #1 *New York Times* bestselling author

"It's a family's worst nightmare. A child is missing and his parents are left with unimaginable choices and the threat of long-held secrets being exposed. Mofina expertly weaves together an anguishing story of a family's trauma with a propulsive, twisty thriller that pays off to the very last page."

—Alafair Burke, *New York Times* bestselling author of *Find Me*

"Focusing on the family's agony and quest for the truth puts the reader directly into the story, and the final payoff is terrific."

—Jeff Ayers, advance review for *firstCLUE*

Everything She Feared

"*Everything She Feared* moves like a raging river. This is a thriller not to be missed!"

—Michael Connelly, #1 *New York Times* bestselling author

"Rick Mofina has penned a creepy, heart-pounding page-turner. Simmering with unrelenting tension and family secrets; Mofina mines the darkest corners of the human heart and explores the age-old question—is evil born or made? A gripping, chilling thriller from beginning to end."

—Heather Gudenkauf, *New York Times* bestselling author of *The Overnight Guest*

"*Everything She Feared* hooked me from page one and didn't let go. An intriguing premise coupled with masterful storytelling and a well-plotted mystery made it impossible for me to put it down. Compulsively readable with twists and turns right up until the stunning conclusion. I loved it."

—Amber Garza, author of *A Mother Would Know*

"A propulsive, page-turning thriller; I couldn't put it down. I was immediately immersed in the different perspectives, all realistic and fascinating characters whom I couldn't help but root for. Mofina has successfully written *The Bad Seed* for the twenty-first century, with even more twists and turns."

—Flora Collins, author of *A Small Affair*

Also available from Rick Mofina and MIRA

EVERYTHING SHE FEARED
HER LAST GOODBYE
SEARCH FOR HER
THEIR LAST SECRET
THE LYING HOUSE
MISSING DAUGHTER
LAST SEEN
FREE FALL
EVERY SECOND
FULL TILT
WHIRLWIND
INTO THE DARK
THEY DISAPPEARED
THE BURNING EDGE
IN DESPERATION
THE PANIC ZONE
VENGEANCE ROAD
SIX SECONDS

Other books by Rick Mofina

A PERFECT GRAVE
EVERY FEAR
THE DYING HOUR
BE MINE
NO WAY BACK
BLOOD OF OTHERS
COLD FEAR
IF ANGELS FALL
INTO THE FIRE
THE HOLLOW PLACE
REQUIEM
BEFORE SUNRISE
THE ONLY HUMAN

RICK MOFINA

SOMEONE SAW SOMETHING

ISBN-13: 978-0-7783-0543-9

Someone Saw Something

Mira
22 Adelaide St. West, 41st Floor
Toronto, Ontario M5H 4E3, Canada
BookClubbish.com

Printed in U.S.A.

This book is for Laura, Mark and Angus

For a moment the lie becomes truth.
—Fyodor Dostoevsky, *The Brothers Karamazov*

PROLOGUE

Several years earlier

THE DEAD STARED open-eyed to the sky.

Women, men, children, mouths agape, their faces breaking the earth's surface in macabre portraits, their bodies entombed in mud. Over here, a leg and shoeless foot protruded. Over there, a hand reached heavenward.

Corina Corado and the other journalists said nothing, taking pictures and video of the horror that stretched into a curving, gruesome river of death, dotted with branches, overturned cars, a bus, and an altar and crucifix from a church, Christ's face in torment.

A breeze carried the stench.

Bodies had started to decompose; birds pecked at remains. Corina and the others moved carefully through the mudslide's aftermath.

She was with NNN, the Newslead Now Network. A week earlier she'd been in El Salvador with Jed Gonzales, the camera operator, finishing a feature on immigrants and another piece on the country's volcanoes.

With her assignments in Central America completed, Corina was happy to be going back to New York, back to her husband and daughter to start her overdue vacation. Anxious to leave before the storms that were expected for the region, she was standing in line to board her flight at the airport in San Miguel when Ken McKee, an assignment editor, called her from New York.

"A hurricane's hit Nicaragua, in Chinandega," McKee said. "Your visas are still valid. You and Jed are our closest crew. We need you on-site, filing ASAP."

Miraculously, Chinandega's airport, using generators, had remained operational and they got a flight into Nicaragua. Upon landing they'd hired a car and driver and begun sending reports via satellite links.

The storm had churned into the region with winds upward of 160 mph, knocking out much of Chinandega's electricity, smashing buildings and tearing off roofs. The rains caused flooding, turning streets into raging rivers, sweeping people away, dragging houses and cars in rushing waters choking with debris and sewage. The known death toll neared three hundred. Rescue and relief efforts were launched, aid was dispatched.

Corina and Jed reported for several days, filing stories and updates nonstop. Most of the world press was in Chinandega when the rumors trickled in that the hurricane's rains had caused massive mudslides inland, in northern Madriz. There were accounts of people disappearing in seconds as the slides wiped out entire towns and villages in the hill country.

News crews scrambled to get there.

Corina and Jed, along with a TV team from Buenos Aires, a reporter and print photographer from a Barcelona newspaper, and a radio reporter from Lima, shared the cost to charter a helicopter to get them into the hardest-hit remote section of Madriz. But government officials stepped in—they wanted to seize the media aircraft for relief and rescue around the city. The press was being intimidated by an increasingly controlling regime. Corina and the others had argued that it was vital to show the world the true extent of the storm's damage, to draw international aid. The officials finally allowed the press flight into the area, provided it deliver a shipment of medicine, food and water, and ferry survivors to a crisis aid camp near the Honduran border.

They lifted off.

Corina gazed at the lush forests, swollen rivers, hills and valleys blurring below. Looking down, she withdrew into her thoughts.

She'd reported on disasters like this in India, Japan, the Philippines and Brazil. Now in Central America, her recently completed stories in El Salvador evoked memories of her parents. How, as young newlyweds, they'd struggled after an earthquake in Guatemala and risked everything for a better life by coming to America where Corina was born.

Like her mother and father, Corina pursued her dream, working hard, becoming a foreign correspondent with a global news network based in New York. There, she met and fell in love with Robert, a widowed engineer, who was raising his young daughter, Charlotte.

"I'm warning you—" Corina had smiled over dinner in Manhattan after accepting his proposal and ring "—ours won't be an ordinary life."

"I can live with the extraordinary," Robert said.

Being dispatched around the world had, at times, challenged their home life, with Corina missing anniversaries and recitals, and having to sing "Happy Birthday" to Charlotte from Afghanistan, via Skype. Still, Corina and Robert not only made their family work, they both wanted a second child. But it wasn't easy, and that was heart-wrenching for them. Corina miscarried twice and was crushed when her doctor told her that getting pregnant again was near impossible.

They were considering fertility treatments, and other options.

All they could do was keep trying and keep hoping.

That's why Corina was anxious to be on her way back home. Then the hurricane hit Nicaragua. Sitting on the helicopter, twisting her rings, she swallowed her guilt at being so selfish. Amid all the suffering she'd witnessed, all the horrible tragedies that filtered through her so she could deliver the news to viewers in America and around the world, all she could think of now was her aching desire to have a child. That's what Corina was thinking when their helicopter landed in a remote corner of Madriz and she stepped into the latest version of hell on earth.

Moving with caution, she and the other reporters spread out, surveying uprooted trees, jagged chunks of houses, a roof, a door, a wall, a tractor, a stove, a refrigerator and beds. The force of the torrent stunned them into a funereal silence, punctuated only by the clicking of the Spanish photographer's camera, and the Lima radio reporter, gripping his microphone, whispering his eye-witness account for listeners in Peru.

Corina could hear him saying how this tiny, remote community had vanished in moments, becoming a cemetery, making one think of Pompeii.

As Jed and the TV camera operator from Argentina videoed the scene, Corina continued alone, deeper into the devastation. She passed more overturned cars, more appliances, a bicycle, a bed, a rocking chair, a doll and framed family photos.

But no survivors. No signs of life.

Only the screeching of the birds and the buzzing of flies.

Corina froze.

Amid the cawing she'd heard a different sound.

A soft moan.

She moved toward it, changing direction, listening intently until she came upon a woman. A young woman, alive and all but encased in the mud, which had hardened like concrete. Only her arms and upper body were free. Streaks of mud and lacerations laced her face. Skin had been torn away in patches from her shoulder by the force and abrasiveness of the slide.

At first glance, the woman appeared to be praying to the heavens, but when her eyes flicked open and found Corina's, she groaned.

"Por favor. Por favor."

The woman was holding a baby, wrapped in a blanket.

"Por favor." The woman pleaded to Corina. "Salva a mi hijo. Por favor. Llevar a mi hijo."

Shouting to the others, Corina dropped to her knees to aid them, taking the baby.

"Por favor. Salva a mi hijo. Por favor. Llevar a mi hijo."

Holding the baby to her chest, Corina felt it move.

The baby was alive.

DAY 1

1

CHARLOTTE TANNER WAS complaining that her mom—her stepmother, actually—was ruining her life.

"Corina doesn't get it. She freaked out. Dad freaked, too."

Charlotte and her friend Harper were at an outside patio table at Bell Ritchie's, a café on Amsterdam Avenue in the Upper West Side.

"Because Vince is twenty-one?" Harper said.

"So what if I want to see an older guy? I should be able to date who I want. I'm seventeen."

"You won't be seventeen for months."

"Whatever. I'll be leaving home for college soon. Corina should let me live my life."

"Vince is hot."

"Yeah, plus, unlike the boys at school, he's mature. I think Corina's afraid I'll get pregnant."

"She knows you're on the pill?"

Charlotte didn't answer, as the barista had emerged and, with a ceramic rattling, set two lattes on the table next to their phones. After thanking their server, Charlotte said: "It's like she thinks Vince is beneath us because he's got a regular job and lives in the Bronx. That just makes him real."

"Did they give you the under-our-roof-our-rules speech?"

"Oh yeah, and they keep saying there are laws in this state about a 'man' dating a minor." Charlotte raised her cup for a taste of coffee. "This is good."

"So, are you going to keep it going with Vince?"

Charlotte's phone rang. It was Corina.

"Speak of the devil," Charlotte said, then answered.

Corina's face appeared on-screen, her office windows behind her. *She's always at work*, Charlotte thought.

"Hi, Corina."

"Hi, honey, I know this is your free afternoon, but something just came up."

"What?"

"We need you to get Gabriel at school and bring him home."

"Isn't Dad getting him today?"

"That was the plan, but he's still in Philadelphia—delayed with a last-minute meeting. I can't get Gabriel either, and it's too close to dismissal for the car service."

"But Harper and I just got here. We just ordered."

Charlotte turned her phone toward Harper, who waved. The café's stylized banner was visible on the awning's edge behind her.

"Hi, Corina."

"Hi, Harper." Corina smiled.

Charlotte turned her phone back to herself.

"I'm sorry to ask this," Corina said, "but Bell Ritchie's is just a few blocks from the school. You're right there and dismissal is at three."

"That's like now. Can't one of the other parents get him or something?"

"You're closest. We'd like you to get him."

"Fine."

"Thank you, honey. I'll alert the school."

Fifteen minutes later, Charlotte paid for the lattes, hugged Harper goodbye and left the café annoyed because Corina's request to get Gabriel felt like another intrusion, another exercise in control. College was now less than a year away. She couldn't wait to leave home, to be on her own, to get away from all this.

No, that's not entirely true.

Distant sirens echoed and horns blasted nearby. Charlotte's attention shifted down the street to where contractors were renovating a house. Farther down the street, movers were loading furniture onto a truck. *Someone's leaving.* Sadness rippled through her now as she trudged past the multimillion-dollar row houses along the tree-lined street.

Raising her phone, Charlotte scrolled to the photos of her birth mom, Victoria. So beautiful. Charlotte's memories of her were vague. She died when Charlotte was four. Then when Charlotte was seven, her dad married Corina, and three years later they adopted Gabriel.

Corina had really been the only mother Charlotte had known. She was a good mother. Charlotte called her mom or mother sometimes, Corina other times. Yes, they argued. But the bottom line was they loved each other. Charlotte respected Corina, was awed by all the crap she'd endured with her job and all she had accomplished. She was proud to tell people that Corina was her mom. And Gabriel was a sweetheart. He called her "Charlie." Dad called her Charlie, too. Even Corina did, sometimes. But she loved it best from Gabriel. He was her buddy. Her little bro. Dad was Dad. Like Corina he was always working, and he was even more stressed lately.

I don't know why. It's like a part of him is broken, deep inside, keeping him distant. Is it his work, or something else? Whatever he's carrying, he's keeping it hidden.

Charlotte would miss her family when it was time for college. But for now, she was a young woman trying to find herself, and Vince excited her.

She knew she was fortunate to live the life she lived. Aside from losing her mom, Charlotte didn't have to struggle—not like Vince, who helped his mom pay the bills. Nothing was handed to him. And he knew more about the world than the boys at her school. None of them had any real-life skills. Most of them couldn't even drive a car. Her parents didn't know it, but Vince was teaching her. Charlotte liked that, his treating her like an adult when no one else did, Vince was showing her how to navigate life in the real world.

Charlotte kept walking.

★ ★ ★

Tooting horns, shouting children and parents calling out mixed with the hubbub of dismissal and pickup at Tillmon Parker Rose.

Built in 1890, the private school occupied a Renaissance Revival brownstone with a limestone facade. It stood four stories on West 73rd Street, where a number of chauffeur-driven black SUVs lined the pickup zone. School escorts brought the children to their parents, or drivers, then followed the security procedure.

Charlotte knew the routine. She'd picked up Gabriel before. She knew most of the faces but not everyone. *No freaks or weirdos. But what do they really look like?* Gripping her phone, she spotted her brother with Hilda, one of Tillmon's staff, and waved. His spaceship backpack was strapped to his back and he was holding a model airplane. He managed to give Charlotte a hug as he ran into her open arms.

"Hi, Charlie," Gabriel said.

"Hey, buddy."

"Ah, Miss Tanner. We've been informed that you would be the pickup," Hilda said.

"And here I am."

Hilda knew Charlotte, so security was a formality. But it needed to be observed. Charlotte held out her phone showing her QR code and Hilda used a barcode scanner gun to read it until it beeped with approval. Soft beeping echoed across the zone as other escorts cleared parents and drivers for approval.

"Thanks, Hilda," Charlotte said.

"See you tomorrow, Gabriel."

"Bye, Hilda," he said. Then to his sister as they walked away: "Where's Dad today? I want to show him my plane."

"It looks cool. Sorry, Dad had a surprise work meeting. You got me." Studying her phone as they neared Central Park West, she said: "I'll get us an Uber or Lyft or something."

"No, no. Let's walk home."

"That'll take forever."

"But I finished building this today. I want to test fly it in the park."

The plane was made of balsa and foam. He'd painted his name, Gabriel, in big letters on one wing, and his last name, Corado, on the other. The plastic propeller was powered by a rubber band.

"It looks great," she said.

Gabriel stopped. "Take a picture of me with it, Charlie."

"Alright. Hold it up."

Others on the street moved around them as Gabriel posed, smiling with pride. Charlotte stepped back to capture the moment, then showed him the image before they resumed walking.

"And it really flies. Can we go home through the park so I can fly it?"

"Okay."

They'd made it a block south on busy Central Park West when Charlotte's phone rang. Looking at it as she walked, she rolled her eyes and answered.

"Hi, Corina."

"Did you get him? Everything okay?"

"Yes. We're going home through the park. He's right here." Charlotte turned her phone toward Gabriel.

"Look, Mom." He held up his plane. "I made this today and I'm going to fly it in the park to see how far it will go."

"Sounds like fun. See you later. Love you."

"Love you, too."

Charlotte turned the phone back to herself and Corina said, "Thank you for doing this."

"Yeah, no problem."

"Let me know when you get home. Love you."

"Love you, too."

When they reached the Dakota, they waited for the light before crossing for the West 72nd Street entrance to the park. Charlotte sent Corina the picture she'd taken of Gabriel. Buses for school and tour groups were parked on the shoulder bordering the stone walls. A steady flow of walkers, joggers, cyclists, pedicabs and tourists moved in and out.

The Strawberry Fields memorial to John Lennon was a short distance inside the park. A cluster of schoolkids all wearing red T-shirts and shepherded by chaperones, then a European tour group, headed toward it. Charlotte and Gabriel didn't go that way. They'd seen the mosaic hundreds of times before and took the paved path to the right, heading south.

In minutes, the traffic noise from Central Park West subsided, replaced by birdsong and the calming shade of the trees, taking them from the city's rush into a tranquil urban oasis. An earthy fragrance floated in the air with a hint of dung and the clip-clop of a horse-drawn carriage along West Drive.

As they walked along the pathway, Charlotte's phone vibrated with a text that made her heart race a bit.

What's up? Vince asked.

Hey, she texted.

At that moment, Gabriel pointed to a rolling grassy section.

"Can I fly my plane there?"

Glancing up from her phone, Charlotte made a quick assessment. Several older people were sitting on the benches bordering the path. And there was a low-rise fence.

"Let's go a bit farther down," she said.

They continued walking and her phone vibrated again.

What're you doing? Vince asked.

Thinking of what to say, it flashed in her mind that she could've asked Vince to drive them home. It would've been nice. It also would've violated the parental edict. Still, she savored the thrill of talking to him. Being forbidden to see him gave her such a *Romeo and Juliet* vibe.

"Here!" Gabriel stopped at a good spot. "Take my backpack."

He began shrugging it off as a tour group huddled ahead of them. Students guided by adults with folding maps—so old-timey.

Other people walking around them were taking pictures.

"Carry on, carry on," someone said as the group moved along. People, some walking dogs, passed by in both directions, and a couple of pedicabs rolled by on West Drive as Charlotte hefted her brother's bag onto her shoulder.

"Want me to hold your phone, too?" She saw it filling his rear pants pocket as he prepared his plane.

Gabriel shook his head, his fingers twirling the plastic propeller, twisting the rubber band that stretched along the plane. Holding it up, he counted to three then released it while thrusting the plane toward the hill. With a soft whirr it soared, climbing beautifully, turning and gliding before disappearing over the crest of the slope.

"Wow. Look how far it went! I'll get it!"

He trotted to where the path bordered dense thickets and trees as it rose to the hill area.

"I'll wait here. Hurry up." Charlotte resumed texting Vince. I'm walking home through C park with my brother.

Want to go to a party in SoHo Fri?

This Fri?

This Fri.

YES!!

How do you want to do it?

Charlotte hesitated, thinking of a way.

I'll go to my friend's place first, tell my parents I'm going to meet up with her friends in SoHo, she texted, then meet up with you at the party.

Good. Send you info later.

Talking with Vince got her pulse galloping, was almost like a high for Charlotte, taking her from her world of private schools, job-obsessed parents, cafés and condos, to real life. Smiling at her phone, she lowered it and looked for Gabriel. He hadn't returned. She adjusted his backpack strap on her shoulder and waited for almost a minute. She didn't see him on the hilltop.

Why's he taking so long? Is he flying it around up there?

She called up to him: "Gabriel, come on. Let's go!"

He didn't answer.

"Gabriel!"

People walked by in both directions. Charlotte ignored them, glancing to look for him across West Drive. They were near the path to the Bowling and Croquet Greens. Not far off was Sheep Meadow. *Did he cross over without me seeing him? No way. He took the path.* She turned back to the hill where he'd run to get his plane.

"Gabriel!"

Charlotte followed Gabriel's route, taking the path to the right that was lined on both sides with shrubs and flowered bushes, ascending the crest of the hilly area. She passed the military statue on the left. In the opposite direction, an old man bent over a wheeled walker went by, followed by a woman pushing a baby stroller.

Arriving at the hilltop and expanse of grass and trees where the plane would've landed, Charlotte saw no sign of her little brother.

"Gabriel!"

Standing there, she looked in all directions without seeing him.

"Gabriel!"

Her focus went to a flash of color at the base of a big tree on the hilltop and she ran to it.

There, on the grass, was Gabriel's plane.

2

CHARLOTTE PICKED UP the plane, checked its wings and propeller. Everything was intact.

She glanced around.

Birds chirped and a squirrel scampered nearby. *Where is Gabriel?*

Adjusting her bag and his backpack, she hurried from the grassy area, returning to the path. Within a few steps, she came across a man walking a small blond dog in the opposite direction. Thinking fast while cradling the plane with one arm, Charlotte scrolled through her phone.

"Excuse me, sir!" She stopped in front of the dog walker and held up the picture of Gabriel taken moments earlier. "Have you seen this little boy? Did he come this way?"

Drawing his face to her phone, the man shook his head. "No, I'm sorry," he said.

Charlotte continued west, stopping where the path intersected with another, known as the Bridle Path.

To the right, it meandered north through the grass and trees with no one in sight. She turned to the left; the southbound path was empty for a few yards before it cut into a dark, dense grove.

"Gabriel!"

Receiving no answer, she kept going west.

A jogger approached. Charlotte held up Gabriel's photo.

"Excuse me," she said.

The panting runner waved her off without breaking stride.

Charlotte's stomach tensed a little. *This isn't happening. He's got to be nearby.*

Frustrated, she looked behind her, turned and kept moving west. In a few steps the traffic noise and her pulse increased as she stepped out of the park at 69th Street.

Gabriel was nowhere to be seen.

She shot a look north on the sidewalk bordering the park—still no sign of Gabriel. She looked south and didn't see him among the walkers, people pushing strollers. Horns blared, motors growled and music spilled from windows of vehicles moving in two lanes north and south along Central Park West. Charlotte studied the people walking along the opposite side of the street. But it was in vain.

Where's Gabriel?

Returning to the park, Charlotte's breathing quickened but she kept calm; her little brother knew the park. They lived blocks from it, and his school took so many class trips here, it was like their backyard. Retracing her steps, she stopped at the path that cut right, south through dense shrubs and trees. It led to two playgrounds, and farther south, to the nearest restrooms.

Maybe he ran down there to use the bathroom?

No, no way! Gabriel wouldn't do that without telling me first. If I run down to check, he might come back and I'll miss him.

She struggled to think.

Wait! I'm forgetting! He's got his phone!

Swiping and tapping at her phone, she called Gabriel's number, pressing her phone to her ear as it connected and rang.

And rang.

Come on.

And rang.

Come on, Gabriel!

And rang.

Answer! Please answer!

Her gut tightening, Charlotte hurried to the bench nearest the grassy hilltop where she'd found his plane. She could see the path below where she had first waited. Another option came to her. Setting his plane down on the bench, then his backpack and her bag, she sat and pulled up the phone-finding app to track Gabriel's phone and pinpoint his location.

Rushing through the steps, her fingers trembled; a map and information appeared on her screen telling her that the last known location of Gabriel's phone was Tillmon Parker Rose on West 73rd Street.

The school?

She stood to hurry back but stopped, looking around again.

Why would he go back? Without telling me? Is the app accurate? She knew sometimes it took time to update. And the school? *It makes no sense. He's got to be in the park—Oh, I don't know.*

Biting her lip—*don't panic*—and acting on impulse, she swiped her phone's screen, searching her contacts for the school and Hilda's number. Thankfully, she still had it from previous times she'd gone to the school. And there it was: Hilda Carrera.

As it rang, Charlotte hoped Hilda was still there. She knew that Tillmon had after-school programs for older students. Finally, on the fourth ring, Hilda picked up.

"Hello."

"Hi, Hilda, this is Charlotte Tanner, Gabriel's sister."

"Yes, Miss Tanner."

"This will sound strange but—" Charlotte was thinking on her feet, not wanting to make any admission, or cause alarm—*or have my parents find out* "—did Gabriel leave his jacket there?"

"His jacket? I don't think so."

"Maybe he came back for it? Could you check, please?"

"Maybe he what? Came back? But he's with you, Miss Tanner?"

"I'm sorry, I mean can you please check for him, I mean for his jacket?"

A static-filled silence followed and Charlotte struggled to control her growing fear seeping into her voice.

"Please, Hilda, would it be possible to check?"

"One moment."

Charlotte hoped with her whole heart that if Hilda checked, she'd determine Gabriel had returned. They could hold him there, consider it all a confused mix-up and maybe even have a laugh. Charlotte rubbed her chin.

"No, his jacket's not here and Gabriel is not here," Hilda said. "Miss Tanner, is something wrong?"

"No, that's fine. Thank you for checking."

Charlotte's stomach spasmed as she ended the call. She refreshed and rechecked her phone's locator app. Now it displayed more information—the time and last location of Gabriel's phone: 11:50 a.m. at Tillmon.

That would've been lunch.

Why isn't it showing an updated time and location? Why isn't it working? Why can't I find him? Why wasn't I watching him?

Stifling a cry, Charlotte looked at her little brother's plane. A blood rush roared in her ears.

Oh my God! I've got to call Mom and Dad! No, I can't. Not yet! They'll kill me! They'll just kill me! I've got to find him!

Central Park was a vast labyrinth of roads, paths, lakes, lawns and darkened woods with hidden realms. All kinds of people passed through it. This was New York. And at times, her family had been confronted by people who were angry or upset. *At times, even dangerous people.* Mostly because of Corina's work. Nightmare scenarios swirled in Charlotte's mind.

Oh God, Gabriel! Where are you? Gabriel, please come back!

3

THE CLOPPING ON the roadway caught Charlotte's attention.

Spotting a mounted cop on West Drive, she ran to him.

"Officer, please help me, I can't find my brother!"

Officer Troy Renner tugged the reins and halted. Charlotte thrust her phone toward him, Gabriel's photo on the screen.

"Please help me!"

"Hold on, miss."

Renner dismounted, his saddle and utility belt made leathery squeaks. Charlotte related what had happened; Renner had just reached for his notebook when he saw an approaching NYPD SUV and waved it down.

Radio dispatches crackling from the car, two uniformed officers, Liz Piccoli and Farid Azar, got out and joined them. Now three cops were listening intently to Charlotte, who was still holding Gabriel's backpack and plane. Showing them Gabriel's photo, she recounted picking him up at Tillmon, how he wanted to fly his plane, how they'd started through the park, bound for their condo on Third Avenue in the Upper East Side.

Within minutes of gathering her information and Gabriel's photo, they alerted their patrol supervisor that a six-year-old boy had gotten separated from his teenage sister in Sector Adam of the park. Renner got back on his horse and left to search the area where Gabriel was last seen.

Charlotte grappled with relief that she had help, but it came with increasing fear as more staccato transmissions bleated from the patrol car and the officers' walkie-talkies, underscoring a rising, ordered urgency.

Gabriel smiled at Charlotte from Officer Piccoli's tablet when she cued up the notice, bearing his picture and details.

Gabriel Santiago Corado, aged six, brown hair, brown eyes, no distinguishing marks or tattoos. Last seen in Central Park wearing a blue plaid short-sleeved shirt, tan shorts, white socks and all-white adidas Superstar shoes and on his left wrist: a blue cord bracelet with a tiny Yankees' baseball and alphabet beads that spell Gabriel.

Charlotte nodded.

Piccoli alerted Central with the missing person notice for Gabriel. Seconds later it was blasted out across the NYPD, and to all park staff, auxiliary units, volunteers, park community organizations and parental groups, as well as the Transit Bureau and Traffic Center, for subways and buses.

More patrol cars arrived with more officers. A quick summary was given along with a time frame and estimates of how far Gabriel could travel by foot. Some officers set off, retracing Charlotte and Gabriel's steps to Tillmon. Others searched the area, scrutinizing every path in the vicinity where he was last seen. During this time, Piccoli called Gabriel's phone, then tried her own advanced GPS tracking features without success.

"Sometimes it doesn't work if the other phone is out of battery power or turned off," Piccoli said to Charlotte. "Who's your carrier?"

"CDSN," Charlotte said. "Chime Digital Sky Network."

Piccoli typed Gabriel's phone information into her own phone and dispatched a new message.

"Our tech guys are better than most people at locating phones by working with the carriers."

Piccoli then asked Charlotte for more background information. Had Gabriel gone missing or run away before? *No, he hadn't.* What was his mood? *He was excited to fly his plane.* Did they argue? *No.*

Did he have a medical condition? *No.* Was he feeling ill? *No.* Could she provide contact information on his friends? *No, she didn't have any with her.* Was it routine for her to pick him up and walk home through the park? *No, but today, her mom asked her to get him, as Charlotte had done in the past.* Did any strangers approach them, follow them or act threatening? *No.* Were there any incidents? *No, nothing like that,* Charlotte said. Could Gabriel find his way home alone? *Probably. Yes.* Did she know if Gabriel was registered with Operation Safe Child? *Charlotte thought he was.* Piccoli radioed her supervisor, who'd been receiving their notes, to check. Then Piccoli double-checked information about Tillmon, Charlotte's parents, their home address and contact information.

"Oh my God, I should call my mom and dad!"

"We'll handle that," Piccoli said.

When Piccoli finished, Charlotte saw that more cops had arrived, their radios chattering. People had stopped nearby to gawk, curious about what was happening. Others held up their phones, recording as Charlotte held back her tears, feeling Piccoli's hand touch her shoulder.

"We'll find him," Piccoli said. "We've got people looking for Gabriel everywhere, okay?"

"Thank you." A small sob escaped Charlotte. "Why wasn't I watching him? My mom and dad are going to kill me!"

"Don't beat yourself up. These things happen." Piccoli moved Charlotte to her patrol car, where Officer Azar opened both passenger-side doors. "We'd like you to drive around with my partner, Farid, to help look. We'll put the plane and your things in the back seat, okay?"

Charlotte was numb when she buckled into the front passenger seat, holding her phone, praying for Gabriel to call.

Azar got behind the wheel, his radio clamoring as he took up his microphone.

"Unit four-five-two-two, Central?" Azar said, then reported how he had sixteen-year-old Charlotte Tanner in his car with him, and together they were going to proceed searching for her brother. He radioed his mileage before they pulled away on West Drive, rolling by a growing crowd of tourists absorbed by the drama of the police units that had collected.

"We'll find your little brother," Azar said. "Don't worry. Our guys in the park are talking to vendors, to horse carriage operators, everybody. We got people in precincts surrounding the park talking to doormen and canvassing businesses and buildings, transit people are looking and..."

As Azar assured Charlotte, his radio hissed with static and dispatches while his console computer screen pinged with messages, pulling her deeper into the horror. She scoured the paths, shrubs and trees, her eyes blurring—this couldn't be real. In a heartbeat, the beauty and immense majesty of Central Park that she loved had been transformed into a nightmare that had taken Gabriel.

Where are you? Where did you go?

Azar continued, "...and we got cameras at all the entrances that we'll check. We've sent people to his school, and your family's condo on Third Avenue. We'll check with your parents in case he's contacted them..."

Charlotte clenched her eyes.

Corina and Dad are going to kill me. They will absolutely kill me.

The radio crackled: "Four-five-two-two?"

It was Azar's patrol supervisor, Sergeant Egan.

"Four-five-two-two," Azar responded into his microphone.

"You're ten-seven Sector Adam with the complainant?"

"Ten four."

"Subject is registered. We pulled Gabriel Corado's Safe Child card," Egan said. "Can you confirm, the father is Robert Tanner with Golden Solution Engineering Consulting?"

Charlotte heard and nodded.

"Ten four, affirmative," Azar responded.

"And the mother is Corina Corado, a journalist with Newslead Now Network?"

Charlotte nodded.

"Ten four, affirmative," Azar said.

Several seconds of static followed before Egan came back.

"We're showing that the family has employed security because of threats the mother received. Can the complainant confirm the status?"

Charlotte's jaw dropped a little. "But that was a long time ago," Charlotte said. "Corina said things were okay and stopped getting security like, a year ago."

Azar relayed her response to Egan.

In the silence that followed, Charlotte scanned the idyllic park scenes of people going about their lives, couples holding hands, cyclists, joggers, tour groups.

But no sign of Gabriel.

She dragged her shaking hand over her face, feeling as if a clock were ticking down on her brother, worry churning in her stomach.

I should've been watching him.

Egan came back on the radio, telling Azar to read the message he'd just sent to his computer. Azar angled the screen so Charlotte couldn't see his supervisor's note. Upon reading it, Azar paused, concentrating, indicating that the call had just taken a deeper turn.

He read it a second time.

"Maybe too late, but keep this off the air. Hang on to the toy plane for ECT. Duty captain alerted. Get people on the gates. We'll issue an AMBER. On my way to scene. We'll activate a Level 1 mobilization for possible kidnapping-in-progress."

4

THE JETLINER SCRAPED along the runway on its belly, leaving a sparking, fiery wake before stopping on the grass median engulfed in flames.

Shaky footage of the disaster had been broadcast continually across the country and around the world by the Newslead Now Network.

The chyron read: **PLANE CRASH-LANDS AT DENVER AIRPORT**.

"For those joining us, Newslead has obtained new, dramatic pictures of yesterday's crash landing of that EastCloud jetliner in Denver," Corina Corado told viewers from the anchor desk as the dramatic scene played over her shoulder, with changing perspectives.

The chyron now read: **AUTHORITIES: NO FATALITIES ALL 91 PASSENGERS 9 CREW ACCOUNTED FOR IN BOSTON TO DENVER FLIGHT**.

"Survivors are sharing their harrowing stories. On the phone now is Rita Green, a Denver teacher, who escaped yesterday's inferno with her ten-year-old daughter, Ashley. Rita, thank you for talking with us."

"Yes."

"First, how are you and Ashley doing?"

"Still a little shaken. But we're holding up."

"Our hearts go out to you, your daughter and everyone who was on board." Corina offered a warm smile. "Now, Rita, if you could, take us back a bit. We understand that the pilot made an announcement as your plane approached Denver."

"He said there was a problem with the landing gear and we needed to brace for an emergency landing," Rita said as an inset photo of her and Ashley appeared on the screen. The chyron now read: **PILOT TOLD PASSENGERS TO BRACE FOR EMERGENCY LANDING**. "People were crying," Green went on. "I saw a man holding a Bible. When we landed there was a horrible thud, jolting us, then a roar, screaming, chaos in the cabin. But the crew took charge. They were so good getting us to the inflatable slides."

"I can't imagine what thoughts raced through your mind at that moment."

"It was terrifying. You think of all the things that matter in your life..."

Corina nodded, and she understood—she'd interviewed so many people facing the worst moments of their lives, reaching into their pain. Rita continued for several minutes before Corina thanked her for sharing her experience. Corina moved on to discuss aviation safety with an expert before wrapping her segment and handing off to a colleague.

"Good job," said Nora Bower, a producer, giving her a thumbs-up.

"Great stuff, Corina." Marty Welman, the control operator, saluted.

"Right back at you guys." Corina waved her thanks to the staff, smiling at the camera operators as she left the news studio, pleased. She'd drawn upon her sources and worked with her producer to find Rita Green and convince her to talk to Newslead. Corina was relieved that no one had died in the Denver crash, but talking to survivors never got easier—it never failed to tear away a piece of her heart, every time.

Making her way through the huge nerve center of the network, she surveyed its open concept and the vast puzzle piece sections of the low-walled workstations. Above them, banks of flat-screen monitors were tuned to Newslead, as well as its competitors in the US and around the world.

Corina scanned the researchers, graphic designers, producers and booking coordinators busy at work. Few stopped to glance out the floor-to-ceiling windows at the views of the Hudson River and the Empire State Building. At times, she couldn't believe she was here. This was Newslead's world headquarters in Midtown Manhattan's West Side. It was located in a 76-story office tower that ascended over Madison Square Garden and Penn Station.

Newslead took up six levels of the skyscraper, starting at the 36th floor, with Sports, Entertainment and International. Corina's division, News, was on the 40th floor. Corporate, with the executive offices, was on the 41st, Newslead's highest floor, which everyone referred to as "Upstairs."

Newslead was a global broadcasting force, one of the world's largest news entities, with bureaus and affiliates in almost every country on earth.

Corina had paid her dues, earning her way to what most considered the apex of her profession. Starting in college, she first learned the news craft working for newspapers. She stopped short of thinking back to her earliest reporting days, in Whittier, California, and facing the tragedy on that one night—the night that changed her. She stopped short of dwelling on it, resuming her thoughts to how she eventually jumped to TV news in small markets, covering everything from dog shows to homicides. Always hustling, always breaking stories, catching the attention of national networks and eventually being hired by Newslead, becoming a foreign correspondent then national senior correspondent and part-time anchor.

She'd worked hard building her career. But it came at a price, exacting a toll from every part of her life. And lately, the cost had risen to an impossible—*no, unconscionable, unacceptable*—level, she thought, spotting Efrem Zyller, head of the entire news division, far across the room.

What's he doing on this floor?

"Corina?"

She turned around to see Gil Dixon, a senior producer.

"Good stuff on Denver."

"Thanks, Gil. Hey." She nodded toward Efrem. "What's he doing down here?"

Following her gaze, Gil shrugged. "Maybe to congratulate you."

"On what?"

Looking around, Gil dropped his voice. "My sources upstairs tell me that you're a shoo-in to anchor the new prime-time show this fall."

"Really? We'll see about that."

"Anyway, don't forget, ten minutes to the next planning meeting for the world leaders conference in Prague next month."

"Right."

"Be sure your passport's up-to-date."

After Gil left Corina, she watched Efrem talking with a couple of interns in graphics. His arms were crossed, and he held a rolled-up piece of paper, as he often did. He was in his early fifties, fit, with coiffed salt-and-pepper hair and a tan, back from visiting his Mediterranean villa. His recessed eyes projected a charming, dangerous confidence telegraphing his power in the industry.

Subtly, he turned to Corina, aiming a brief laser-focused glance at her as if to acknowledge the tension broiling secretly between them.

Corina's jawline muscles bunched as she returned his stare, ever so slightly raising her chin in defiance. Then she entered her office slowly, not in surrender, fear or retreat, but in steadfast refusal.

Closing her door and leaning against it, Corina shut her eyes. Seeing Efrem Zyller chilled her, especially after what Gil just said about her being promoted to the new show.

Did Efrem send Gil to strategically drop that on me?

She bit down on her bottom lip.

I don't know who I can trust anymore.

The memory of the recent incident with Efrem was seared in her mind. It happened several weeks ago. She was working late when Gil popped his head into her office and said Efrem wanted to see her for a meeting upstairs. They went up together, but Gil didn't stay. Corina and Efrem were alone in his corner office, the city lights twinkling below, talking about how she'd be perfect for the new show, when all of a sudden Efrem's hand was on her leg and moving up.

No, she told him, thinking it would end there.

But it didn't.

She stepped away and told him that she would report him. He raised his eyebrows ever so slightly, the hint of a grin surfacing.

"No, you won't. This was an embarrassing miscommunication and I apologize."

She insisted it was clear what he'd done, and it was wrong.

After a moment, his demeanor turned cold and his eyes narrowed.

"Corina, if you do what you're threatening to do, you'll force me to take steps. And when I go to war I never lose."

Now, with her back against her office door, Corina took a slow breath, pushing her issue with Efrem aside. Then she got her phone from her purse and looked at recent photos. There was Charlotte's picture of Gabriel with his plane. *My sweetheart.* Along with her text that she had picked him up. And there was one of Charlotte. *My beautiful rebel angel.* Corina was pleased she'd agreed to pick up her brother at school. Charlotte might be a handful these days, but she was reliable.

Corina checked her messages. *Maybe my lawyer's got an update?*

Nothing on that front.

She went to her Newslead laptop and checked her social media feeds. In recent months, most messages and posts were positive, like today's stream:

Corina showed so much respect to the mother in the Denver crash.

CC is a compassionate professional through and through.

Corado's the best of them all; she's why I watch NNN.

Then she found those that were negative.

As usual Corado sucked today.

A talentless vain bimbo.

Purveyor of BS.

The vitriol would always be there, but it had long since slowed to a trickle. Corina knew that it had always been part of the job.

During her early TV days, it had been criticism about her hair, her clothes, her voice, her weight. Eventually it grew more menacing and was aimed at the profession. In one of many cases, Corina was among scores of news crews that had descended on a small town after a school shooting. Some people confronted the line of cameras, shouting at them.

"Burn in hell, media scum!"

"You're all liars, all part of the plot to destroy the Constitution!"

"You're the enemy and we're going to put you in prison!"

Some wore T-shirts or carried signs depicting a noose, a tree and the word *Journalist*.

The abuse became common, especially during election campaigns. It culminated for Corina personally a few years ago after she'd interviewed Max and Marnie Ritzzkel, a husband and wife team. The couple led a controversial group known for extreme views connected to disturbing conspiracy theories.

Corina's live interview lasted about seven minutes but was a charged exchange, making for gripping TV. Every time the couple made a wild, incredible, untrue statement, Corina countered with facts. The couple's jaw-dropping responses to her questions made them appear unbalanced, even silly. It angered them. Their faces reddening, they soon abandoned any civility and attacked the news profession, then Newslead, then Corina.

"We know all about you… You never adopted a kid—you stole him… Your whole life is a lie! You're the Queen of Lies!" Marnie Ritzzkel spat as the interview ended.

Within minutes, the couple's legion of followers unleashed a hurricane of hate-filled posts online attacking Corina.

You lie, you die!

The Queen of Lies needs a bullet!

We're coming for you QOL!

It continued for weeks and included voicemails like, *"Your days are numbered!"* Relentless social media posts targeted her with fabrications, altered photos and manipulated videos accusing her of every imaginable evil, linking her to a murderous sect of child-stealing, blood-drinking devil-worshippers.

It reached its most frightening stage when a troubled, incoherent man was arrested in Newslead's lobby. He was carrying a fake security pass, a map of the 40th floor, a gun and a hand-scrawled *Order of Execution for Corina Corado, aka "Queen of Lies."*

The man ended up in jail, and, in a way, so did Corina and her family. Because immediately after the incident, Newslead and the police determined she required private, personal security.

She accepted the need but hated the upheaval in her life. She mourned the fact that things had devolved to such a point in the country that a journalist needed an armed guard to join her on assignments, or when she got groceries or when she and her family went out to a restaurant.

The security firm hired by Newslead had concluded that Corina and her family were safe in their Upper East Side condominium, so the guard didn't stay in their home. But in most facets of their lives, a guard was present. Charlotte disliked it: *"It's weird, like we're being punished."* Gabriel's fascination soon faded. *"How long will we have guard people, Mom?"* Corina's husband, Robert, took comfort in the added safety but as time went on, he grew weary of "our extended family," as he called it.

As a working mom, Corina already carried a measure of guilt. But the dramatic change was crushing. It was because of her job that her family had to live this way. The security employees were good people, but she resented needing them. It was suffocating and it angered her. She wrote an opinion piece for the *New York Times*, stating that she refused to be silenced or live in fear for doing her job, which was to report the truth.

Time passed after the controversial interview. The volume of malicious messages and posts against her diminished. Eventually, things had calmed. Soon it had been a year, and after consulting with Newslead and the security firm, Corina succeeded in quietly having the personal security removed.

In the first weeks without a guard, she wondered if she'd done the right thing. But any doubt she'd had was eclipsed by her family's happiness, and hers, at having their lives back. For more than a year now, they'd lived a normal life without a security team.

Corina looked again at the picture Charlotte had taken today of Gabriel. Their miracle. She and Robert had tried so hard to get pregnant, a dream made difficult because Corina was in and out of the country so much at the time. Compounding the challenge, Corina struggled with fertility because of ovulation problems. It broke her heart, especially on some foreign assignments. Often when she interviewed refugees and asylum seekers in Central American camps, mothers with infants would invite Corina to hold their babies. It tore her up inside each time she looked down at the child in her arms, because no matter how tragic the family's history was, the mothers never gave up hope for a better life. Corina realized she was fortunate, that her life was easy compared with those of the displaced women she talked with who'd suffered atrocities.

Privately, she still ached for a child.

Gabriel was her answered prayer. Now, looking at the picture of him with his model airplane, she blinked and smiled. Her little boy was growing up too fast.

She swiped to her photos of Charlotte. She was so beautiful, like her late mother. Charlotte was a high-maintenance teen, a rebellious free spirit. Corina admired her for that. But Charlotte was misguided in wanting to date a twenty-one-year-old rideshare driver from the Bronx named Vince. Corina and Robert—as well as state law—drew the line there.

She smiled at Charlotte's pretty face, her heart bursting with love for her and for Robert.

He was an engineer. They'd met at a party and something about him struck Corina. A widower with a little girl. Corina fell in love with them both. Robert possessed a gentle sadness, and the warmth and understanding of a good man. It seemed to Corina that they were in sync, that they fit together.

This was her family.

But lately, at home, something didn't feel right with Robert. Whenever they had a moment alone, he was distant. At times, she'd overheard him having subdued phone conversations with someone.

"Oh, it's work," he'd say when she asked him about it. But once, she walked by his study and glimpsed him talking softly on what appeared to be a new blue phone. She wasn't sure, though—maybe it was simply a new case. Was that call also work related? she'd wondered at the time.

Her thoughts returned to Charlotte. Despite their rules, Corina was certain Charlotte would defy them and secretly see Vince.

Maybe Robert and I need to talk to him?

She then thought of Gabriel, which gave her a fresh stab of guilt, because he seemed left out these days.

Am I neglecting my family?

She'd been distracted by the matter with Efrem. The stakes were rising and she needed to make a decision on when to report him, but she wanted to talk more with her lawyer. As she checked again for messages, her laptop pinged, informing her of an internal note from Gil Dixon with a link to a New York tabloid.

You'll see this sooner or later—don't believe it! Gil wrote.

She scrolled through the gossip column that had just been posted: *"...and sources tell us Newslead is considering dropping one of its most seasoned journalists, Corina Corado, because of low ratings..."*

I can't believe this!

Before she could read it a second time, a soft knock sounded at her door, then a woman's voice.

"We're heading to the Prague meeting, Corina. Are you coming?"

"Be right there."

She'd just began collecting her things—and her composure—when her phone rang. The caller ID displayed *NYPD.*

Police?

She answered.

"This is Sergeant Egan, NYPD Central Park Precinct. Is this Corina Corado?"

"Yes."

"Ma'am, your son, Gabriel, appears to have gotten separated from his sister in the park."

"Separated! But I don't—" Corina suspected the call could be a hoax.

But how would a hoaxer know Gabriel was with Charlotte in the park?

"Ma'am, has Gabriel attempted to contact you since leaving his school?"

"No." Corina's voice wavered. "Oh my God, where's my son?"

5

AT PHILADELPHIA INTERNATIONAL AIRPORT, Robert Tanner's seating group was called for the one-hour flight to New York.

His line advanced to the desk. He tilted his phone, showing his boarding pass barcode to the gate agent. She scanned it and thanked him, then he proceeded down the jet bridge, rolling his carry-on behind him.

At last.

Robert was happy to finally be heading home.

The best-laid plans…

He would've been back in New York on a morning flight with plenty of time to get Gabriel at Tillmon. But things changed after the contracting company he'd met with called a second, unscheduled, meeting, which he couldn't miss. It meant delaying his return to New York and not being able to pick up Gabriel this afternoon.

I'll be home in time for dinner.

Stepping into the plane, Robert fell in with the usual buildup of passengers wrangling bags into the overhead bins. Things progressed until the woman now in front of him, who appeared to be in her eighties, stopped in the aisle. She looked at the open bin above and her carry-on bag she was pulling as if she were at the foot of Mount Everest.

"Would you like me to store your bag for you?" Robert asked her.

"Oh, I don't want to trouble you."

"No, no trouble." Robert hefted her bag into place.

"You're a kind gentleman." She patted his arm and took her seat.

He pressed on, keeping a lookout for his row and seat number. His head was splitting from last night; he was a bit woozy and relieved he'd reserved the aisle, as it was his preference. He came to a man in his twenties: three-day scruff, ball cap, headphones, Rolling Stones T-shirt, nodding his head to a beat while watching the ground crew through the window. The empty aisle seat next to him was Robert's.

He stored his bag above, sat and buckled up.

Settling in, he looked at his phone, smiling at the picture Charlotte had sent earlier of Gabriel with his rubber band–powered plane.

Maybe he'll follow in my footsteps and become an engineer.

He swiped to one of his favorites of Corina, Charlie and Gabe.

Charlie's a force of nature. Sixteen going on twenty-six, wanting to date a grown man. That's not going to happen.

The plane's door thudded shut and was secured. Then an attendant started making the preflight safety announcements. Massaging his temples as the jet pushed off, Robert was thinking of where he could take his family for dinner that evening. They needed time together. He and Corina had been working too many long hours over the last few weeks and soon Newslead would be sending her off to Europe.

"...airplane mode during this flight. But for now we request that all electronic devices be switched off during takeoff and landing..."

Robert placed his phone in his lap and pulled his burner from his inside jacket pocket. No new messages. Cursing to himself, he reviewed his overnight trip to Philly and all that was supposed to have happened.

There was the woman.

They'd planned to meet last night at his hotel, the Elysium Winds. She'd texted him on his burner suggesting 8:30 p.m. at the Atlantis Bar near the lobby. She said she had short brown hair and would be wearing a red, formfitting dress. In her messages she promised, "I'll give you what you need. But there's much at risk."

Yes, a lot was at stake, but he needed her.

She'd never showed. Never texted. Nothing.

He'd sat waiting for a while at the bar. He was hungry so he got a burger and a beer, watched the game. Maybe it was the burger, or the onion rings, but something didn't agree with him, so he called it a night.

He had no idea why the woman stood him up, or if he would ever see her. His head and stomach were in a spin cycle by the time he got to his room. He took a shower then fell asleep watching *The Treasure of the Sierra Madre.*

In the morning, he woke with his head throbbing and his mouth dry, and he was naked. He'd been so foggy last night, he didn't remember if he'd put on sweats and a T-shirt when he went to bed. He untangled himself from the sheets and took some headache pills, had a hot shower to wake himself up and got dressed for his meeting.

Robert's main reason for the trip was to obtain facts and supporting records from a Philadelphia contractor concerning their role in constructing a 94-story luxury condo in Manhattan. But they were vague, evasive and came up short on the documents they were supposed to provide him.

Robert left the meeting frustrated and was halfway to the airport when they called him back for a second meeting. This time some new, and somewhat nervous faces were at the table. Robert was hopeful until he wasn't. During meeting number two he was told the same BS and he left thinking, maybe these guys, and all the others, preferred lawsuits, discoveries, subpoenas and scandal?

Because that's where this is headed.

Billions were at stake with so many companies implicated.

At play was a huge conglomerate, linked to several international groups concerned about their investment. Robert's consulting group was caught in the middle.

The underlying issues were not publicly known.

On the chance of this surfacing in the media, Robert had the impression that the players in this thing had no idea what his wife did for a living. He gave his head a mental shake. No, he couldn't pull the pin on that grenade. Corina didn't know exactly what he was involved in. He needed to keep everything confidential because so much was on the line right now—people needed protecting.

It was that serious.

He rubbed his head again, his discomfort coming and going as he thought about the woman and how badly he'd needed to see her last night.

Robert felt someone touch his arm and looked up to a smiling attendant.

"Please turn off your phones, sir."

He nodded, then powered off his burner and returned it to his pocket. As he picked up his personal phone to switch it off, it rang. The attendant was a few rows away, but she lifted her head in Robert's direction.

The caller ID came up as *NYPD.*

Robert's brow furrowed, a question emerging on his face before he answered.

"Is this Robert Tanner?" a male voice asked.

"Yes, who's calling?"

"Sergeant Egan, NYPD Central Park Precinct. Sir, are you the father of Gabriel Corado and Charlotte Tanner?"

Robert's breathing halted.

The attendant eyed him talking on his phone and started back. No smiles.

Robert's thoughts swirled. Was this one of those scam ransom calls?

"What's going on?" Robert asked.

"Can you confirm I am speaking to Robert Tanner?"

"Yes. What's happening? Are my children hurt?"

"Sir, please switch off your phone?"

Robert kept it to his ear, lifting his head to the attendant.

"Sir," the caller said, "has your son, Gabriel, contacted you recently, with a call, text, email, anything?"

Robert's stomach tightened.

"You need to switch off your phone, sir!" the attendant said.

"No, he hasn't." Robert pushed his phone harder to his ear. "What's happened?"

"He got separated from his sister in Central Park."

"Separated? How? What're you talking about?"

"Sir, we've activated resources, we're looking for him."

"Sir, if you don't turn off your phone now, I'll alert the captain to an uncooperative passenger, which may result in us turning around and your removal from the aircraft."

The police call hit Robert with the force of a tsunami. Confusion scraped through his throbbing head as he stayed on the phone with Egan and turned to the attendant.

"Please," he said. "I just need a moment. I've just been called by police in New York. My son is missing, please…let me…"

Her officious demeanor shifted instantly to concern.

"Alright," she said, waving over another crew member. "But we'll have to alert the captain. That'll give you some time, sir, it's okay."

On the phone, Egan assured Robert that police were doing all they could to find Gabriel. The plane was taxiing when Egan ended the call. The attendants hovered to ensure Robert was not attempting to disrupt the flight, allowing him to try reaching Corina, then Charlotte. Each time it was futile.

So Robert turned off his phone, showing the attendants.

Numbed, he looked ahead at nothing, struggling to process the call.

The guy beside him stared, his jaw dropped. "Holy crap, man!"

6

HORNS HONKED AT the yellow taxi threading through traffic lanes northbound on the West Side Highway.

In the back seat, Corina was on her phone with Charlotte.

"I don't understand, what happened?" Corina asked as Charlotte sobbed through her account of how Gabriel had disappeared.

"I'm sorry… I'm so sorry."

"It's okay," Corina said. But it wasn't. Working to get her head around the crisis, all she could say was, "It's going to be okay. I'm on my way."

Minutes earlier, Corina had promised the driver a massive tip to get her to Central Park's 69th Street entrance as fast as possible. Heart racing, she'd hurried from her office, phone welded to her ear, getting all she could from Sergeant Egan while nearly trampling over producer Nora Bower in the hall.

"Heads up, Corina. The Prague meeting's this way, in the big room."

She kept walking.

"Corina?"

"I can't make it." She turned briefly. "Family emergency. I've got to go!"

After jabbing the elevator button, thankful it had arrived quickly and made few stops descending to the lobby, she trotted to the street, then into the middle of the road, flagging down the first cab she saw.

Now, roaring through West Side traffic, Corina took action. She called Gabriel. It rang, pulling her back to her decision to get him his own phone. It gave her hope at a time like this. Yes, absolutely, he was too young to have a phone. Her insistence was a consequence of when they had personal security. It gave her peace of mind.

Answer, sweetie!

Gabriel's phone had strict parental limits. He could only make and receive calls from the family numbers she'd stored in his contacts. He didn't have to dial.

Please answer!

She'd showed him how to press the buttons labeled with their names: Mom, Dad, Charlie. No emails or texts with friends.

Countless rings.

Gabriel didn't answer.

Where is he?

Then Corina tried finding his phone with her app.

It was futile.

Why isn't it working?

She called Tillmon and was put through to Alice Donovan, the school's director.

"Yes, Ms. Corado, the police are here asking about Gabriel. All we know is he was dismissed into the care of his sister, Charlotte Tanner, as you'd instructed, and in keeping with our policy. We've shared that with police. We'll send out a bulletin straight away about Gabriel on our school family email network."

"Yes, maybe he saw friends and went with them."

"Let us know if there's more we can do to help."

"Call me if you hear anything."

Corina's next call was to the security desk at their condominium. Paulo Lugano, the building security manager, answered.

"I'm sorry, ma'am. No news here on your son yet," Lugano said. "The NYPD has been here to alert us. I've sent one of our people to scout the street for him. We'll alert you if we see him."

The taxi made good time on the highway, exiting to navigate

through the Upper West Side, now closer to the park as Corina struggled to think.

What could've happened?

She prayed that Gabriel had met friends with their parents in the park. All the kids at Tillmon knew the park. The school had class outings there almost every other day. *But why wouldn't a parent call me to say he was with them?* Maybe they got distracted, went to the zoo, the carousel or the conservatory? He loved playing with the remote control boats.

Maybe something else happened?

Scenarios wrenched her to that night at her first news job in Whittier, California, where she grew up.

Her parents couldn't afford the entire tuition, so Corina helped put herself through local college, studying journalism while working at the newspaper. That night she was on the crime desk, hearing the police scanner crosstalk—"*...all units, report of an eleven-eighty...*" Hank Clayton, the night editor, never took his eyes from his screen, saying, "Sounds serious, better go check it out, kid."

Speeding in the news photog's Jeep, navigating the quickest route, deciphering updates on his portable scanner. The first responding officer's emotions seeping into his transmissions: "...sheared this thing...two fatalities..." Rushing to the scene, police, fire and ambulance lights illuminating debris scattered like shrapnel after a detonation...catching her breath...malformed metal and plastic yellow tarps covering the dead... Approaching to talk to a cop, Corina stepped carefully around the debris strewn on the pavement, spotting...there's something familiar here... A worn ball cap...identical to her dad's...then a shoe...identical to her mom's...the logo on the wreckage—her mom and dad's office cleaning service...

The taxi swerved, yanking Corina from that night.

She took a breath now, telling herself no, this couldn't be like California.

Please, not again.

Corina tried Robert's phone.

No answer.

He was likely in the air flying home from Philadelphia.

Her phone pinged; she opened the message from Egan and caught her breath.

There was Gabriel beaming at her from her screen, in the NYPD's missing person notice.

She wanted to caress Gabriel's face, but her hand flew to her mouth. The notice was a gut punch, her skin prickling at the reality.

My son is missing!

Corina forced herself to remain calm. On dangerous stories, especially those where she was under fire, she'd learned to stay focused and think.

It's how she survived.

Oh God! Hold on! Wait, there's something to try!

She'd hidden a travel tag, a button-shaped tracking device, with Gabriel. He didn't know. No one in the family knew. An additional precaution she'd taken, like his phone. She never had to use it before. Fingers shaking a little, swiping to the device's tracking app on her phone, the taxi swayed and Corina steadied herself. The driver moved around a loading truck, cursing at the crew for blocking the street.

Corina concentrated on the app, activating a search. The tracking device she'd gotten had an extended range and a precision finder. A map appeared on her screen, and on it was a tiny pulsating green dot.

"Oh my God, it's working!"

A truck's horn blasted when the cab wheeled to the curb at the Central Park's 69th Street entrance. Scrambling for her wallet, Corina gave the driver a fistful of cash, covering the fare and tip.

Hurrying out of the car, holding her phone as if it were a lifeline, the dot was blinking for a location in Central Park. *Maybe he ran off to be alone? Maybe he fought with Charlotte?* Not wanting to lose the position, she used driving mode and voice command to call Sergeant Egan.

It rang twice while she eyed the dot on the map and moved toward it.

"Egan."

"It's Corina Corado! I'm at the 69th Street entrance and I have a location on my son!"

"You found him? Where?"

"Yes. I placed a tracking device with him, like a luggage tag, and it's showing me a spot in Central Park!"

"Alright, give it to me."

Corina gave him the location.

After taking it down and double-checking, Egan said, "Meet us there."

Hope and relief flooding her heart, she continued hurrying east along the park's paved walkway. The dot blinked steadily on the map on her screen. *It says I'm close. Very close.*

She rushed along the walkway, past shrubs where it intersected with the Bridle Path, and she looked down a pathway, where there were two officers on horseback searching the bushes. In the opposite direction, she saw a uniformed cop and parks worker, probing shrubs.

She resumed examining her phone and kept going, to where the grassy hill sloped downward by the military statue. Then she came to the array of pulsing lights, vehicles and police officers clustered on West Drive.

This is it.

The app confirmed it, the dot growing and flashing faster. This was the spot. West Drive near the bowling greens. She looked around.

Where's Gabriel? I don't understand. I don't see him.

Her hope frozen, she scanned the scene. Beyond the knot of police cars, a crowd, including a couple of news crews, had gathered at the periphery. Seeing her, someone said, "Hey, that's Corina Corado from Newslead!" Phones and news cameras turned to her.

"Ms. Corado."

A uniformed cop with sergeant's stripes approached her.

"Sergeant Egan," he said. "This way."

"Where's my son?" She glanced at her app, then at the scene and Egan. "The tracker tells me Gabriel is here!"

Corina extended her phone, showing Egan. He studied it for a few seconds as she surveyed all the police units, their radios crackling.

"Did you find Gabriel?" she asked. "Where is he?"

"Where did you place the tracker?" Egan asked.

"Hidden in his backpack."

"Come with me."

Egan led her to an NYPD SUV and at that moment, not far off, Corina thought she saw Charlotte, leaning on the side of another patrol car, hugging herself, two female uniformed officers rubbing her shoulders.

The SUV door handle clicked and Egan watched Corina carefully as he opened the rear door.

Her knees nearly buckled.

Gabriel was not there. Instead, she saw his backpack with the spaceships on it and his plane.

The tracker was where she'd put it—shoved deep in the small sleeve holding his ID tag.

7

CORINA REACHED FOR Gabriel's backpack.

But Sergeant Egan didn't want her handling it, saying something about processing it and the plane. He showed her photos he'd taken of the contents, Gabriel's jacket, some books, an open package of vanilla crème cookies, his favorite. Stepping back, Corina looked toward Charlotte, distraught in the distance.

"Charlotte said she was holding his backpack when they got separated," Egan said.

"I want to talk to my daughter."

"Okay, but first, I need to ask you a few things." Egan weighed the proximity of the news cameras. "Come with me, over here."

Egan's car was parked amid the others and afforded more privacy. They got in the front, the interior smelling of synthetic leather, coffee and cologne, the radio bleating with transmissions.

Egan took up his microphone and made a short, coded report with Corina understanding only snippets: "Sector Adam… Central… I've got the mother on scene…"

He copied her identification from her driver's license, took a photo of it, then set his phone to Record.

"For my notes," he said. "Now, I alerted your husband, Robert Tanner, before his plane left Philadelphia."

Egan then asked Corina to walk him through the day's events, creating a timeline leading up to Gabriel's disappearance. He asked if Gabriel had ever run off in the past, if there'd been anything, or anyone, suspicious in the time before; if he needed medication; if he knew his way home; anywhere he might go; any stress in the home; and how he got along with his stepsister.

Corina looked toward Charlotte again in the distance.

As Egan continued, adrenaline surged through Corina, her voice tremoring as she answered. She knew he was doing more than collecting vital background. He was also confirming if her account was consistent with whatever account Charlotte had given them, or whatever Robert said.

"Have you received any calls from strangers since your son got separated?"

"No."

"Anyone claiming to know something, instructing you not to tell us, like ransom demands from a kidnapper?"

"No. You don't think Gabriel's been—"

"I understand that you've previously had private security because of threats you received related to your job with Newslead?"

"Yes, but that was a while ago. We ended security after things calmed down. Do you think—" Corina turned to the scene, a new horror dawning "—do you think that this has something to do with the threats? After all this time?"

"We can't rule out anything at this point." He paused. "Did you receive threats today?"

"Just the usual insults. Nothing specific," she said, her voice quivering. "Nothing targeting my children."

"We're doing all we can to reunite Gabriel with his family."

Egan listed off much of the response: how they'd dispatched units to Gabriel's school and condominium; how they'd activated an intensive search of Central Park—the bathrooms, the playgrounds, everywhere; they were canvassing doormen and buildings surrounding the park; had alerted the transit and traffic systems; called in the aviation unit and canine teams; put out bulletins through social media; and were preparing an AMBER Alert.

"Charlotte said he had his phone with him. Our computer crimes people are on it, and they're good at tracking. They're working with your carrier. We have agreements with most for exigent circumstances like this."

"Don't you have cameras in the park?"

"Not inside the park. It's a privacy issue. We've got cameras at all the park entrances. We'll review the footage. We have transit and traffic system cameras, too. And we have agreements to look at security footage from local residential and commercial buildings. We can request the public to share any images from phones or dash cams."

Lifted a little by the police response, Corina nodded.

"And I don't have to tell you—" Egan indicated more news crews arriving at the scene's edge "—the press coverage is intensifying. I'm told they're already at the school and your condo building."

Corina shut her eyes for a second.

"And detectives from the One-Nine, your resident precinct, will need to talk to you and your family at your home. We're going to find him," Egan said, stopping his recording and ending his questions.

Corina blinked back tears as she left Egan's car. Through the web of emergency people coming and going, she found Charlotte and hurried toward her. Their eyes locked, a cold terror passing between them, Charlotte bolting to Corina, fusing herself to her with a crushing hug. Charlotte shook, her words coming out in choking sobs.

"I'm so sorry! It's my fault!"

Holding her, Corina was too afraid to be angry. She needed facts. "Tell me again what happened."

"He wanted to walk home through the park to fly his plane."

Charlotte pointed nearby to where benches and a low-rise fence bordered the walkway at the bottom of the grassy slope.

"I held his backpack for him and he flew the plane, but it went up there." She circled her trembling finger at the slope. "He ran around the fence over there." She pointed to the pathway that rose up the hill and led to 69th Street, the very path Corina had used. "He ran up to get it and I waited and he never came down. I called his phone. He didn't answer. I tried to find his phone with mine. Nothing worked!"

Charlotte sobbed.

"It was just up on that little hill. I should have gone up with him but—I didn't because, because—I'm so sorry."

"Because you were on your phone while he was looking for his plane?"

She didn't answer. She didn't have to. Corina knew the answer. Corina reined in her fury, deciding to retrace Gabriel's steps on the hill. Then she heard a dog's yelp.

An NYPD canine team was at Sergeant Egan's car. The officer handling the dog had retrieved Gabriel's backpack and was opening it. Egan signaled to Corina. They needed her.

"This is Officer Esser with Patrol Services, and his partner, Blaze."

"Ma'am," Esser said, withdrawing Gabriel's jacket. "Is this your son's jacket? And has he had recent contact with it?"

Corina nodded. "He put it on this morning."

Esser ensured Blaze got Gabriel's scent from his jacket, then they headed up the hill, disappearing into the bushes.

Corina started to follow them.

"Hold on," Egan said.

Other officers began stretching yellow plastic tape, cordoning off the entire area, as if it were a crime scene, as more specialized units arrived.

"Corina!"

"Ms. Corado!"

Reporters with New York City news outlets had arrived and called to her from the boundary police had created to hold them back beyond the emergency vehicles.

"Talk to us, Corina!"

"Police told us your son is missing!"

"What's your reaction to what's happening?"

She saw the faces, the cameras, microphones, lights and phones. How many times had she been among them, or in a press group, covering some terrible story somewhere? Now she was on the other side of the cameras. Now she was the story. And she couldn't face them. She couldn't deal with it. Shaking her head, she raised her palm.

But this is about Gabriel.

Corina wasn't thinking clearly. She had to find him, and here, before her, stood one of the greatest resources to help her. She strode toward them while cuing up Gabriel's photo on her phone. As she held it up, the group jostled, tightening in a horseshoe around her.

"This is my son, Gabriel Corado—he's six years old. I'm sure most of you have the police notice with a more recent picture—from today, maybe less than an hour, I don't know."

"What happened, Corina?"

"His sister was walking him home from school when they got separated in this area of the park."

Then questions came together: "Was he taken by a stranger?"

"Do you have any idea why this happened to your son?"

"What's your daughter's name?"

Corina held up her palms, forcing her voice to be calm and even.

"We just want to locate Gabriel and get him home safely. That's all I can say right now."

Corina turned but more questions followed her.

"Has anyone claimed responsibility?"

"What're your thoughts at this time?"

Making her way back into the activity of the scene, she rejoined Charlotte, holding her while the sky above them thudded as an NYPD helicopter passed. Corina knew the park had several lakes and ponds. The helicopter was scouring them for a body. The realization, the radio chatter, the police dog, officers searching, the news media, the gawkers—it all deepened her fear. Corina noticed Egan was on his phone, huddling with other officers, some of them talking into their radios. Their faces taut, their conversations amped up.

Something big was happening.

8

In the Queens neighborhood of Rego Park, an old blue Ford F-150 waited at a red light to turn left onto 67th Street.

The front doors bore a logo of a stylized hammer and the words *Super Eezzee Contracting.* The truck had a crew cab and a short bed; the left fender was wrinkled from a collision last month but the turn signal worked.

While it blinked, smoke curled from the cigarette in Ivan Beckke's hand. The window had been lowered; Beckke's arm rested on the frame. A grinning skull shrouded in a Grim Reaper's hood was tattooed on his bicep, visible because of the sleeveless Metallica T-shirt Beckke wore. He also had a stained Jets ball cap, the brim pulled down to his dark glasses, wild blondish locks loose around his unshaven face.

Beckke glanced around the intersection at the CVS, and the old discount clothing store, the multilevel parking garage and the apartment complex. The Ramones flowed from his radio, his head almost bobbing along with "Blitzkrieg Bop."

All was looking good now, Beckke thought. The job in the Upper West Side went better than he'd expected. He was figuring he'd be paid extra for his work as the light changed to green.

Beckke had just made a left onto 67th Street when the air split with piercing yelps of a siren. He stomped on the truck's brakes. An unmarked SUV emerged from nowhere, lights wigwagging in its grill and dash. It cut across within inches of Beckke's front bumper, stopping in T-bone style, blocking him.

"What the—!"

Beckke's jaw dropped, and his cigarette bounced off the wheel and out the window. In an instant, a white unmarked police sedan, with sirens and lights going, pulled tight to Beckke's passenger side. Then another SUV angled on the driver's side blocking his rear left quarter, boxing him in.

Beckke's head twisted as NYPD cops wearing body armor, badges clipped to their belts, guns drawn and aimed at him, closed in from all sides. The one in front of him, his handgun aimed at Beckke's head, shouted, "Toss the keys to the ground! Hands out the window! Now! Now! Now!"

Beckke complied.

One of the cops opened the driver's door, forcing Beckke out at gunpoint.

"On the ground, on your knees, hands behind you!"

The acrid smell of burning rubber filled the air. One cop snapped handcuffs on Beckke, then hefted him to his feet. Another patted him down, taking his wallet and phone from his pockets.

"What the hell?" Beckke said. "What'd I do?"

Other officers, their body cameras recording, searched Beckke's truck. One found a Glock 17 and two mags holding seventeen rounds each, wrapped in a towel under the passenger seat.

The officer moved to check the cab's rear seat.

He paused.

A heavy blanket was heaped in a corner.

The toe of a child's sneaker peeked from under it.

Adjusting his grip on his weapon with one hand, the officer reached his free hand to the blanket and drew it back slowly, finding a stuffed toy panda and a pair of empty, child-sized shoes.

Officers searching the bed of the truck found crates with cans of paint, heavy plastic storage bins holding tools, coiled extension cords, rope, duct tape, a collapsible table saw and boxes with compartments for nails, screws and smaller tools, like utility knives.

One side of the bed held a supply of lumber: more than a dozen two-by-fours, all cut in about six-foot lengths. As the officers studied the loose wooden bundle, light flickered in a gap, a reflection of the sun on glass on the floor.

The officer picked up the item: a phone.

He held it up in his gloved hand.

"Bingo!" he said to the others on the team.

The phone fit the description of Gabriel Corado's phone, which IT had tracked, pinpointing it to this pickup truck.

One of the cops standing before Beckke, holding Beckke's driver's license and phone, said: "Where's the boy?"

"I don't have him."

The cop's jaw muscles tightened as he eyed Beckke.

"You're under arrest. You have the right to remain silent..."

9

Burn in hell skank!

You lying POS!

If I see you, I'll gut you!

We're going to hang you in Times Square!

At her desk in the squad room of the Upper East Side's 19th Precinct, Detective Vicky Lonza studied the history of threats against Corina Corado. It was a sampling from a couple of years ago. Some were more personal, like the one where a strange woman walked up to Corado at LaGuardia and said, "I pray every night for you to get raped!"

Then Lonza came to the history of bomb threats at Newslead's building. Four in eight months. No bombs or packages had been found. But the incidents had forced evacuations, created chaos and fear. Ultimately, Corado got private security. It all went back a few years before tapering off, Lonza thought, with Corado and Newslead ending the security about a year ago.

Could this history be connected to her son being missing?

No new threats had arisen since.

Lonza closed the threat files on her computer, intent on taking a harder look after interviewing Corado and her family. But first things first, Lonza resumed checking updates out of Central Park. She reread the summaries of how Gabriel Corado got separated from his sister and saw how, taken together with the circumstances, the location, the family's profile and the background, the response had been elevated.

A possible kidnapping-in-progress.

A lot of resources had been activated and the police were going all out. And a potential break was emerging in Queens.

Lonza glanced at the hinged double photo frame beside her computer: Eva, her four-year-old daughter, and Marco, her nine-year-old son. Absorbing the light in their faces, her scarred heart fractured for Eva.

My angel.

Losing Eva had proved to be too much. It broke her marriage. And now Lonza worried about the toll the separation was taking on Marco, bouncing between their home and visits every second weekend to Staten Island. Marco's father, Tony, was a ferry captain. Lonza and Tony's divorce would be final in a few months. She was grateful her parents had stepped up to help, coming over, or watching Marco at their house. They worshipped Marco, and took care of him whenever she needed. Marco loved his grandparents and his grandparents' retriever, Luna, who was Marco's best pal.

Lonza looked to her partner at his desk across from hers: Harvey Grimes. He'd played for the US national hockey team and Boston College, and had been drafted by the Islanders. Cut after two seasons, he decided to follow in the steps of his dad and brother, becoming a cop with the NYPD. Grimes and his wife, Nadine, were expecting their first child.

Lonza and Grimes had been tapped to lead because Gabriel Corado's family resided within the 19th's command.

"Ready?" Lonza stood to leave. "We'll pick it up at Central Park."

Grimes pulled his eyes from his monitor, rising to go.

"That threat history's something," Grimes said as he and Lonza turned to see Garlan Weaver, their lieutenant, filling his office doorway.

"Hold up," Weaver said. "We got something in Queens. The One-Twelve just picked up a male suspect with the boy's phone in Rego Park."

Lonza and Grimes traded glances.

"Is this our guy?" Grimes asked.

"He didn't have the boy," Weaver said. "But they're tossing him to us. I expect delivery any minute. You two will question him."

10

Believing police had learned of a break, Corina went to Sergeant Egan, urging him to step away from the officers at the scene in Central Park.

"What's going on?" she said.

He shook his head slowly.

"I don't have details."

"You know something."

Looking at her, Egan appeared to grapple with revealing anything to Corina.

"We've got a lot of people investigating. I'm sorry, that's all I can say."

"Is Gabriel hurt?"

Egan didn't answer.

Corina's eyes bored into his.

"Is he dead? *You tell me right now if Gabriel's dead!*"

Egan blinked a few times.

"I don't have answers for you. I wish I did."

Searching his eyes for deception and finding none, Corina walked away. She knew cops were tight-lipped about investigations, fearful of jeopardizing a case, or releasing incorrect information.

But it's not going to stop me from finding out.

She adjusted her hold on her phone to call her newsroom. Like all newsrooms, Newslead assigned people to listen to emergency radio scanners. They were skilled at deciphering transmissions, determining what was happening in real time. But before calling, she cast a glance to where the news crews were gathered. Some people were on their phones; some were packing up, hurrying to their vehicles.

They know.

She moved toward a crew she'd spotted from Newslead: Dakota Adams, a new reporter who covered the city, and Del Sotto, a veteran camera operator.

Del was on his phone, but Dakota spotted her.

"Corina, everyone at Newslead's so concerned for what's happened to your son," Dakota said. "We just arrived and Del says there's been a development."

Phone to his ear, camera under one arm, Del gave Corina a finger wave then said, "An arrest has been made in the case." He slid his phone into his pocket, repositioning his camera. "They're bringing the person to the One-Nine now. We've gotta go."

"Wait! I'm going with you! Just wait!" Corina said, then rushed back to Charlotte, who was nearby with officers, and took her aside.

"Charlotte, I have to go."

"Where? Why?" Charlotte flung her arms around Corina. "Mom, please don't go!"

"I need to go with a news crew."

"What?" Charlotte pulled back; eyes narrowing. "You're working?"

"No, something's come up."

"What?"

"I don't know everything, just listen, I need you to stay here with police to alert me if they find him. I need you to do that." She took Charlotte's face in her hands, staring hard at her. "Can you do that?"

Forcing back tears, Charlotte nodded.

"I'll keep you posted, too," Corina said, hugging her.

Seconds later Corina was trotting with Dakota and Del to their SUV. Del started it and got onto the 65th Street transverse road, the motor roaring as he shoved a stick of gum into his mouth. The park blurred by as Corina fought to find calm in her nightmare.

"I saw the police reacting to something," she said from the back seat. "Del, what do you know about the arrest?"

"It's not clear." Del chewed. "From what we picked up on the scanners there was a takedown in Queens."

"Anything about Gabriel?"

Working his gum, Del shook his head.

"Maybe we'll get more at the precinct," Dakota said.

"Corina." Del met her face in the mirror. "You're going to find him."

She patted his shoulder.

The 19th Precinct was four blocks from the park's east side. Del scoured the area to find a parking space, pulling tight to the rear of a Mercedes and encroaching on the entrance to the garage door of a condo. They hustled down the street, which was dotted with parked patrol cars as they neared the precinct. A traffic cop kept media trucks from stopping, keeping access to the street clear for the firehall next door. Corina, Del and Dakota joined the other news crews just in time. A siren issued a sharp bleep as an unmarked SUV arrived, its grill and dash lights flashing.

"Here we go! That's him!" someone said.

TV lights came on and, under the glare of news cameras scrambling into position, Ivan Beckke was perp-walked in handcuffs on East 67th Street. Corina concentrated on him, her mind swirling, heart hammering, and then she charged toward Beckke. The detectives on either side of him shot out their hands. Beckke's jaw opened as she stood toe-to-toe with him.

"Where's my son?"

Beckke stared back, confused, shaking his head, saying nothing. The cameras tightened in on the scene, still photographers clicking away.

"Back off!" a detective shouted at Corina. "Ma'am, step away now!"

The detectives ushered Beckke past Corina and into the five-story brick and granite station house of the 19th Precinct. She stood alone outside the entrance as the press moved in. Corina was deaf to reporters extending microphones, calling for comment. Refusing defeat, she entered the station house.

Seeing no sign of the arrested man, she went to the sergeant at the desk.

"Where's the man they just brought in?"

Recognizing Corina, he said, "Ms. Corado, he's going to be processed and interviewed. It could take a while."

"What does he know about my son?"

"Ma'am, you should go home. You'll be notified."

"Notified about what? I want to speak to whoever's in charge."

The sergeant held up his hand then reached for his phone and said something into it. Behind her, officers closed the door reporters had opened, denying the news media entry, stating: "Stay out with those cameras. You know recording is not permitted in here." A moment later Lieutenant Garlan Weaver emerged.

"Lieutenant, this is Corina Corado," the sergeant said.

"I know. Hello, Ms. Corado." Weaver nodded, inviting Corina to sit with him on a bench nearby.

"Did you find my son? Why was this man arrested? Who is he?"

"We're going to talk to him."

"Is Gabriel hurt? Is he dead?" Corina's voice cracked.

"We're going to talk to the person we have here but it's going to take some time. Let us investigate. Let us do our job."

"But my son?"

"I can only imagine what you're going through right now. I know it's hard. Our detectives will be in touch later and we may know a little more then. So, the best thing for you to do now is go home."

Weaver offered to have a patrol car take her home or back to the park, whatever she wanted.

She declined.

A short time later, Corina was standing outside the precinct in front of the news cameras, facing questions.

"All I know," she said, a tissue balled in her fist, "is that they're going to question the man they've brought in. And no, I have no idea who he is."

After Corina left with Dakota and Del, some of the TV reporters did stand-ups in front of their cameras.

"…in a dramatic moment, Newslead journalist and anchor Corina Corado arrived at the precinct just as the man arrested for questioning in the disappearance of her son was brought in, in handcuffs. Corado confronted the man, demanding to know where her son is… Let's play that scene again…"

11

INSIDE THE 19TH PRECINCT, Ivan Beckke was searched, photographed and fingerprinted, and his identity was confirmed.

He didn't need to be Mirandized again. Before he was put in a holding cell, he was permitted to make calls. Beckke reached Thad Charters, the lawyer who'd nearly impoverished him after handling his divorce. Charters, who spoke with a rasping voice, arranged for a criminal defense attorney. Charters, his words grating over the line, told Beckke: "Sure, Ivan, sure, very modest rates and she's on her way now."

The arrest had set more investigative wheels in motion. After handing off Beckke, the detectives from Queens briefed Lonza and Grimes. Then, through video calls, Lonza and Grimes collected every iota of up-to-date information from officers at the Central Park scene.

While Beckke waited for his lawyer, NYPD forensic experts were examining Gabriel's phone and Beckke's truck. It appeared the kids' shoes weren't a match for Gabriel's. Still, a canine team was brought in to determine if Gabriel had been in the truck. Warrants were being obtained for Beckke's phone records and for other searches at locations linked to him.

The gun and ammunition found in Beckke's truck were being examined.

Detectives from other precincts were dispatched to canvass Beckke's employer, his colleagues and people in his circle. Investigators scrutinized his social media posts and accounts. At the 19th Precinct, Beckke's name was run through the system for any outstanding warrants, a summons, unpaid traffic tickets, any and all court records.

Lieutenant Weaver got a call from 26 Federal Plaza; the FBI was standing by prepared to provide support, if requested.

In just under an hour, Beckke's lawyer, Sophia Saint Paul, arrived and talked briefly with the detectives. She was unsmiling, all business, with a lot of nodding and note-taking on a yellow pad. Then for forty-five minutes, she spoke privately with Beckke before they were escorted into the interview room.

Weaver, Lonza and Grimes watched from the observation room. The detectives were prepared with all they had from the work done so far.

Ivan Hector Beckke, 37—high school dropout, subcontractor, renovator. Divorced Deidre Beckke, 35, two years ago. Deidre got custody of their son, Bobby, now age 4. Ivan resides with his widowed mother, Irma Beckke, 66, in a two-story frame house in Flushing Meadows, Queens.

Staring at Beckke through the one-way mirror, Lonza suddenly thought of Corina Corado, who she'd seen many times on Newslead, and how she'd come to the station house to confront Beckke.

In that moment, Corina was no longer the journalist, but an anguished mother, and, like any mother, she would be here fighting for her son.

I so get that. It's crystalline to me.

Because as a mother, Lonza knew about monsters and what they could do. But she swallowed the sentiment. She couldn't afford to feel what Corina might be feeling right now. Lonza was not there to help shoulder the agony; she was there to find the truth, to find Gabriel.

Lonza looked at Grimes and saw an intensity burning in his deep-set eyes, his jaw clenched.

"All set, Harvey?"

"Let's do this."

They entered the interview room. The scraping of their chairs bounced against the bare white walls as they sat across the table from Beckke and his lawyer.

Saint Paul's eyes flicked to the small camera lens in the corner near the ceiling, aware their session would be recorded. She clicked her pen, poised over her pad.

"For the record, my client is cooperating with the investigation and denies any involvement in the disappearance of the boy in Central Park."

Grimes's eyebrows edged up. "Yet he was driving around with Gabriel Corado's phone in his truck."

"He has no knowledge of how, or why, the phone was in the open back of his vehicle," Saint Paul said.

Lonza glanced at her notebook.

"Ivan," Lonza said, "you've got a sheet here that goes way back. Deidre called 911 to say you were assaulting her, then withdrew the complaint. You were charged with drunk driving but pleaded down. You assaulted Deidre again, but got that down to a misdemeanor. Then you fractured her jaw. You did ten months for that. She finally divorced you, took Bobby and the house, and now she has a new man in her life, Raylon Lewis."

"As we speak," Grimes said, "we've got people going through your truck and your mother's house for any trace of Gabriel Corado. What do you think we're going to find?"

Beckke looked into his hands and shook his head.

"Can you tell us why—" Lonza looked at her notes "—when the arresting officer asked you about the missing boy, you said, 'I don't have him'?"

"My client thought he was being asked about his son, that it was a custody issue," Saint Paul said. "My client has nothing to do with this case. You have weak circumstance, no grounds for holding him. I request his release."

"We're holding him," Lonza said.

"On what grounds?" Saint Paul asked.

"Besides being in possession of Gabriel Corado's phone?" Lonza said. "The Glock found in his truck was among the weapons reported stolen two months ago from the home of a retired marine in Nassau County."

"Ivan," Grimes said. "If you're going to cooperate, then cooperate and tell us what you did with the boy."

Beckke remained silent.

"We've talked to people at your job, your friends," Lonza said.

"You're being squeezed," Grimes said. "You're behind on child support, alimony, truck payments."

Beckke pushed back tears and looked away.

"At the bar you cry to your friends about how Deidre's draining you, killing you," Grimes said. "But she's living with Raylon, who's in your face over visitation, acting like he's Bobby's father. You say you're thinking of grabbing Bobby and disappearing to someplace in Oregon, starting clean, if you only had enough money to do it."

"We know you've done a lot of work in this part of the city," Lonza said.

"You see how the people live," Grimes said. "How some are dripping with money. So you think, grab a kid, hold him for cash, then let him go and you're on your way with Bobby. Kinda like going to an ATM."

Beckke shook his head.

"Ivan," Lonza said. "We've tracked your phone movements today and spoken with your boss. You were in the Upper West Side near Central Park when Gabriel Corado disappeared."

Grimes said: "Did you follow him from the Tillmon school and into the park? Did you act on an impulse and opportunity? Maybe you got close enough to see his name on his airplane, to know who he is. Maybe you tricked him into coming with you. But then something went wrong. You thought you got rid of his phone, tossed it, but it bounced into the back of your truck. And we tracked you before you were even set up for a ransom call."

"Is that what happened, Ivan?" Lonza said. "Are you hiding the boy somewhere? Are you working with someone?"

"Now's the time to set things right," Grimes said. "Help us help you. Where's the boy?"

"Make it easy on yourself," Lonza said. "Tell us where the boy is and we'll tell the district attorney how you cooperated and never hurt the boy."

"You didn't hurt him, did you, Ivan?" Grimes asked.

Beckke shook his head, his eyes brimming with tears. "Everything's so messed up."

12

Gabriel's out there.

Corina stood at the floor-to-ceiling window of her 38th-floor condominium overlooking Central Park, her heart imploring heaven to help find her son.

The blue sky was fading to pink coral, lights flickering like hope in Manhattan's skyscrapers. She was on her phone concentrating on her call to New York City's police commissioner. Corina had the commissioner's private number. They'd spoken on stories before. The commissioner was a lawyer, a former detective, never one for BS. Corina knew the woman would take her call, even if it meant interrupting a charity gala at the Ritz-Carlton.

"I have no word on the arrest. What I know is they're looking at…hang on…" the commissioner spoke over the clinking cutlery and conversations "…they're looking at cameras at the park entrances and the entire area outside the wall. As you know, we don't have any cameras inside the park."

"And hospitals?" Corina asked. "He could've fallen, bumped his head—maybe someone found him and took him in."

"They've circulated alerts to hospitals and EMS with his photo."

A tense moment ticked by.

"Corina," the commissioner said, "everyone has your son in their thoughts. I give you my word, we'll spare nothing to bring him back to you."

Ending the call, her mind swirling, Corina looked down at the park. The ocean of green darkening in the sunset had become a black hole—*where no light can escape.*

Guilt gnawed at her for not thinking, for not simply getting a car service, or friends, to pick up Gabriel, but wanting Charlotte—*was it to keep a tight rein on her?*—to get him; guilt for insisting they end private security a year ago; guilt for working so hard for so many years to come this far, only for her family…

Oh God…is this the price?

Corina turned to the table nearby—it looked like a computer store display. Three laptops—hers, her husband's and Charlotte's—each sat open, NYPD officers monitoring them for possible ransom demands, talking in subdued tones. Across the room, friends had gathered in front of the flat-screen TV, surfing channels for news and scrolling their phones. It could almost pass for an informal party, she thought, if the room didn't hold a funereal air, a sense of anticipated tragedy.

Charlotte was near her, curled in a sofa chair, knees to her chin, face in her phone.

Robert stood with them, on his phone talking to police, one hand gripping his temple, lines of anguish creasing his face.

Upon landing in New York, he'd rushed to the park and found Charlotte with Corina, who'd returned after the confrontation at the precinct.

He'd hugged Charlotte.

Then he took Corina in his arms, feeling the strength of her embrace.

"We'll find him," he said. "It'll be alright."

"I know, I know," Corina said.

His presence had helped. Whatever frustration Corina had felt about him earlier that day was eclipsed as he absorbed what had happened, challenged police about their search for Gabriel and received the same answers she had. News helicopters thundered over the park just before afternoon faded into evening. Ultimately, Robert gave in to investigators at the scene, conceding that it was best for the family to wait for word at home.

News crews were collected on the sidewalk in front of their building when the family arrived in a marked patrol car. Corina had declined to use the secure garage entrance, choosing again to go to the cameras and plead for Gabriel, this time with Robert and Charlotte at her side.

"Someone knows something. Someone saw something," she said, her voice strong, eyes glistening in the lights. "Please, help us find Gabriel."

Now, in the suffocating, taut air of their home, she looked at Robert on his phone trying to extract information from Lieutenant Weaver about the man arrested in Queens.

"They've had him for hours," Robert said. "He must've told you about our son. Why was he arrested? Your people here don't know anything. No one's telling us a damned thing, not a word… How much longer…"

Suddenly, the TV's volume was raised. Friends in the living room stood and a few turned to Corina, summoning her to watch.

It was tuned to Newslead. Her colleague Tina Asher was on the desk saying, *"…involving a member of our news family today… Gabriel Corado, the six-year-old son of Corina Corado, a Newslead journalist, went missing in Central Park while walking home from his Upper West Side school with his older sister…"*

Moving toward the TV, Corina brought her hand to her mouth when Gabriel's smiling face appeared on the screen. Then came footage of Tillmon, Central Park West and the park, with quick cuts to an NYPD officer at the scene earlier, updating reporters on the search. Corina's stomach twisted watching the dog team scour the hill, then police in a grid search, police searching subway stations, canvassing doormen along the streets bordering the park, looking in dumpsters as the helicopter thumped overhead.

Steadying herself against a sofa arm, Corina glanced at Charlotte, her face a mask of distress as she watched the report. Corina looked to Robert; his jaw clenched as he watched. He moved next to her, took her hand in a reassuring squeeze, and she turned back to the story.

"...ongoing major effort covering the vast area..." Asher said, noting how the 843-acre park received more than forty-two million visitors annually. *"...a development that came within hours, police in Queens made a dramatic arrest of a man...and we've obtained pictures..."* Shaky video captured on someone's phone rolled. *"...he was then taken to the 19th Precinct in the Upper East Side..."* Then came footage of Corina facing the man, demanding to know about Gabriel.

"A short time later, Corina spoke with our own Dakota Adams." The interview she had given after Del and Dakota drove her back to the park played.

"Our children know the park," Corina said. *"We live blocks away. The school's nearby. They use the park every other day. They feel safe here."*

"As we know," Dakota said, *"some time ago you, and Newslead, experienced serious threats from people who took issue with your reporting..."*

"They took issue with the truth, with reality."

"Do you think it's possible that what's happened today could be connected to those threats?"

"I don't know," she said. *"With the arrest, we have so many questions. All I can say is someone must've seen something."*

The report ended and came back to Tina Asher. She looked down at a sheet of paper on the desk, then directly at the camera.

"Okay, this just in," she said, urgency in her voice. *"Newslead has learned that the man arrested is Ivan Hector Beckke, a thirty-seven-year-old contractor from Queens. We're told, and this is key, that police tracked Gabriel Corado's phone and Beckke was in possession of the phone when he was arrested. No word on Gabriel Corado. That's all we have at this time. We'll update you when we can. Alright, we'll go to a break..."*

"Oh my God—what?" Corina shouted at the screen, raised her phone and called her newsroom. "It's Corina. Who's on? Phil? Put him on!" She stared at the ceiling, blinking, waiting. "Phil, I just saw it—what is this? You guys knew about Beckke having Gabriel's phone and you didn't tell me?"

"Corina, we just got it from sources at the One-Twelve. We were going to call, but we had to get it on."

While Corina was on the phone, she saw Robert demanding answers from the officers in their condo about a suspect having Gabriel's phone. As the officers shook their heads, Robert raised his voice.

"Well, someone sure as hell knows something!"

Going back to her call, Corina asked: "What else did you find out?"

"That's it, that's all. We're digging into it and we'll reach out to you when we know more. Everybody here's thinking of you."

Clenching her eyes, she nodded.

"Alright."

Seconds after her call, her phone vibrated with messages as more people learned about Gabriel. Then it rang and she answered.

"Corina, it's Beth-Anne. I just heard." Corina welcomed the familiar British voice. She'd interviewed Beth-Anne Bridger, the Oscar-winning British actor, years back, when Bridger was unknown. They'd been friends ever since. "I just got back in the country for work on a film upstate at Evans Mills and saw the news about Gabriel. Please, please let me know if there's anything I can do. I could ask our security to send people to help in the search?"

"Thank you—" Corina pushed back a sob. "I'll let you know."

Other messages and calls followed. Journalists from rival networks offered Corina and her family their support, while making interview requests. Robert received well-wishes from friends, colleagues and clients. Community and neighborhood groups sent messages saying they'd coordinated teams to search for Gabriel and would launch a campaign online, offering a reward for information. Corina received a text that said: We're going to find Gabriel, Corina. Be strong. It was from the governor.

A loud gasp seized Corina's attention, and everyone's focus shifted to Charlotte in the chair, her eyes wide, staring at her phone, shaking her head.

"Why—how could they—why, why?"

The officers went to her, along with Robert and Corina, who angled the phone so they all could see.

A new post said: *Corado got what she deserved cuz she's THE QUEEN OF LIES!!!*

Accompanying the text was a crude, animated video depicting a cartoon figure with Corina's real headshot atop a cliff alongside a cartoon figure with Gabriel's face, from the photo Charlotte had taken. The action showed Gabriel slipping from Corina's grasp, plunging to the ground and shattering into pieces.

13

EFREM ZYLLER LIKED his whiskey neat.

The crisp, honeyed taste of the brand he'd discovered at a distillery in Ireland warmed his throat as he sat alone at his desk in Newslead.

Manhattan's lights shimmered through the windows of his 41st-floor office. But Zyller's attention was on the monitors and the deluge of news reports on Corina Corado's missing son.

It was gut-wrenching.

Gabriel Corado's face blossomed on his screens.

Then footage of police searching the park, while a helicopter hovered above. Here were police talking to doormen and staff at businesses. Here was Corina in the park before the cameras pleading for Gabriel. Now here she was in front of the police precinct confronting a suspect.

Zyller thought Corina's ferociousness, her intensity, magnificent. Memory took him back to the night when Corina was here in this office alone with him, a late meeting after she'd filled in anchoring a nighttime show. How he savored what she wore, her smile, her dark sheath dress, a hint of L'Air du Temps.

Corina knew what she was doing when she came to him that night.

For her to deny it, to twist reality into a threat against him, well, *that would not be permitted.* She hadn't done anything yet, as far as he knew. Maybe because he'd made clear what was at stake if she complained.

Such a terrible coincidence what was happening with her son.

Now Zyller's nostrils flared with sharp breaths as he sipped his drink and watched Corina beg for Gabriel on the TV and computer screens before him. Maybe this tragic incident would distract her from their private war? That was cold but so be it. Better the distraction, because there was no way he would let Corina, or anyone, end what he'd taken years to build. No matter the cost, whatever it took, he would not allow them to write the last chapter in his career.

Because Corina Corado had known what she was doing.

Just like the others.

For the few who'd attempted to pervert what he knew in his heart was a consensual communion, for those who'd threatened to ruin him, it never ended well. He'd always taken steps, to unearth something about them—*and there was always something*—to defuse the situation.

Taking another drink, he empathized with Corina in her anguish.

This is real. This is happening. She must be going out of her mind.

Zyller could only imagine what she might do, or say.

I have to stay on top of things.

Loosening his tie, he picked up his phone to make a call.

14

AnonTruthAngel_666.

It was the name linked to the mocking, hurtful posting depicting Gabriel's death.

The officers at the condominium got on their phones, setting out to work with other investigators to identify whoever was behind it.

The post, rapidly racking up hundreds of views, had struck a nerve with Charlotte. Corina and Robert brought her into his study for some privacy. Robert closed the door, and Corina helped Charlotte to the sofa. Looking at them, Charlotte asked: "Why do people hate us?"

"They have problems," Robert said. "They like causing pain."

"I get that, Dad, but why do they hate *us*?" She locked onto Corina. "And especially *you*?"

"Charlie, don't," her father said.

"No, she's always working, working, working!"

"All I did," Corina said, "was ask you to bring your little brother home."

"Charlie." Lowering himself, Robert took her hands. "Tell us again what happened."

She pulled her hands away.

"For the millionth time, I fucked up, okay?" She glared at her parents, dropped her head.

"You were on your phone," Corina said. "Instead of watching Gabriel, you were texting with that man, that driver, we told you not to talk to."

Charlotte's head snapped up, and she scowled at Corina.

"Let me live my life!"

"He's twenty-one and you're sixteen!" Corina said.

"Why do you work at a job that makes people hate you so much? You love your job and being famous more than you love us!"

"Oh my God," Corina said.

"Stop, Charlie," Robert said. "You know what Mom does is important, and lately she's been under a lot of pressure."

Corina looked at Robert in disbelief. Was he blaming her, too?

"It's all my fault, alright?" Charlotte got up from the sofa and left the study, slamming the door behind her.

"Oh my God." Corina turned to Robert. "Do you think this is my fault?"

"No, I don't," he said. "But before this, you seemed stressed. Then today, I saw the tabloid item about your position at Newslead being tenuous."

"What about you, Robert? You've been secretive, distant. What's up with you? What happened in Philadelphia?"

"What do you mean, *secretive*? I went there for the contract for the building. You know all about it."

"What about those calls? You practically whisper into the phone lately."

"There's a lot at stake on this contract," he said. "It's complicated."

"Uncomplicate it," Corina said as her phone rang. Gil Dixon from Newslead. Figuring it could be about Gabriel, she answered.

"Corina, it's Gil. I talked to Phil about the piece that just ran."

"Gil, I need to know what you guys know."

"You're right, I'm sorry. Listen, we're all behind you on this. I spoke with Efrem and he says the network will do whatever it can to—"

"I don't want *his* help."

"If this is about the tabloid hit, I don't know where it came from, and for God's sake, don't believe—"

"Gil—" Corina's voice trembled "—I have one priority: to find my son. And I need—" A knock sounded on the door.

Robert opened it to one of the officers, who said, "The detectives are here."

"Gil, you guys have to keep me updated on anything you learn. I've got to go."

Detective Vicky Lonza never got used to the luxurious homes in the Upper East Side.

The soaring glass towers were a world away from her semidetached frame house in Woodhaven, Queens, and her partner Harvey Grimes's townhouse in Brooklyn's Bed-Stuy.

But working in the 19th, Lonza had become familiar with these places. Even with all their amenities, like twenty-four-hour concierge service, God's-eye views of the city and spas for dogs—*bet Luna would love to be pampered in one of those*—she'd learned a few universal truths. One was that no one was above the law. Everyone's a potential suspect. Another was that fear didn't care about status. It cut across the board, and Lonza saw it cutting deep into the faces of the family when she and Grimes stepped into Robert Tanner's study.

Charlotte was called back to the room.

They'd barely gotten through introductions and Lonza's request to record the interview on her phone—"Yes, yes," Corina Corado said—when the questions began.

"Did you find Gabriel?" Corina asked.

"No, not yet," Lonza said. "We're doing all we can."

"What about Beckke, the man you arrested?" Corina asked. "Did he have Gabriel's phone? What did he tell you about Gabriel?"

Lonza gestured for them to join Charlotte on the sofa. Lonza leaned on the edge of the desk and Grimes took a chair.

Corina remained standing. "Did Ivan Beckke have Gabriel's phone? Did he take Gabriel?"

"He had his phone, but we're still determining whether he's involved in Gabriel's disappearance."

Charlotte let out a pained squeal she muffled with her hands.

"But you think he is, right?" Robert said.

"Is he a pedo creep?" Charlotte asked.

"We can't say much," Lonza said, "because Beckke's facing charges."

"What charges?" Corina said.

"We're investigating," Lonza said. "I'm sorry. I know that's not what you want to hear right now. But we need to go over a few things. Please, sit. Please."

Corina slowly eased down beside Robert, who put his arm around her. Grimes opened his valise and withdrew his tablet. Lonza took her notebook from her bag and paged through it.

"Our officers here indicate that, so far," Lonza said, "you've received no communication, such as ransom calls or claims of involvement?"

"No, none," Corina said. "Should we expect one? Is Beckke working with someone?"

"That's an unknown at this point," Lonza said.

"What about all the cameras you have?" Corina said. "Gabriel must be on some of them?"

"We're still looking—it takes time," Lonza said.

"Isn't Beckke on them? How did you find him?" Robert asked.

"We tracked Gabriel's phone," Lonza said.

"Then he knows where Gabriel is," Robert said.

"We can't confirm that just yet," Lonza said.

"I don't understand!" Corina shook her head.

"All we can tell you at this point is we're investigating," Lonza said. "We're reviewing available security footage of Beckke's movements, establishing a timeline, linking his path of travel to when your son was reported missing."

"It would help us get a clearer picture," Grimes said, shifting the focus, "if we went over your statements. Do you have a routine getting Gabriel to school and picking him up?"

"In the mornings, Robert or I will drop him off on our way to work," Corina said. "Depending on when we leave. In the afternoon, same thing, one of us will pick him up. Or we notify a car service we know and trust, Empire CloudGlide. Or, sometimes, Charlotte will help."

"Can you give us an average for the last three months?" Grimes asked.

"It varies," Corina said. "On average, I'd say we each get him once a week, then use the service a couple times a week."

"And the way you go home?"

"Car, cab or walking," Corina said.

"So, if someone were watching, stalking you," Lonza said, "would you agree they could see something of a routine?"

"It's possible," Corina said. "Do you think that's what happened?"

"One avenue of investigation," Lonza said. "Could you go back as far as possible and log dates, routes, travel methods for us?"

"We can do that," Corina said.

"We can check with Empire, too," Lonza said. "Okay, so, you didn't notify Empire today?"

"No, because their policy requires twenty-four-hour advance notice for school pickups," Corina said.

"Alright," Grimes said. "Corina, you were working at Newslead when you asked Charlotte to bring Gabriel home from the Tillmon school. Why did you ask her to get him?"

"Robert had planned to get him, but he was delayed getting home from Philadelphia. It was sudden. I knew from the app on my phone that Charlotte was close by and I thought it best if Charlotte got him."

Making notes, Lonza turned to Charlotte. "And where were you when your mom asked you to get him?"

"Bell Ritchie's on Amsterdam with my friend Harper Hall."

"Who else knew you were getting him?" Grimes asked.

"Just Harper, and I left her at the café."

Grimes cued up a map on his tablet and asked Charlotte to trace the path she took from the café to the school.

"Then you proceeded to the park," Lonza said, "with your brother openly carrying his plane with his name on it?"

"Yes," Charlotte said, tracing the map. "We went this way to the 72nd Street entrance."

"Did you stop anywhere? Go inside anywhere?"

"No."

"Did anyone talk to you along the way?" Grimes asked.

"No. Well, just my mom."

"Did you notice anyone following you?" Lonza asked. "Anything strange, out of the ordinary?"

"No."

"So, you've entered the park," Grimes said, indicating the map.

Charlotte's shaking finger traced their path in the park along West Drive to the spot near the Bowling and Croquet Greens and Sheep Meadow.

"This is where he flew his plane." Charlotte's voice trembled. "It disappeared over the top of the hill, so he ran to get it."

"You were waiting near West Drive when he ran out of your sight?" Lonza said.

"I was watching, but I was also texting with a friend."

"Harper Hall?"

Charlotte shook her head. "His name is Vince Tarone."

"Boyfriend?" Grimes asked.

"Maybe, I guess." Charlotte glanced at her parents. "We met a few months ago when he picked me up with my friends. He's a ride-share driver."

"He's twenty-one." Corina's tone dipped.

Lonza was slightly taken aback. "Tarone's twenty-one and you're sixteen?"

Charlotte hesitated before nodding. Lonza made a note.

"So, you're texting Vince," Lonza said. "Does he know you're in the park with Gabriel?"

"Yes."

"What were you texting Vince about?"

"He invited me to a party Friday night in SoHo."

Robert muttered a curse and shook his head.

"We didn't know this," Robert said. "We told you to end your relationship with him, Charlotte."

Lonza and Grimes traded glances.

"Has Tarone ever been a problem for you?" Grimes cast the question more to Corina and Robert.

"No," Corina said. "Nothing we're aware of."

Lonza focused on Charlotte.

"You were texting Tarone when you lost sight of your brother?"

Nodding, Charlotte shut her eyes, squeezing out more tears.

"I called for Gabriel and when I couldn't find him, I called his phone. He had it in his back pocket when he went over the hill."

"And he knows how to use his phone?" Lonza said.

"Yes," Corina said. "We set it up and showed him."

"Do you know if it was turned on?" Grimes said.

Corina looked to Charlotte, who whispered, "No," pushing back sobs.

"I looked everywhere. I couldn't find him and I went to a police officer on a horse and—I'm sorry, I'm so sorry!"

Letting a moment pass, the detectives turned to Robert.

"You're an engineer. You were in Philadelphia for work?" Lonza said.

"Yes."

"Why did your work take you to Philadelphia?"

Robert straightened a little.

"To meet with a building company, a contractor."

"Why were you meeting this company?"

"Why?" Robert repeated. "It was business, but I don't see what this has to do with Gabriel."

"It will help us."

Robert rubbed his temple. "I'm a forensic structural engineer. I've been contracted by a condo board that's in a dispute with developers of one of the new supertall luxury condominiums here in Manhattan."

"To do what?" Grimes asked.

"Residents want us to prove their allegations that their building is unsafe. They're threatening legal action if expensive repairs aren't made to maintain the value of their units. A lot of money is at stake on all sides. A lot of contractors, a lot of big players."

"Sounds stressful," Grimes said.

"Yes, a lot of pressure is being exerted. None of this has been made public."

"And you were supposed to fly home this morning, in time to pick up your son, but were delayed by an additional meeting?" Lonza said.

"Yes."

"This additional meeting was unscheduled, unexpected?" Lonza asked.

"Yes. I let Corina know that I wouldn't be back in time to get Gabriel."

Lonza made notes.

"Did anything unusual happen to you in Philadelphia?" Grimes asked.

Robert hesitated before he said, "No, nothing unusual."

"You say a lot of pressure's being exerted," Lonza said. "Is it possible it could take the shape of threats, actions or leverage against you?"

Robert blinked at the implication someone linked to his work might have kidnapped Gabriel. Weighing the question, he said, "No, I don't think so."

"Could you provide us names and contact information of the people you met in Philadelphia, and those with your company here?" Lonza asked.

"Yes."

Lonza turned her focus to Corina.

"Today, one of the tabloids suggested your job at Newslead may be at risk."

Corina shook her head. "I'm not thinking of that now."

"I know, but it must be upsetting. And, taken with Charlotte's relationship with Tarone, your husband's situation, it seems like there's a lot of tension in your home. Is it possible Gabriel picked up on it and maybe ran off and threw his phone away?"

"Absolutely not," Corina said, battling to restrain anger at the suggestion. "He's never run off, he just wouldn't."

Robert dragged both hands over his face, then said, "Why aren't you out there looking for him?"

"We've got people combing the park, canvassing everywhere, alerts everywhere," Grimes said. "We've got detectives from the major case squad, computer crimes and missing persons on the case, and the FBI is assisting, as are State Police. We've also got people talking to Newslead's security people."

"Corina," Lonza said. "One critical concern is the history of the threats against you in the past. You received a flow of attacks online culminating with an armed, disturbed man entering Newslead intending to hurt you."

A deepening fear mixed with regret arose on Corina's face. "It was horrible. I hated that we needed personal security. But that incident was nearly two years ago."

"And you discontinued security a year ago?" Lonza said.

Corina nodded.

"Things have calmed down. It's mostly just insulting messages now."

"We don't want to make any assumptions," Lonza said, "or jump to any conclusions, but, Corina, do you think it's possible that these threats could be related to Gabriel's disappearance?"

"Oh God, I don't know," Corina said with an underpinning of self-condemnation.

"With the world as it is these days, it's hard to determine what is a serious threat and what is rhetoric. We need to assess every message and posting aimed at you."

Corina nodded.

"That's a lot of work," Robert said.

"We've got people set to start," Grimes said. "It's one more aspect of the investigation."

"And we'd like you to review all your past interviews and news stories," Lonza said.

"My reporting?"

"Since the worst threats arose from your interview a couple of years ago, we need you to take a look at them with an eye for any possible links. We can't rule anything out," Grimes said.

"We understand Gabriel is adopted?" Lonza said.

"Yes, when he was a baby."

"Did you use a surrogate, an agency? What were the circumstances?"

"It was a private adoption," Robert said.

"Do you keep contact with the biological mother?" Grimes asked.

"No."

"Do you think the biological mother could be a factor in what's happened?" Grimes said. "Sometimes they come back into the picture, for various reasons."

"God, no," Corina said. "Not at all. No."

"Could you give us her name?" Grimes said.

Corina took a moment, looked at Robert, then said, "We vowed, as a condition of the process, to always protect her identity."

The detectives exchanged glances.

"We can't. It's all sealed in the adoption records," Robert said. "A court won't unseal them unless it's a medical emergency."

"Yes, we know. Still, it's an avenue we might pursue, if necessary," Lonza said. "Is Gabriel aware he's adopted?"

"Yes, we consulted a psychologist and started talking about it with him when he turned four, to build trust," Corina said. "He's done well, knowing the truth."

The detectives traded glances.

"So," Grimes said, "you're confident the adoption aspect has no bearing on Gabriel's disappearance?"

"We are," Robert said.

"Almost done," Lonza said. "Before we leave, we'd like to take a walk through your home here."

"But the other officers did that already," Robert said. "They searched through everything."

"Yes, but we need to, as well, particularly your son's room," Grimes said.

"First we just have a few more things to go over," Lonza said.

The detectives collected the names and contact information of everyone mentioned, including Harper, Vince and the people and companies Robert was dealing with. Grimes also explained how they needed everyone's fingerprints and devices, including phones.

"Our phones?" Robert said.

"Yes, all your phones," Grimes said.

"But—" Robert hesitated.

The detectives stared at Robert, then Corina.

"But what?" Lonza said. "Is this a problem?"

"We need our phones to do our jobs, to function," Robert said.

"It's purely procedural for the investigation, to help us build a timeline," Grimes said. "We have warrants. We'll take your SIM and SD cards from your phones. You can replace them to keep using them in the meantime, but we may also request those cards later, too."

Lonza updated them on other aspects of the investigation: how the canine teams had not yet yielded a solid lead, nor had the ongoing searches of the park, the lakes; how they were following scores of tips; how they were checking the sex offender registry and working with missing persons groups. As they summarized the investigation, Lonza could see a tightness intensifying with Corina.

"Is there anything else we need to know?" Lonza asked, eyeing the family carefully, mindful of another universal fact: everybody rations the truth when first questioned. They do it for any combination of reasons—they're scared, they're anguished or *they're guilty.*

Robert and Charlotte were silent, but Corina said, "You're not telling us everything."

Lonza didn't answer.

"You arrest Beckke with Gabriel's phone," Corina went on. "Beckke's facing charges, but your information stops there."

Lonza exchanged a quick glance with Grimes.

"We want the truth, *whatever it is.* We deserve that much." Corina's voice cracked. "Is Gabriel dead? You tell me now!"

Lonza took a sharp breath, coming quickly to a decision. "We have no evidence to suggest that Gabriel's been hurt."

"How did Beckke get Gabriel's phone?" Corina asked. "Is he working with someone?"

Grimes looked at Lonza again.

"We don't know," Lonza said.

"You don't know?"

"We're investigating. We need to confirm it," Lonza said.

"But?" Corina shook her head, processing the revelation. "If Beckke has no connection to Gabriel," she said, standing, "then you don't have anything! That's why you were holding this back!" She began hugging herself, as if to stem pain. "Time is running out and you have nothing!"

15

"You have nothing!"

Repeating the words in shaky breaths, Corina swayed, prompting Robert and the detectives to support her. She declined to sit.

"I'll get Joan," Robert said. "She's out there with everybody." Then to the detectives: "She's a family friend, a retired doctor."

"I don't need Joan." Corina pulled a tissue from a box on Robert's desk, then said, "I'll take you to Gabriel's room now."

Leading them down the hall had, for a moment, distracted Corina from her grief, stirring memories of the day when the agent first showed her and Robert the condo.

"...radiant-heated marble floors throughout...and here, the kitchen, with custom Danish cabinetry...here, we have the great room...this way, the secondary baths and powder room have Italian sculpted accents...and the primary bedroom, with its spacious bathroom, handcrafted coral tiles, walk-in wardrobes... This suite offers stunning sunset—sunrise exposures, gorgeous views of the park and skyline..."

Corina remembered how, during the process of buying their condo, she thought of her parents and their struggle. How the earthquake had killed most everyone in their village. How they'd come to America as a young couple and built their small cleaning business.

After school, helping them scrub office toilets, clean windows, learning not to leave streaks…watching her mom and dad working so hard…then that night at the paper…rushing to the crash…walking through the debris…

She saw how they'd struggled for a better life, and she wished they could have seen how far she had taken that dream.

But that dream had become a nightmare now as she entered her son's room with police investigators. They were met with a subtle mingling scent of shampoo and fresh linen, alongside a stillness that bordered on dread.

Lonza and Grimes took in the decor—the tic-tac-toe–patterned comforter on his bed; his dresser, with his pajamas, speckled with spaceships, spilling from a drawer; on the wall, an autographed poster of the quarterback for the New York Giants; bookshelves with toys and Dr. Seuss books stood against another wall. They saw Gabriel's superhero nightlight and the glow-in-the-dark stars on the ceiling. Near his little desk was the corkboard, papered with artwork and pictures.

"Does Gabriel have online access? Could he have communicated with friends, or strangers posing as friends?" Grimes asked.

Corina shook her head. "We put in parental safeguards."

"Can you think of anyone in this building who's been paying an unusual amount of attention to him, anything that comes to mind?" Lonza asked.

"No." Corina shook her head then sat on her son's bed, caressing his comforter. Hours earlier Gabriel was here, safe.

She turned to the corkboard and a photo, one of her favorites, showing Charlotte and Gabriel, who was one at the time. Charlotte was holding him, arms wrapped around him, his big sister, his guardian. Corina thought of how Gabriel had come into their lives. He was their answered prayer, their miracle. She thought she'd never have him.

And now she feared losing him forever.

She saw Gabriel's drawing of his family on the board, everyone holding hands and smiling. Reaching toward his dresser drawer, she pulled his pajamas to her as a great sob erupted from her core.

Lonza went to her, bent down and took her shoulder.

Robert appeared at the door and rushed to his wife, putting his arms around her. "I'm getting Joan."

"No!" Corina held Gabriel's pajamas, looking to the window, into the night, her heart breaking.

She got up and left the bedroom.

With Robert and the detectives following, she went to a storage closet, pulling a flashlight from a shelf. She tested its brightness, satisfied that the batteries were good.

"What're you doing?" Robert said. "You should take a sedative. You need to sleep."

Corina pointed to a window and the night.

"Our son is out there! He could be hurt, or worse!"

"Corina—"

"There's no way in hell I can rest here. I'm going to find him!"

Corina left her building through a rear delivery door, avoiding the media people keeping vigil out front.

Glimpsing her reflection in a window, she realized she was wearing the same skirt and top she'd worn on-air before rushing from Newslead earlier. At least now she'd put on sneakers. Sirens echoed, horns and traffic carried in the night as she power walked and trotted the few blocks to Central Park, coming to the entrance at Fifth Avenue and East 65th Street.

She moved west, scrutinizing the shadows under lamplights, people resting on benches, every runner, every cyclist, every person pushing a stroller or walking a dog that she encountered. Illuminating dark pockets, she probed shrubs with her light, calling out to Gabriel.

Along the way, she found a measure of comfort in seeing officers with flashlights, their beams sweeping through forested sections, while patrol units crawled along paved pathways, their powerful searchlights raking swaths of the grassy, hilly areas.

Glancing over her shoulder, she saw Robert a protective distance behind with Lonza and Grimes. The detectives had persuaded Robert to let her leave their condo to search, sensing that no one would be able to stop her.

Hurrying farther west, the beauty and glory of the park evolved into a vast living thing, a threatening colossus, pulling her into all of her darkest fears, threatening to rip her family apart. Her battles with Charlotte, her suspicions of Robert, the history of wicked attacks against her for telling the truth. Then the rumors and abhorrent incident at Newslead no one knew about, and her guilt for working her way to the top and the toll it took on everything—all of it churned inside her.

She looked up at the skyscrapers that soared to the stars around her, glowing pillars that now seemed like bars in a gilded prison.

Is Gabriel the price I paid?

Approaching the area where he'd vanished, Corina saw the flashing lights of parked patrol cars. She saw the reflective vests and flashlights of volunteers of a community group talking with officers. The brilliant lights of TV cameras illuminated faces as crews from local stations reported on the search. An officer had just collected the yellow tape cordoning the area where Gabriel had disappeared. A moment later, Corina made her way unnoticed to the grassy hill near West Drive and the path to 69th Street.

I need to be at the spot where he last was.

Coming to the place where Charlotte had found Gabriel's plane, she searched the area, turning full circle with her halo of light, hoping, begging, praying for some sort of cosmic connection to help her.

Pulse quickening, tears brimming, she recalled her last photo of Gabriel, the one Charlotte took, aglow with excitement. As she turned, her mind filled with a montage of Gabriel; images of when he was a baby, a toddler, a little boy, all blazed in meteoric splendor in her mind.

As she turned, she burned inside because of what she knew from news stories she'd done on missing children.

Corina knew the odds, knew the statistics.

Most abducted children are killed within hours.

As she turned, she was lost in the night, taken into the abyss until something inside her cracked and a scream broke free.

"GABRIEL!!!"

Dropping her flashlight, she screamed his name again, and again, her cry launching birds from the trees, to the heavens, alarming anyone who heard. Robert, the detectives and others, strangers, rushed to her, reaching her in the moments after she collapsed.

DAY 2

16

THE NEXT MORNING in Midtown Manhattan.

High up in the 64-story utilitarian steel-and-glass tower that exuded corporate power, the staff of *The Wynne Files* started its first story meeting of the day.

Hosted by Wynne Varden, the *Files* trafficked in controversy, drawing nearly five million prime-time viewers nightly to the ReLOX Broadcasting Network, making it one of the highest-rated shows in the country.

Ceramic mugs, muffins, donuts, yogurt and fruit cups were necklaced around the table as the team brainstormed.

"How about this?" Peering into her tablet, Zoie Glick, assistant news director, jumped into her pitch. "We've learned of rumors that the key components in new voting equipment are from China. And get this. Not only are the components controlled remotely by China, the technology allows for the secret capture of your DNA when you touch the keypad."

"And where do we go with this story?" Dominic Conte, a hard-nosed producer, sipped coffee.

"We put it out there now," Glick said. "And we bring it up again later, applying it to jurisdictions in swing states. We can raise questions about the integrity of the voting process."

"How do we support this claim?" Conte eyed a muffin.

"We point to one of the websites where I saw it. We'll get some kind of denial from the PRC. Then we get denials from the companies that made the components, elections officials, the State Department, whatever. We'll get experts debating the rumors on the show. Is the claim valid? Is it possible? Who knows?"

"Is it all pure BS? Who knows?" T.J., a writer, muttered, biting into a glazed donut.

"Hey," Glick said. "We ask the questions Americans want us to ask, the questions other news outlets are afraid to ask. That's why we're number one."

"This could be an item for us." Conte selected a banana muffin. "If we can get it by Legal. What do you think?" Conte turned to their boss.

Attention shifted to the head of the table and Wynne Varden, one of the most recognizable people in the US. Age forty-eight, a Harvard grad, Varden had made a name for himself writing controversial op-ed pieces, then started a magazine, *Eagle Eye Revelations*. Razor-sharp, articulate and quick-witted, he became a frequent combative political commentator on national TV news programs. His profile grew over the years until ReLOX offered him his own TV show. Since then, *The Wynne Files* had come to be a powerful political force, worshipped and loathed by millions.

Leaning back, gently rocking in his chair, Wynne propped an ankle on his knee, his laptop resting on his lap. He studied the screen, nodding to his own thoughts while twirling a pen in his left hand to aid his thinking.

"I like it, Zoie. But it'll have to stand," Wynne said, keeping his eyes on his laptop. "Something timelier is unfolding in front of us. Something we're going to move on."

"Corina Corado's missing son?" Glick said.

"That's right," said Amanda Lutz, a senior producer, tapping on her tablet while glancing to the large monitor filling the wall at one end of the room. "Wynne and I were working out ideas this morning."

"What's happened to Corina Corado is profoundly tragic," Wynne said, placing his pen hand on his heart. "We all feel for her."

"Oh my God, yes. It's horrible what's happened," Lutz said.

"Let's take a look at some things." Varden indicated the large screen.

From her tablet, Lutz controlled the video, which began on the big screen with current news coverage of the search for Gabriel Corado in Central Park, the photo of Gabriel with his plane.

"Oh, he's so cute," Glick said.

The images were followed by footage and sound of the huge police effort—in the park, on the subways, on the streets and in the sky. It showed Ivan Beckke's arrest, the confrontation with Corina Corado, and her heartbreaking pleas for her son.

"Very dramatic. Makes for good TV," Lutz said.

"Let's look at some other aspects," Varden said. "My sources at Newslead hinted to me that recently there's been some unspoken strain, perhaps even enmity between Efrem Zyller, head of the news division, and Corado. We have no idea what the root of it may be. There are rumors Corado was being considered to anchor a new show."

The screen changed to show the gossip section of one of New York's tabloids, with its headline and a highlighted paragraph.

"Then, earlier yesterday," Varden said, "this little nugget appears, indicating that Newslead may be dropping Corina Corado, one of their most respected journalists. What the heck is going on with her at Newslead? Bearing all this in mind, let's go back."

A series of TV clips showed Corina reporting from one of the campaigns. She's doing live stand-ups with members of the crowd surrounding her. Their faces twisted in anger, they hurl insults, trying, and failing, to disrupt her report from the floor of the rally.

"As we know, Corina's catching it here," Lutz said, "because supporters accuse her of being nasty, unfair and untruthful in her coverage."

Wynne watched without comment.

"And we can't forget a couple of years ago, her infamous interview with Max and Marnie Ritzzkel, the couple who founded Greeters of the Rising Storm," Lutz said, cuing up and freezing the Newslead segment. "When Wynne had the Ritzzkels on the *Files*, it was a respectful discussion of ideas. Albeit some were interesting, but it was positive. But with Corado, it was entirely different—it was combative and didn't end well."

Lutz ran a portion of Corina Corado's interview with the Ritzzkels.

"We know all about you!" Marnie said. *"Your whole life is a lie!"*

"My whole life is a lie? Excuse me? What does that mean?"

"You never adopted a kid! You stole him! Your life is a lie! You're the Queen of Lies!" Marnie spat as the interview ended.

"That interview was disastrous for Corado," Lutz said. "It brought on a tsunami of impassioned reaction. She wounded, no, attacked, the psyche of many members of the group and others who sympathized with them. There were protests in front of Newslead's headquarters."

Tapping on her tablet, Lutz launched several older segments of Corina's reports from across the country and trouble spots around the world, including disasters in Central America. After watching everything, Wynne leaned forward, propped his elbows, steepled his fingers and touched them to his lips, almost in prayer.

"We're going to put something solid together for our next show," he said.

"Tonight's show?" Dominic Conte repeated.

"Yes, Dom. We need to move on this now. We're going to take a deep look at Corina Corado. What's happened is tragic, but it also raises questions. Troubling questions our viewers need us to ask."

17

ADIDAS SUPERSTARS.

Officer Bonnie Graham had been searching for them through her whole midnight-to-eight shift, examining video from the NYPD's security cameras.

In a softly lit room of the Central Park Precinct, she'd continued the work of the earlier squads, analyzing recorded images on large monitors.

The footage was collected from the police security cameras that ringed Central Park. Over thirty in all, placed outside the park—along its northern perimeter; along the east side; along Central Park South; and on Fifth Avenue and stretching up Central Park West.

Graham worked from the timeline established by investigators of when Gabriel Corado got separated from his sister. She was guided by the photo Charlotte had taken moments before he went missing.

Blue plaid short-sleeved shirt, tan shorts, white socks and all-white adidas Superstar shoes, and a blue bracelet, featuring a tiny New York Yankees' baseball strung with similar-sized beads spelling the name Gabriel.

For hours, Graham scoured the footage focusing on shoes—searching for Superstars as a starting point. In cases like this, footwear could be an identifying factor.

Again, she returned to the beginning and the footage that picked up Gabriel leaving Tillmon with his sister, walking south on the west side of Central Park West. There was Gabriel carrying his plane. They stop for Charlotte to take the photo using her phone, then, later, she talks on her phone.

No one appeared to be following them.

When the siblings reached the Dakota and waited for the light, Graham surveyed the area. A man and a woman with backpacks, giving off a tourist vibe, were taking photos in front of the building; a man with a dog was waiting to cross, along with half a dozen other people.

Nothing appeared suspicious.

The light changed, Gabriel and his sister, along with the others, crossed to the park's busy West 72nd Street entrance. Graham scanned the cyclists, walkers and runners flowing in and out of the park. Older people sat on benches along the sidewalks, and tour groups and pedicabs passed in and out.

It was impossible to gauge if anyone was following as Gabriel and Charlotte moved deeper into the park and out of camera range. Minutes later, Charlotte appeared alone, briefly exiting the park at 69th Street. She looked up and down Central Park West, lined with tour and charter buses, before disappearing back into the park.

Graham typed on her keyboard, calling up footage for the 72nd Street entrance. From the moment Gabriel stepped into the park, she paid close attention to the footage. This time for people leaving the park. Again, for any child fitting Gabriel's description, closely checking clothes and shoes.

Nothing surfaced.

Graham did the same with the park's entrance at 69th Street.

Again, nothing.

Then she went back to reviewing footage recorded by the other NYPD cameras around Central Park, one by one. Sometimes she saw white Superstars, but on adult women, or men, or teens, or children who looked nothing like Gabriel. Often with the wrong-colored stripes.

Nothing consistent with Gabriel Corado's description.

The other precincts bordering Central Park were also studying the NYPD security camera footage in their respective commands. The MTA was scrutinizing every surveillance camera in New York's subway and bus system. Nothing on any front had emerged so far. Graham knew it was a needle-in-a-haystack search.

But the needle was there, somewhere.

Across Manhattan, other critical efforts of the investigation were ongoing. Not far from City Hall and the Brooklyn Bridge, in a windowless room of One Police Plaza, was the NYPD's Real Time Crime Center, the RTCC.

At computer stations situated before an array of flat video panels, known as the data wall, detectives and analysts, using state-of-the-art technology, worked on the Corado case.

One aspect involved facial recognition. They submitted Gabriel's photo into their facial recognition systems. They were attempting to find if his face appeared in video feeds or recordings within the NYPD's security camera network throughout the city.

The technology analyzed various characteristics—such as Gabriel's facial features, his hair, skin tone and clothing—in an attempt to pinpoint his location since his disappearance.

Nothing had surfaced so far.

Detectives also ran his photos and his name through social media, monitoring to see if he appeared on any platform, or in any discussion, that would indicate his location, or knowledge of it.

Nothing significant had emerged on that front.

In one of the most difficult and crucial elements of the investigation, detectives at the RTCC were using signals they'd obtained from Ivan Beckke's phone. Applying coordinates and using satellite GPS mapping, they established his route of travel within the time Gabriel was reported missing. They wanted to determine if Beckke was in Central Park at the time, and when and where Gabriel's phone ended up in Beckke's truck.

They were able to track the truck starting from the Upper West Side, not far from the Tillmon school.

While tracing Beckke's movements, the analysts tapped into detailed city maps to display nearby landmarks. They used the NYPD's surveillance cameras to get recorded video of his blue Ford F-150, with the *Super Eezzee Contracting* sign, as it moved along the route, ending with his arrest in Rego Park, in Queens.

The challenge was that Gabriel Corado's phone, which stopped pinging where he vanished in the park, didn't start pinging again until Beckke had left Manhattan via the tunnel and traveled a couple of miles along the Long Island Expressway. It was possible the phone could've been switched off, or delayed connecting to the carrier network, but that made it difficult to pinpoint when it was first in Beckke's vehicle.

The additional challenge was that along the route Beckke took, there were gaps in camera coverage at some key locations due to software updates. And some segments of the route were obscured by trees. At times, in traffic, Beckke drew up alongside any number of vehicles where a suspect could've tossed the phone into the back of his truck, including a double-decker open-top tour bus. Someone on the street could've also thrown the phone into the truck. Or it could've happened in the Midtown Tunnel.

The detectives were uncertain if Beckke could be involved in Gabriel Corado's disappearance. Or if somewhere in Manhattan, the person, or persons, who had the boy's phone, switched it off and removed the cards, only to replace them and turn it back on in the moment before tossing it into Beckke's truck, deflecting suspicion.

But so far, nobody had been able to determine where that might have happened.

At the Central Park Precinct, Officer Bonnie Graham downed the last of her tepid coffee. Continuing to scrutinize footage, she grappled with theories and observations other investigators were floating.

In abduction cases, people moved fast to alter or disguise an abducted child's appearance. In this case, it would likely have been done quickly in a bathroom stall or concealed wooded area.

The abductor could have left the park immediately with the child, or waited any length of time.

There was the sex offender registry to consider, child traffickers and so many other chilling scenarios.

Yes, Graham thought, scrutinizing her screens, this was needle-in-a-haystack work.

But the needle is here, somewhere. I just know it.

18

CORINA FOUGHT HER way to consciousness.

Like a panicked swimmer, she struggled to the surface, escaping the remnants of a terrifying dream that Gabriel was missing.

It was a dream, she told herself. *Only a dream.*

But becoming alert, feeling her bedsheets, opening her eyes, recognizing her bedroom, the morning—the sudden, awful reality hit her with the force of a locomotive.

I'm not dreaming!

Sitting upright, Corina's hands flew to her mouth, stifling a groan.

Robert rose from his chair beside her, taking her hand. Then Joan appeared.

Corina's words were raw in her throat. "Did they find him?"

Robert and Joan, faces flooding with concern, shook their heads.

"Everyone's still searching," Robert said.

"I need to look for him!"

"You need rest," Joan said. "You're traumatized. You collapsed in the park last night. We got you home and I gave you one of your prescribed sedatives in your medicine cabinet."

Corina gave her a weak, thankful smile. Joan was a longtime friend of the family, a retired doctor who lived in the building.

Joan's eyes had lit up when they all met for the first time, especially when she was introduced to Charlotte and Gabriel.

"My goodness, look at the both of you! Aren't you a couple of balls of sunshine! Just what this condo of stuffed shirts needs!"

Joan never had children of her own, but she practically watched Charlotte and Gabriel grow up, treating them like they were her kids. She often came over for dinner, or hosted them, or babysat. Joan was always there for the family. Doing whatever she could do for them whenever they needed it done.

"Thanks, Joan." Corina looked around. "Where's my phone?"

"In the kitchen," Robert said. "The detectives took our SIM and SD cards last night. I arranged to get us new ones this morning. Gil Dixon called earlier. He had Newslead rush over a laptop after I told him about our phone and computer situation. It's in the kitchen, too."

Raking her hand through her hair, thinking, Corina glanced at the time on her digital clock: 7:59 a.m. She grabbed the remote from her bedside table, switching on the TV on the wall, scanning channels for any word, any hope.

"News at the top of the hour," ABC's *Eyewitness News* anchor said as Gabriel's face appeared over her shoulder. *"The search continues for a missing six-year-old boy..."* Corina switched to other channels—CBS, Newslead, NBC. Seeing nothing new, she swept away the sheets.

"I have to look for Gabriel."

"You should rest," Joan said.

"I can't."

Corina requested privacy then went to the bathroom and showered, emerging minutes later dressed in jeans, a T-shirt, sneakers and no makeup. A band was clamped between her teeth; she pulled her hair into a ponytail, tying it as she left the bedroom. Seeing her, the new shift of two NYPD plainclothes officers monitoring for ransom calls at the large table in the living/dining room area stood.

"Detective Jerrod Russell," the taller man said.

"Rafael Delgado," the second one said.

"Any word?"

"Nothing yet, ma'am," Delgado said.

"Anything on Beckke? How he got Gabriel's phone?"

The detectives shook their heads.

"Where're Lonza and Grimes?"

"At the precinct, still holding Beckke," Russell said.

"And the park's cameras?"

"The whole system's being analyzed," Delgado said. "Ma'am—"

Corina cursed under her breath. "So nothing, then?"

"Ma'am, the investigation's growing," Delgado said. "We're working with the FBI and Newslead's security, assessing potential threats directed at you and the network, recently and historically."

"We're looking for anything that gives rise to a person, or persons, of concern," Russell said. "We'd like you to start reviewing your news stories, recent and older, for any potential leads that could help us."

"Now? With everything else? I want to go back to searching the park."

"That's being done," Delgado said. "We're going full bore, investigating in all directions, leaving nothing to chance."

Corina clenched her eyes, the truth stabbing her with guilt.

If only I'd kept our security detail. If only Charlotte was watching him. If only I…

"I'll check on Robert and Charlotte," she said. "Then I'll get started in the study."

Corina found Robert on a stool at the kitchen counter. The lines in his unshaven face were pressed deeper, aging him, as he nodded to her while on his phone.

"Yes, whatever you can do. Thank you," he said, ending his call.

"Anything?" Corina asked.

He shook his head, stood, and took her in his arms.

"My company is putting up thirty thousand toward the reward for information. Others want to help. We're in this together, Corina."

She nodded, then her phone vibrated and a pinging noise came from the Newslead laptop sitting on the counter.

Corina checked her messages, scrolling through a stream of interview requests. It seemed like every news outlet in the country wanted to talk to her. The messages of support continued, including one from the White House, which Corina scanned.

We're praying for Gabriel Corado's safe return to his family...

"Did you see this?" She held her phone out to him.

Robert nodded, his eyes red-rimmed from lack of sleep. "I should've been there, Corina," he said, his voice straining. "I should've been at the school to get him."

She went back to him and they hugged, hard.

"We'll find him," she said, pulling back, closing her laptop and picking it up. "Where's Charlotte?"

"In her room."

The door to Charlotte's bedroom wasn't closed all the way.

Raising her hand to knock, Corina paused upon hearing Charlotte's end of a conversation spilling into the hall.

"...they blame me...you've got to help me, Vince, please..."

Corina rapped on the door before swinging it open to see Charlotte, phone to her ear, eyes widening at her entrance.

"Gotta go!" She hung up quickly, putting her phone down.

"Are you okay?" Corina asked.

"Yes, you startled me. How're you feeling?"

"Who were you talking to?"

"Just—a friend—I—" Charlotte said.

"It was Vince, wasn't it?"

"It's not like you think!"

"*Oh my God, Charlotte!* What have we told you?"

"Please. He was just—"

"This is why Gabriel's missing!"

"Don't say that!"

"Because you were talking to Vince when you should've been watching him! And now you're talking to him again!"

"No, God, please, don't— Yes, Vince just called. He's helping. He's asked all the drivers to look, and everyone at Uber and Lyft, and the taxi companies—"

"What's going on?" Robert stood at the door.

"She's been talking to Vince Tarone."

"What?"

"I can't believe this, after all that's happened!" Corina said.

"Okay." Robert held up his palms. "Everyone, dial it down."

Corina leveled a finger at Charlotte. "Detectives are going to question him, Charlotte! Do you understand?"

"Corina," Robert said.

"Yes! I understand everything!" Charlotte screamed. *"It's all my fault!"*

"Corina, just step back," Robert said. "Charlotte, please take a breath."

An uneasy moment passed before Corina left the room.

Corina went to the study.

After shutting the door, she put her phone and laptop on the desk, then thrust her face into her hands, her pulse rippling.

Finger-pointing was not going to bring Gabriel home. Nothing would be gained by blaming Charlotte. Yes, she should've been watching her brother, but Corina realized her anger was fueled by Charlotte's fixation with Vince.

And that anger is misdirected.

I'm to blame.

Exhaling, she collected herself and focused on what the detectives needed her to do. She opened her laptop, her keyboard clacking as she cued up Newslead's secured portal. Using her network employee card number and her PIN, she logged in. She entered the database holding archived stories and submitted her name in the search window.

The screen filled with summaries of items of her work, each including headlines and dates, starting with the most recent. The search offered twenty entries to a page, hundreds of stories, page after page, going back years.

It was daunting.

Unsure of where to begin, she thought for a moment. Then, using keywords and names, she pulled up her old piece on Greeters of the Rising Storm, clicked on the video icon and replayed her interview with Max and Marnie Ritzzkel.

Watching her exchange with them, challenging their troubling statements and outrageous claims, still stunned Corina as the segment ended with Marnie Ritzzkel accusing Corina of stealing a baby, calling Corina the Queen of Lies. Corina reflected on the deluge of online attacks that had followed. Those attacks soon evolved into the demonstrations.

Corina moved on to the reports showing more than a hundred people outside the Newslead building, chanting, singing, waving signs; some placards said:

QUEEN OF LIES

FAKE NEWS

CORADO'S LIFE IS A LIE

All of them condemned her and the network, linking them to wild conspiracies and government secrets.

"The Greeters nailed it," one woman told a reporter for a controversial blog. *"Corina Corado is a liar spreading lies."*

"They're afraid to report the truth," a man said. *"Wynne has it right. We have to expose them for what they are."*

Corina studied the faces in the footage. After the rallies in front of Newslead, things had escalated. Days later, Trayman Herman Shrike, who had been among the protestors, entered the building with a gun, intent on finding her.

Could there be a connection to Gabriel?

But Shrike's in jail.

And the Ritzzkels are still pedaling conspiracies and life-extending elixirs online.

Corina left the stories of people embracing absurd and dangerous theories, moving quickly through the array of her reports over the years; she sampled those she'd done on people who'd faced tragedies.

She came to a clip of a grieving father and checked his name in the summary: Lee Farnley. His twelve-year-old daughter, Addison, had gone missing for days and was later found murdered. *"The last thing she did was turn and wave goodbye to me that morning."*

Corina went on to other stories on families whose children had vanished. In some cases, their remains were found months, or years, later. In others, they were never found. *"Burke was playing in our yard, then he was gone,"* said Cathy Miller, participating in a support group of parents who met in the basement of a church in Brooklyn. Burke, her ten-year-old son, had never been found after he'd gone missing in the small Pennsylvania town where she used to live. *"After all these years, he comes to me in my dreams."*

Corina then came to one of her reports on Julie Landon, whose son Logan was eleven when he vanished from a park near his New Jersey home. He'd been missing for a little over a year before he was found and returned to her. *"Never give up hope,"* Julie said in the report. *"I learned that a mother cannot ever give up hope because hope connects you to your child."*

Tapping on her keyboard, Corina viewed some of her international reports, gut-wrenching pieces she'd done from war zones; she scrolled through footage of the dead, including people pulled from the rubble of bombed buildings. There were her stories from disasters around the world: hurricanes, floods and earthquakes. She catalogued human tragedies—the worst being mothers holding their dying, or dead, children—at times feeling evil for intruding on their grief when they deserved privacy. But often a relative invited her to record their pain, for the world to know. She remembered displays of dignity when bereaved mothers who had nothing comforted her while she wept for them. Absorbing their suffering, through the camera, was Corina's job. To shine a light on the truth, in all of its horrifying manifestations across the country and around the world.

But even now, Corina was consumed with guilt, combing through her work, uncertain what she was looking for and how it related to her missing child. She looked to a photo of her family on Robert's desk and stared into Gabriel's eyes, remembering his words while he showed her his plane.

Love you.

The photo blurred as Corina feared a karmic wheel had turned on her.

Am I paying the price for all I've done? For all I've failed to do? Oh God, please help me.

Her phone rang. It was Gil Dixon.

Time froze before the second ring, and Corina inventoried her unsettling, unresolved difficulties at Newslead: what Efrem Zyller had done; how no one knew, and his warning if she took any action;

the rumors of her promotion to a new show; then being jolted by the hurtful suggestion of her dismissal. Corina had to move past it all.

Maybe Gil, or someone at Newslead, has learned something?

She answered.

"Hi, Gil. You guys have anything new?"

"No, I'm sorry. We've got everybody pushing their sources. How're you holding up?"

"Not good. I got the laptop, thank you."

"Listen, if you want to talk to us again, we can set it up."

"I know."

"Efrem told me to tell you we'll give you the air, anytime."

Corina's jaw tensed as she struggled to respond. "Thank you, Gil, I'll let you know. Keep me posted."

"You bet."

Hanging up, she gazed at the laptop's display of her listed stories, not knowing what to do. As she contemplated whether any of them provided a lead, or a person of concern, she heard a vibration. Thinking it was her phone, she looked but noticed it hadn't illuminated.

Likely a text message.

She checked. No message.

The vibration had been faint.

It couldn't have been my phone.

The sound seemed to have come from behind her. She turned her attention to the bookshelf, spotting a pencil-like strip of metallic blue slivered between two books.

A phone. She pulled it out.

What's it doing here?

She didn't know this phone.

Is this Robert's? Is it a burner. Why is it concealed?

Suddenly she recognized the metallic blue as similar to what Robert was holding that night when he disappeared into the study.

Now, a text message bloomed on the screen.

I'm so sorry for what I did. I'm so scared.

19

"Do you know where Gabriel Corado is now?"

"No."

"Do you know how his phone came to be in your possession?"

"No."

"Are you involved in Gabriel Corado's disappearance?"

Ivan Beckke hesitated.

Poised for Beckke's answer, Detective Kris Holmes, one of the NYPD's polygraph examiners, concentrated on the moving, colored graphs on her laptop's screen. Holmes sat behind Beckke. Near her was Beckke's lawyer, Sophia Saint Paul.

Beckke sat in a cushioned chair with armrests, his feet flat on the floor. A network of wires connected sensors from Beckke's chest and fingertips to Holmes's equipment, recording his responses to her questions.

Beckke had agreed to submit to a polygraph, through his attorney.

"The results won't be admissible in court. They're not considered reliable," Saint Paul had told him. "But this could remove you from suspicion."

The process had begun that morning in a stark interview room in the 19th Precinct. Holmes had first been briefed by investigators. Then, after reading Beckke's earlier statements, she conducted a pretest interview with him before preparing her questions and moving on to the exam.

Lonza knew that the NYPD had no departmental policy on using polygraphs, which left it to her, Grimes and Lieutenant Weaver to decide whether to request one. At this stage, with every minute counting, they believed administering one to Beckke could point their investigation in the right direction. They were also well aware that some suspects believed they could beat a polygraph.

Now, standing with Weaver in the observation room, Lonza and Grimes watched Beckke through the one-way mirror.

The investigation into Gabriel Corado's disappearance had several elements, but Lonza had no doubt that it was solvable. *Follow the facts and the evidence*, she told herself. And right now, a critical aspect was Gabriel's phone and Ivan Beckke. They'd been digging deeper into Beckke's background, studying his social media profiles, looking to see if he'd ever made threats against Corina Corado or her family. Whether he'd had any contact at all with the family. Nothing had surfaced so far. The polygraph was just another tool, Lonza thought as Holmes repeated the question.

"Are you involved in Gabriel Corado's disappearance?"

"No."

"Do you know how Gabriel came to be missing?"

"No."

"Are you familiar with Corina Corado the network journalist?"

"Yes."

"Do you harbor any animosity toward Corina Corado?"

"No."

"Have you associated with anyone who has harbored ill will toward Corina Corado?"

"No."

"Did you conspire with anyone to cause Gabriel to disappear?"

"No."

"Do you know any staff members or families associated with the Tillmon school?"

"No."

"Are you divorced from Deidre Beckke?"

"Yes."

"Do you have a son with Deidre Beckke?"

"Yes."

"Do you have custody of your son?"

"No."

"Did you ever assault your wife?"

Beckke let a long moment pass, causing Holmes to repeat the question.

Beckke responded: "Yes."

"Have you ever been incarcerated?"

Beckke closed his eyes. "Yes."

"Do you reside with your mother?"

"Yes."

"Do you reside in Manhattan?"

"No."

"Do you reside in Flushing Meadows, Queens?"

"Yes."

"Did you ever express a desire to abduct your son and flee the state?"

A moment passed.

"Yes."

"Did you possess a stolen firearm?"

"Yes."

"Is it a Glock?"

"Yes."

"Did you steal the Glock?"

"No."

"Did you buy it illegally?"

"Yes."

"Have you used it to commit another crime?"

"No."

"Were you intending to use it to commit a crime?"

"No."

Holmes continued for another fifteen minutes before winding it down with her last question.

"Did you mislead police earlier when you denied having any involvement in Gabriel Corado's disappearance?"

"No."

The examination ended, and Beckke and his lawyer were escorted from the interview room. A moment later, as Kris Holmes gathered her polygraph equipment, the investigators entered.

"What do you think?" Weaver asked.

"I'll need to analyze the results. As I said, there are three possible outcomes: Beckke is truthful, Beckke is untruthful, or the results are inconclusive."

"Can you tell us what he looks like now?" Grimes asked.

"No. I have to look at how he scored."

"How long will it take before you know?" Lonza asked.

"It normally takes twenty-four hours," Holmes said. "But given the urgency, and with my supervisor standing by to review, we'll get results to you within a few hours."

"Good," Weaver said. "I'm alerting the DA's office."

Less than two hours later, the detectives were called to Weaver's office.

Lonza crossed her arms in front of her, leaning her back against a file cabinet as Grimes closed the door. Weaver punched numbers on his desk phone keypad to reach Audrey Retson at the Manhattan District Attorney's Office.

"Audrey, it's Weaver. Ready to go?" Weaver was looking at his computer, scrolling through Holmes's expedited report on Beckke's polygraph.

"Hi, Garlan. Yes." Retson's voice rose through the speaker phone.

"I got the leads here, detectives Lonza and Grimes. We got the results of Beckke's polygraph. Inconclusive."

"Inconclusive. That doesn't help," Retson said. "Alright, where are you on the investigation?"

"Interviews with residents and contractors put Beckke on a job in the Upper West Side, near Tillmon, within the time frame," Weaver said. "Through Crime Stoppers we got a photo of Beckke's truck parked at the job site at that time."

The detectives related the snippets from the security camera network and what RTCC had recovered so far.

The speaker carried the staccato clicking of Retson's keyboard as she took notes. "What about latents or trace?"

"Nothing from Beckke on Gabriel Corado's phone," Weaver said. "Only partials, consistent with Gabriel and his family. Anything else was smudged, smeared."

"And," Lonza added, "no indication from the canine team that Gabriel Corado had been in Beckke's truck. Forensics has found no trace evidence showing Gabriel Corado had been in Beckke's truck, or his mother's house."

"What about the plane?" Retson asked.

"Nothing but DNA from Gabriel Corado and his teacher who helped him with it at the Tillmon school, Zak Medleroff," Weaver said. "He was solidly alibied as having never left the school at the time of the disappearance and has no record."

"Where are you with the school?"

"Checking background and interviewing all staff, and families linked to Tillmon," Weaver said. "And we're talking to the students. To date, nothing has emerged."

"Alright, this remains wide open," Retson said. "With Beckke you got a huge amount of reasonable doubt. Anyone could've tossed the phone into his truck to throw you off."

"Right," Weaver said.

"He's cooperated. Release him," Retson said. "Or you could keep him on the gun."

"Sure," Weaver said.

"Keep working it. You guys know what to do," Retson said. "Run down the offender registry. Look at who else knew Gabriel was leaving the school with his sister. Keep looking at the mother and the history of threats. Look at what was going on in the family at the time."

Weaver glanced at Lonza.

She was nodding and thinking about the world of possibilities they were facing while time was slipping by.

20

PERPLEXED, CORINA HELD the phone in her hand for a long moment, staring at the message.

> I'm so sorry for what I did. I'm so scared.

It was a New York City number but she didn't recognize it. Standing alone in Robert's study, her mind spun questions.

Who sent it? What does it mean?

Inspecting the phone, Corina was now sure that it was not Robert's everyday phone. It was a burner.

Why hide it?

Her breathing quickened.

Is he having an affair? Is it a text about Gabriel?

Not wanting to waste another second, she left the room.

Robert was at the table in the living/dining room area talking with detectives Russell and Delgado.

"Excuse me." She clasped Robert's arm. "Can I talk to you in the study, alone?"

Robert and the detectives traded glances.

"Just for a moment," she said.

"Is there something we should be aware of, ma'am?" Russell asked.

Corina gave him a hint of a smile. "I'd just like a private moment with my husband."

In the study, Corina placed the phone in Robert's hand.

She watched his face closely as he read the message.

"Does this have anything to do with Gabriel?" she asked.

His Adam's apple rose and fell, then he shook his head.

"What is it, then?" she asked. "This is a burner, a prepaid phone. Why hide it in the bookshelf? What's the message about?"

He took a breath, then let it out.

"Are you having an affair?" she asked.

Hurt, guilt and fear merged on Robert's face.

"No."

"Why didn't you give this phone to Lonza and Grimes?"

"It's about work, the condo contract—it has no bearing on Gabriel."

"No bearing? How would you know? You told them there's a lot of money, pressure and power at stake here. Now this text. Whatever's going on, we can't hold back, Robert! We need to give police this phone!"

Snatching the phone from him, Corina started to leave. He took her hand, she glared at his grasp with disgust. He let go as if she were on fire.

"Please don't tell them." His voice filled with remorse. "Don't tell them! Don't tell them anything! Wait!"

"Wait? You want me to wait? My son is missing!"

"Corina, please. He's my son, too, and I would never keep something back from the police that could help us find him."

"Then why are you keeping secrets and hiding this burner? Why is the person on this text sorry for what they did? Why are they afraid? What were you doing in Philadelphia?"

His shoulders sagged, indicating surrender.

"I went to see a whistleblower who was going to give me critical records on the project. There could be lives at stake with the building. I know you don't care about that. I get it. But I have to see this through. I promise you this has nothing to do with Gabriel. Give me time to resolve it. And then I will hand the burner over to the police and tell them everything. Give me twenty-four hours, or a little more, to lock this down. Please, Corina."

She weighed his plea in silence.

"You have to trust me," Robert said. "This is someone trying to help me confidentially. It's complicated—they're taking risks, and they're worried, anxious. You're on edge, I'm on edge. We're going out of our minds trying to find Gabriel. I swear, I'm telling you the truth."

Another moment went by. She clenched her eyes and covered her mouth with one shaky hand, then she gave him the phone.

"I don't know what to believe," she said, fighting tears. "I'm not sure you're telling me the truth. But I'll give you time. But, Robert, if I find out you're lying about this—" her gaze burned into him "—it'll be over for us."

He took a deep breath, his voice cracking. "I know."

A knock sounded.

"Come in," Robert said.

Detective Delgado opened the door.

"You have a call, Corina. It got bounced from Newslead to us. It's from Mexico."

"Mexico?"

"The caller says it's important and they'll only talk to you." Delgado passed a phone to Corina.

"Yes?" she said.

Delgado gestured for Corina to use the speakerphone and set another phone down to record the call.

"Corina Corado," a deep male voice said. "Javier Santos, with the Globo Prensa Agency in Mexico City."

A second passed.

"We met when you were working in South and Central America," Santos said.

"Yes, I recall. I have you on speaker, Javier." Corina looked to Delgado and Robert, indicating Javier could be trusted.

"We saw the wire stories on your missing son, Gabriel," Santos said. "We pray you will be reunited with him."

"Thank you."

"I'm calling because of a strange thing that happened recently that may be related. I'm now a senior editor at Globo Prensa here. Word came to me from our bureau chief in Managua that our correspondent in Chinandega got a call, a call about your son."

"What? What sort of call?"

"Someone was calling from New York City and wanted to reach someone with Globo Prensa, specifically in Chinandega."

"Why? Who was calling? Javier, I don't understand."

"We don't know who was calling, or why. I'm told our correspondent was traveling in a remote region when she received the call. It was a bad connection, a lot of static. All that she heard was, and I am quoting here: 'Tell me all you can about Corina Corado's son, Gabriel.'"

21

ONE HAND ON her forehead, one hand on her hip, Corina paced, mystery twisting around the development out of Central America.

Why would someone in New York ask a reporter in Nicaragua about Gabriel after he disappeared from Central Park?

"It makes no sense," Robert said, looking at the others in the study.

Unease gnawed at Corina as she tried to comprehend her call with Javier Santos. It had ended with Javier promising to have Globo Prensa reporters dig deeper, to learn more at his end. Corina thanked him, picked up her phone and left a message with Gil Dixon to find out more on what Santos told her.

At the same time, Detective Delgado was getting in touch with Lonza and Grimes. The detectives joined them at the family's condo, where they listened to the recording, then advised the FBI, Homeland Security and the Transportation Security Administration.

"It's possible to fly from New York to Managua in about six hours," Lonza said. "The TSA is double-checking screening, flights, airlines, looking for Gabriel."

Grimes paged through notes he'd taken from a call with an agent at the FBI's office in Lower Manhattan.

"The bureau's reaching out to its legal attaché at the US Embassy in Panama City, which covers Nicaragua," Grimes said. "They'll coordinate with Nicaraguan authorities and special agents at the US Embassy in Managua to check all inbound flights to the region for possible leads.

"And Nicaraguan authorities will also use their intelligence sources and informants to determine if there's a kidnap-for-ransom scheme in operation."

"Kidnapping for ransom," Robert repeated.

"Dear God." Corina steadied herself at the table.

Robert went to her but she waved him off.

"Corina," Delgado said. "It might help if you reviewed your reports from Central and South America for any possible connections."

Corina agreed and returned to her laptop, keys clicking as she searched Newslead's archives, starting with her reports out of Central America.

The images pulled her back over time to stories about gangs; about cartels; poverty; human trafficking; corruption; successful and failed economic actions; conflicts; and disasters—hurricanes, flooding, mudslides and earthquakes.

Corina worked through the afternoon while Robert and Charlotte took part in the efforts of a community search group, distributing flyers with Gabriel's picture in neighborhoods around the park.

Alone, examining her stories, Corina struggled with her memories in a whirlwind of emotion as the faces of the damned, the desperate, the dying and the dead haunted her. All the human suffering she'd witnessed, smelled, touched and felt had cost her a piece of her soul.

Early that evening Javier Santos called again. "All we've learned are the rumors."

"Rumors?"

"Around the time our correspondent was called, other calls regarding your son were made by someone in New York to other Nicaraguan news agencies in Managua and Chinandega. We don't know who it was, or why they were calling. Or why they focused on the west and northwest region."

Corina thanked Santos again.

As she informed the detectives, Gil Dixon called.

"Unfortunately, we've not learned much more from our people in the region, except for a couple rumors floating around."

"A rumor about other news outlets getting similar calls?"

"There's that, and another strange one."

"What is it, Gil?"

"An anonymous tip suggested you watch *The Wynne Files* tonight."

22

THE OPENING THEME, a marching orchestral fanfare swelling and rising, played under a montage of major news events. It was followed by an animation of file folders being fanned as a show title erupted out of it.

The Wynne Files.

A spectrum of lights and huge screens in a glitzy studio set dazzled in the point of view of an overhead camera. The angle swooped down, framing the man alone at an anchor desk—the star—who greeted viewers with a smile.

"Hello, I'm Wynne Varden, and welcome to another edition of *The Wynne Files.*"

The camera stayed on him.

"You may be aware of a heartbreaking story unfolding here in New York."

The camera angle shifted and Gabriel Corado's face filled the large screen over Varden's shoulder. Varden's expression and voice softened to suggest sadness.

"This little boy you see right here is six-year-old Gabriel Corado, the adopted son of TV network journalist, Corina Corado. Gabriel apparently vanished while walking home from school with his big sister in Central Park."

A large studio monitor played news footage of Corina holding up Gabriel's photo on her phone to a crowd of reporters gathered in Central Park.

"This is my son..." she began before the questions came, pleading, *"We just want to locate Gabriel and get him home safely. That's all I can say right now."*

The camera switched to Varden at his desk.

"By all accounts this is a gut-wrenching story. And, I hate to use this cliché, but it is every parent's nightmare. All of us here on *The Wynne Files*, just like all of you watching tonight, I'm sure, pray that Gabriel is found safe and is reunited with his family."

Varden blinked. He lowered his head slightly then raised it.

"But who is Gabriel Corado's family?"

Varden's face hardened. "Let's consider the facts. Gabriel disappeared walking home with his big sister through Central Park. That's all we really know so far."

Photos of Corina and Robert appeared side by side on the screen.

"His adoptive parents, Corina Corado and her husband, Robert Tanner, are a power couple here in Manhattan. Tanner is an engineer who's worked on the city's skyscrapers. Corina Corado, as most everyone knows, is a journalist for NNN, the Newslead Now Network. They have a pricey condo near the park in the Upper East Side, where a lot of the city's elites live.

"So why would Corina allow her children to walk alone through the park? Why not have a nanny or car service collect Gabriel from the prestigious Tillmon Parker Rose private school in the Upper West Side? I mean, not long ago she didn't go anywhere without the security NNN hired for her. So why would she put her children at risk now, letting them go off on their own?"

Varden turned to another camera.

"Let's open the files. Corina Corado's immigrant parents came to America from Guatemala. We don't know if they came legally or not. But supposedly, she was born here, had some sort of humble upbringing, pursued her dream, became a reporter and married Robert Tanner, who was widowed with a young daughter."

The screens showed an array of photos of Corina and Robert—walking in New York City, at a gala, dining on a patio.

"Not long after they were married, Corina Corado opened up about her life in a magazine interview."

A photo of *Vanity Fair* magazine appeared, and there was Corina's photo alongside an article about her.

"She talked about facing personal tragedy as she climbed to the upper ranks of TV news, all before she'd met Robert Tanner. And how after their marriage, how challenging it was for her to get pregnant, the miscarriages she experienced, how Gabriel became their son, as a baby, adopted through private adoption."

Now, a sequence of video clips of Corina reporting from across the US and around the world played behind Varden.

At their condo, Corina and Robert sat together, watching in astonishment.

"Where's he going with this?" Robert said.

"He's stigmatizing Gabriel for being adopted," Corina said. "Why?"

They watched as the show continued.

"But," Varden said, *"something about her work caught our attention. Several years ago, she was reporting on the hurricane, floods and mudslides that devastated parts of Nicaragua."*

A selection of Corina's reports from Chinandega and Madriz ran.

"At the time, the news surfaced—not widely but it was known—that a group of reporters had made their way to a hard-hit remote region in Madriz where an entire town was destroyed. They discovered a baby that had survived. Corina Corado was one of the reporters in that group. And it wasn't long after that time, when she was back in New York, that Corina and Robert welcomed Gabriel into their family via a private adoption. The timing is very interesting."

A selection of images of controversial websites and social media posts appeared.

"Keep in mind, it was around the time the baby was found in Nicaragua, and around the time Corina and Robert adopted Gabriel, that theories about Corado's activities while reporting on the disaster began surfacing in some deeply inquisitive corners of social media. Back then, it was reported that Corado 'rescued' the baby from the arms of its dying mother. But questions and theories about Corado's actions were dismissed. They faded, and were forgotten by most everyone. Until now."

"What?" Corina said to the screen. "What is this?"

Varden turned to face another camera.

"Flash forward to recent events leading up to Gabriel Corado's disappearance. Here in New York, rumors were circulating that Corina was in line to anchor NNN's upcoming prime-time show. Industry sources also indicated there was tension in the NNN's news division, possibly involving Corina Corado. Then there was this."

Varden pointed his thumb over his shoulder at the screen. It now displayed a headline for the gossip column of a New York tabloid. The section relating to Corina was enlarged and highlighted.

Newslead is considering dropping one of its most seasoned journalists, Corina Corado, because of low ratings...

"These recent events leading up to Gabriel's disappearance are interesting, don't you think? Almost alarming. There's more. Let's go back to her reporting on the hurricane years ago and the baby rescue.

"Remember, a few early theories claimed that Corina had taken the baby from the arms of its dying mother. There was never really any proof of that. Until now. Our investigative team, and they are among the best, spoke to the Nicaraguan helicopter company hired at the time by the press group. The company confirmed who was on the flight. Among the group was a freelance news photographer who was working for a Spanish newspaper. We found him and obtained these never-before-seen pictures."

The big screen showed images of Corina Corado holding a baby in her arms, boarding a helicopter with it, then images taken inside the aircraft in flight with Corina still holding the baby.

"These pictures confirm Corina Corado did indeed have the baby. A noble thing to save a child. But the fact is, she had some form of custody over the child at that moment. What we don't know is where the baby went from there. What ultimately happened to that child? To be sure, The Wynne Files *reached out to Corina Corado for her reaction. She didn't respond.*

"But I am pleased to welcome back two people who some say were the first to raise questions about Corina Corado's reporting activities in Nicaragua all those years ago. They've had dealings with her, and they're scrutinizing the most recent dramatic events involving Gabriel Corado."

The camera shifted and Varden turned to a screen showing a man and woman looking directly at the camera. The graphic at the bottom said: **MAX AND MARNIE RITZZKEL, FOUNDERS OF GREETERS OF THE RISING STORM**. It included their website, which, in addition to bizarre theories, offered health products whose benefits were, at best, questionable.

"Marnie and Max, welcome back."

"Thank you, Wynne," Max said.

"What is your take on this heart-wrenching story, the disappearance of six-year-old Gabriel Corado?"

"It's awful," Marnie said. *"And our hearts go out to any parent in that situation."*

"Without question," Varden said. *"But given your study of events, does anything stand out for you? Do you have concerns?"*

"We do," Max said. *"As you said, we were among the first to question the story involving Corina Corado's rescue of the hurricane baby. We put it out on our site years ago and were attacked online for it."*

The monitor showed a screenshot of the Ritzzkels' controversial conspiracy site, with a photo of Corina reporting from the disaster in the Chinandega and Madriz regions alongside the headline: **DID THIS REPORTER STEAL A BABY FROM THE ARMS OF ITS DYING MOTHER?**

"That's it," Marnie said. *"We know Corina Corado misleads people with her reporting. Her bias was off the charts during major election campaigns. We know from our own experience with her that she twists people's words."*

"You called her the Queen of Lies," Varden said.

"If the crown fits," Marnie said.

"I don't believe this." Robert put his hand on Corina's shoulder.

Corina shook her head.

"Let's go back to her activity in Nicaragua," Varden said as the Spanish photos of Corina with the baby in her arms were displayed again. *"What's your read on that?"*

"Well, these pictures prove what we said back then, when few people believed us," Max said.

"Which is?"

"That Corado," Marnie said, *"who'd told* Vanity Fair *that it was virtually impossible for her to get pregnant, is seen in these photos taking a baby from the arms of its dying mother. She obviously smuggled it back to New York and worked out some black-market adoption, raising the 'rescued child' as her own, calling him Gabriel."*

"You believe that to be true?" Varden said.

"We believed it then and we believe it now," Max said.

"And what about Gabriel's disappearance?" Varden said.

The monitor ran the news footage of Corina confronting Ivan Beckke in front of the 19th Precinct, then repeated the clip of her pleading for Gabriel.

"You've pretty much connected all the dots," Max said.

Marnie held up her hand and counted off points with her fingers. *"Look at what was happening with Corado's job—she was about to be fired. Why did she let her children walk alone through Central Park? Ivan hasn't been charged with anything related to this. We think he was paid to act his part, to dupe the police. We think this was all staged, a desperate bid to shift attention, create sympathy and save Corado's job."*

"Wow," Varden said. *"You raise valid points."*

"We're calling this the great deception," Max said.

"And you are not alone in questioning this. Take a look," Varden said.

Older footage played, showing conspiracy believers demonstrating in front of Newslead, waving signs:

QUEEN OF LIES

FAKE NEWS

CORADO'S LIFE IS A LIE

The footage cut to believers rallying at the court in support of the man who wanted to execute Corina. Their signs read: **CORADO SHOULD BE ON TRIAL, LOCK HER UP, QUEEN OF LIES**, and one that was almost blocked, except for the words… **WITH HIS MOTHER**.

Turning from the footage, Varden said: *"So much to think about."*

"Watch our site," Max said.

"I urge everyone to do that," Varden said. *"Thanks for being with us."*

"Thank you, Wynne," Marnie said.

Varden turned to face the camera.

"What's happened with Gabriel Corado is tragic and difficult, but it also raises troubling questions that need to be asked. Because, as we say on

the Files, *our duty is to look at the evidence, connect the dots and question whether this is all part of a deeper truth.*

"Is Gabriel actually Corina Corado and Robert Tanner's lawfully adopted child? Could his disappearance be an elaborate, staged event? Is there another reality than what's being presented to us?"

Varden paused, looked down, shook his head as if puzzled, then looked into the camera.

"Thank you for joining us on The Wynne Files.*"*

23

CORINA FELT LIKE she'd been punched in the stomach.

After watching *The Wynne Files*, she remained standing in her living room, anger rising, her world spinning. Robert was rooted beside her, staring at the black screen after switching off the television.

"What the hell was that?" Robert said, turning to the detectives who had seen it with them. *"Corina stole Gabriel? We staged this with actors?"* Robert looked to Corina, who was speechless. He glanced at Charlotte, on the sofa, lips pursed while looking at her phone. Then back to the detectives. "We should sue him. How are they allowed to vomit this hateful crap? Why?"

"They push falsehoods," Lonza said. "It's what they do." Then, to Corina, "It must've been Varden's people making the calls to Nicaragua."

Corina didn't answer.

Her eyes went to her phone, which was vibrating with messages from reporters requesting her reaction to Varden's conspiracy theories. She didn't respond to them. Fingers trembling, she scrolled through older messages, finally landing on a text from Amanda Lutz, a senior producer at the ReLOX Broadcasting Network. It was true that Lutz had invited Corina to be on *The Wynne Files*. And Corina had ignored it, like she did with the other media requests.

She called the show now and Lutz answered after three rings.

"Amanda Lutz."

"Corina Corado. I want to talk to Varden."

"Oh, Corina—I—yes. Well, Wynne's tied up. Could he call you back?"

"Get him now, Amanda!"

Corina heard muffled talking, then a man's voice.

"Corina, it's Wynne. How're you holding up?"

Corina took a sharp intake of breath, like an archer drawing the string of her bow, then she aimed, concentrated and released.

"You callous monster!"

Clearing his throat, Varden chose his words.

"I understand you're upset, Corina. I do. I can only imagine what you're going through."

"No, you can't. Because you'd have to be human! What you did was vile and unconscionable!"

"What we did is journalism. It's what you do. We asked questions."

"You twisted facts with lies, Varden! You accuse me of stealing a baby! You accuse us of staging Gabriel's disappearance for my job!" Corina's voice cracked as Robert and the others watched. "Then you have on two people with no grasp of reality, people who hawk snake oil, to push your lies!"

"You didn't respond to our invitation to be on the show, Corina."

"Oh! My! God! My son is missing!"

"Come on the *Files*. Come on our next show. We can help you."

Corina choked with revulsion. "I'd rather die!"

"I understand you're upset. I hope you find Gabriel."

Corina hung up and dropped to the sofa. Robert moved to console her but there was little he, or the detectives, could do or say. Contending with a maelstrom of emotions, she opened her phone to her last picture of Gabriel. Even as her phone continued vibrating with pop-up messages—a rush of new interview requests from Reuters, NBC, the Associated Press, CNN and the *New York Times*—she gazed at Gabriel. She struggled alone with how *The Wynne Files* had woven the truth with innuendo, speculation and lies.

As Gabriel smiled at her from the screen, the accusations and those photos of her taken by the Barcelona news photographer sent her back through time, to Nicaragua, the destruction wrought by the hurricane, the rains, and the mudslides in Madriz.

Corina was pulled back to the woman entombed in the mud holding the baby…*her cries… Por favor… Salva a mi hijo. Por favor. Llevar a mi hijo. Corina dropping to her knees, taking the baby into her arms… The woman pleading… The others trying in vain to dig out the mother…to save her…but it was futile. Her last words to Corina before she died… Por favor… Salva a mi hijo… Overcome, Corina making her way into the helicopter with the baby…the ground dropping as they ascended… bound for the relief post…*

A voice echoed in Corina's home.

"Charlotte?"

It was Robert calling for his daughter, bringing Corina back to the present.

"I think she went to the bathroom in the front hall," Lonza said.

Robert checked it, then returned.

"She's not there," he said. "Charlotte's gone."

24

DESCENDING IN THE ELEVATOR, Charlotte Tanner tucked her hair up under her Yankees' ball cap.

She pulled the bill down, keeping her face in shadow, veiling herself under her oversized black hoodie.

The doors opened.

Her head lowered, her hands in the front kangaroo pocket, she walked through the lobby of her family's condo building to the street. Charlotte wasn't famous like her mother, but she didn't want to chance being recognized. A few news people were keeping vigil on the sidewalk. She passed by unnoticed, relieved.

Then a photographer shouted after her. "Hey! You live there? Do you know Corina Corado?"

Without turning, Charlotte gave her head an exaggerated shake and kept walking, picking up her pace.

Distant sirens howled, the wailing floating on night breezes threading through Manhattan's towers along with the honking and murmuring of traffic. After going a block, Charlotte turned to see if she was being followed. Satisfied she wasn't, she crossed the street.

A half block later she entered the More Mirth Café, pushed back her hood and removed her cap. Taking in the coffee aroma, the workings of an espresso machine and soft jazz, she scanned the patrons at their tables.

A hand shot up.

Charlotte waved, then went to Harper.

"Thanks for coming," Charlotte said.

"No problem, I'm visiting my aunt and uncle. They live right over there on Third. I told them I was going to meet some girlfriends."

"Okay, let's go."

"We're not doing this here?"

"No."

Harper had trouble keeping up with Charlotte, who had asked her to meet because she didn't want to go alone to their next destination. Harper also knew just about everything concerning Gabriel because Charlotte had kept her informed. As they walked, Charlotte obsessively checked her phone.

A new text from her dad: Where are you?

Taking a walk with Harper. I need fresh air, she texted him back, then looked behind her for any reporters on the street.

Please come home.

Yes, soon, she texted, adding a heart emoji, then she lowered her phone hand and exhaled. "That was my dad."

"Is there any word?" Harper asked.

"No."

"I'm so sorry—it's so awful," Harper said. "I can't believe nobody has seen Gabriel. His face is on the news, it's trending, it's everywhere."

"It's my fault."

"No, you can't blame yourself."

"My parents blame me."

"They're just freaking out. Everybody is."

They reached 61st Street. When they arrived in front of a restaurant called No Place on Earth, Harper said: "You really think you should be doing this? You think this will work?"

"I have to do something. I have to try."

The diner's art deco feel was underscored by its linoleum floor, chrome and vinyl stools, and the booths, most of which were occupied. She scoured the dining room amid the smell of deep-fried food, clink of cutlery and din of conversations. Finding Vince Tarone in a corner booth, she went to him with Harper in tow.

"Hey," Vince said, flicking a guarded look at Harper as the pair slid onto the bench across from him.

"It's okay," Charlotte said. "This is my friend Harper. She knows everything."

Harper gave Vince a tiny wave.

Then Charlotte said, "Thank you for coming."

"Yeah, about that." Vince leaned forward, quickly surveyed other diners and dropped his voice. "Look, Charlotte, I want to help, but I don't know if this is a good idea meeting like this."

"I didn't want to call you or put this in a text," she said.

"Still." Vince shook his head slowly. "The NYPD went at me hard."

"But you didn't do anything."

"Tell that to the detectives at the 48th Precinct. They took my phone. I had to get a new one." He held up his phone. "They grilled me big-time because I was the person you were talking to when your little brother went missing."

"They're talking to everybody. That's what they do."

"I know. What's going on is wild. It breaks my heart about your brother."

Charlotte's chin crumpled. "My parents hate me," she said. "They blame me. You got to help me find him, Vince. There must be something you can do?"

Vince looked into his hands and said, "I don't know."

"You told me you know people, who know people."

"Yeah, well, being a driver I meet a lot of people."

"You gotta do something. God, please, Vince."

Charlotte turned her phone to show Vince Gabriel's picture.

"His face is everywhere," she said. "We've got media calling us, media outside our building." She looked out the diner's window into the night. "When I think of him out there and all the things that could happen to him— It's my fault and I gotta make this right."

Vince looked at the image of Gabriel on Charlotte's phone.

"You know," Charlotte said, "in a way, it's kinda your fault, too."

Vince's face flushed. "My fault? How?"

"Because you texted me right when I was walking with him. I mean, I looked away to answer you."

Vince flashed his palms. "Whoa. Hey, like I told the detectives, I was working at the time. I was on the Long Island Expressway and lawfully using voice texting when it all went down. I didn't know where you were."

"I know, but—" Charlotte looked away, cursed under her breath. "Please, Vince, I'm begging you. Promise me you'll try. You know people, and you know how things work. There must be something you can do."

Vince bit his bottom lip, his heart roiling with his feelings for Charlotte. In that moment, he thought of his father, dying, leaving just him and his mom. Just plain working people trying to get by. He thought of the rich people he drove around every day. Most treated him like he was a million miles beneath them. Like he was part of the car. Charlotte was different. She stepped out of her Upper East Side life and looked up to him. Vince Tarone. She gave him the respect he sought and, God, he loved her for it. And now, more than ever, he wanted to protect her. He took one of Charlotte's hands.

"This goes nowhere," he said. "This stays with the three of us, okay?"

Charlotte and Harper nodded.

"Okay, I do, kinda, maybe, know someone. It's a long shot but I'll see what I can do."

"You give me your word?" Charlotte said.

"You have my word."

Charlotte stood and hugged him.

"Thank you, thank you."

Outside the diner, Charlotte hugged Vince again, kissing his cheek this time, making him smile before he left in the opposite direction, trotting across the street. Charlotte and Harper started down the sidewalk, with Charlotte buoyed by Vince's promise to help. They'd gone about fifty feet when Harper said: "What the—"

Two people blocked their path, stopping them dead.

Detectives Lonza and Grimes.

"What was your meeting about?" Grimes asked, pointing his chin a distance behind them, where Vince stood, his hands on the fender of an unmarked car, its lights flashing as two detectives in plainclothes patted him down.

25

"You followed me?" Charlotte asked.

"Your mom and dad were concerned," Lonza said. "You left without telling them, or us, where you were going, or why."

"I'm not a prisoner. I'm not under arrest, right?"

"No, you're not," Grimes said. "But why did you, and your friend here, meet with Vince Tarone?"

Charlotte hesitated.

"Let me spell it out," Grimes said. "Gabriel went missing while he was in your care. You were the last person to see him. You were communicating with Tarone when Gabriel disappeared. Now you rush out to meet with Tarone." Again, Grimes nodded down the street. "What did you two talk about?"

Charlotte had no response; her face tensed and she turned to look toward Vince.

Finding no weapons on Vince Tarone, the detectives who'd stopped him had him stand next to their sedan as they checked his ID and questioned him.

"Why'd you meet with Charlotte Tanner?" Detective Stu Pankin asked.

His partner, Detective June Keene, made a call, reading off the address on Tarone's ID to someone on the other end of the line, then making a request with Tarone watching nervously.

"She just wanted to talk about her missing brother," Tarone said.

"Yeah?" Pankin said. "What about him?"

"She wanted me to help find him."

"Help how?" Pankin said.

"I'm a driver—she wanted me to ask other drivers to look for him. You know, ask my friends at Lyft, Uber, cab drivers, to keep an eye out. That sort of thing. You guys know all this."

Keene returned Tarone's ID, then said, "Mind letting us look at your phone messages? If you want to cooperate, to help us find Gabriel Corado, it would be a good thing to do."

Emergency lights pulsed in Tarone's face as he logged into his phone and handed it to Keene, shaking his head.

"I already cooperated," Tarone said. "Your guys in the Bronx already took my phone. Now you go through my new one. Why? The cops already talked to me, like for hours, right after it happened."

"Yeah, well, Vince," Pankin said, "we're talking to you *now*, right after your little get-together with Charlotte Tanner in the diner over there. You know what exigent circumstances are?"

Tarone had some idea but looked to Pankin for him to explain.

"It means an urgent, possibly life-and-death situation," Pankin said. "It allows us to immediately enter and search, which is what we're doing right now on your home in the Bronx," Pankin said.

Up the block, Grimes and Lonza continued questioning Charlotte.

"Why did you meet Tarone?" Lonza asked.

"I asked him to help us find Gabriel."

"So, without informing anyone, you leave for a secret meeting with the person you were talking to when Gabriel got separated from you?"

"I asked Vince to ask other drivers to look for Gabriel. I asked him because he knows the city, he knows stuff."

"Can I have a look at your phone?"

Lonza held out a hand and Charlotte surrendered her phone.

"And how about you?" Grimes said to Harper. "Can we see some ID?"

Harper passed her ID to Grimes, who studied it.

"Harper Hall," he said. "Right, we have your statement. You were the last person with Charlotte before she went to Tillmon to pick up Gabriel."

"Yes."

"You live on the Upper West Side," Grimes said. "How'd you get here?"

"Uber. I was actually visiting my aunt and uncle. They live on Third."

"Write down their names and address clearly for me," Grimes said, handing Harper a notebook and pen.

After she wrote down the information, Lonza asked for Harper's phone. She agreed to let the detective search her messages, as well.

Grimes took his notebook from Harper, stepped away to make a call, then returned, nodding an affirmation to Lonza. Lonza took a moment to examine the girls' phones, taking pictures of some of the texts.

"You were present at Charlotte's meeting with Tarone, Harper?" Lonza said, returning their phones.

"Yes," Harper said.

"And Charlotte asked for his help?"

"Yes."

"What else did they discuss?"

"That's it," Harper said.

"That's it?"

"I think Charlotte needed to get out of her house, she needed a break, you know?"

"My parents blame me for losing Gabriel," Charlotte said. "They absolutely hate me for what's happened."

Lonza kept her eyes on Charlotte, glanced to Harper, then acknowledged two uniformed officers who appeared. "You two stay right here with these officers."

Lonza and Grimes walked down the street. At the midway point, out of earshot, they huddled with Detectives Keene and Pankin while uniformed officers watched over Tarone. More patrol units arrived, red and blue lights splashing against the building, reflecting off windows and parked cars. The investigators made calls, radios crackled and a few gawkers clustered on the sidewalks.

Everything was in motion now.

A few blocks away on a tree-lined street, marked and unmarked units from the 19th Precinct wheeled up to a white brick building. Officers entered the recently renovated lobby, barreled past the surprised doorman and filled the elevator, taking it to the 14th floor.

They went to a corner apartment and knocked on the door.

Albert Collings opened it. His eyes widened as he took in the number of officers. He confirmed his name, that he was Harper Hall's uncle, and that his wife, Veronica, was the only other person inside. Then his jaw dropped as officers took him out into the hall and began patting him down.

"This is a mistake," the sixty-seven-year-old retired accountant said.

Officers also took Veronica Collings, a sixty-six-year-old retired museum coordinator, into the hall. A female officer checked her for weapons while other cops began searching their home—for any telltale signs of Gabriel Corado.

None were found.

Albert Collings was then escorted to the basement, where he was told to unlock their storage unit so it could be searched.

Across Manhattan, between West End and Riverside, Beatrice Hall's mind raced the instant she opened the door of her 1890s brownstone to police.

In a heartbeat, her thoughts blazed for her daughter Harper's safety, entwined with her worry for her friend Charlotte's missing little brother, Gabriel, before thinking that maybe something had happened to Elliot, her husband, who was out walking Buddy, their retriever.

But something was wrong.

Several NYPD officers, along with plainclothes detectives, stood on her step.

The next moments blurred as a detective confirmed details: her name and address; that Harper was her daughter; and that Harper was visiting her aunt and uncle, Albert and Veronica Collings, who resided in the Upper East Side.

"What's wrong?"

No one answered.

This couldn't be real. It was as if everything was collapsing around her. That little boy was missing. Her husband and daughter were not home and grim-faced police were not telling her anything.

Beatrice was told to turn around and raise her hands, press her palms to the wall. She stared at the new painting she bought in the East Village, a Vermont landscape with colorful leaves, and felt humiliated when a female officer checked her for weapons. Behind her, officers streamed into the three-story home. Beatrice heard them rushing up the stairs, felt the thudding of them moving through the bedrooms, doors opening, closing, going through the bathrooms, and thumping up and down the stairs.

Tears came as she pleaded. "Why're you doing this?"

At the same time, in the Bronx, Brenda Tarone was watching *Wheel of Fortune* when lights flared through the front window of her home on Prospect Avenue.

Oh God, this is it, she thought, rising from her sofa to see officers pounding on her door.

It's Vince. I know it's Vince.

Brenda went to her door.

Flashing badges, the officers stormed by her and began searching the house. One officer let others in at the back. Two women confirmed Brenda's identification through her driver's license and asked questions.

"Yes, Vincent Tarone lives here. He's my son," Brenda said. "What's going on? Is Vince hurt?"

The female officers nudged Brenda to the wall and began patting her, while others searched her house. One cop seized her phone and scrolled through it.

"What're you doing? Do you have a warrant?"

Brenda's house shook as the cops searched upstairs and downstairs. Someone muted the TV. Brenda was directed to sit on the sofa, where fear gnawed at her.

"Please just tell me, is Vince hurt?"

Reluctantly, after trading a glance with another officer, one of the female cops looked at Brenda.

"He's not hurt."

The search continued before tapering off to a series of radio transmissions and phone calls. Waiting and watching from the sofa, her heart nearly bursting, Brenda felt like she'd fallen into a dream. Confusion swirled in her mind before it hit her, and she grappled with dread—*the truth*—and what this police action might really mean.

She stared numbly at her TV, the moment a *Wheel of Fortune* contestant solved a puzzle phrase:

THE CALM BEFORE THE STORM

On 61st Street, near the No Place on Earth restaurant in the Upper East Side, Detective Grimes took another call, then turned to Lonza.

"That's the last one, Vicky," Grimes said. "Negative on all searches. No sign of the boy."

The detectives glanced toward the cars holding Charlotte, Harper and Vince Tarone, respectively.

"Okay, let them all get home." Grimes noticed that Lonza was holding her gaze on Tarone. "What's up, Vicky?"

Lonza bit her bottom lip. "I've got a bad vibe about this."

"What do you mean?" Grimes asked.

"Just a feeling we're not getting the whole picture."

26

Robert rubbed the back of his corded neck and Corina's face reddened as they scowled at Charlotte.

"With all the horrible things going on, you pull a stunt like this!" Corina said through a sob. "What were you thinking?"

Assessing Charlotte, Robert said: "Harper's family called. Police searched their homes, treated them like criminals." He shook his head in disbelief. "Why did you defy us and meet him? Why?"

"Because you hate me for losing Gabriel!"

They were in the kitchen but their voices carried through the condo.

"We don't hate you!" Corina said.

"You do! It's why I needed to talk to someone who could understand and help me fix this!"

"And how is Vince Tarone going to do that?" Robert asked.

"Dad, he knows other drivers who could help us find Gabriel."

"You already told us that!" Corina said. "Why did you meet him?"

"I told you! To ask for his help!"

"And that's the only reason you snuck out to meet him?"

"Yes."

Robert looked at Charlotte for a pained moment, his heart breaking again with a spectrum of emotions. "Just go to your room, Charlie."

"It should be me who's missing!"

"Charlotte, don't—it's not about—!" Corina said. "Just don't!"

After Charlotte left, Corina gripped the edge of the counter. "I can't handle this," she said. "Gabriel's gone! Varden's telling his minions we faked it, and she goes out and— Oh God, everyone and everything's coming at us!"

Rubbing his face, Robert turned to the dining area and the detectives, at the table, studying their laptops and phones. They were right there, talking quietly as if unaware of the argument. He asked them: "Was it necessary to search the homes of Harper's family?"

"We can't make assumptions, Mr. Tanner," Lonza said. "We have to pursue every aspect, wherever it leads."

"Do you have anything?" Robert's desperation strained him. "Anything from the searches, the cameras, tips? You must have something?"

"We're working on all fronts," Lonza said.

Watching Robert with the detectives, Corina's nerves rippled through her. Her family was being torn apart by Gabriel's disappearance, Wynne Varden's accusations, and her own fears and suspicions. Charlotte's obsession with Tarone was disturbing. Her actions tonight were frightening.

Then Corina studied her husband.

And what about Robert?

Prior to Gabriel's going missing, he'd been acting strangely, secretively, and then she'd discovered his hidden burner phone and that message.

I'm so sorry for what I did. I'm so scared.

I want to believe Robert. I want to trust my husband. But…

Corina's phone continued vibrating as the pressure to respond to Wynne Varden's conspiracy mounted. She glanced at the messages. The interview requests had not subsided. There were a couple from Newslead—one from Dakota Adams and another from Gil Dixon—that swept her back to her unresolved trouble with Efrem Zyller.

She shuddered at the memory of what Zyller had done to her; how she had stood her ground, vowing to reveal it to the world; and how he'd threatened to destroy her if she did.

"And when I go to war I never lose."

Corina's life was spinning out of control.

Her pulse beating under her skin, she stood at the window of her condo, probing the night, the glittering skyscrapers and the vast darkness of Central Park thirty-eight stories below.

Gabriel is out there.

Again, memory suddenly pulled her to Nicaragua and the mother dying in the mud, how she'd lived long enough to keep her baby boy alive.

...begging Corina to take her baby. Corina holding the baby...her ache to have a child...staring at the baby in her arms... Was this a sign to honor the mother's dying wish? Her last words echoing... Por favor. Salva a mi hijo. Por favor...

Corina's vibrating phone brought her out of the past to a new text, this one from a British newspaper, the *World Sun Express*, owned by the ReLOX corporate empire and legendary for being aggressive and breaking stories.

This message contained a couple of still images: one showing Corina entering a Nicaraguan government office, and another showing her gripping a file folder and leaving the offices of a law firm in Nicaragua. The date stamp was consistent with the time frame of the hurricane that devastated parts of the country.

How did they get these pictures?

The accompanying questions from the *World Sun Express* reporter asked: We're preparing a story and seek your response: Are the accusations made by The Wynne Files true? Did you take a baby from a dying mother in Nicaragua and raise him as your son, Gabriel? Did you stage his disappearance to deflect attention from your tenuous position at Newslead?

27

RETURNING TO THE BRONX, Vince Tarone took stock of his mom's two-story house wrapped in robin's egg blue aluminum siding.

He remembered when his dad, Sal, who was a mechanic, had died of a heart attack. How the place was jammed with people, most Vince didn't even know, and how he'd watched them drinking away their grief.

"Geez, there he was leanin' over the fender of a Cadillac," Richie, his dad's friend, had staggered among the mourners, ice clinking and booze spilling from his glass. "Geez, I swear, I thought Sal was sleepin'. Wake up, come on, Sal, wake up, I'm tellin' him, but geez he won't wake up."

Not long after they'd lost his father, Vince's mom, Brenda, got a job at the Bronx Zoo restaurant. He was about fourteen then and he'd walk from Prospect Avenue to see her. Sometimes he'd look at the tigers, pacing in their enclosure. Pacing like something inside them was going to explode. Which was how he'd felt at the time, back when he cursed God for taking his dad.

It's how he felt now, too, for Charlotte and her little brother.

Like those tigers, pacing and pacing.

Steeling himself, he came in through the back into the kitchen, where his mother was waiting for him at the table.

"You weren't driving tonight, were you?" Her husky whiskey voice signaled the coming inquisition.

Vince went to the fridge for the milk.

"I think you were with that girl again."

Vince was pouring milk into a glass when her palm slapped the table.

"Police were here! They searched everywhere! They frisked me like I was a gangster! God Almighty, Vince! What did you do?"

He kept his back to her.

"How many times have I told you to stay away from her? I wish to God Vinnie that your dad was here so he could talk some sense into you."

"Well, he's not. I'm the man of the house."

"You're a man obsessed with a rich young girl. A girl, Vinnie!"

"Stop. Charlotte's different. She's mature for her age, she treats me with respect. I'm going to protect her."

"Oh my God! She don't need you to protect her! What does it take to get through to you?"

"I love her."

"You love her? You love her? She's a child! Are you nuts?"

"You don't get it."

"Give your head a shake!"

"No, you don't get it! I've got to help her. She's beggin' me to help her."

"No! No, no, you can't!"

"I've got to."

"No! If you don't stop this, I swear, Vince, they're going to find out the truth about us!"

DAY 3

28

THE NEXT MORNING in Central Park, Corina stood at a portable podium that was heaped with microphones.

Gabriel's disappearance was entering its third day and she felt an internal clock ticking down. Corina had lived much of her life facing deadlines, but now time was running out on her son's life. Hammering at her was the reality that most abducted children were murdered within hours of being taken.

Taking slow breaths, she surveyed the news people gathered before her, recognizing national and local reporters. They were sending last-minute texts, or talking on phones, while photographers adjusted tripods and cameras. Police were observing from the periphery, and walkers and joggers stopped to watch.

Last night, after Charlotte's incident, Corina had studied her older stories while enduring on coffee and little sleep. She'd made calls and got word out that she'd hold a press conference in the park where Gabriel had disappeared. She'd had Charlotte's photo of Gabriel made into a head-to-toe poster that was now displayed beside her.

Earlier today, while getting ready at home, Corina had caught herself slipping into reporter mode as if she were on an assignment, preparing a stand-up. For a second, she considered makeup and clothes.

It's wrong. I'm not doing a story. I'm pleading for my son.

Still, she knew the increasing coverage would be her best weapon for finding Gabriel, and she had to take charge, convey control. She put on jeans, a dark blazer over a T-shirt, some eyeliner and blush. Corina was a natural beauty; her famous face and voice held authority.

"Okay, Corina," one of the reporters said.

Nodding under the camera lights, adrenaline surged through her in a near out-of-body sensation. So many times, she'd been on the other side of the microphones asking questions of people at the worst moments of their lives. Now the tables had turned. She introduced Robert and Charlotte, who stood behind her with a handful of supporters, then she took hold of the podium's edges and began.

"Our son, Gabriel Corado, is missing," she began. "He was last seen here in this very spot playing with the airplane he'd made—" she turned to the grassy slope "—while walking home from the Tillmon school with his big sister, Charlotte. He was wearing a blue plaid shirt, tan shorts, white socks and all-white adidas Superstar shoes. On his left wrist he's got a handmade, blue, stretchy cord bracelet, with a small Yankees' baseball and beads that spell out *Gabriel.*"

Corina blinked thoughtfully, her eyes glistening.

"Someone knows what happened to Gabriel. Someone saw something. Please, if you are the person who has Gabriel, let him come home to us now. Please. If you know something, anything, no matter how seemingly insignificant, call the police tip line, now. Please. A reward will be paid if it leads to Gabriel's safe return. Please help us find Gabriel."

Corina paused, looked to Robert, Charlotte and their supporters, then turned back to the news people, whose questions came fast, mashed together until the loudest got through.

"Do you believe Ivan Beckke took Gabriel?" Mario Guzman from the *Post* asked.

"We don't know. Police are still investigating him."

"What did Beckke tell you upon his arrest?" Guzman asked.

"Nothing."

"We understand Beckke had Gabriel's phone. Is he still a suspect?" Helen Yee from Reuters asked.

"That's for the police."

"Sources tell us Beckke was polygraphed. Do you know the result?" Ron Manjoo for *Newsday* asked.

"That's for police."

"Any ransom calls?" Manjoo asked.

"No."

"Could this be linked to threats you may have received?" Juliet Rentas with the Associated Press asked.

"Nothing can be ruled out."

"What's the reward up to now?" Kim Siftman with *Vanity Fair* asked.

"Seventy-five thousand," Corina said into the microphones.

"Do you often let your children walk through here, through Central Park?" Sheldon DuHame from the *Star-Ledger* asked.

"They've done it many times."

"Is it a routine someone stalking you could learn?" DuHame asked.

"Not really a routine," Corina said as a hand touched her shoulder. Charlotte leaned past her, toward the microphones.

"We live next to the park, it's like our backyard," Charlotte said. "I was walking Gabriel home from school, and we stopped here so he could play with his airplane. It went up over that little hill." Her voice trembled as she pointed. "I was texting on my phone and that's when he went missing, so it's my fault. Okay? It's my fault."

"Who were you texting?" Nell Dinsmore, a reporter for the *World Sun Express*, called her question.

Another shouted: "Did you notice anyone following you?"

Charlotte didn't answer. She buried her face in Corina's chest. Corina hugged Charlotte, then Robert took her aside, comforting her.

"Corina, what do you think happened to your son?" Susanne Lacey with the *New York Times* asked.

"We believe Gabriel was abducted."

"Why would someone abduct your son?" Brooke Browne, a local TV reporter, asked.

"I don't know."

"If police determine Beckke played no role in Gabriel's disappearance, who do you think would be responsible and why?" Lacey asked.

"I don't know."

"Corina?"

Heads turned to Vonn Bittner, a deep-voiced reporter with the ReLOX Broadcasting Network, which carried *The Wynne Files*.

Corina's jaw tensed as Bittner continued.

"Corina, you say you have no clue as to who would take your son, but I think my colleagues are giving you a pass on the obvious here. Haven't serious threats been made against you previous to this incident?"

"Yes. All of us in this profession face threats every day in this country. In the course of doing our jobs we've been called lying, disgusting people. We've been kicked, punched, spat upon—and, in cases here and around the world, journalists have been murdered."

"True, indeed," Bittner said. "But I'm thinking of your on-air exchange with Max and Marnie Ritzzkel, who head Greeters of the Rising Storm. Many viewed your handling of the interview as rude, unprofessional. Your treatment of the Ritzzkels antagonized the Storm's community to the point a man showed up at the Newslead building to implore you to be fair."

"Implore me?" Corina shook her head slowly, barely masking her anger. "That man had a gun and wanted to execute me. Now he's in jail. Do you have a question, Vonn?"

"I do. I'm sure everyone here is aware of last night's edition of *The Wynne Files*. It made some disturbing revelations, supported with photographs that have surfaced, as to whether you lawfully adopted Gabriel. Or if, in fact, you took him from a mother dying in a Central American disaster and arranged to secretly bring him to the US. Furthermore, there was the question of whether you staged Gabriel's abduction to divert attention from your looming termination from Newslead. What is your response?"

"My response? My son is missing. You and Wynne Varden defame me as being a baby-stealing monster who staged my son's disappearance, and you want me to respond to a ludicrous conspiracy theory?"

"If you would."

Corina raised her taut face, blinking, biting back on her fury. The silence that followed was punctuated by birdsong and the subdued rush of traffic on Central Park West.

"It's true." Corina looked at Bittner. "I took a baby boy from his mother who was trapped and died in a mudslide in northern Nicaragua. I did. I took the baby from her arms and left."

A few gasps rose from the group. Bittner's eyebrows lifted slightly.

"The fact is—" Corina cast her hand to the group "—the woman begged me to take her baby boy, to save her baby. Those were her last words to me before she died." Corina paused. "This brave mother had fought to live long enough to save her child. The photos show me carrying the baby to our press-chartered helicopter. We delivered him to a hospital in Somoto. I relayed the details to local officials and international aid groups so the boy would be cared for. These other photos from the *World Sun Express* show me checking in, following up with officials."

"What happened to the baby?" a reporter asked.

"The father was also killed in the disaster, but the mother's sister was located in another town and she took him into her family."

"Could you give us their names?" Susanne Lacey with the *Times* asked.

"The government posted the names of the dead and the missing at the time. You would have to know the town, and where to look on the lists. It was in the Madriz region of northwest Nicaragua." Corina straightened, then said with reverence: "The boy's mother was Evelin Flores—she was twenty-four. The sister who took the boy is Gloria Salgado from Sébaco. The boy's name is Octavio Salgado. I'll spell those names for you."

Lacey and other reporters made quick notes.

"Have you kept in touch with the baby and the family?" Lacey asked.

"I tried to." Corina brushed at her tears. "The last word I had was that Gloria Salgado passed away from illness and Octavio was taken in by in-laws, or distant relatives. That was a few years ago." Her voice weakened. "I lost contact after that."

"Corina," Bittner said, "we can all appreciate this is what you *claim* to have happened—"

"Claim?" Corina said.

"Yes, because no one else was there—"

"That's not true. There were other reporters from Spain, Argentina and Peru."

"So you say, but it appears difficult to locate them—"

"Someone found the photographer from Spain—"

"The fact is, in the time before the hurricane, you gave a candid interview to *Vanity Fair*, in which you said you desired a second child but had trouble getting pregnant. But lo and behold, your discovery of the orphaned baby, Octavio, aligns with your desire to have a child and took place right around the time you claimed to have adopted Gabriel. All about six years ago."

"What is your point?"

"Did you legally adopt Gabriel in this state?"

"Yes."

"Would you provide us his adoption records?"

"No. You know very well that the court seals adoption records," Corina said.

"So you refuse to disclose them?" Bittner said.

Robert stepped to the microphones. "They cannot be disclosed. And you know that," he said. "I can't believe this! What Wynne Varden did is unconscionable. The damage to our family is incalculable. And still you make these ludicrous allegations to drive ratings for your network! Our son is missing!"

For an instant, the surreality of what was happening overtook Corina. She saw how the crowd of onlookers had grown.

"We'll take one more question," Corina said.

"Corina, what is your response to the tabloid item suggesting your possible termination from Newslead?" Juliet Rentas with the Associated Press asked.

"It's a gossip column. Gossip is often unkind and untrue. What is true is that ours is a high-pressure industry."

At that moment, Corina caught her breath when she noticed Gil Dixon standing at the edge of the gathering. He stood next to Efrem

Zyller, who met her gaze with a slight nod and the beginnings of a grin.

"I think we're done. Thank you, everyone," Corina said.

Before turning from the podium, Corina glimpsed Lonza and Grimes again. The detectives were concentrating on their phones with a glint of gravity before they left.

Quickly.

29

NOT FAR NORTH of where the news conference was taking place, Jasmine Butler was running along the perimeter of Central Park Lake.

It was one of the park's largest bodies of water. To the north, it was bordered by the Ramble, a dense woodland of paths, trails, streams and bridges. This was Jasmine Butler's favorite place.

She used to run this route at dawn when there were fewer people. She loved the near solitude and sunrises of Manhattan waking up to a new day.

But that all changed.

One morning, a few months ago, she was running alone, just as the first light appeared, when she realized she was being followed by a figure that got close. Feeling uneasy, she increased her speed until she left the park and made it home, breathless.

The incident creeped her out.

Now Jasmine Butler only ran during daylight. As a freelance editor who worked from home, she had the option to do that.

The park was so pretty in the different seasons: autumn colors, winter snowfalls, spring, and Jasmine's favorite, summer. She liked how the lake's shoreline changed from rocky, to treelined brush, then to grassy sections. The bridges, like the Bow Bridge, were straight out of a fairy tale.

It was so sad about that little boy who'd gone missing from the park. She thought of his mother, his father and sister. How anguishing for them. She hoped they'd find him alive and well.

Jasmine Butler sent good thoughts to the boy's family.

Running was her favorite time to think about her work—it was a great way to clear her mind and get the ideas flowing. She was happy with the book she was currently editing. The author had a strong voice and was a natural storyteller. She was considering a few suggestions, deciding the middle chapters could be improved by—

Something ahead at the shore's edge caught her eye.

What is that?

Bobbing and sinking in the water, it became evident as she got closer.

That looks like— Oh my God!

Jasmine Butler reached for her phone.

30

UNDER SIX FEET of water, with inches of visibility, NYPD diver Detective Nick Lustig was feeling his way around the bottom of the Central Park Lake.

A jogger had spotted "human limbs" floating in the lake and alerted 911.

The NYPD Scuba Team had been dispatched, arriving within minutes. More emergency resources followed. They launched rubber rescue boats and got divers into the water, while team members unraveled safety lines. Orange markers bobbed where the divers worked, air bubbles breaking the surface. Radios crackled with transmissions, and the sky thudded as a police helicopter searched from overhead.

News teams had hurried from Corina Corado's press conference to report on the recovery action in the lake. People collected on the lakeshore to watch the grim operation—Robert, Charlotte and Corina were among them.

Charlotte clamped her teeth onto the tips of her thumbs and fought her tears. The muscles in Robert's gut tensed. Watching the horror of divers searching for body parts, Corina prayed.

Please, God, don't let this be Gabriel.

The pounding helicopter, crackling radios and meticulous work of the dive crews drew Corina into a near-surreal trance.

Watching from down the shoreline, almost hidden among the other bystanders, was Efrem Zyller. Not far off, in the opposite direction, detectives Lonza and Grimes were observing Corina and her family's reaction.

Working under the surface, diver Nick Lustig was nearly on his stomach, crawling along the murky bottom, when he was nudged by an object above.

Ascending, he came upon a foot.

No shoe. No sock.

In the muddied cloudiness, he saw the foot was attached to a leg, then his gloved hand found the second leg and foot, also bare. The legs continued but that was it.

Lustig could see the bottom half of a naked torso, child-sized, wedged in rocks and nearly breaking the surface. Grasping the lower calves, he found the remains extremely stiff and hard.

He began tugging.

At that moment, not far from Lustig on the surface, diver Detective Rhona Bailey discovered a single arm entangled in weeds along the shoreline. Grasping it, Bailey found that the hand was solid, frozen in a graceful gesture. The shoulder of the arm was fibrous, and Bailey, along with Lustig below, realized what they'd recovered were not human body parts.

They were discarded pieces of a mannequin.

The dive team's command was informed of the discovery. Word was relayed and the operation wound down.

Corina, Robert and Charlotte embraced, relief rolling over them as reporters sought their reaction to the false alarm.

"We'll never give up hope we'll be holding our son again soon," Corina said.

Before leaving, Efrem Zyller and the detectives assessed the family one more time, perhaps out of sympathy. Perhaps out of fear.

Perhaps out of suspicion.

31

Gabriel Corado is walking on the west side of Central Park West.

At the light, he takes the 72nd Street entrance, holding his airplane. His sister, Charlotte, is with him.

Come on, come on. Give us something.

Vicky Lonza crossed her arms. Again, she and Grimes studied the footage Officer Bonnie Graham was displaying for them on her monitors. Standing next to Graham's workstation in the Central Park Precinct, Lonza's concentration bounced between the photo of Gabriel Corado on the adjacent monitor and the footage of Gabriel and Charlotte vanishing among the runners, walkers, cyclists, horse carriages, pedicabs and tour groups streaming in and out of the park.

Then Graham reran the new sequence recorded at locations near Columbus Circle, the Guggenheim and the American Museum of Natural History. Cameras had captured instances of boys who appeared to be Gabriel's age; wearing similar clothing. But every time Graham zeroed in, it was not the right shirt, shoes or shorts—or the right boy.

"So, nothing on any camera?" Grimes kept tapping his notebook against his thigh.

"We're working on it," Graham said. "We've been processing hours of video from our cameras surrounding the park, our security and traffic cameras across the city and commercial cameras in our network. We've been working with MTA on subway and bus cameras. And people have come forward with video from phones and dash cams."

"Whoever took him could've changed his appearance," Grimes said.

"Right," Graham said. "Our Real Time Crime Center's been all over this with facial recognition. They could still pick him up if his clothing had changed. We're drilling down, separating video data for granular searching," Graham said.

"Keep us posted, Bonnie. We'll take your update into the meeting," Lonza said before she and Grimes left.

As they headed toward the precinct's glass atrium and the front desk, where officers were dealing with walk-ins, fragments of conversations spilled as Lonza and Grimes passed.

"It was a black wallet, lost it near the carousel." A man gestured with his hands. "It had an anchor imprinted on it."

The officer took notes. Next to him, a white-haired woman, who was helping an older man using a wheelchair, complained to another officer.

"That damned horse carriage nearly ran us over!" the woman said.

Near them, a man with a British accent spoke to a young officer. "That pedicab driver was bloody rude! He said his timer was accurate, but I know he overcharged us! He had a blue machine with a flower on it."

The scenes took Lonza back to her early days, dealing with complaints. You got all kinds.

Then a young woman with a child in a stroller stopped an officer passing by and held out her phone, which showed a map. "Excuse me, my GPS isn't working. I'm looking for the zoo."

Rounding the spacious lobby, Lonza and Grimes went to the room to the right of the precinct's entrance. Given recent events, it was decided to hold the latest case-status meeting here, rather than at the 19th. Plainclothes and uniformed cops jammed the room, sitting at classroom-style desks. Subdued conversations floated to the low ceiling.

Blowups of Gabriel Corado's photos stared at the investigators from the whiteboard and a large, wall-mounted flat-screen, positioned behind the table at the front. Garlan Weaver, their lieutenant, glanced up from his laptop, acknowledging Lonza and Grimes settling in at the table.

Lonza's phone vibrated, a message from her husband. Her stomach twinged. *Not now, Tony.* She put her phone away without reading his text. This was not a good time for her. She knew his anxiety over Marco's allergies—and that's all they were—stemmed from losing Eva.

"All set?" Weaver asked before turning to the group of investigators from a growing range of agencies.

"We'll get going." Weaver raised his voice. "With the press conference and the lake business earlier today, we've got a lot to cover. I'll turn it over to our leads, Vicky Lonza and Harvey Grimes, to tell us where we're at, and then we can brainstorm."

Working at her laptop, Lonza displayed a timeline with maps on the large screen. She gave an overview and provided key points, one being that nothing had emerged from the jailhouse interview of Trayman Herman Shrike.

"We're told Shrike was uncooperative and provided no useful information," Lonza said before summing up.

Then questions were raised, and theories on all aspects were discussed for nearly an hour before the meeting ended with investigators gathering phones, notebooks and tablets.

Lonza and Grimes were frustrated.

"We haven't advanced much," Grimes said. "It's not like *Law & Order*, all neat and tidy. This thing pinballs in a thousand directions."

Lieutenant Weaver joined them. "We're talking to the DA about getting the court to unseal the adoption records so we can locate the birth mother."

"But court orders to unseal adoption records are rarely given," Lonza said. "Maybe for medical reasons."

"We can make a case for the health and well-being of the child," Weaver said. "It'll take some time, but let us work on that. Meanwhile, Vicky, we'll need your next written status report for the captains and commanders first thing tomorrow."

"Yes, sir."

As they exited the room, Lonza's phone rang—her husband. His text had said he was picking up their son tomorrow, to stay with him in Staten Island for the weekend.

"Yes, Tony?" she answered.

"I just want to be sure...so I give him the blue pill in the morning and his new pink pill at night?"

"No. The blue pill in the morning but the pink pill at lunch. I'll write it down for you, don't worry."

Tony never overcame his guilt over his family being at a higher risk of cancer; that because of it, he was somehow responsible for them losing Eva. No matter what she told him, Tony would not accept it. His grief and guilt consumed him. He'd sit alone in the dark, refusing to talk to her, until eventually it became entwined with other marital problems between them, ultimately putting them on the road to a divorce.

"Did you hear me, Tony, don't worry about his pills?"

"Okay."

"I gotta go."

Eva's face flashed in her mind. She needed so many medications. Lonza understood how Tony was so anxious about getting it right with Marco.

But in the end, *in the end...all is vanity. Isn't that what the Bible says?*

"Detective Lonza?"

Lonza looked at the woman holding a tablet.

"Margaret Corley, Computer Crimes. I'm sorry I missed this meeting." Corley glanced at the last officers leaving the room, then at her tablet. "We've found something that nearly got by us. A deleted draft message created a few days before Gabriel's disappearance. It was created on Corina Corado's phone and never sent. Here."

Corley turned the tablet so Lonza could read the message.

Am I ready to reveal the truth about what happened? What will it do to my family?

32

At home, Corina Corado's laptop keyboard clicked as she resumed searching her archived stories in Newslead's database.

Scrolling through headlines, dates and summaries, she wondered if any of her reports would actually help her find Gabriel. Or if it was futile, nothing more than a police request to keep her occupied.

Exhausted from lack of sleep, Corina fell into a memory of Gabriel learning to ride his bicycle in the park. Robert had removed the training wheels, holding him up, rolling him toward her ten yards away, then letting go. Gabriel squealing with delight, contending with nervous exhilaration, balancing the bike to her, as she caught him, lifting him in a hug.

Wanting to hold him forever.

But the memory vanished.

Now Corina closed her eyes, her thoughts shifting as something undefined pinged in a corner of her mind. She took a shaky breath, contending with the fallout of the press conference, Wynne's vile allegations and the horrible moments at the lake.

Seeing Zyller in the park had turned her stomach. In the aftermath, his attempt to embrace her had failed. His presence attracted cameras, and reporters swarmed, pressing him to comment.

"We're all praying for Gabriel's safe return," Zyller said.

"Sir," a New York radio reporter said. "Is Newslead poised to terminate Corina Corado?"

"That's an inappropriate question at this time. I'm here because the network supports Corina and her family."

"That's not a denial, sir!"

Corina had moved off with her family and supporters while Zyller headed in the opposite direction, with cameras following both of them.

Zyller was there for appearances only, Corina thought, typing a few commands and turning to social media, finding a clip of her press conference. It cut to Gabriel's face. Corina traced it on her screen, her heart aching. She withdrew her fingers when the feed flowed to recent posted comments:

Don't believe a word out of her mouth she's the Queen of Lies!!!!

No sympathy for a baby snatching demon!!!! said another.

Another said, The liar used actors to fake the kid's disappearance!!!!

Corina's phone continued chiming and vibrating with interview requests, coming from every news outlet. All the while, time hammered against her.

Moving through her stories, she reflected on the comfort she took in how Robert and Charlotte had unexpectedly stepped up to the microphones. In that moment, her family was united in its fight for Gabriel.

But worry gnawed at Corina. She couldn't dismiss Charlotte's relationship with Vince Tarone—that they were texting when Gabriel went missing, and that Charlotte had snuck out to secretly meet him. And she couldn't ignore Robert's acting strangely before Gabriel disappeared, or that message on his burner phone, his plea for time to resolve his issue with the condo project.

My God, Robert, our son is missing. What's happened with us? We should be united in every way to find him, but I fear you may have betrayed me.

Her troubled heart pulled her back to when they met. How Robert told her about losing Cynthia, his first wife. How she told him about the night she'd lost her mother and father. In their understanding of loss and grief, they'd found each other.

Corina's thoughts shot in a thousand directions as she continued mining the headlines of her stories, and she forced herself to focus.

What am I really looking for?

Again, she stopped on a few of her older reports: stories about support groups for victims' families, fragments of the parents' voices echoing in her mind.

Why am I drawn to these stories?

Corina weighed everything, again and again, the history of threats against her, like those from Trayman Herman Shrike. Then Max and Marnie Ritzzkel, with Greeters of the Rising Storm, who'd generated so much hate against her in the past. And, more recently, on *The Wynne Files*, they'd spread the conspiracy that she'd stolen Gabriel and staged his disappearance.

But police had found no evidence any of them were involved.

Corina's anger meshed with her anguish when she looked closer to home at her family's turmoil, at everything leading up to Gabriel's disappearance, racking her brain for an answer.

Then it struck her, niggling in the corner of her mind.

That's the answer.

She froze. She knew.

It's crystalline.

Picking up her phone, she called down to the security desk and arranged for a cab to pick her up in the condominium's secured underground parking garage.

Grabbing her things, Corina hurried through the condo. Robert and Charlotte paused their video call with a community group as she rushed past.

"I have to go," Corina said.

"Where?" Robert asked.

The two detectives at the dining room table turned to her, one asking, "Did you find something in one of your news stories?"

"I have to check something out," she said.

"What is it?" Robert asked.

"We'll go with you," the detective said.

"No, I need to do this alone. I'll let you know."

"Corina, what is it?" Robert said.

Corina left, with the detectives trading glances before one made a call and the other reached for a radio.

By the time she reached the underground garage, the cab was waiting. She exited through the automatic delivery door at the condo's rear. A solitary TV crew aimed a camera at the taxi, but within seconds it was cutting across Manhattan.

Corina knew the detectives, or the FBI, would likely assume a ransom call or something, and have her followed.

I don't care what they think.

Twisting her ring, heart pounding, skin tingling, she questioned whether she was thinking clearly as buildings flowed by.

Yes, I'm right about this.

Gripping her phone, she opened the sites for the city's major newspapers. She called up the *Post* first, seeing the page on the story with the first headline:

THE DESPERATE SEARCH FOR GABRIEL

She saw the array of photos—Gabriel's, hers and a tight shot of divers surfacing in the lake with the headline:

TERRIFYING CLOSE CALL—LIMBS IN LAKE MANNEQUIN PARTS

The most recent *Daily News* headline read:

'HELP US FIND GABRIEL!' TV JOURNO MOM PLEADS

It was followed with photos of the search in Central Park and the headline:

SOMEONE KNOWS WHAT HAPPENED

Corina took a pained breath, fighting tears as her cab moved farther across the city.

33

I KNOW WHO took Gabriel.

Corina was closer now.

Her cab driver sailed smoothly through Midtown traffic to Manhattan's west side while Corina did all she could to keep from coming apart.

Pull yourself together.

Her destination in sight, she withdrew enough cash from her wallet to exceed the fare. She gave it to the driver when he stopped at the office tower that soared over Madison Square Garden and Penn Station.

Newslead's world headquarters.

Trotting to the main doors, she fished her Newslead ID from her purse, then tapped her way through the security turnstile. A few heads turned as she whisked through the lobby, hurrying to the bank of elevators.

She stepped into a car with about six other people, relieved no one paid attention to the fact she was in the building.

The answer was here all this time.

She ascended beyond the 36th floor, then past her own, the news division on the 40th floor. *Where I first learned that Gabriel had gotten separated from Charlotte...* The bell dinged, and Corina stepped off at Corporate, and the executive offices, on the 41st floor.

Striding through realms of executive units and support desks, her heart raced as recognition flashed on faces. Jaws dropped as she rushed by. She made her way to the vast corner office, where Muriel Dwyer, the executive assistant to Efrem Zyller, came around from her desk.

"Corina? Oh, dear, what is it? Did they—"

Waving Dwyer off without breaking step, Corina opened Zyller's heavy oak door. He was working on his computer while on the phone, his head lifting at the interruption. Startled, he ended his call with, "I'll call you back." Then he stood, surprised. "Corina? What is it? Has there been a development?"

"I know!" she said.

"You know? I don't under—" Zyller cast behind Corina to Dwyer, who was watching from the open door.

"Can I get you anything, Corina?" Dwyer said.

"No, thank you!"

"Muriel, let us talk alone," Zyller said. "Please, close the door and ensure we're not disturbed."

The door closed and Zyller indicated the sofa.

The same sofa.

"Sit down, Corina. What's happened? Is this about the chaos at the park? Is there anything I can do to help?"

She moved toward him. "Where is my son?"

"What? I don't know—"

She thrust her finger within inches of his face. "You know!"

Searching Corina's expression, an icy puzzlement crept into Zyller's eyes.

"Corina, you're traumatized, you're not thinking clearly."

"You said you'd destroy me if I exposed you for what you did to me. You found out I was talking to a lawyer, didn't you?"

"You're not making sense."

"You threaten me. You put out rumors you're firing me. Maybe you worked with Wynne Varden to resurrect the old conspiracy theory that I stole a baby in Nicaragua?"

"Corina, you're stressed."

"And who knew that Charlotte had to pick up Gabriel from Tillmon? I called her from this building. Everyone's heard the stories, the rumors, that Newslead monitors—or should I say eavesdrops?—on calls in the building for security."

Zyller shook his head. "You're going through hell, the situation with your son goes beyond our misunderstanding—"

"No! It all fits. Who would benefit the most from what's happened? You! You stood to gain! YOU!" Corina's voice rose to a scream: "YOU TOOK MY SON TO SILENCE ME!"

Closing her fingers into fists, Corina let go with a barrage of blows to Zyller's face and chest.

"GIVE GABRIEL BACK TO ME!"

"Corina! Stop!" Zyller fought to seize her wrists.

The door opened on Dwyer and two uniformed security guards, who helped get Corina away from Zyller and onto the couch, where she sobbed into her hands. Dwyer sat with her as security radios sputtered dispatches. In time, more people arrived. Paramedics assessed Corina, and Detectives Lonza and Grimes emerged with Robert, who, concerned at Corina's anguish and lack of sleep, wanted to get her home to rest.

Reading the situation, Zyller said: "I was telling Corina that there was no truth to all the rumors, that we support her and will do all we can to help find Gabriel."

"He's lying!" Corina said. "He took Gabriel! He's the one!"

Lonza's and Grimes's eyes went to Zyller, who shook his head.

"She was upset about the rumors," Zyller said.

"Liar!"

"Corina," Robert said. "She's had no sleep. We need to bring her home."

"You don't know!" Corina shouted. "None of you know what he did!"

As Robert and the paramedics began helping, Lonza and Grimes eyed Zyller, the blood draining from his face.

Raising his phone, Grimes turned away to make a call.

34

NOW HOME, in her living room, Corina squeezed a crumpled tissue.

Robert, the detectives and Deidre Thompson, Corina's attorney, waited for her to begin.

Charlotte was with family friends in the building, two floors down.

"You have to arrest Zyller!" Corina said.

"We've got people with him," Lonza said. "One step at a time. We need your background here."

"Take a breath, then go ahead," Thompson said.

Corina cleared her throat.

"I was filling in for a week. Anchoring a prime-time slot. I had completed the last program and I was still in the studio when Gil Dixon, a senior producer, came to me and said Efrem wanted a quick meeting upstairs, something quite rare. On the way up, I pumped Gil, but he just smiled and said it was exciting news.

"When we got to Zyller's office and sat down, he revealed that the network was launching a new prime-time news program in the style of *60 Minutes*, *20/20* or *Dateline*. The aim would be to dig deep into stories, and Efrem said I was the leading choice to anchor.

I was thrilled, it's what I've dreamed of. Gil fetched champagne to celebrate, then he got called away—some personal thing."

Corina looked down at her wedding ring, twisted it, then went on.

"Zyller moved next to me on the sofa and poured drinks, then he patted my knee, casually, in a celebratory way. But he left it there. I moved his hand and tried to shift away but I was next to the sofa arm."

Corina steeled herself before continuing.

"I thought it was just an awkward moment and that it had ended. Zyller went on about the show's budget, how it would pull in big numbers, how I was going to be fantastic. Having just anchored, I was wearing a sheath." She paused, blinking at the memory. "Then he put his hand on my knee again. I grabbed it, but he was strong and slid it up my inner thigh—" her voice broke "—touching me, saying, 'Come on, Corina.'"

Corina covered her face with her hands momentarily before lowering them and pushing through.

"'What're you doing?' I shouted at him, and I started to leave. He grabbed my wrist and said, 'I don't get you. You've come this far in this business. You know this is how the world works, how we both get what we need. *This is how I seal my deals.*' I slapped his face, cursed him and left."

Corina met Robert's gaze, rage and hurt seething behind his eyes.

"I'm so sorry," she said.

"No, don't apologize," he said, clenching his jaw.

"What happened numbed me," she said. "That night, I wrote down every detail and saved it. I didn't know what to do. In the time that followed, I kept asking myself if I was ready to reveal the truth about what happened. Was my family ready? If the truth came out, it could hurt us."

These thoughts were consistent with the draft message Computer Crimes had found on Corina's phone, Lonza thought.

"Not long after it happened, Zyller was on our floor. He took me aside and tried to frame it as a misunderstanding to keep between us. 'It was no misunderstanding,' I said. 'You assaulted me. I have to report it to HR.'

"Like a switch, his demeanor became malevolent and he warned me to think long and hard before I did anything. He also said that others were being considered to anchor the new program.

"I still hadn't told anyone. I was grappling with a million emotions—trauma, shame, guilt, even though I knew it wasn't my fault."

"That's a normal response," Thompson said.

"I agonized over what I should do. Should I remain silent, live with it, or go to HR? But Zyller came around again, saying the whole thing was consensual, a misunderstanding, and this time, he threatened me."

"How did he threaten you?" Grimes asked.

"He said if I was still going to report him, he'd take steps, he'd go to war. He implied that he wouldn't lose, that I would be destroyed."

Lonza and Grimes took notes.

"That angered me. And I thought back to what he said that night. *'This is how I seal my deals.'* I realized that the rumors about him were true. That he'd done this with other women. I thought how if I remained silent, he'd prey on more women. I thought, what kind of world am I shaping for my daughter if I stay silent? But I was afraid. I kept thinking what would be the impact on my family if the truth came out. But no one, no matter how powerful, should be permitted to prey on people, threaten them into silence and live above the law. Then I called Deidre, who I'd met from doing stories on harassment cases, to alert her and discuss how to proceed. She's the only person I've told. Until now."

"When did the incident happen, in relation to Gabriel's disappearance?" Lonza asked.

"About six weeks prior." Corina stood. "Don't you see? Maybe Zyller had people follow my family? And if the rumors about phone monitoring in the Newslead building are true, Zyller would know about Charlotte picking up Gabriel and he could take action to keep me silent."

"Did Zyller indicate he knew Gabriel's location?" Grimes asked. "Or attempt to gain anything from you in exchange for his return?"

"No, not directly. Not yet. But it fits, don't you see? He threatened me!"

Robert began pacing. "I'll kill him. If he took Gabriel or harmed him, I swear I'll tear him apart!"

"Hold on," Grimes said.

"Did you take action with regard to Zyller assaulting you?" Lonza asked.

"Nothing yet," Thompson said. "After Corina contacted me, my firm began studying Newslead's complaint policy. We also needed to weigh the repercussions of a formal complaint and whether a civil or a criminal path is best. Either way, the personal risks are severe. But the matter has been overtaken by recent events with Gabriel. I think it's clear that we'll wait until Gabriel is found."

"Corina," Grimes said. "Why didn't you tell us about Zyller at the beginning?"

"Because of the guilt, the shock of it. It was a separate shameful problem I didn't want revealed," she said. "But now it's clear what Zyller's done! You've got to arrest him!" Corina said.

"Alright," Lonza said. "There are steps we'll take."

The detectives consulted each other in the kitchen, standing near the island, where they sent messages and made phone calls, triggering measures targeting Efrem Zyller, the corporate head of Newslead's entire news division.

35

WITHIN NINETY MINUTES of Corina's allegation against Efrem Zyller, the detectives had obtained expedited warrants, via email, launching a new element of the investigation at Newslead's headquarters in Midtown.

"What is this?" Zyller said when Lonza, Grimes and other investigators, including a canine team, arrived at his office, where they provided him with the warrants. Reading quickly, Zyller's face reddened and he summoned Garnett Sloan, who headed Newslead's legal division, from down the hall.

"This is outrageous!" Zyller said, watching Sloan study the warrants. "Corina came here upset about the rumors. Then she tells you a bizarre story about a misunderstanding, and says I'm somehow behind her son's disappearance? It makes no sense."

"No one's being charged, or arrested," Sloan said. "These search warrants are in order. They apply to every floor, and we must comply."

The warrants allowed investigators to seize all phones and computers related to Zyller and his support staff. They also allowed police to search for any evidence of Gabriel Corado's presence in Zyller's office and on all floors associated with Newslead. Police wouldn't seize computers or phones from the other divisions, but the warrants permitted search of the cloud and all servers for any evidence linked to the case.

The canine handlers had cautioned investigators that the physical search would be a challenge for the dogs because the offices were contaminated with so many people's scents, along with odors left from the cleaning staff.

Shock waves rolled through Newslead as police executed the warrants. The sudden appearance of NYPD police dogs even prompted some staff, fearing a search for illicit drugs, to hurry to the bathrooms.

In his office, Zyller rubbed his neck as he watched a panting police dog stick its snout into his sofa, his private bathroom, his closet and his desk.

"We're also searching your residence," Lonza said.

"My home?"

"They are," Sloan said after scrolling through the warrants sent to his phone. "You might want to seek a criminal defense attorney, Efrem."

Zyller closed his eyes and took a slow breath.

Across the city, FBI agents were going room to room at Zyller's penthouse on Madison Avenue.

At Newslead, where the canine team had finished probing Zyller's office, investigators began removing his computers. Lonza held out a gloved hand for Zyller's phone.

Something was seething behind Zyller's eyes, and as Lonza closed her fingers around his phone, she remembered a fundamental tenet of criminal investigations.

No one tells the truth until it's too late.

36

"NAME?" THE WOMAN sitting at the first table asked.

"Cathy Miller."

"Do you have photo ID, Cathy, so we can sign you in?"

Cathy presented her driver's license. As the woman scanned it in, then typed into a laptop, Cathy surveyed the people already at work and others arriving, estimating more than a hundred.

That morning, word spread that a search center for Gabriel Corado had been set up on East 62nd Street, a few blocks from the park. A landlord had offered the vacant ground floor in his Upper East Side building. Located between a small museum and a parking garage, the space, last used as a dance studio, was large and open, with utilities and bathrooms.

The woman returned Cathy's license. "They'll make you a laminated search center ID at the next table before assigning you. Thanks for volunteering, Cathy."

"I want to help any way I can," Cathy said. "Corina Corado once interviewed my support group for parents of missing kids. She was so kind."

"A lot of people here know her from her work. Others are walk-ins who just want to help." The woman angled her head around Cathy and waved to the next person, a man, in the growing line behind her.

"I'm a retired firefighter," he said, stepping up. "My grandson's Gabriel's age. I want to help."

Cathy got her new ID for the search center and was directed to her area. She moved deeper into the activity toward a group of tables arranged in a horseshoe pattern, covered with laptops, flyers, maps and walkie-talkies. Several large flat-screens were tuned to local and national TV news networks.

In a far corner, one table held coffee urns, a supply of sandwiches and soft drinks. The air, smelling of cleaner and dusty plaster, echoed with dispatches from searchers in the park and the city, checking in with those at the center. People were busy working on the phones or computers, or organizing canvass or search teams.

In another area, the bright light of a TV news camera was focused on a woman who appeared to be in charge.

Vanessa Chang was telling the reporter how she'd used vacation time from her job as an investment analyst to help organize the center.

"I also volunteer with a local missing children's group," she said. "Many of us coming to the center are from those groups. Some are residents, or volunteers who help maintain Central Park. More people are coming in every minute."

As Cathy settled in nearby at the table she'd been assigned to, she heard the reporter ask for permission to interview a few volunteers. Someone named Valerie handed Cathy a laptop, explaining that Cathy's job would be to track areas that had been canvassed by volunteers. They both paused to listen to the volunteers being interviewed near them. The first was Lee Farnley, who drove a sanitation truck for a living.

"Why did I volunteer?" Farnley said to the reporter. "My twelve-year-old daughter, Addison, vanished after walking home from a party at her friend's house. Days later her body was found, but not her killer. She'd been assaulted and strangled. I talked to a lot of reporters. Most all of them asked me, 'How does it feel?' But then they never really listened to my answer. I could see it in their eyes—they were thinking about the next question, or lunch, or whatever. But not Corina Corado. She was compassionate, understanding, asking me what thoughts were in my heart. She asked about my memories of Addison that day. Corina seemed to have a depth to her—she was truly caring. That's why I arranged to be here, to help any way I can."

The next person to be interviewed was Julie Landon, a New Jersey mom, whose son Logan had vanished from a park near his home in Teaneck when he was eleven.

"Logan had been missing for a year. Then a police officer spotted him at a mall in Ohio with the man who'd abducted him," Julie said. "But in that whole time Logan was missing, I was interviewed by the press countless times. Corina Corado, and NNN, got Logan's case a lot of exposure, which I believe helped. And she was so kind, so thoughtful, telling me to never give up hope. That's why I'm here to help Corina, to pray for her, to tell her to never give up hope."

Blinking at her tears, Cathy thought of her missing son, Burke, and how she'd identified with Lee and Julie. In her case, Cathy remembered how Corina had interviewed her support group in the church basement so many years ago.

Cathy let out a long slow breath.

That's why she was here, to do what she needed to do.

"I can't believe this." Valerie had turned to one of the big TV screens. It was tuned to the ReLOX Broadcasting Network, replaying parts of *The Wynne Files* and Vonn Bittner's interview questions—they were clearly continuing to accuse Corina Corado of being a liar and staging her son's disappearance.

"How can they get away with spewing such horrible things?" Valerie said.

Staring at the screen, listening to the allegations, the accusations, the outlandish claims, Cathy pursed her lips and shook her head slowly.

"The lies," Cathy said. "The lies."

37

VINCE TARONE WATCHED the waterfront, the East River, and jets lifting off and approaching LaGuardia outside his bus window.

While the search for Gabriel Corado was unfolding in Manhattan that day, Vince had left his home in the Bronx that morning, made his way to Queens and boarded a Q100 bus.

He didn't have to work until tonight, so he had the whole day. If his mom knew what he was doing, she'd freak out. Maybe this was a huge mistake.

It didn't matter.

I gave Charlotte my word I'd help her.

Vince thought back to the sign they'd passed before the bus drove onto the bridge: *Department of Correction, Rikers Island, 'Home of New York City's Boldest.'*

His mother didn't know, but he'd first secretly applied to visit about six months ago, using an email account he'd created on a computer at the public library. At that time, he'd wanted to go because he had questions. He'd changed his mind, though, couldn't go through with it. But now, in the wake of what had happened to Gabriel Corado, he had to take the risk and act on his existing application, which was already in the system. No flags were raised.

To his surprise, it was still valid, giving him a green light. It also surprised him that the NYPD never got in his face about Rikers. Maybe it didn't matter to them, or maybe they missed it.

That's another risk I'm taking.

Now here he was, making his first visit to the notorious jail. A deplorable place of suffering, one agency called it. The conditions were so inhumane, the city had given Rikers a death sentence, initiating plans to permanently close it within the next few years.

There's no turning back. I have to do this because Charlotte's right, it's kinda my fault. Only it's way more than that—this is my penance. Besides, she makes me feel like I'm the only one who can protect her. It's like I matter to someone.

After crossing the nearly mile-long bridge, the bus stopped at the complex where a corrections officer boarded and listed off the rules. The passengers, mostly women, some with kids, were directed to a building where they began the security process of being sniffed by dogs for drugs, being patted down for weapons and storing their personal belongings in a locker. They passed through metal detectors at security points. IDs were confirmed and they were issued temporary photo passes. They progressed to an empty room where they waited until the name of the inmate they were visiting was called.

Vince was directed to the visiting area, which for him and the inmate was a table and bench separated by plexiglass. He was now seated face-to-face with a man in a tan jumpsuit.

Trayman Herman Shrike.

Over two years ago, Shrike had gone to Newslead intending to kill Corina Corado. His trial had been delayed with continuances; he'd continually fired and hired lawyers.

In his late forties, Shrike had the build of a middleweight boxer.

His face looked as if it had been sculpted in stone. It bore a few scars, was void of emotion. His small, piercing eyes squinted as he took stock of Vince.

"My sheet says we're family," Shrike said. "I don't know you."

"I'm Salvatore and Brenda Tarone's boy."

Tilting his head, Shrike looked at him.

"You're a cousin on my dad's side," Vince said, "after his sister,

Cecilia, remarried and moved to Garden City. Her people moved around."

It didn't register with Shrike.

"The only time we met," Vince said, "I was a kid and you came to my dad's funeral."

"Funeral? Tarone?" Shrike thought for a few seconds. "In the Bronx?"

"Yeah. On Prospect."

Recognition dawned and Shrike nodded.

"Sal Tarone, the mechanic. He fixed my old Ford for me. Never charged me. I remember him, he was a good guy. How's Brenda doing?"

"Okay. She works at the zoo." Vince paused. "She went to a couple of your court appearances, sat at the back."

Shrike hesitated at the shift in subject.

"I didn't know." Shrike eyed Vince.

"I think she had questions, like me, about why you did what you did."

"Oh yeah? So, why're you here?"

Vince glanced around, drew his face to the glass.

"I need your help."

Shrike stared at him.

"You're aware of where I am—there's nothing I can do in here."

"It's related to your case."

"My case?"

"Do you know that Corina Corado's son is missing?"

Shrike's eyes narrowed and he grinned. "Wonderful, isn't it?"

Briefly taken aback, Vince then asked: "Have police talked to you about the kid?"

"They sent people. Like you, they had questions. I'll tell you what I told them. I don't have him here and I'm not involved."

Vince lowered his voice. "I need your help."

"I can't help you."

"You must've been connected to people who, you know...people who don't like Corina. You must have an idea who might've done this?"

Shrike leaned back, folded his arms in front of him and stared at Vince.

"You sound like a cop. How do I know you weren't sent here by police?"

Vince shook his head. "Hand to God, I swear. I'm not."

"Why come to me?"

"I need your help. Look, the kid disappeared from Central Park when his big sister was supposed to be watching him."

"The park's a long way from Rikers."

"I'm kinda dating the kid's sister. I mean, I like her and she likes me. We were texting when it happened. It tears me to pieces, so I come to you, knowing your situation, and I ask you, I beg you, as family, to tell me if you know who might've done this."

Shrike began laughing. "You're a sweet kid. But you're a simpleton. A clueless, freaking simpleton. You know that?"

Vince flashed his palms. "Okay, okay, I'm sorry, I upset you. I apologize."

"You know what Corina Corado is, don't you?"

Vince waited for Shrike to answer his own question.

"She's the Queen of Lies!"

Vince nodded politely.

Shrike leaned closer to the glass.

"You know what I hold in my heart, Vince?"

He didn't know.

"The truth. I know what happened to the lying queen's boy," Shrike said.

"You do?"

"And there's one thing I can tell you."

"What is it?"

"I don't think she's ever going to see him again."

38

THE AFTERNOON SKY bled into another evening without Gabriel.

Corina, nerves shredded from lack of sleep, pressed her fist to her lips while studying her phone, constantly refreshing her emails and social media.

In the hours since police had launched their searches of Zyller, there'd been no word from Lonza or Grimes that they'd found Gabriel, or any evidence leading to him. Corina glanced at the new shift of detectives sitting at the table with their laptops: DiMaria and Alvarez. They had nothing to report, leaving Corina grappling with her torment.

Did Zyller hire Ivan Beckke? Zyller wouldn't hurt Gabriel, would he?

Corina went to Robert, who was surfing TV news channels, and he put his arm around her. Charlotte was on the sofa scrolling on her phone. Next to her, Joan Plaxon. Robert had accepted Joan's offer to return after all they'd endured that day. As their friend, Joan had been unwavering in her support to help the family in every way she could.

At that moment, Detective Lisa DiMaria finished a call and approached them.

"We've got people in the lobby who want to see you. Nora and Marty."

Corina's face brightened and Robert's gaze shifted to Joan, both indicating that a friendly visit from colleagues might help.

Robert turned to Corina. "Are you up to seeing them?"

Regaining her composure, Corina nodded.

Robert met them at the door.

Corina's producer, Nora Bower, and Marty Welman, the control operator, were barely visible coming through the entry hall. They had bunches of Mylar helium foil balloons bearing the words *Hope*, or *Courage*, or *Faith*. Others were plain, mostly blue or silver. Many were tethered to plush toys—bears or rabbits. They also carried cards and flowers.

"People have been dropping these off at Newslead nonstop," Nora said. "We brought what we could manage."

DiMaria and Alvarez began inspecting the items before Marty spoke.

"Your uniformed guys at Newslead and down in the lobby went through everything pretty good. I think they tagged this batch."

"Thank you for this," Corina said.

"There's a lot of support and love for you," Nora said. "And the emails keep coming."

After a tear-filled embrace, Nora and Marty deposited everything on the island in the kitchen. No one seemed ready to address the underlying tension of the search at Newslead hours earlier. Nora and Marty helped Corina sort through the messages on the cards and gifts. Some had been sent by journalists, celebrities, politicians or people she'd interviewed for news stories, but most were from strangers.

"With every beat of my heart, I beg heaven to return Gabriel," one card said.

"Wishing you strength at this time," said the next. Then the next: *"Cherish every memory of him, pray for his return."* Corina paused. That one was signed by Lee Farnley. His daughter went missing years ago and was found murdered. She remembered interviewing him, how his grief had turned his hair prematurely gray. She was touched that he would send her a message.

Moving on, Corina picked up a stuffed teddy bear, its arms extended for a hug, and read the attached message. *"Gabriel is such a beautiful boy. I wish for him to be back in your arms."*

She tugged at a balloon with the word *Courage* to reach the attached note, which said: *"Everything will be okay, Corina."* It was unsigned.

"Look at these, Mom." Charlotte passed her more cards.

"Gabriel is in our prayers," a state senator had written, and *"You're going to find him,"* from a retired FBI agent Corina knew.

The messages and gifts warmed Corina's heart, especially those from parents she'd interviewed in the past. She was awed by people who'd faced unimaginable tragedies yet had found it in their hearts to comfort her.

"See, Corina. Robert. Charlotte. You're not alone in this," Nora said. "And everyone at Newslead is with you."

"Thank you," Robert said.

Charlotte returned to the living room, took up the remote and watched TV.

"After all that's happened today—" Marty shot a look toward the detectives. "Is there any word?"

"No," Corina said. "Have you heard anything?"

"The search at Newslead today rocked every floor," Nora said.

"Rumors started flying about Efrem. And you," Marty said.

"What rumors?" Corina asked, exchanging a glance with Robert.

"That you were in the building today on the forty-first floor," Nora said. "That you confronted Efrem."

"We've heard that Efrem was the target of the warrants," Marty said, "that maybe he's connected to the investigation somehow, or that it might be connected to Wynne's conspiracy theories that you staged Gabriel's disappearance. We heard Efrem's got a criminal lawyer."

"It's confusing. Nobody knows what's going on," Nora said.

"I was there today," Corina said. "I can't tell you why, but if the warrants aren't sealed, media can access them."

"Yes, we've got people on it," Nora said. "But the warrants don't always tell you the full reason for the search."

"Did you guys come here as friends?" Corina asked. "Or journalists?"

"We came as friends," Nora said.

Weighing the response, Corina glanced at the detectives. They were talking on their phones and looking at her just as Charlotte raised the TV's volume. She'd landed on the ReLOX Broadcasting Network News. A report in progress pulled the others closer to the screen. The chyron banner at the bottom of the screen said:

SEARCH WARRANTS EXECUTED AT NEWSLEAD IN ANCHOR'S MISSING CHILD CASE

"To repeat, sources have told RBNN that in the case of Gabriel Corado, the missing six-year-old son of Newslead journalist Corina Corado, search warrants were executed today at Newslead's New York headquarters."

The anchor looked at his copy in his hands. Then there was video of investigators carting off boxes and computers.

"We've also learned that search warrants were executed at the Madison Avenue condo of Efrem Zyller, the head of Newslead's news division. Now, a freelance news team got this exclusive footage—" a clip of Corina's cab leaving her condo's rear security garage door played *"—of Corina Corado rushing to Newslead a few hours before the warrants were executed."*

While all of the footage replayed continually, Wynne Varden appeared below it on a split screen with the anchor.

"For his take on these developments, we go to Wynne Varden, host of the highest-rated news analysis show, The Wynne Files. *Wynne, what do you make of today's events?"*

"Thank you. Well, it underscores our belief this could've been a staged inside job with something much deeper at play. We must not lose sight of the fact a little boy is at the center of this heartbreaking case. We can only hope and pray for his well-being and that the truth will—"

"Wynne, hold on, I have to stop you. We have to cut away to Vonn Bittner, who is live at Central Park. Vonn, what do you have there?"

Bittner appeared on screen, turning to the rhythmic glow of police lights and yellow crime scene tape illuminating a darkened area of the park.

"Yes, I'm at the east side where a body has been discovered in a wooded area of Central Park, near 65th Street, bordering the Upper East Side neighborhood where Gabriel Corado lived—"

39

The breaking news catapulted Corina to her door with the detectives calling after her.

"Wait! Don't leave!" Alvarez said, phone to his ear.

DiMaria, also on her phone, cautioned: "Don't go to the park, please! We're getting more information!"

They were too late to stop her; she'd rushed to the elevator and jabbed the button. It was quick to arrive. She saw Robert and Charlotte rush into the hall, but she got on and the doors closed before they could reach her.

Downstairs, Corina exited her building. News crews were waiting on the sidewalk. In a sudden blaze of lights, they assailed her with questions that went unanswered as she flew past them with a brief look over her shoulder. Some trotted after her before giving up; others hurried to vehicles.

Corina was unsure if media—or her family, friends or detectives—were following as she ran. She didn't care. The location given in the report was less than five blocks away. Her heart pounded, panic rising as she ran, pleading for Gabriel.

He can't be dead! It can't happen like this!

Sirens screamed in the night, underscored with horns, traffic.

Breezes carried take-out wrappers and the smells of the city. Corina ran toward a galaxy of police lights, strobing against the park wall. The wailing of the sirens was endless…taking her back through her life to California…replaying that night…

Please don't let this be Whittier again…not again…

The lights were brighter, sirens louder, as Corina arrived. Inside the park entrance she found controlled chaos as she shouldered through bystanders to the yellow tape. She clasped the arm of a cop.

"Help me, please!"

"Ma'am, remove your hand and stand back!"

"Please, I need to talk to a detective. I'm Corina Corado and my son Gabriel's missing."

A moment. Then recognition registered.

"Wait here." The cop turned away, speaking into his shoulder microphone. A static response sounded and he lifted the tape. "This way."

With a sharp intake of breath, Corina ducked under the tape.

"Corina!"

Robert and Charlotte emerged, out of breath, and identified themselves to the officer. Assessing them, the cop then led the family along the inside perimeter, advising them where to step.

Still distant from the scene, they moved along, near another cluster of emergency vehicles situated deeper in the park, lights strobing, radio crosstalk crackling. Beyond them, Corina glimpsed more crime scene tape. Then, on the ground, just as she saw a yellow tarp covering a body, investigators huddled near it, she heard the fragment of a radio dispatch.

"…male…deceased is male…age…stand by…"

Corina's legs gave way, but Robert and Charlotte steadied her.

Moments later, two detectives, Aubato and Plunkett, stood before them; their badges swaying from neck chains glinting in the lights. They nodded when the cop confirmed who they were.

"I'm sorry you had to come down here like this," Aubato said, gripping a notebook.

"Didn't DiMaria inform you?" Plunkett asked.

Corina covered her mouth with her hands and shook her head.

"Corina ran over when she saw the news," Robert said. "We followed her. In the confusion, we only know that you have—" His gaze went to the tarp. "Is that—"

"Did you find our son?" Corina asked.

"No," Aubato said. "We have a male in his late seventies. He may have fallen due to a medical condition. He may have been assaulted. But we assure you, it is not your son."

Corina groaned. Robert reached to comfort her but she shook him off. Something inside her was fracturing, her thoughts were whirling. Robert tried to comfort her again, nodding to Charlotte.

"You have to sit down, Mom."

This time, with Charlotte's support, Robert helped her to a bench nearby.

But the world continued spinning for Corina, swirling faster, her heart going out to the dead man's family, her fears streaking before her: fears that Zyller had taken Gabriel; fears over Ivan Beckke; fears that Robert was hiding something; fears that fate had control of her and she was breaking apart.

"No, no, nothing's true! I can't believe anyone anymore! I can't even believe you, Robert! Is this all happening because of you? What're you doing, Robert? You're lying to me? Why?"

"No, no, Corina."

Suddenly, the laments of suffering people replayed in Corina's mind.

"The last thing she did was turn and wave goodbye…"

"He comes to me in my dreams…"

"Salva a mi hijo. Por favor. Llevar a mi hijo."

As her anguish churned, Corina saw the park as the abyss that had stolen her little boy, and whatever threads of control she had snapped as she fought off Robert's attempts to hold her.

"Gabriel!" Corina screamed, her cry rising above police radios, the sirens, to the sky. "Gabriel!"

Police helped Robert get Corina home, where Robert and Joan got her into bed. Joan gave her a sedative from the medicine cabinet.

Robert lay with her, holding her until she fell asleep. After he left, he checked on her from time to time, tenderly brushing her hair or adjusting her blanket.

Joan stayed as well, joining Robert in the living room. At times she struggled with her own composure at seeing Corina, Robert and Charlotte, the family she often regarded as her own, being torn apart by Gabriel's disappearance.

"I'd do anything to bring him home to you," Joan said, burying her face in her hands. "Anything in the world."

Meanwhile, Charlotte found refuge in the shower, where she slammed her back to the wall and sank to the floor, drawing up her knees and sobbing, great choking, heaving sobs.

Robert retreated to his study, where he closed the door.

In the darkness, he sat at his desk, caressing his wedding band, casting his thoughts back to the dinner party at the opening of a new condo tower where he and Corina had first met. How they talked like they'd known each other forever. How they met for coffee, then again for dinner. How they were so comfortable with each other, both carrying deep wounds from pain they'd suffered in their lives. They fell in love and had lived an extraordinary life, but one not without its heartaches—the miscarriages, the strain of all-consuming careers. Above it all, they were blessed with Charlotte and Gabriel.

How could Corina think he would ever lie to her?

Easy, he thought. *Because I look guilty of betraying her. I can't blame her. But I have to make things right. I promised her I'd resolve the crisis with my building project and tell the detectives everything. But I'm running out of time and hanging by a thread. Truth is, I don't know if I can do it.*

Robert held his face in his hands and fought to keep himself together. He'd lost sense of time, praying for Gabriel, Corina and Charlotte, when a vibration hummed.

He had a message on his burner.

He didn't recognize the number.

The message came with an attachment containing images.

His heart dropped to his stomach; his face twisted.

The message began: You know what we want...

40

Late that night across the city, in her semidetached home in Queens, Detective Vicky Lonza worked on Gabriel Corado's case.

Her laptop chimed with the email from Lieutenant Weaver on the preliminary results from the warrants executed against Efrem Zyller. Nothing from the searches so far. Zyller's got a lawyer now and they're talking to the DA. We'll know more in the a.m.

Lonza tapped her pen. She wasn't surprised he'd lawyered up. They needed hard evidence to arrest Zyller. And Corina Corado didn't want to swear out an assault complaint yet, making things more of a challenge.

We've got nothing to tie him to this. Still, I don't trust that guy. Something's not right with him.

Lonza surveyed the remnants of the pizza her mom and Marco had left her on the counter. She took a few bites and massaged her neck, which felt like steel. She got fresh coffee and soon her keyboard was clicking as she worked on her report arising from the case-status meeting earlier that day. Weaver needed it by morning.

She wrote that Ivan Beckke had been released but faced weapons charges. His polygraph: inconclusive. Other than Gabriel's phone, they had no evidence tying him to an abduction, leading them to believe that the phone was tossed into Beckke's truck.

She weighed other aspects.

Gabriel's appearance could've been changed; he could've been absorbed into a tour group and ended up on a bus. Investigators were pursuing tour and charter groups at or near the park at the time. Nothing had emerged from RTCC using facial identification. Gabriel's route and timeline from Tillmon to the park were under continual analysis. The transverse streets that took traffic through the park were checked and rechecked.

Vendors, street performers, park regulars and doormen were being canvassed. All school staff had been interviewed and were alibied and cleared. The sex offender registry was being analyzed and alibis confirmed. Investigators were also working with missing children's groups and neighborhood associations, and monitoring social media. The FBI was checking the dark web for chatter and trafficking.

No communication from a kidnapper. Nothing to indicate involvement of religious groups, cults, Satanists or extortioners.

To date, over six hundred tips had been received. Two women had been overheard talking on a crosstown bus: "...like they had something to do with that boy in the park." Another tip concerned guests at a motel in Schenectady with a boy resembling "that missing boy in the news." In Manhattan, a jogger reported a woman scolding a boy at the Central Park entrance near East 76th Street. A tipster in Rhode Island said she saw Gabriel Corado with older teens at a mall in Providence. So far, every lead dead-ended, was unfounded or too vague, but every tip that could be pursued was being pursued.

Lonza continued writing her notes. *No evidence of abuse in the home, a runaway, an internet lure, substance abuse, or financial stress or gambling debts. Stress in the home, originating from Corina Corado's job and Robert Tanner's current engineering project on a supertall condo—both parents have high-pressure professions. Additional stress in the home arising from Charlotte Tanner's relationship with Vince Tarone—she's sixteen, he's twenty-one. They were communicating when Gabriel disappeared. Their meeting after the incident was investigated; nothing substantive was found, but their communication and relationship remains a concern. Tarone, a ride-share driver, lives with his mother in the Bronx, has no criminal history. He was driving on the Long Island Expressway while the boy was in the park. Tarone's passenger, a Queens College professor, alibied him.*

At the time of Gabriel's disappearance, Gabriel's father, Robert Tanner, was in Philadelphia on business. He was expected to return to New York in the morning and pick up Gabriel in the afternoon, but got delayed with another meeting, leaving Philadelphia on a later flight. All confirmed.

Gabriel's mother, Corina Corado, who was working at Newslead across town, directed Charlotte to pick up Gabriel from the Tillmon school.

Lonza paused, drank coffee and resumed writing in the section titled "Threat History."

Corina Corado has received many threats throughout her career, on campaigns and contentious stories, from extreme elements who consider journalists criminals. A pivotal point came a few years ago with her interview with the leaders of Greeters of the Rising Storm, a controversial group who called Corado "The Queen of Lies." That prompted a viral tsunami of hate, which culminated in an armed man, Trayman Herman Shrike, entering the Newslead building intent on killing her. Shrike is in Rikers awaiting trial. Working with the FBI and other jurisdictions, investigators have run down people behind other serious threats against Corado, going back years. No links have surfaced. Storm leaders, Max and Marnie Ritzzkel, reside in California and appear to have no link to Gabriel's disappearance.

Additionally, Corado is reviewing her news stories with an eye to alerting us to potential threats or suspects.

Allegations that Corado "stole" her son while he was an infant and she was on assignment in Central America, then staged his disappearance to create sympathy, distraction or leverage from rumors of her impending termination at Newslead, have yet to be substantiated. However, potential ties to the recent controversial claims, and Corina Corado's allegation of being sexually assaulted by a Newslead executive, led to the execution of warrants; all are under investigation.

What cannot be ruled out is the possibility that family members have, inadvertently or intentionally, withheld useful information or misled investigators.

Wrapping up her report, Lonza finished off her coffee just as her laptop chimed with an email from Bonnie Graham.

We've just pulled this new one together, Graham wrote. Nothing on it yet, still needs analysis. But it fills in a few gaps. Sharing it with you and the others to get more eyes on it.

Graham's note said the short video was a succession of footage patched together from NYPD cameras and the commercial security network. Lonza hit Play and found Beckke's truck as it moved east on 59th Street. The footage jolted from perspective to perspective between Fifth and Park Avenue. In those few blocks, cameras showed a delivery truck to maneuver around, bicycles, a pedicab, pedestrians, traffic lights. There were still camera gaps, but Lonza saw nothing out of the ordinary. Beckke did not exit his vehicle, and no one approached or got into it.

For the next twenty minutes, she replayed and scrutinized the short video until her vision blurred.

She closed the file, rubbing her eyes, every fiber of her body trembling. She opened the last photo taken of Gabriel Corado.

Six years old.

Something scraped against the walls of Lonza's gut. She yearned to find him, not because this was one of the biggest cases she'd ever led, but because as a mother she knew the pain of losing a child.

As if on cue, the patter of paws on the floor preceded Luna, her parents' retriever. Lonza's mother always brought her along when she looked after Marco. He called her "Luna Lonza." Now Luna joined her in the kitchen, nuzzling her lap. Lonza brushed her coat, hugged her, got her a treat and freshened her water bowl.

Listening to the comforting sounds of Luna's lapping, Lonza got up and walked through the house. The bedroom door was half open in the room where her mother was sleeping, her breathing even. Lonza smiled, then went on to the next bedroom. In the soft light she saw Marco's poster of vintage NHL goalie masks that Grimes got him. She moved to Marco's bedside, brushed his cheek and kissed him on the forehead.

She turned to the twin bed across the room.

Empty, still made.

It had been Eva's.

Before cancer.

Lonza sat on the mattress, caressing the pillow and finding herself floating back to the hospital, sitting with Eva. Holding her hand in those last days. Eva, looking so tiny in the bed, so fragile, so weak. But her eyes held light that brightened into a smile when a couple of interns and nurses came to the ward dressed as clowns. Those last moments came softly, quietly, Eva weakening and slipping away. But Lonza carried her laugh with her, from the way Eva reveled in joy watching street artists in the park creating giant bubbles and saying, "If I could ride inside one, I think I would float to heaven, Mom."

Losing Eva was like a claw, ripping the fragile web of their existence. The therapists had said tragedies of this magnitude either brought families together or tore them apart. Lonza and Tony had done all they could to hang on, but it was too much, just too much.

I have to find Gabriel Corado. I can't let the world take another child.

Pulling herself together, Lonza returned to her work.

The laptop screen gave the room a glow as she concentrated again on the video. Stroking Luna, who'd rested her head on her lap, Lonza played it again and again.

DAY 4

41

An hour before sunrise, Robert Tanner was at a twenty-four-hour coffee shop on Lexington, praying he could bring Gabriel home.

He refused to believe that the pictures he'd been sent were real. Sitting at his table, cautioning himself to be careful, he reflected.

Since receiving the disturbing message, he hadn't slept. The hours had swept by, only increasing his dread. Then, after receiving additional information from whoever was behind the message, he'd gotten up from his desk and checked on Corina and Charlotte. Both were still asleep. He went to the living room, where Alvarez and DiMaria were talking quietly at the table.

"I'm taking a walk before Corina and Charlotte wake," he'd told them.

"Has something come up?" Alvarez asked. "Want company?"

"No. Thank you."

"You sure?"

Clearing his throat, he'd struggled to sound calm. "I'm sure."

The detectives considered his tousled hair, bloodshot eyes and unshaven face, the lines carved deep into it.

"Is something going on?" Alvarez asked. "Are you holding something back?"

"I need some air, need to think, you know?"

It took a moment for the undercurrent of suspicion to diminish, then DiMaria said, "Sure, might do you some good. Got your phone?"

Robert held up his personal phone before he pulled on a jacket and a ball cap.

Alone in the elevator, his nerves rippled through his body from lack of sleep and the soft drone brought a memory of Gabriel. How he'd invited him to speak to his class about his job. Robert had brought models, explained how skyscrapers were built, showed them old photos of work crews eating lunch on a beam high over the city, making the class gasp. Later, when Robert left, Gabriel followed him into the hallway, telling him, "You're the best dad ever!"

Coming out of his reverie, Robert's fingers shook as he looked at his two phones. At the outset of Gabriel's disappearance, the police had taken his SIM and SD cards, allowing him to replace them so he could still use his phone. How long did he have before police wanted the replacement cards?

He looked at his burner phone, which he used for confidential calls for his condo tower contract; it had aroused Corina's suspicion when she discovered it. Did she still believe him? How long until she asked him about it again? Or told police?

I can't lose this phone. Not now. It's my lifeline to Gabriel.

He'd left his building through the underground parking garage, hoping there was little chance he'd encounter media at this hour. Relieved that it was clear of reporters, he walked the few blocks to Lexington, battling to keep his wits about him, aware he may have been followed. Along the way he saw a couple of joggers and people walking their dogs. The grind of delivery trucks and quieter strains of traffic rose from the darkened streets.

Now in the coffee shop, he took quick inventory of the few people near him. An older couple at one table; across from them, a man reading the *Wall Street Journal*; in the corner, two women talking.

Fear and self-doubt coiled through him.

Am I a fool to think I can handle this myself? Or, should I tell police?

He stared at his phones, using his day-to-day phone to search news sites for updates. Then he switched to his burner and scrolled to the older message from Jennifer, the woman who'd stood him up in Philadelphia.

I'm so sorry for what I did. I'm so scared.

Looking again at the photos sent to his burner phone a few hours ago, bile oozed up the back of his throat.

How? These pictures can't be real. Who sent them?

Rubbing his lips, he struggled to piece things together.

Jennifer had promised to give him the records he needed to make his case for the residents of the New York tower. The building's wealthy, powerful residents were alleging their new building had serious defects—that it was unsafe, and that this had reduced property values. The group was threatening to go public with legal action if expensive repairs were not made. They'd hired Robert's engineering consulting group to examine the defects and submit a report crucial for them to proceed with their case.

He'd discovered potential problems with the construction from the beginning, but he needed contractors' records to support his findings. All the while, Robert encountered hearsay about the conglomerate behind the $2-billion tower. Unfounded rumors held that behind a web of LLCs and numbered offshore companies, the investors were cartels, oligarchs and other nefarious groups. It was also rumored that the New York building, one of the world's tallest, was to be the first jewel in a crown of luxury multibillion-dollar towers the group planned for Dubai, Tokyo, Paris, Jakarta and Cairo. Robert was told the group would not let anything tarnish or impede its global vision.

Having no evidence concerning who truly invested the money for the building, Robert set the rumors aside. As he continued working, looking at a number of aspects for possible issues, such as the quality of concrete used in the foundation to support the structure's weight, and a review of wind bracing to counter sway. He was also looking into possible issues with elevators, plumbing and the electrical system. And he'd heard talk of bribery and cost-cutting. He hadn't yet reached the point of making any conclusions on potential structural failure, because he needed reports and inspection records to check against industry thresholds. A whistleblower had emerged, an anonymous woman who called herself Jennifer. She advised him to get a burner phone for communicating with her and others on the inside. She promised to supply him with the documents he needed, if they met in Philadelphia.

Now, looking at the horrifying pictures that had been sent anonymously—*oh God, these would destroy Corina*—he felt the tentacles of the nightmare constricting around him and stifled his sobs.

Do not go to police. Tell no one, the last message stated, then directed him to this coffee shop, where he'd be watched to ensure he was alone. Then we'll end this.

Robert turned to the window, the first light painting the sky.

His burner phone vibrated.

You know what we want.

Gritting his teeth, he wrote: Give me my son.

Do what we want and this will end.

Where is my son? I don't believe the pictures are real. Show me proof you have Gabriel.

Moments passed, then his burner vibrated. The new message had a short video that appeared to be from a security camera. The footage clearly showed Gabriel walking with Charlotte, entering Central Park.

Robert jammed his knuckle into his mouth and bit down on it. *They must've followed the kids.*

Let me talk to Gabriel!

Are you going to do what we need you to do?

Let me talk to my son! Show me he's unharmed!

Seconds passed with nothing—no images, no connection, nothing—twisting Robert's gut, until finally, a response.

We'll give you a few hours to decide. If we don't see action, if you inform police, you'll force us to take irreversible measures.

Show me my son!

The exchange ended, leaving Robert numb. He sat stock-still for a full minute, then managed to get to the bathroom. He splashed water on his face. His mind swirled; he needed to act but he didn't know what to do.

He stepped into the street.

The sun had risen and two detectives came toward him, showing Robert their badges.

"Hi, Mr. Tanner," one of them said.

Robert gave a small nod.

"Sir, we'll get to the point. Do you know something about this case you haven't told us?"

"I just wanted some fresh air and time to think."

"Would you mind surrendering your phone to us."

Robert opened it and handed it to the detective, who scrolled through his recent search and message history. He showed it to his partner, and they studied it until they were satisfied, then handed it back.

"Thank you, Mr. Tanner," the detective said. "We're leaving no stone unturned to find your son."

Robert started for home, his burner phone tucked low in his sock and time ticking down for Gabriel.

42

CORINA WAS RUNNING with the baby, searching for a way out, the faces of the dead cracking through the ground, breaking the surface, issuing a macabre chorus: 'Salva a mi hijo'...thundering in the gloom until she...

Woke.

Struggling out of her dream, waking to her nightmare, Corina sat up, her thoughts forming: a fourth day without Gabriel. Scrolling through her phone, finding no updates, she dressed and rushed through the condo. It was 5:45 a.m. Detectives Lisa DiMaria and Dan Alvarez had extended their shift and were sitting at the kitchen counter.

Corina's mouth was dry, her voice raw when she asked: "Anything?"

The detectives turned from their laptops.

"No, I'm sorry, nothing yet," DiMaria said.

Drinking a glass of water from the tap, Lonza took a quick survey of their coffee mugs, phones and notebooks on the counter.

"Did you arrest Zyller, question him?"

"We're still investigating," Alvarez said.

Seizing on a thought, Corina left them for the kitchen, raising her phone and punching in Lonza's number. It rang three times before Lonza answered. "Hello?"

"It's Corina—what's happening with Zyller?"

"Our people and the FBI have been working through the night on the items seized with the warrants. It's a meticulous process, and we can't report on anything yet."

"You have to arrest him now and find Gabriel!"

"Zyller's got an attorney. We're moving as fast as we can, but it's going to take time. I know it's not what you want to hear, Corina, but it's all I can tell you right now."

Hanging up, Corina looked around, then returned to the detectives to ask about Robert's whereabouts.

"He went out earlier to take a walk," Alvarez said.

Raking a hand through her hair, contending with mounting desperation, she entered the living room. The TV was on, the sound low, as a cable news channel reported on growing tensions with North Korea. On the sofa, knees drawn under her chin, Charlotte was scrolling through her phone.

Sitting down beside her, Corina stroked her daughter's hair.

"Why do people keep attacking you?" Charlotte asked, turning her phone for Corina to see social media posts and images about Gabriel's disappearance and her.

Wynne Files nailed it. Corina Corado's hiding the truth.
QOL steals a baby raises it as her own then stages stunt.

Fake news purveyor pathetic attempt to save her job.

Lock her up.

"Everyone hates us," Charlotte said.

At a loss, Corina looked up at the balloons, stuffed toys and cards Nora and Marty had brought. They were arranged in colorful juxtaposition on the table nearby.

"No, honey. Everyone does not hate us."

"You hate me for losing him."

"No, I don't."

"But it was my fault!"

"No. No, it wasn't. I was just... I was angry. Angry at myself, angry that Dad got delayed. I don't hate you, and I'm not angry with you. I am angry that it happened."

They both turned to the TV when Gabriel's face appeared on the screen. The news anchor said, *"Today is the fourth day in the case of six-year-old Gabriel Corado, who vanished from Central Park while walking home from his Upper West Side school with his sister..."* The report continued on with footage of police executing warrants at Newslead and Efrem Zyller's Madison Avenue condo. *"Police are tight-lipped on speculation of possible links to the boy's disappearance and someone within the news organization..."*

After digesting the report, Charlotte turned to Corina. "You really think Efrem Zyller did this?"

Corina stared in silence at the TV, oblivious to the next news story.

"I don't get it," Charlotte said. "I mean, I didn't see Zyller in the park."

Corina continued staring, sinking into her thoughts, oblivious to the report on wildfires in California and Arizona.

"Like, why?" Charlotte said. "Why would Zyller take Gabriel? I mean, he's your boss. It's nuts. Your work friends who came here think he's a suspect or something. Do you really think it's him?"

Staring at nothing, Corina said, "I'll tell you more later. It's complicated."

"It's because I lost him, isn't it? That's why you won't tell me."

Corina searched Charlotte's eyes.

"No, honey. I want to tell you but now is not the time."

"Why?"

"Because we have to get Gabriel back. It's just so complicated."

"This is bull." Charlotte's voice broke as she got up to leave. "I deserve to know what's going on! Because whatever you think, whatever you say, it's still my fault!"

"No—the police— We just have to be strong."

Charlotte waved her open palm like a leave-me-alone flag, then left.

Corina let her go, trying to pull herself together by going to the balloons, stuffed toys and cards. She welcomed the supportive messages from colleagues, from friends, from people she'd never met. She was especially touched by the kind messages from strangers. She drew strength from them, as she did from the notes that she'd received from people she'd interviewed in the depths of their own tragedies. Checking them again, she saw a nice one from Cathy

Miller, and another from Julie Landon in New Jersey—*"Never give up hope."* Their messages were attached to stuffed teddy bears and balloons, their words taking Corina back again, making her remember the pain in their faces.

She was awed that they would reach out to comfort her.

Where do they find the grace?

Caressing one of the toy bears, Corina considered the bottomless chasm between their acts of kindness and the vile acts of Efrem Zyller.

It had to be Zyller who'd taken Gabriel. Everything fit. He'd threatened her. He had the resources to arrange the kidnapping. But why? What Corina couldn't grasp was how it made any sense.

My son for my silence in some twisted Faustian bargain, with a new anchor job tossed in? Was he allied in some way with Wynne to destroy me? Was Zyller that desperate, or that dangerous? He wouldn't harm Gabriel, would he? If he would go to the extreme of stealing my son...

Corina had to call Zyller. She scrolled through her contacts and tapped his number. As it rang, her pulse raced. She'd plead again for Gabriel. Could she reason with Zyller? As the line rang and rang, Corina realized that police had seized his phone. Abandoning the call, she stared out her condo window at the city below, her mind numbing with the fear that she might never see Gabriel again.

43

SITTING ON HER bed with her door closed, Charlotte raised her phone.

Last night, she'd installed the best app she could find for self-destructing messaging. She didn't care if police found out and recovered her texts later.

I've got to do something. I lost Gabriel, my parents hate me, the world hates us, everything's gone nuts and I've got to fix it.

Charlotte's fingers blurred as she typed, You there?

Minutes went by before she got a response.

Hi, Vince answered.

He had the same app, providing them with a degree of confidence for the moment.

What did you find out? she asked.

Do not breathe a word of this to anyone.

What is it?

Met with someone who says they know what happened.

OMG really? Swear to God?

Yes.

Where is Gabriel? Is he okay? I'm shaking.

I don't have answers yet.

What?

Don't tell anyone anything. I need more time. It's dangerous.

After texting Vince, Charlotte, her heart racing, raked her fingers through her hair, then stood.

She had to do something besides sitting at home like a prisoner while waiting for Vince's help. Dad had gone out. She wanted out, too. She had to do more to fix this.

Charlotte went to the living room. "Could I go back to the park?" she asked her mom.

"Why? Did you remember something?"

"No, but when it happened, they asked me if I'd noticed anything. I was so upset at the time. Maybe I missed something. I'd like to go back, retrace my steps."

"Alone?" Corina said.

"Whatever you guys think. I just want to help."

DiMaria and Dan Alvarez exchanged a quick, positive glance.

"It could jog your memory," Alvarez said.

"We'll set it up." DiMaria made a call.

A short time later, Detectives Sally Teel and Ross Kozoll brought Charlotte to the Tillmon Parker Rose school. From there, they followed the path Charlotte and Gabriel had taken. Along the way Charlotte stopped here and there to study the surroundings before moving on.

When they were near the Dakota, Charlotte recalled that the rock star, John Lennon, one of the Beatles, lived there back in the day. She smiled because it brought her a warm memory of Gabriel; how he loved one of the group's old songs, "Ob-La-Di, Ob-La-Da." And sometimes Gabriel would sing it, clapping his hands and raising them in his own little dance when he walked home with her.

Now, inside the park, traffic noise subsided as Charlotte led them along West Drive. She surveyed the horse carriages clip-clopping by, the tourists, walkers, joggers and pedicabs, straining her mind to remember. Things were coming back to her as they approached a rolling grassy section.

"But we moved farther down," Charlotte told the detectives as they passed a low-rise fence and benches. "Some older people were sitting here, nothing strange though."

Charlotte recalled a group ahead of them, students with adults carrying folding maps. People were walking around taking pictures. She remembered dog walkers and some pedicabs. Then Charlotte and the detectives came to the spot where Gabriel flew his plane while she texted.

"This is where I stood. He launched his plane, and it landed out of sight at the top of that hill. He ran around the low fence to the other path by the bushes to go up the hill. That's the last I saw him."

She caught her breath.

"Did you see anyone familiar, or anyone who looked out of place?" Kozoll asked.

"No." Charlotte shook her head. "First, I looked around this way, that way. Wait..."

"What is it?" Teel asked.

Charlotte shook her head. "No, it's nothing."

"You can tell us," Teel said.

"I can't be sure." She blinked. "Maybe I saw a person far away, that way, but holding their phone up like they were recording."

"That's common in the park," Teel said.

"But it was kinda, maybe, like they were recording me and Gabriel."

"Do you remember anything about the person?"

"I'm not sure. I didn't get a good look because I was starting to worry about Gabriel." Charlotte covered her mouth with her hand while shaking her head. "It could've been a woman."

44

THAT MORNING LONZA and Grimes were in an elevator at the FBI's New York headquarters, time ticking with each floor they passed.

Lonza counted off the illuminated indicators while sorting her thoughts.

An hour earlier, she'd submitted her case-status report to Lieutenant Weaver. He'd just gotten off a call with the DA's office—an agreement had been negotiated to interview Efrem Zyller.

"It'll be with the FBI." Weaver clenched his jaw. "He'll have his attorney present. We don't have any hard evidence. Nothing from the warrants, so far. No real grounds. Until we find something, this may be our only shot with him."

At the 28th floor, they stepped off the elevator and were met by agents Stan Bodziak and Pam Wolbert, who'd overseen the warrants executed at Zyller's condo.

"You got our inventory from the Madison Avenue warrants?" Bodziak asked.

"Yeah, thanks," Grimes said. "Not much there."

"Right, and we're still analyzing the digital collection," Bodziak said.

"This is your case," Wolbert said. "We'll let you lead with him."

They left reception, its walls showcasing the framed photos of executive agents. Nearby was the display honoring agents killed in the line of duty as the result of a direct adversarial force, the Service Martyrs.

They soon came to a panelled meeting room where Efrem Zyller and a man with a walrus mustache, round glasses, rolled shirt sleeves, tie and suspenders stood to greet them.

"James J. Spindler." The man extended his hand. "Mr. Zyller's attorney."

They all settled in with notebooks, tablets and phones at the table.

"You're aware—" Wolbert pointed to a camera mounted in a ceiling corner "—our conversation's being recorded?"

"Yes," Spindler said. "My client has consented and we request a copy at the conclusion."

"Agreed," Wolbert said.

"For the record," Spindler said, "my client faces no charges and has no obligation to step forward. He's volunteered to fully cooperate."

Grimes threw a glance to Lonza, subtly registering a shared thought: an employee's son is missing, yet Zyller *volunteers to cooperate through his attorney.*

"Yes," Wolbert said. "I'll turn things over to Detective Lonza."

"Mr. Zyller, you're the head of Newslead's entire news division, domestically and internationally, correct?"

"Correct."

"Now, how did you first become aware that Gabriel Corado was missing, and where were you at the time?"

"I was at Newslead's headquarters, in my office, when Gil Dixon, a producer, informed me."

"And what was your response?"

"I made calls, monitored developments. I was, and remain, concerned."

"Who did you call?"

"Our newsroom."

Lonza scrolled through her tablet. "Mr. Zyller, do you know an individual named Ivan Hector Beckke, aged thirty-seven, of Queens?"

"No. Well, through news coverage, but not personally."

"Have you ever had any direct or indirect communication with Ivan Beckke?"

"No."

"Are you aware of a recent item in a New York tabloid suggesting Corina Corado's upcoming termination from Newslead?"

"Yes."

"Is the item accurate?"

"No."

"Are you the source of that item?"

"No."

"As the head of news, you have the authority to hire, promote or terminate employees, correct?"

"Yes."

"Do you ever seek favors of a sexual nature from employees in exchange for advancement?"

Taken aback, Zyller tilted his head slightly, as if seeing Lonza in a new light.

"I advise my client not to answer," Spindler said.

"Did you recently touch Corina Corado inappropriately after summoning her to your office to discuss advancement?"

Zyller blinked but remained silent.

"Mr. Zyller, after Corina Corado objected, rejected and voiced her anger at your act, did you not then suggest that was how all your 'deals are sealed,' then threaten to destroy her if she reported the incident?"

"Again," Spindler said, "I advise my client not to answer."

Any warmth in Zyller's eyes vanished with the stirrings of a grin.

"Let's get to the crux of the matter," Spindler said. "My client acknowledges a misunderstanding with Corina Corado. The fact she has not issued a formal complaint supports his statement."

"No, it doesn't," Lonza said.

"We're suggesting," Spindler said, "that she didn't make a complaint because there's no basis for a complaint. It was a consensual misunderstanding, in a moment of joy at learning she was a candidate for promotion. She enticed him, he responded. He then apologized for the misunderstanding. And, as for anchoring a new show, yes, she was, and is, being considered. But no decision has been made and that's how business is done."

"Is it?" Lonza said.

"And, if I may..." Spindler continued. "My client puts no stock in the allegations, conspiracies, gossip and rumors swirling about Corina

Corado. As for her missing son, my client has offered his full support. He's been to the park, attended her press conference. He empathizes with her agony and he's offered the full resources of the news organization. You must bear in mind, Corina Corado is, understandably, under tremendous stress."

"She's traumatized, facing what she's facing," Zyller said. "She's traumatized to the point of being unstable, irrational. We respect that you must be thorough in your investigation. But I assure you, I had nothing to do with her son's disappearance."

A moment passed before Lonza traded a glance with Grimes. Then, like a poker player, she opened a folder, studying the pages inside.

"Interesting you should say that, Mr. Zyller. Do you know what we found after executing the warrants?"

Zyller froze.

Lonza closed the folder, staring into Zyller's face.

"Well, we're not required to reveal it to you. At this stage."

"And," Grimes said, "there are the other people we talked to about you."

"That's right," Lonza said.

Zyller's jaw muscles tensed as Lonza leaned toward him.

"Mr. Zyller, do you know the whereabouts of Gabriel Corado?"

"No."

"Are you involved directly or indirectly in his disappearance?"

"No."

"Do you know anyone who may be involved in his disappearance?"

"No."

Lonza sat back, the uneasy silence punctuated by the creaking of her chair. "Alright," she said. "Thank you for your cooperation."

Zyller offered a small nod.

"Oh, one last thing," Lonza said. "If you remember, or want to volunteer, information to help us, now is the time. Because when this case is resolved—and it will be resolved—any deception on your part will have serious consequences for you, sir."

Zyller looked to Spindler.

"My client has nothing further to add, at this time," he said.

Lonza held Zyller's gaze until he and Spindler left the room, remaining silent as they progressed down the hall toward the elevator.

45

THE DOOR OPENED and Robert stepped into the condo.

Corina met him in the front hall.

"Any news?" he asked her.

She shook her head.

"They're still going through things with Zyller. He's got a lawyer now. Where were you?"

"I couldn't sleep, I went for a walk, for coffee. Where's Charlotte?"

"She's at the park with police. She wanted to retrace her steps again, something to help with the investigation."

Corina studied the lines in Robert's face, his red-rimmed eyes. "You look terrible. What is it?"

He shook his head.

"Is it Zyller?" she said. "I'm sorry I never told you what he did."

"No, Corina." He took a moment. "Hearing what he did to you tore me up. But you dealt with it as best as you could. I get that."

She stared at him hard, recalling his burner phone and that strange message, straining her trust in him.

"Something's wrong, something's going on, Robert. Tell me."

"Nothing's going on. I just needed fresh air."

"That's it?" she said, looking at him for several seconds. Corina wasn't sure she believed him. She glanced over to the detectives, who'd been watching them. Alvarez was on the phone. Ending the call, he nodded to DiMaria.

"Robert," Alvarez said. "Is there something you haven't told us?"

Robert was silent.

Corina studied her husband, and struggled to navigate the jumble of trepidation and emotion twisting in her heart.

"No, I just needed fresh air to think. I'm sorry for alarming anyone."

The detectives eyed him, then Corina said, "He's been under pressure with the condo tower project, and I think you guys might need to look hard at the people involved in that."

"No, I don't think—" Robert started before Corina cut him off.

"You don't think what, Robert?" she said. Then to the detectives, "You guys have to look at every angle, right?"

A few minutes later, alone in his study, Robert dragged the back of his shaking hand across his lips.

Do something! Time is running out! Do something!

He'd carried the heat of Corina and the detectives' mistrust into the room with him, as the walls closed in. Gabriel, Charlotte and Corina smiled at him from the framed family photo he caressed. Tears webbed down his whiskered cheeks, his life blurring before him.

His father, reeking of alcohol, whipping him with his belt for defending his mother. "You're worthless, Bobby! You'll always be worthless like your whoring mother!" Fleeing in the night with his mom, to live in a trailer park in Bayonne, New Jersey. Working every job, putting himself through college, where he met Cynthia, his first wife. She was so strong, so beautiful, on her way to being a lawyer; he was on his way to becoming an engineer. Then having Charlotte. Everything going well, living their perfect lives in their Manhattan apartment...until two cops show up at his door, holding their hats.

"Are you Robert Tanner, husband of Cynthia Tanner?"

"Yes, she's visiting a friend across town."

"Sir, we regret to inform you..."

Cynthia was shot dead by drug dealers targeting the wrong address. His world collapsing. Years later...his darkness turning to light when he met Co-

rina, giving him a chance to heal a wound that he thought would never heal. Then adopting Gabriel… Gabriel that day at school, telling him, "You're the best dad, ever!"… God help me, please…

Robert took up his burner phone. Bracing himself once more, he looked at the photos and video they'd sent him.

I know what they want.

They wanted his report on the condo to state it was structurally sound, to diminish any complaints noted by the residents. But Jennifer was supposed to give him the records that proved it was unsafe.

Robert shifted his focus to the locked file cabinet holding his work on the alleged defects of the supertall tower. So far, his team was looking at the integrity of the steel and concrete, the foundation, the sway rate, the elevators and several other aspects. But he hadn't made any conclusions.

Do something!

In sudden desperation, he reached for his phone and called Cal Darden, his team leader. Cal answered after two rings.

"Hey, Cal, it's Robert."

A few seconds passed.

"Robert? Oh man, everybody's heard and we're all praying."

"Thanks." Robert calmed his quavering voice. "Do you think we could produce a positive preliminary report on the supertall today?"

A moment of silence.

"What?" Darden said.

"Just a draft."

"We're not even close to being done."

Robert drove the heel of his palm into his temple as hard as he could.

"Just a preliminary analysis that I could sign off on."

"Bob, what's— Are you alright? We can't do that."

Robert choked back a sob.

"Bob?"

"No. I mean, you're right. Just forget it. Sorry, Cal. Forget I called."

Robert dropped his phone and plunged his face into his hands, his thoughts whirling.

"Jennifer" had promised to give him the records he needed when they met in Philadelphia. But she didn't show.

She was too afraid.

I know they want a fake report in exchange for Gabriel.

Robert picked up the phone, staring at it as he paced around his study.

These pictures can't be real. But what if they are? Oh God. What's wrong with me? I can't take the risk with my son's life.

They'd warned him against going to police.

But they could hurt Gabriel.

And if he gave them a falsified report in their favor, on a building that could be unsound, he'd be risking people's lives, criminal and professional devastation at every turn.

I'm wasting time. I've got to do something.

Staring at the photos, swiping through them, he didn't hear his study door open. He thought he was alone until Corina, standing behind him, looking over his shoulder, saw the pictures on Robert's phone.

Her scream reverberated throughout the condo.

46

Robert is lying *naked on a bed.*

In the next photo, a naked young woman, her face angled from view, stands over him, stroking his chest. A tattoo of angel wings is visible on her inner forearm.

Next, the woman is straddling Robert.

Then a cut to a video of Gabriel and Charlotte entering Central Park.

Corina screamed.

Robert turned and the detectives rushed to his study.

"Show them, Robert!" Corina said. "Show them everything!"

He surrendered his burner phone to DiMaria, who, tilting it for Alvarez, looked through the photos.

The blood drained from Robert's face. Corina flew at him, slapping, punching. He seized her wrists, and Alvarez pulled her away, struggling to get her to the sofa in the living room while she screamed at Robert, "Where's Gabriel? What did you do?"

"No, no, no! I didn't— It's not what you think! It's not real!"

"Where's my son? You knew all along! Where is he?"

"It's not what you think!"

They turned to Charlotte, who'd returned from the park. Standing in the living room, she was horrified by the scene playing out before her.

"What's happening?" Charlotte asked, her voice breaking. "What is it?"

"Go to your room," Robert said.

"No! Stay! Let her hear!" Corina sat on the sofa, doubled over, holding her stomach.

Robert got on his knees before her.

"I swear, I swear it's not what you think!"

"Oh my God! Is Gabriel dead?"

"No!" Robert said.

"You don't know that! Stop lying to me!" Corina screeched.

Hugging herself, Charlotte turned from her parents, pushed her face into the wall and sobbed while Alvarez and DiMaria made calls, sent texts.

And copies of the images.

In the time that followed, more police arrived.

Lonza, Grimes, FBI agents and officers with specialized units were alerted and involved, because now the situation had been taken to a new level. Now they had contact with Gabriel's kidnapper. All police communications were encrypted, to guard against leaks to the news media. Analysis of the images and video had begun. All phone and digital surveillance of the family's devices was enhanced, extending to Robert's office and Corina's newsroom, as investigators set out to track who was behind the threat.

Federal law enforcement and police in countries around the world began probing the corporations connected to the supertall condo project. Detectives descended on the coffee shop Robert had visited earlier to interview staff and review security cameras and receipts. The investigation also reached back to Philadelphia, to security at the hotel where Robert had stayed and background on the company officials he'd met.

As it all went into motion, Lonza and Grimes, with FBI agents Stan Bodziak and Pam Wolbert, took Robert into the kitchen, where he was read his rights, a precaution in case he was involved.

Declining an attorney, Robert began relating more on the history of how he headed an engineering team contracted by a condo board in a dispute with developers of a 94-story luxury condo. The board alleged the $2-billion building was unsafe, and residents were demanding expensive repairs be made to maintain the value of their homes—something the developer had refused.

There was a lot at stake for both sides.

Listening, the detectives asked the occasional question, nodded and took notes.

Robert told them he'd been approached confidentially by a nervous whistleblower, "Jennifer," who'd urged him to communicate with a burner phone, which he had now surrendered to police. Jennifer said she worked for the developer and told Robert that safety had been skirted, and bribes were paid to inspectors to meet deadlines and cut costs. She'd promised Robert secret records to prove the allegations and support his work for the residents, and had set up a meeting in Philadelphia.

"But she never showed. She said she was scared," Robert said. "I ate a burger and had a beer at the bar while waiting for her, and then I remember not feeling so good. I left and went to bed. The next morning, I woke up woozy before meeting with one of the contractors."

"You woke up woozy?" Grimes said.

"Yeah."

"And you never met this Jennifer, ever?"

"No."

"Who is the woman in your hotel room with you?"

"I don't know. I don't know who she is, how she got in. I never woke up," Robert said. "Now they say they have Gabriel and they want me to create a report saying the building's safe. Oh God. You gotta look closely at those photos. My eyes are closed. I'm not even awake. And how did they get the video of Gabriel and Charlotte? I thought I could handle this on my own. But I don't know what happened or what to do anymore."

Robert's face was a mask of torment as their questioning ended.

Lonza and Grimes stepped away, huddling with the agents.

"What do you think?" Grimes asked.

"We keep going flat out on all fronts," Wolbert said. "It's our best chance at getting the boy back."

"What about the demand?" Grimes said.

"Did they set up the husband for extortion, then add a kidnap-for-ransom demand?" Bodziak bit his bottom lip. "It doesn't fit."

"How so?" Grimes asked.

"It's a strange demand, because it seems easy to tie to somebody in the conglomerate behind the condo."

"Maybe yes. Maybe no," Lonza said. "Let's just say that the conglomerate people are behind it. I'm thinking they could've botched things but are still attempting, are desperate, to use Gabriel as leverage."

"What do you mean?"

"They never showed Robert proof they have Gabriel, or that he's alive."

47

ALONE IN GABRIEL'S ROOM, her arms wrapped around his pillow, Corina inhaled her son's scent.

In that instant, she was pulled back to the moment when Gabriel, still a baby, had started walking. She was working at home at her desk when he toddled to her, sucking on his bottle, and wriggled up on her. She took him into her lap and he fell asleep, bottle in hand. She typed, kissing his head, breathing in his sweet scent.

Oh God, she could almost feel him again now, her fear shifting to his terror alone out there.

Gone.

Corina tried to dissect what she knew. But she kept coming back to those horrible photos, and her fear that Robert was having an affair with a dangerous woman who was blackmailing him and took Gabriel. Robert claimed it was an extortion tied to his condo contract, but those images of him with the woman were burned into Corina's heart.

How could Robert play games like this with our son's life?

Corina was lost.

Before she'd seen the photos, she was convinced Efrem Zyller had taken Gabriel, carrying out his threat to prevent her from revealing who he was and what he'd done. And then there was Wynne Varden's conspiracies and the believers, continually damning her with intense vileness.

I don't know what's true anymore.

Corina turned to the stuffed toys, cards and balloons. Charlotte had moved some from the living room to the head of Gabriel's bed, where she'd arranged them.

Like a memorial.

Corina had seen so many like it while covering shootings, fires and other disasters where she'd reported on someone else's pain. Gasping, she reached for a stuffed bear, and for the next several minutes she found solace in the messages.

"Sending you all our prayers and love."

"Hope with all our hearts that you find your son."

"Wishing you have him in your arms again."

She returned to the message from Cathy Miller, a mother she'd interviewed in Brooklyn. She was part of a support group. Her ten-year-old son, Burke, went missing several years ago from their small town in Pennsylvania and had never been found. Corina remembered Cathy telling her, "He comes to me in dreams. They're so beautiful, I never want to wake up." Her message, affixed to a balloon, read: *"Always believe, Gabriel will be reunited with his mother."*

She thought of Cathy. *How does she go on? How does she endure with a broken heart?*

She marveled at all of these people who'd endured unimaginable horrors and still found the grace to reach out and comfort her, giving her something to hang on to.

Her hands trembling, Corina wiped her eyes and nose with a crumpled tissue while taking in the colorful memorial, realizing, *It has happened. I am now among the parents who'd lost children—the community of sorrow.*

I am now one of you.

48

WALKING FAST, the woman stole another look over her shoulder, scanning the faces behind her.

She didn't see her pursuers.

Letting out a shaky breath, she studied people nearby, unable to distinguish the two men.

I've got to keep moving.

She was in her thirties and in good shape, but with dark circles under her eyes, operating on adrenaline. She feared the two men, who'd spotted her near the Whitney, had followed her here to the High Line, the narrow pedestrian park built on an abandoned elevated railway, stretching for a mile and a half through Manhattan.

They wanted her because of what she knew.

They wanted to stop her from telling the truth.

How did it come to this?

She had to get out of the city before they caught up to her. *Because if they do…*

She'd gotten rid of her phone, but they'd found her. Adjusting her small leather long-strapped purse so that it rested in front of her, she struggled to think of a way out. She couldn't go back to her room for her things, and she couldn't use credit or bank cards; they could track that. Brushing by tourists, she calculated how much cash she'd managed to pull together. Maybe enough for a one-way bus fare to Boston, Baltimore or DC. She knew people in those cities who could help her.

If I can just get a cab or subway to the Port Authority.

Moving fast, she looked back again, her eyes darting and hunting as she came upon the aroma of the open-air food court. Passing through it, she soon heard salsa music from street musicians she couldn't see.

She hurried around people, the park's beauty, the murals, the gardens, water features and buildings with stunning architecture that bordered the walkway, all of it rushing by. She took another look back. Her heart skipped as recognition sprang on her.

It's them!

They'd spotted her and they were gaining.

Like a sprinter exploding from the starting block, she ran, bumping into a woman holding hands with a man, his arms sleeved in tattoos.

"Hey!"

"What the hell..."

Their protests faded as she threaded around people at top speed, daring to glance back at the men, who were running now, too.

Panicked, she searched for help: a cop, a security guard. But her search was in vain. *Keep moving! Keep moving!* She considered going into a bathroom, then dropped the idea. They were too close. They'd come in for her. Breathing hard, she reached the northern end of the High Line.

Racing through Hudson Yards, frantically looking for a cop or a security guard, gasping for breath, she chanced another look back, not realizing she'd run into the street, never seeing the dump truck.

Before the driver reacted, before his foot stomped on the brake, the loaded thirty-six-ton truck launched her like a rag doll high into the air, her body landing on the windshield of an oncoming taxi then bouncing to the street, her blood flowing onto the asphalt.

49

In her home in the Bronx, amid the smell of lavender-scented laundry detergent, Brenda Tarone stood at her washing machine preparing a load, going through the pockets of her son's jeans.

A crisp crumpling made Brenda pause, thinking it was a cash tip Vince had forgotten. But she withdrew a credit card–sized piece of paper.

Reading it, she froze.

Vince stared back from a visitor's photo ID for Rikers Island.

Brenda marched through the house to Vince's bedroom, where he was standing before his dresser mirror, getting ready for his shift.

"What?" he asked, adjusting his tie, checking his reflection.

Holding his jeans in one hand, as if the pants were supporting evidence, she thrust the ID toward his face.

"You didn't go to Rikers. Tell me you didn't see him!"

He blinked a few times, cursing under his breath for forgetting the expired ID in his pocket.

"I saw him."

"My God, Vince, why? Why, when I told you to stay out of it?"

"I had to. I have to help her."

"I begged you not to do this." Shaking her head, eyes brimming. "Police were already here once."

"Mom, I think he knows what happened."

"Then go to police, Vince!"

"I can't."

"Why not?"

"I've got to go back, get him to tell me more. Then I can help."

Brenda sank to the edge of the bed, holding his ID and jeans, and stared into the past.

"When I went to his early court proceedings," she said, "the things I heard about him, and people like him—what they believe and what they want to do—terrified me, Vince. I'm begging you to stop this now. They are going to find out about us."

"I can't. Not just yet."

"Is it because of the girl? Vince, she's a child!"

He lowered himself to search his mother's eyes.

"It's not just that."

"Then what is it?"

"Charlotte's mature, she treats me with respect. I want to protect her."

"She don't need you for that."

"Did you know I'm teaching her how to drive?"

"Vinnie, you're thinking with your heart and not seeing the big picture."

"You're not listening. She looks up to me like I am somebody. Look at where she lives, and who she is. And she looks up to me. Me. Vince Tarone from the Bronx who lives with his mother."

"Vinnie." She cupped her hands to his face and shook her head. "You shouldn't get involved with her."

"There's more. It's hard to explain. It's strange, and it's killing me."

"What?"

"I feel like I'm involved in Gabriel Corado's disappearance."

"What? Oh God, Vinnie. Did you do something you're not telling me?"

Brenda covered her mouth with both hands, eyes ballooning with horror.

"Vince?"

"I gotta go, Mom."

50

A 911 OPERATOR took the call.

She directed it to Lonza, who alerted detectives Jerrod Russell and Rafael Delgado, the returning shift at Corina and Robert's condo. After listening, his face tensing, Russell passed his phone to Corina, who'd come out of her room for water.

"Detective Lonza," he said.

Corina put the phone to her ear.

"A woman injured in a traffic accident says she has information about Gabriel." Lonza sounded like she was in a moving car.

"Oh God, what's happened? Where is he? Did she say?"

"No. She'll talk only to you. She's at Bellevue. The detectives will take you and Robert there as soon as possible. Grimes and I are already on our way." Lonza paused. "Corina, everybody needs to hurry—she may not survive."

Sirens echoed the screaming in Corina's head as the detectives' sedan followed a marked unit, both cars weaving through traffic. Manhattan blurred by her window. Grappling with their thoughts, she and Robert didn't speak.

At the hospital, the uniformed officers and detectives hurried them toward the ICU. The air was heavy with the smell of antiseptic, and the public address system carried notifications and prerecorded messages. They came to a cluster of detectives, officers and hospital staff. Lonza and Grimes broke from a subdued huddle to meet them.

"Here's what we know," Lonza said. "A woman, hit by a truck on West 33rd near the High Line, says she has information about Gabriel."

Lonza nodded to Dr. Amanda Martina, who continued.

"We did all we could for her, but her injuries are significant. After treating her, she began talking incoherently, as most trauma patients do. But a nurse recognized she was speaking English with a Russian accent."

"Russian?" Robert said.

"Yes," Dr. Martina said. "She said she had information about Gabriel, the missing boy on the news. But she insisted she'd only tell the boy's mother."

"Okay." Corina's eyes searched Dr. Martina's, then Lonza's. "What do we do now?"

After a few seconds, Dr. Martina said: "The patient's condition is critical." Dr. Martina then looked at Corina, Robert, and the rest of the group, which included NYPD officer Oksana Petrov, who was fluent in Russian and had been summoned in case translation was needed.

"For the moment, she is conscious," Dr. Martina said. "But there's no telling how much time she has left."

The woman was in a private room.

The small screen above her bed was connected to equipment monitoring her heart rate, blood pressure, breathing and other vital signs. An IV pole with a drip stood beside her, and oxygen flowed through the tube running under her nostrils. Her face was swollen in a grotesque mash of contusions, lacerations and abrasions.

Corina looked upon her.

Who is she? What does she know? Is this a cruel hoax, or my only hope?

Directed by Dr. Martina, Robert and Grimes remained at the foot of the bed. Officer Petrov and Corina were at the head, on either side, with Lonza nearby, making a video recording on her phone. Dr. Martina and a nurse stood close by, observing and watching the patient's signs on the monitor. The doctor nodded to Petrov.

Petrov leaned close to the woman, whispering in English, then Russian, identifying herself as a police officer, summarizing how they were recording her statement and that Corina Corado was present, as she had requested.

Her eyes half open, the woman scanned the room.

Petrov nodded for Corina to move closer so the woman could see her, then Corina began. "I am Gabriel's mother. What do you know about my son?"

Creaking, hissing tones issued from the woman. "I am sorry," she said in accented English.

"Is my son dead?"

"I am sorry for my actions."

Biting back on her frustration, Corina then asked: "Who are you?"

"I am Jennifer. I am the woman in the video from Robert's hotel room."

Robert's jaw dropped as everyone looked to the inside of the woman's forearm, where, partially obscured by the bandages holding the IV, there was a tattoo of angel wings.

The woman coughed, then spoke.

"Robert was drugged. The video was fabricated. He was unaware. He never betrayed you."

Corina looked at Robert, then Lonza. "Where is my son?"

"It was never meant to be an abduction."

"Where is my son?"

"It was never meant—see my video—it was never meant to be an abduction... I beg forgiveness..."

"Where is Gabriel?" Corina raised her voice.

The monitor began beeping.

Corina leaned closer to better hear the woman.

"Forgive me, cleanse my soul..."

The woman's head fell to one side, her eyes closed.

The monitors bleated warnings, and the lines tracking the woman's vital signs flattened.

"Everyone leave!" Dr. Martina slapped an alarm button above the bed as she and the nurse moved in. "Out! Now!"

As Corina, Robert and the police left, staff rushed in. For the next twenty minutes, they made a futile attempt to resuscitate the woman.

51

In the hall, Corina slammed her back against the wall.

Contending with the thudding in her chest, the roaring blood rush in her ears, she tried to make sense of what had happened.

The woman who knows about Gabriel is dead.

Her tattoo confirmed that she was the woman who'd been in Robert's hotel room.

She was real. It was no hoax.

Corina was scared, as terrified as she'd been when she first learned Gabriel was missing. The hospital walls swirled; her anguish deepened as Robert paced in front of her.

The sounds of low-volume radio transmissions, soft conversations on phones, pulled their attention to the end of the hall where Lonza and Grimes had gathered with detectives and officers.

Corina and Robert went to them.

"Did you find Gabriel?" Corina said.

"No, Corina," Lonza said. "We're calling in more people."

"Who is she?" Robert nodded toward the hospital room.

"Pieces of information are coming in now," Grimes said. "It might be best for us to get someone to take you home. We may need to move fast."

Fragments of radio transmissions and phone conversations floated over to Corina and Robert.

"No, we need to stay," Corina said.

"We have her name," said an investigator wearing blue latex gloves, holding a small leather purse, its long strap swaying. "This was brought in with her to the hospital. Admitting had it."

What appeared to be a passport was passed to Lonza and Grimes. Photos were taken of it, then calls were made. While the purse was searched for further information, Lonza showed the passport to Corina and Robert. It was a Canadian passport issued in Montreal.

Irina Anna Kortova, aged thirty-two, born in Saint Petersburg, Russia.

"Do you know this woman?" Grimes asked.

Robert shook his head.

After studying it intensely, Corina said, "No."

A radio crackled and another investigator approached.

"First responders have witnesses saying that before she was struck, it appeared the woman was being chased by two males along the High Line to West 33rd."

"Alright, let's grab security cameras," Lonza said.

The detective searching the purse found little else—a wallet with more IDs for Irina Kortova, credit cards in her name, some cash, then: "We've got something."

He held up a plastic key for the Apple Top hotel.

52

DETECTIVE MOE GRADY tightened his one-handed grip on his weapon, then raised the plastic key for Room 1112.

His colleague behind the ballistic shield, Detective Rashon Harlow, was also braced at the room's locked door. Behind them, in the narrow hallway, waiting in silence, were other members of the NYPD's Emergency Service Unit, heavily armed, wearing helmets, protective body armor and tactical gear.

They'd been called to a hostage situation at the Apple Top hotel.

It was a 14-story stone and brick structure built in the ornate Beaux Arts style. A short walk from Times Square, the hotel was on 46th Street, where the operation unfolded. Police had moved quickly, choking traffic around the entire block, quietly evacuating guests to safe zones, positioning officers at the back of the building, on the roof, the fire escapes, in the stairwells, and shutting off the elevators.

The area was sealed.

A hostage situation was among the most dangerous an officer could face. You never knew what you'd find behind the door. Grady and Harlow drew on their training, remaining calm, focused on the rescue.

Grady moved the room key near the door reader, initiating a

mechanized buzz and a winking green light, and the lock opened. Grady seized the handle and entered with Harlow, followed by the other ESU members, filling the room and shouting: “Police! Police!” They raked their weapons over and under the bed, the floor, the open closet and the bathroom.

Nothing.

Empty.

Clear.

Grady radioed to his lieutenant.

“No sign of the boy.”

With Room 1112 secured, detectives Lonza and Grimes tugged on gloves and searched it further.

The queen-sized bed was unmade. They pushed aside the sheets, then checked the pillowcases, the nightstand, the dresser drawers. They checked under the bed, then inside the room’s waste cans. Splayed on the desk were recent print editions of the *Daily News* and *Post* with headlines like **‘HELP US FIND GABRIEL!’ TV JOURNO MOM PLEADS** and **THE DESPERATE SEARCH FOR GABRIEL**.

Under them, Lonza found two charging cords, but no laptop, tablet or phone. She found boarding passes for a round-trip flight from La Guardia to Philadelphia. The closet held clothes on hangers, and a near-empty suitcase on the floor. There were a few toiletries on the bathroom counter.

Lonza bit her bottom lip.

“We need crime scene to go through this,” she said.

Carrying her take-out coffee, Dericia Cook walked up to the people craning and staring ahead at the police activity not far from Times Square.

Something’s going down, she thought.

Cook was coming from a long break before starting an extra shift. Needing to get to work, she maneuvered through to the front of the crowd, where yellow tape stopped her from progressing on 46th Street.

She waved, catching the attention of a uniformed cop.

“What’s going on?”

"A police operation. This is as far as you can go, so you might want to circle around."

"But I got to get through to work." Cook pointed with the coffee cup.

"Where do you work?"

"The Apple Top. I'm an assistant manager." She one-handed her ID from her purse and held it up. "See?"

"That's where the operation is," he said. "Hang tight, it's wrapping up."

Studying the emergency vehicles, the blazing lights, police coming and going from her hotel, Cook considered her next choice.

"Hey, officer?"

He turned to her, deciding whether to engage when she tossed a question to him.

"Would this have anything to do with the woman in Eleven-Twelve?"

"Why?"

"Because I may know something."

Ten minutes later, Dericia Cook was leaning against an unmarked police vehicle with Lonza and Grimes listening to her account.

"Yeah, like, so earlier today, these two men, all serious, came to the desk and said they're with Homeland, National Intelligence... or something."

"Did you get names or copy their IDs?" Grimes asked.

"No, they flashed them—they looked official—but they were in a hurry and kinda scary, saying they had authority for an immediate search of the room."

"Did they say why?"

"No, only that I faced a serious charge if I didn't cooperate immediately. Look, I need this job, so I cooperated."

"You gave them a key to Eleven-Twelve?"

Cook nodded. "They went up, but they weren't long—ten, fifteen minutes before they left. I'm pretty sure one of them was carrying a laptop."

"They took a laptop from the room?" Lonza said.

"Yes."

"Did they give you a receipt, or anything that looked like a warrant, or have you sign for anything evidentiary?" Grimes asked.

"No, nothing. I was distracted. We had a charter group come in at the same time."

Lonza and Grimes traded glances.

"I remember," Cook said, "the woman's name was Eleena, Lydia, something. I can look it up inside. She had an accent, like Russian, right?"

Grimes nodded.

"What's going on with her?" Cook asked.

"She passed away," Grimes said.

"Oh God!" Cook stiffened and turned away, then back. "In our hotel? What happened?"

"Hit by a truck near Penn Station."

Cook whispered to herself, "I can't believe it!"

"What?" Lonza asked.

"Please," she said. "I don't want to get into trouble because I didn't tell those other guys. I mean, they missed it. I mean, they never asked me and I got thrown off, got busy. This is just too wild, it's just—"

"Dericia, what is it?" Lonza asked.

"Look, we get lots of guests—most are tourists who want to see the town. But we also get people in all kinds of horrible situations and this woman, she seemed troubled, like I'm saying, scared."

"How so?" Grimes said.

"It was just the other night, she was crying when she gave me an envelope, all taped up, and said that if anything happened to her, I should give it to the press, or the police. I kind of laughed to myself, thinking this was like a movie or something, but she was dead serious."

"Where's the envelope?" Lonza asked.

"I put it in our hotel safe."

53

Irina Anna Kortova stared into the camera, crying softly.

Her face was framed by the hood of her white I ♥ NY hoodie.

From the background, it appeared she was in Room 1112 of the Apple Top hotel. Her video was the only file loaded onto the USB flash drive that was in the envelope Dericia Cook had given Lonza and Grimes.

Looking at Kortova's video, Lonza thought: *This should get us closer.*

All procedures for processing and preserving evidence had been followed. A copy of the video had been made for the detectives. The NYPD and FBI analysts were examining the original, as they were doing with the video showing Robert in his Philadelphia hotel, and the short sequence of Gabriel and Charlotte entering Central Park. At the same time, several law enforcement agencies were investigating Kortova's background.

It was now late afternoon. Lonza and Grimes were in a meeting room at the 19th Precinct working with FBI agents Stan Bodziak and Pam Wolbert, and Officer Oksana Petrov was present, again, for any needed translation. Lonza had cast the Apple Top video from her laptop to the large wall-mounted monitor. Lieutenant Weaver joined them, and Lonza replayed the video again from the beginning.

"My name is Irina Anna Kortova. My English is not good, but I will use it for this message. If you are seeing this, I have disappeared. Or… I am dead." She held up a passport. "This is the passport I am using. I have others, forged for other countries.

"I had been in the military intelligence. When I left the military, I was approached by certain people who offered me high-paying employment. They said I had been selected for assignments for unnamed global entities, as they described them. The people I worked for directly—" she looked down at notes she held in her lap "—use the names Anton Valiev, Tatiana Galkina and Sergey Tellev."

She spelled them slowly. The names would be passed to the FBI and Interpol.

The video continued.

"These three people are at the operational level and they report higher in the network to people I never knew. My employer would identify a target. Usually, a corrupt person in a position of power. Contact would be made—it could be a social gathering, event, or a meeting, or a secret communication. I would entice or involve them in an illicit relationship we would secretly record. We would threaten to expose it in exchange for certain actions, or monies, that would benefit whomever my people were working for. My work took me around the world and it paid well.

"This was the case with Robert Tanner. Certain people wanted him to complete a report to their benefit concerning the new skyscraper in Manhattan. I posed as a person on the inside with information to aid him. But I soon became aware that he was a good man, not like the others.

"Then this."

She held up the *Daily News* and *Post* reporting Gabriel Corado's disappearance.

"When I saw what had happened, I suspected my employer was responsible. I was angered. I didn't want to be involved in the abduction of a child and I told my employer that I wanted no part of it. But they said that it was critical that we were successful with the New York building and threatened to harm my mother, brother and sister in Saint Petersburg if I refused or went to the authorities. This was the first time such a threat had been made to me."

She paused.

"They showed me the camera footage they had of Tanner's children before the boy was missing. It scared me. Then they forced me to continue sending Robert Tanner messages, pressuring him to take the steps they desired on the skyscraper. I wanted out. I wanted to go home—"

The room phone rang and before answering she abruptly ended the video.

"Alright," Weaver said. "Do we have anything here that leads us to Gabriel Corado?"

"Other than Kortova's account and relationship with Tanner," Lonza said, "nothing solid yet. We're working on tracking down that call to her room."

"Any evidence putting the boy in the hotel room?" Weaver asked.

"Nothing so far," Lonza said. "But we requested extra patrols, issued alerts at every transportation point in case he is being taken from the city."

"What about the people she named?" Weaver asked.

"We're pursuing her alleged accomplices. We've submitted notices to Interpol. We've alerted agents at our embassies around the world," Wolbert said. "We've checked with other federal agencies, who report no operations that would involve agents going to the Apple Top and taking Kortova's laptop. We believe the two men were impersonating agents and were likely the same people she was running from on the High Line."

"Does this fit in any way with Efrem Zyller, Ivan Beckke or the history of threats against Corado?" Weaver asked.

"Nothing's surfaced so far," Grimes said.

"Any other updates, thoughts?" Weaver said.

"This is classic honey trapping," Bodziak said. "It's what the KGB did during the Cold War with foreign diplomats to spy on enemy countries."

"We're looking at the conglomerate that built the supertall that Tanner's company was contracted to study," Wolbert said. "There are eleven major and nine smaller US and international groups behind it, a few with ties to nefarious groups. It's a sophisticated labyrinth."

Lonza's keyboard clicked and she replayed the video sent to extort Tanner, showing Gabriel and Charlotte entering the park.

"Our analysts say the footage sent to Tanner," Lonza said, "was somehow hacked from the exterior security cameras on a building on Central Park West."

"So, it was shown to Tanner to prove they have Gabriel," Grimes said.

"But they never showed him proof of life," Lonza said.

"Could they have messed up things with the boy?" Wolbert said.

"It's a possibility," Lonza said, her voice trailing as she and the others studied the video.

They saw Charlotte and Gabriel, with his airplane, near the Dakota, crossing to enter the park. Down along the street, parallel to the park's walls, were the tour buses. Traffic filled the streets in both directions. Then Charlotte and Gabriel disappeared into the stream of cyclists, joggers, walkers, pedicabs and tourists flowing in and out of the park.

Lonza shook her head slowly.

54

After boarding Amtrak's Northeast Regional train to Boston at the Moynihan Train Hall in Penn Station, Sergey Tellev relaxed in his aisle seat, relieved to be leaving.

He didn't know if the others had gotten out, or where they were. His squad had ceased contact and split up, in keeping with pre-arranged strategies after the work in New York City didn't go as planned.

Too many complications.

The girl, who'd always been an asset, had become a liability.

Unfortunate how it had ended, Tellev thought.

But it was out of his control and now he needed to leave.

After he got to Boston, he'd take a direct Lufthansa flight to Frankfurt. From there he'd connect to Baku for his return flight to Azerbaijan. He'd recover there, and if necessary, disappear to Kuwait or Bahrain. Once he cleared Germany, none of his destinations had extradition treaties with the US. He'd be out of reach.

He glanced at his copy of the New York newspaper in the seat pocket. It was folded to the latest story he'd read on the continuing search for the little boy who had disappeared in Central Park. He shrugged to himself.

Too bad about the kid. But in this life, things never go as we hope.

Tellev had just begun dreaming of home-cooked food when a voice came over the public address.

"We're working on a mechanical issue. Our departure will be delayed, but we'll make up the time along the way."

A few murmurs and soft groans rolled in the car.

Keep calm, these things happen, Tellev thought, glancing at the paper, thinking of the boy. Then two men clad in coveralls with reflective safety strips moved through his car. Confident that the reason for the delay was indeed a mechanical issue, he dropped his head back in his seat and closed his eyes. A moment later, voices rose.

Tellev opened his eyes.

A man and a woman in plainclothes, their badges swaying from chains and catching the light, were followed by a line of armed police in tactical gear. They moved down the aisle, stopping at Tellev's row. The woman checked photos on her phone before making eye contact.

"Detective Lonza, NYPD," she said. "Can you show me identification, sir?"

"Why? What is wrong?"

"Your identification, sir."

Realizing it was pointless to resist, Tellev provided it.

After looking at it and showing it to her partner, Lonza said: "Sir, you are under arrest. Stand up and place your hands behind your back."

Passengers gasped, and some held up phones, recording the drama.

As his wrists were zip-tied by a tactical cop, Sergey Tellev was read his rights and removed from the train.

55

Did Gabriel's abductor kill him?

Corina's anguish pulled her to the last words Irina Kortova spoke before dying.

It was never meant to be an abduction…forgive me, cleanse my soul.

What was it meant to be? Had they taken Gabriel? Could she trust that a monster like Kortova was telling the truth—even on her deathbed?

The questions tore her apart. Police hadn't found him in Kortova's hotel. That's all detectives had told her and Robert, refusing to reveal any other details.

Now, at home, with Robert on the phone getting more information on the players in his condo project sent to investigators, Corina suddenly saw him in a new light.

He didn't betray me.

Still, she was at war with her emotions, struggling to let go of her anger at him for not revealing what he knew from the beginning.

Ending his call, he turned to her. "I'm so sorry, Corina. I should've told police about all of it, from the start. I didn't believe it could've been tied to Gabriel. I thought I could handle it, make it go away. I thought I was doing the right thing. I was wrong. I should've told police."

"You could've put him in danger, Robert!"

"I'm so sorry."

Corina paused, pursing her lips as she considered her own actions. "And I'm sorry for not telling you about Zyller."

"No, don't be. I know. I get that. It was a different situation for you. But for me, I thought I was doing what was best at the time. I thought I could get him back—he's my son, too, but...but it... I lost control. I swear I never slept with her. She promised me critical documents. But they drugged me, set me up and took Gabriel to pressure me. *They took our son!*"

"But if they took him, where is he? He can't be dead!"

"No." Robert took her in his arms. "No, we can't believe that! We need to be strong, together!"

"You have to promise me, right now, no more secrets. No matter what. We tell each other the truth. We stand together. It's the only way we can bring him home, united, together."

"Absolutely."

"We cannot accept that he's dead!" Corina said. "Maybe there's a connection to Zyller and Beckke? I don't know. We never saw proof that anyone's hurt him, that anyone has him."

"That's right. We can't give up hoping."

"We'll never give up. We'll fight for him together, all of us!"

Listening in the hall, out of sight, Charlotte overheard pieces of her parent's anguished conversation—"Gabriel can't be dead!... We cannot accept that he's dead!" She heard snippets about a dying woman's confession at Bellevue.

Charlotte concluded that Gabriel was likely dead.

No one had told her anything, and she couldn't bear to hear any more. Charlotte fled to her room, closed the door, then collapsed onto her bed. Minutes later, she texted Vince using her app for self-destructing messaging.

Hi, Vince responded.

Gabriel's dead.

What? No. That can't be right. Who told you he's dead?

My parents came back from the hospital where police had a woman who took him and she told them before she died.

You know for sure he's dead?

I don't know. Oh God. Can you help me?

What can I do?

You said you met with someone who knows what happened.

Yes.

Was it this woman who died?

It was not a woman.

Can you find out what happened to Gabriel?

Vince didn't respond.

Can you? she texted. Please!!!

I'll have to go back to the person who might know.

Please, Vince, I have to know if it's true, because it's my fault! Vince, please, please help me!

I'll help you.

A short time later, Corina and Robert took a moment alone together in Gabriel's room.

She touched Gabriel's pajamas to her cheek. Robert surveyed his football poster.

"I remember the moment he became ours," Robert said. "Holding him. He was so small, so tiny. And I thought, with all you'd been through, and all I'd been through, and the way Gabriel came into our lives—the heartache, the joy—he truly was our miracle."

Corina took Robert's hand.

"We were so blessed," he said.

"Yes."

Turning to the night, her insides twisting, Corina watched the lights of Manhattan's skyscrapers twinkling and was pierced with dark thoughts. *But where is he now? Is he in the ground? Is he in the East River? Is he in some backstreet trash bin?*

No, stop it, she told herself, looking to the tribute on Gabriel's bed. Some of the balloons had started to deflate, wrinkling the words *Courage*, *Faith* and *Hope*.

Hope.

Hang on to it, draw strength from it.

She squeezed Robert's hand.

They would be stronger together, for Gabriel.

A soft knock sounded on the door and Detective DiMaria entered.

"One of the networks has breaking news."

56

Unsteady footage of a man being arrested on a train at Penn Station by cops in tactical gear filled the large TV screen in Efrem Zyller's luxury condominium on Madison Avenue.

The chyron banner across the bottom said: **MAN REMOVED FROM DEPARTING TRAIN AT PENN IN MISSING CHILD CASE**.

"...no details on charges, identity or nationality, but sources tell RBNN his arrest is related to the case of Gabriel Corado, the six-year-old son of Newslead Now journalist Corina Corado. The dramatic incident took place on a Boston-bound Amtrak train moments before departure from Penn Station. The boy was not on the train and he has not been located... The search continues..."

Footage in the breaking news report shifted to a clearer angle on the handcuffed man being escorted to a police vehicle.

Zyller didn't recognize him.

Alarmed by the development, Zyller analyzed his own situation and the steps he needed to take. He reached for his new phone, obtained after the FBI and NYPD had seized all of his devices. He recalled his attorney cautioning him to use it with the expectation that it, too, would be seized.

"Use it for business and everyday living, do not use it for anything that might be questionable or draw attention. Do not even get a burner," Spindler had said. "My understanding is that investigators have found nothing detrimental so far on your devices. You will overcome Corina Corado's allegations, Efrem, if you are careful."

Zyller rubbed his bottom lip, eyeing his TV.

He clicked through channels. Only ReLOX had the arrest story, so far. Zyller figured he could call the NNN desk, check if his people were on the story and request updates, but he dismissed the thought for now.

Better to keep a low profile.

He searched online instead.

The *New York Times* had a breaking item on the arrest. But the *Times* advanced it with a revelation no one else had—they raised the possibility of a connection to the case of a woman fleeing pursuers on the High Line before she ran into the path of a truck and died from her injuries. Citing unnamed sources, the *Times* reported that before she died earlier today, the woman admitted to involvement in the case of Gabriel Corado.

Who is she? What's going on?

Zyller needed more information now.

Staring at his phone, he wondered: *Can I take a risk to get it?*

He was jolted from his thoughts by the chime of his condo intercom and a call from security downstairs.

"Yes?"

"Your food order has arrived, Mr. Zyller. Will it be on your account with a gratuity?"

Remembering that he'd ordered a take-out dinner from a deli nearby, an idea dawned.

"No, thanks, send the delivery person up. I'll pay with cash."

Zyller went to his home office, unlocked a desk drawer, withdrew a metal box. It held cash he used for poker nights. Pleased that the FBI hadn't seized it, he withdrew a rolled bundle.

A minute later, his doorbell rang, and he opened the door to a man in his late twenties, wearing a jacket, hoodie, torn jeans and Air Jordans. He held a brown paper bag with a check stapled to it.

"Thanks. What do I owe you?"

"Thirty-four."

Zyller gave him a fifty, ensuring the delivery guy saw the roll in his hand. "Keep the change," he said, taking the bag.

"Thank you." He gave Zyller a half salute and turned to leave.

"Wait a sec. Maybe you can help me?"

"Help you?"

"You have a phone, right?"

"Yeah."

"My phone just died and I need to make a quick business call. I don't have a landline and my laptop's no good—it's complicated. I'm in a jam. If I give you five hundred—" Zyller saw the delivery guy's eyes flick to the cash bundle "—can I use your phone to make a call?"

The delivery guy looked at Zyller, then the cash, then Zyller again.

"You'll give me five hundred dollars to make one call?"

"It's critical—it's a contract with a deadline. How about I make it a thousand, five now and five when I'm done and you delete the call log."

Without waiting for an answer, Zyller peeled off five hundred in bills, then held it out. Although he seemed wary about the offer, the delivery guy gave in to the promise of easy money and took the cash. He reached for his phone, typed in his password, then handed it to Zyller.

"Thank you," Zyller said. "Wait here. I'll make it quick."

Zyller stepped into his condo, shut the door, set the food down, then dialed the memorized number. It rang and rang. Six rings.

Come on. Come on.

Finally, it clicked with a low voice saying: "Hello."

"It's me," Zyller said. "I had to borrow a phone."

"I thought we weren't supposed to talk until things cooled."

"Things have changed. Have you seen the news?"

"Yes."

"Do you know the people from Penn and the High Line?"

"Maybe I do and maybe I don't. But I do know a business opportunity when I see one."

"Are you involved?"

"We're all involved, Efrem."

"Not me! I told you to stand down when things went awry. I called it off."

"No, what you did was set something in motion that's turned into a runaway train, so to speak. And, because of you, I have something of enormous value."

"What're you talking about?"

"Take a guess."

"I'll go to the police."

"No, you won't, because I'll tell them about all I've done for you and how this all ties to you. It'll be over for you. You'll go down with me."

"Don't do this."

The line went dead.

The call sent a chilling fear coiling up Zyller's spine, leaving him fixed where he stood until his doorbell rang.

Remembering the phone in his hand, noticing the New York Knicks phone case, Zyller opened the door to the delivery guy.

"I gotta go. I got deliveries. So, if you could pay me the rest."

"Sure, but first, delete the call and the number I called."

Taking back his phone and swiping through it, he showed Zyller the last call entry, then the deletion button before he tapped it and the record of the call disappeared.

Zyller put another five hundred in the delivery guy's hand.

57

SECURITY CAMERAS ALONG the High Line had captured Irina Anna Kortova running in fear during the last moments of her life.

They also recorded her pursuers.

Using facial recognition, and passport records, analysts at the NYPD's Real Time Crime Center identified Sergey Tellev as one of the men chasing her.

Watching the footage now playing through Lonza's laptop on the monitor of a meeting room in the 19th Precinct, Tellev was silent.

Seated beside him was Aleena Shadrin, his Russian-speaking attorney. Born in Omsk, Russia, Shadrin's family had moved to the US when she was just a child. She'd graduated from Columbia and helped clients with legal issues in the US, Russia, Belarus, Kazakhstan, Uzbekistan and Azerbaijan.

Shadrin glanced at the time. It was late into the night. Several hours had passed since Tellev had been removed from the train and was detained for questioning.

"How much longer? My client faces no charges. All you've presented is hearsay. Again, I respectfully request his release," Shadrin said.

"He's not telling us the truth," Grimes said.

"Mr. Tellev," Lonza said, "you entered the US on a temporary B-1 visa. What was your business here?"

"We've been over this," Shadrin said. "He's a security consultant and the purpose of his visit was to consult with business associates."

"What type of security and for which businesses?"

"Russian and American-based companies," Tellev said, "with offices in New York and Moscow. Mostly IT work to synchronize office systems."

"IT work," Grimes said. "Computer stuff."

"Yes," Tellev said.

"What is your relationship with Irina Anna Kortova?" Lonza asked.

"My client has stated that he does not know her," Shadrin said.

"No?" Grimes said. "Why was he chasing her on the High Line?"

"I was running to aid this woman. I saw her for the first time on the High Line. She was distraught, talking in Russian about someone following her. I was afraid she may hurt herself, or others."

"And yet," Lonza said, "you were so concerned that you ran off when she was struck, as we've seen in the security video. Fled like a guilty man."

Tellev was silent and Lonza leaned closer to him.

"Here's what you don't know, Mr. Tellev," she said. "Before she died, Irina Kortova named Tatiana Galkina, Anton Valiev and you as her accomplices—she revealed your criminal activities."

Pausing to process the new information, Tellev looked at Lonza, who entered commands on her laptop.

"This is what our computer experts found on your phone and your tablet that were seized after your arrest," Lonza said.

The video of Kortova and Robert in the Philadelphia hotel room played. Then the brief video of Gabriel and Charlotte entering Central Park.

"Our people tell us a hidden camera was placed in Robert Tanner's hotel room. And in Manhattan, the old security system on a building on Central Park West was hacked to obtain the video footage of Gabriel Corado and his sister entering the park."

Shadrin made notes as Lonza continued.

"Our analysts concluded that these videos were manipulated, and the hack was completed on the devices in your possession, Mr. Tellev. It's strong evidence of your involvement."

Knowing that the law allowed police to use deceptive methods to determine the truth, Lonza looked at her notes.

"We've spoken with Tatiana Galkina and Anton Valiev. They've confessed their role, *and yours*, in the extortion against Robert Tanner, as it relates to a multibillion-dollar condominium."

Grimes, like Lonza, maintained a poker face, knowing that the other two accomplices had not yet been located.

"And we have a team processing your last known address in the city at Brooklyn Plaza Court," Lonza added. "Extortion and kidnapping a child are extremely serious crimes. You face life in prison."

"As you know, Sergey—" Grimes stood "—criminals who harm children are not well regarded in prison."

"Tell us where Gabriel Corado is," Lonza said.

"We know you're involved." Grimes placed his hands on the table, drawing his face close to Tellev's. "Where is the boy?"

Tellev never removed his eyes from Grimes.

"If you guarantee me immunity from charges," Tellev said, "I will tell you what we did."

DAY 5

58

Sunrise over Brooklyn.

Wheels humming under them, Grimes guided their unmarked SUV over the Manhattan Bridge. Lonza took another hit of stale precinct coffee from her commuter cup and searched the early light bathing Brooklyn's skyline.

Dismissing the tension in her neck, she blinked at a memory; that autumn day before Eva was sick. She and Tony had taken the kids to the park. Eva and Marco got down in a pile of leaves begging her and Tony to cover them. They did and after a few seconds of ruffling, the kids were gone. But she could hear Marco giggling and Eva's squeals of laughter, until they faded, and she looked at Gabriel Corado's face on her phone and concentrated on the case.

It was now the fifth day of his disappearance.

A few hours ago, their interview with Sergey Tellev halted so the US attorney could weigh Tellev's request for immunity from charges in exchange for information about the boy. Lonza and Grimes used the time to check Tellev's last address, Brooklyn Plaza Court near Flatbush.

"Not far from my place," Grimes said, parking next to the Crime

Scene Unit van in front of the brick building. They were met by a woman tugging off gloves at the rear of the van's open doors.

"Jean Linski, CSU. You guys the leads, Lonza and Grimes?"

"That's right," Grimes said. "Got anything for us?"

"Let me lay it out for you." Linski reached for her laptop. "ESU found nothing after they'd secured it. Canine picked up nothing. The downside is housekeeping went through the unit after he checked out. See?"

She played a video of the extended-stay suite, basic with bed, bathroom, kitchenette, counter, TV and desk.

"That presents a challenge. Our people worked through the night, processing. And we worked with cleaning staff, tracking all trash, linen. We halted all garbage pickup. Got people sifting through everything, with an eye to articles worn by the boy."

"And?"

"Nothing so far that puts the boy in the unit."

"So do we rule this out—" Lonza nodded to the building "—as a crime scene?"

"No, we can't. Because we're still working on things. We've got to test and swab everything we can, like hair, fibers. A lot of testing. Just because we haven't found anything yet doesn't mean it's not there."

Lonza's phone vibrated with a text from Lieutenant Weaver. Time to come back.

At the 19th precinct, in the interview room, they resumed sitting across from Sergey Tellev and Aleena Shadrin.

"The US attorney is unwilling to make any deals, or take charges off the table," Lonza said.

Tellev took a moment to absorb the decision.

"Why not?"

"The case against you is strong. You will be going to prison. However, if you provide information that leads to the safe return of the boy, that would be considered. But nothing more. Do you wish to proceed?"

Shadrin then asked, "What did Galkina and Valiev tell you?"

"We're not going to reveal that."

"Did you make a deal with them?" Tellev asked.

"Mr. Tellev," Lonza said, "do you wish to proceed?"

Shadrin requested a private moment with her client. The detectives left for about twenty minutes, then Shadrin signaled for them to return.

"My client will tell you all he knows," Shadrin said.

Tellev spoke, with the detectives occasionally interrupting him to clarify a point.

"We needed Tanner to authorize a positive report on the building," Tellev said. "One that would not result in extensive repair requirements. Kortova posed as a friendly source to provide Tanner documents and arranged to meet him at a hotel, where a drug, similar to GHB, was surreptitiously placed by one of our team in his food at the bar."

Tellev went on.

"That's how the compromising images of Tanner and Kortova were acquired. The plan was to use them to force Tanner to cooperate. It has worked in the past."

Tellev paused to think.

"But then his child went missing, which changed things. We were not involved in his son's disappearance, but we wanted Tanner to believe we were, to convince him to give us the report. We saw the boy's case as an advantage for us. Kortova really believed we were involved in the kidnapping, which was not true. We told her it was a ploy, but she refused to believe us, or to be part of any ruse using the boy. We tried to convince her to work with us, but she became a problem."

Tellev leaned back.

"That is the truth. And now that I have told you, I request Witness Protection to stay in America because I can never go home again."

"Why not?" Grimes said.

"They will kill me."

The interview ended.

Shadrin returned to her office and Tellev was escorted back to his holding cell without any commitments from the US attorney or the investigators.

Lonza and Grimes regrouped in Lieutenant Weaver's office to review Tellev's admission.

"Right off," Weaver said, "we'll hold him and initiate charges for extortion and computer fraud, to start."

"Do we believe him?" Grimes said. "Was he giving us a version to save himself?"

Looking at the notes he'd made while observing the interviews through the room's one-way mirror, Weaver said, "We've found no connection between Tellev, Kortova and Ivan Beckke or Efrem Zyller."

"Not so far," Grimes said.

"We have a provable link between the Russians and Robert Tanner," Weaver said. "But so far, we have no evidence that the boy was being held by Kortova or Tellev."

"But we haven't located the other two, Galkina and Valiev," Grimes said. "They could've slipped out of the country."

"Or maybe they haven't left." Lonza folded her arms and bit her bottom lip. "And they could have Gabriel, if they haven't…"

Lonza stopped herself from finishing her thought.

59

Observing the stubble on Grimes's haggard face, the dark circles under Lonza's eyes, Lieutenant Weaver tossed his pen onto his desk.

"Go home. You've been going at this all day and night. Grab some sleep while we're waiting on test results."

"I'm okay," Grimes said. "I got fresh clothes in my locker. I'll take a quick shower here."

"I just need more coffee," Lonza said. "There's stuff to follow up on."

"We got an army of people working all fronts," Weaver said. "I'm ordering you to rest a few hours."

Massaging her temples and nodding, Lonza left Weaver's office. Collecting her things at her desk, she waved to Grimes as he headed out, but then her phone vibrated with a text, one she'd been expecting.

Her stomach tensed.

Corina Corado wanted answers.

The family's condominium wasn't far from the precinct.

On my way, Lonza texted.

As the elevator ascended to the 38th floor, Lonza accepted that she could've called or texted the family.

That would be cowardly. I need to face them. And their pain.

Robert met her at the door, looking hollow-eyed. Lonza first talked privately, and briefly, with the on-duty detectives. They said the family had been inundated with a new wave of media requests for interviews, which they had declined, for the moment. Lonza then joined Robert, Corina and Charlotte in the living room.

The TV was muted on a news network, the air heavy with apprehension. Corina stood, hands clasped in front of her, her voice tremulous.

"Is Gabriel alive?"

"We've found no evidence to suggest he's been hurt."

"Where is he?"

"We're still determining that."

"You don't know?"

"I wish I had better news."

"What have you determined, then?"

"I'm sorry, but I can't discuss everything in the invest—"

"Don't do this to us, Vicky. Please. You get us to rush to Bellevue where that woman, Kortova, confesses 'it wasn't supposed to be an abduction,' then begs my forgiveness on her deathbed."

Lonza nodded as Corina pointed at the muted TV.

"Then we see news of a man arrested on a train at Penn Station, reportedly involved with Kortova. Did they take Gabriel? We deserve to know, Vicky, please."

"All I can tell you is that we found no evidence that Gabriel's been harmed."

"That tells me nothing."

"We're doing all we can to find him."

"You keep saying that! It tells us you don't know where he is and you don't have any leads, and time's running out!"

"You know more," Robert said.

Charlotte held her knuckles to her mouth.

In the face of the family's agony, Lonza blinked back tears. She was slipping. Perhaps from exhaustion, perhaps from the unbearable anguish of the moment. She agreed, the family had the right to know something.

She cautioned them once more.

"I know media want to talk to you, and they can be helpful. But again, we ask that you not reveal details of the investigation that might aid people involved in Gabriel's case."

Corina stared at Lonza, who began telling them more.

"What we've learned is that the suspect from the train denies any involvement in Gabriel's disappearance," Lonza said. "Instead, he claims to have used that information, wanting Robert to believe they had Gabriel, to further pressure Robert to issue a positive report on the condo."

Robert cursed and Corina shook her head slowly.

"We have alerts for two accomplices who remain at large," Lonza said. "We're processing every related location, searching for evidence, awaiting test results."

Corina stared at her. "But you have nothing telling you where Gabriel is?" Corina closed her hand into a fist and gently pounded her forehead.

A terrible silence filled the room before she spoke again.

"Five days now—" Corina's voice cracked "—and we know nothing."

In that moment, Lonza met Corina's haunted gaze.

In that moment, they were two mothers sharing a horrible unspoken secret truth, that death was brushing its wings over their hearts.

Later, alone in the descending elevator, Lonza leaned against the wall and gripped the handrail to keep herself from losing all control.

60

THE CORRECTIONS OFFICER at Rikers examined Vince Tarone's ID.

He entered commands on the keyboard of his terminal. His chair squeaked, and he studied his monitor as if something had registered. He looked at Vince standing before him, long enough to make Vince uncomfortable. He'd already been patted down, sniffed by a corrections dog and gone through metal detectors.

The corrections officer's keyboard clicked again before he returned Vince's ID. Without speaking or smiling, the officer then directed him to the area where Vince was given a photo-pass with an expiration time.

Then Vince passed through the process with the other visitors, coming to a stark room where they waited for the next step. Most people stared at the walls. Vince stood with them in silence, unease rattling through him.

The news stories about arrests in Gabriel Corado's case unnerved him. Charlotte's belief that her brother was dead devastated him.

It can't be true. It just can't.

Vince had lied to his mother, telling her he'd taken an extra driving shift. This was his second visit to Rikers, his second attempt to keep his promise to Charlotte to find the truth about Gabriel.

His deepest fears were swirling when a corrections officer came into the room, calling out inmate names, including…

"Shrike, Trayman Shrike…"

Vince and the others moved to the visiting area. He was directed to the table and bench separated by plexiglass. Shrike sat on the other side, in his jail jumpsuit, arms folded across his chest.

Eyeing Vince, he said, "You again."

"I need your help."

"I can't help you. In fact, I believe you're working with police to screw up my case."

"I'm not. I swear to you. Please, help me understand how you know what you know about the boy's disappearance."

Shrike didn't answer. His jaw tightened.

"Please," Vince said.

Shrike's eyes gleamed like bullet tips as his breathing quickened.

"You must've seen the latest TV news reports on the case. Help me understand what you know. Please, I'm family. You came to my dad's funeral. Please help me."

Shrike began shaking his head slowly. "They're wrong," he said.

"Who's wrong?"

"The police. They don't know what I know."

"How are they wrong? Tell me."

Shrike's eyes shifted across the visiting area to two officers talking and taking stock of all the visits, their focus pausing ever so briefly at Tarone and Shrike.

"Please," Vince said. "Tell me."

Shrike leaned as close as he could to the glass.

"Alright, I'll tell you."

61

THE PITTER-PATTER of Luna's paws greeted Lonza when she arrived at her empty home.

Marco had gone to Staten Island with his dad. Lonza's mother was visiting a friend at the seniors' center. The only one home to welcome her was Luna, who nuzzled against her.

"It's just you and me, girl."

After hugging her, Lonza freshened Luna's water bowl, got her a treat and stroked her head. Minutes later, Lonza was in the shower, needles of hot water prickling her skin, steam clouds rising around her as she searched for a grip on her case, and her life.

I'm failing at everything.

A sob escaped her as she recalled their work at Bellevue, how the hospital's antiseptic smell had triggered a memory, taking her back to another hospital and the doctor with a dot of dried blood on his jaw, a nick from shaving. Concern was layered behind his blue eyes as he gave her and Tony the outcome for Eva, his words hitting them like bursts of gunfire...*rare genetic disorder...no treatment...no survival rate...terminal.*

The agony of losing their four-year-old little girl had been unbearable. They sought counseling, but Tony was consumed with guilt because the disorder stemmed from his side of the family. He drank, became withdrawn; Lonza did all she could to help him, but it was taking a toll on Marco.

It was too much.

No matter how hard Lonza tried, she couldn't keep her hurting family together.

Children are not supposed to die. They should be light-years from death. Losing a child is a cruel violation of the order of things, leaving a wound that never heals.

And now with this case, Lonza saw—*and felt*—the pain in Corina Corado, in Robert and Charlotte Tanner.

We can't lose another child.

The investigation was going nowhere, but she refused to be defeated.

Lonza stepped from the shower, got dressed, made coffee, opened her laptop on her kitchen table and got to work, beginning by checking the status of all aspects of the investigation.

She read Lieutenant Weaver's recent email concerning the move to get the adoption records unsealed in order to locate Gabriel's biological mother, to clear her.

> The judge says we don't have enough evidence to warrant pursuing the birth mom. We've argued that we need her information to pursue a case. It's a catch-22, and it's going to take time, but we'll keep on it.

Shaking her head, Lonza then looked into where they were with alerts at airports, borders, international notices, facial recognition. Lonza knew it was possible to leave the country with an abducted child, disguised, or made to appear sleeping, or ill. The abductors would blend in. It could be done at an airport or driving across the border. A challenge, of course, but it could be done if someone had let their guard down.

Gabriel could be miles away or in another country.

She checked on the alibis arising from the sex offender registry, the history of hate messages sent to Corina Corado, and the tips that had come in. She read through reports and summaries provided by investigators from numerous agencies. She looked at additional videos from personal phones and dash cams people in the area at the time had volunteered.

Nothing strong, so far.

It forced Lonza back to the fundamentals of investigation. Anything and everything could be evidence, whether physical or in a given statement.

They'd gone from arresting Beckke with Gabriel's phone, where things stalled, to Zyller, who Corina alleged had threatened her. They looked at the threats against Corina, had her check old stories for leads against the backdrop of Wynne's conspiracies and his believers' claims that Corina stole a child and staged her son's disappearance to save her career.

Then they moved to the admitted extortion attempt against Robert Tanner that appeared to entail Gabriel's abduction.

But that made no sense. An abduction would only draw attention to their covert objective. Were Tellev and the others that desperate, that shortsighted? Or were they under that much pressure to take such a risk?

We're pinballing all over the place when in actuality we're no closer to Gabriel than we were the moment he disappeared.

Lonza dragged both hands over her face.

This is not a TV show where everything makes sense and every puzzle piece falls into place.

Cursing under her breath, Lonza drew upon one of her own fundamentals of investigation: *the pebble-in-the-pond principle.* The pebble breaks the water's surface, sending out ripples.

Go to the first ripples.

They'll bring you closer to the truth.

Lonza went back to what she considered were the best videos: those recorded in the moments before and after the abduction, and the hacked video used to convince Robert that the abduction was part of the extortion. For more than an hour, she studied the footage, replaying it again and again until the images began swimming on her screen.

The answer has to be here.

Her eyes began to close, her head swayed, and she felt it sinking to the table, where she soon fell asleep.

She was dreaming of Eva, holding her hand and walking on a beach when a ringing phone stopped them, pulling her back to her kitchen.

Waking, she saw it was her lieutenant and answered.

"Vicky, it's Weaver. Sorry to wake you."

"It's okay." Her voice was ragged. "What's up."

"We got something."

62

Vince Tarone's left leg bounced ever so slightly under the table in the small room at Rikers Island, where two corrections officers had taken him after his visit with Shrike ended.

He'd been sitting in here alone for more than an hour.

"What is it?" Vince had asked when they'd pulled him aside after double-checking his photo-pass.

The officers didn't speak until they'd brought him into the room.

"What's wrong?" Vince asked.

Before closing the door, one of them said, "Security protocol."

But Vince knew.

He'd been caught red-handed.

His luck had run out.

And now he waited for what was coming.

Grimes closed his notebook then surveyed the office at Rikers.

A framed photo of a man, a woman, a young girl and a boy stood next to the computer. Near the bookcase were diplomas and awards for Leo Maclary. Then photos of the commissioner, mayor and governor. There were the flags, and a hint of Old Spice.

"Tarone's on our playlist," Lonza said, scrolling through her tablet.

"Yeah," Grimes said. "So how did this get by?"

The door opened and a senior officer entered.

"Leo Maclary. Sorry for the wait." After shaking hands, he began working at his keyboard.

"Our records show we had guys from the One-Fourteen in here to interview Shrike right from the get-go," Lonza said, "and that Rikers had been advised to alert us to any visits or communication with Trayman Herman Shrike."

"Yeah," Maclary said.

"So," Grimes said, "Tarone, who is connected to the family of our missing boy, is visiting Shrike in your house here, the guy who wanted to kill Corina Corado, and we're just now hearing about it?"

"A glitch in the overburdened system," Maclary said. "He got by us only briefly. We caught it today. Turns out he's a relative and, as you know, inmates have the right to family visits."

"How many visits have they had, and when?" Lonza asked.

"Two. The first was two days ago, and then today." Maclary removed his glasses. "As soon as we caught it, we secured him and alerted you."

"We'll want to talk to Shrike, too," Lonza said. "And we want your records of everyone who's visited or contacted him since he's been here."

"We'll take care of that," Maclary said. "Are you set to talk with Tarone?"

"We are," Lonza said.

Maclary led the detectives through several security points to the sound of buzzers, and metal clanging on metal, until they reached the room.

When Lonza and Grimes entered, Vince Tarone began to rise.

"Don't get up," Grimes said.

The detectives positioned their chairs across from him.

"We met on the Upper East Side the night you had your meeting with Charlotte Tanner," Grimes said.

Vince nodded.

"Why didn't you come forward about your relationship to Trayman Herman Shrike?"

Vince's Adam's apple rose and fell.

"I was afraid," he said. "He's, like, a distant relative. An in-law. But no one knew, and my mom and I figured if people found out we'd lose our jobs, no one would associate with us, kinda thing."

"Why did you come to see him days after Gabriel disappeared?" Lonza asked.

"I thought he could help find him."

"Why did you think that?" Grimes asked.

Vince looked at the ceiling then back to the detectives. "Months ago, even before I first met Charlotte—"

"Wait, tell us again, how did you meet her?" Lonza asked.

"She was a passenger. We hit it off, exchanged numbers, like that."

"Go ahead."

"Yeah, so it was months ago, before I met Charlotte, when Shrike's case was back in the news—something about a court delay, I think—I was driving a woman in Manhattan, you know, giving her a little tour, customers will ask and pay extra for that. So, I'm driving this woman, pointing out the sites, and she got talking about the news and Shrike's case and how she thought Shrike got a raw deal.

"I thought it was strange, but later, when Gabriel disappeared…it kind of brought things back and I got thinking about Shrike and his situation, what he did, and all the people who think like him, you know? And Charlotte, she doesn't know I'm related to Shrike; she's out of her mind, begging and pleading for me to help her any way I can. She thinks because of my job, I know a lot of people, probably because one time, I said something, kinda half joking, about knowing all kinds of people as a driver, even dangerous types, like wise guys. Guess maybe she took it the wrong way, like I'm mobbed up or something. And I'm feeling guilty because I was the person she was talking to when Gabriel went missing.

"So that's why I came to see him, thinking that because of his situation, he may actually know someone involved, and maybe since I'm kind of family, he might help me in some way, and then I could tell you."

"You're very civic-minded, aren't you?" Grimes said.

"And what did he tell you?" Lonza asked.

"He's really kind of out there, you know?" Vince said.

"We know," Lonza said. "What did he tell you?"

"He said he knows what happened."

"What does he say happened?" Grimes said.

Vince took a second.

"He made it sound like a riddle."

"A riddle?" Grimes said.

"He said, 'If you look closely, you'll see what happened, *because it had to happen.*'"

63

A THOUSAND DOLLARS.

Clifton Chase brooded over the money as the train rocketed north to his destination. Staring at the tunnel walls racing by his window, he replayed the unusual way he got the cash that was thickening his wallet.

Last night's delivery to a Madison Avenue condo in the Upper East Side. The customer had paid in cash at his penthouse door, then gave him a grand, in cash, to make a call on his phone.

Weird.

As he headed home after his shift, Clifton couldn't believe his luck.

A thousand dollars to make a phone call.

One phone call.

Finally, a good thing happened.

Four months ago, he'd lost his courier driver job and benefits. *"Budget cuts, sorry, Cliff, if it was up to me..."* his supervisor said. Then Shawna, his girlfriend, left him. We're on different paths, she'd texted after clearing out most of their apartment. He suspected she'd found someone else. Unable to pay the rent, Clifton moved in with his mom and dad. His father had been disabled after being shot during the robbery of a corner store where he'd gone for milk and eggs.

Clifton found some lower-paying, part-time jobs: a dishwasher at a SoHo restaurant, a maintenance assistant at a Midtown hotel and a bike food delivery worker. He worked three jobs to help his parents, and to save for courses to become a unionized licensed electrician.

Getting a thousand bucks for one phone call was a lottery win.

He didn't tell anybody when he got home. It was late. His parents had gone to bed. He could hear his dad's snoring. His mother had made up the sofa, where Clifton had been sleeping the last few months in their cramped place.

Excited about the money, he couldn't sleep. He could get his dad a new four-wheel walker with handbrakes. His mom needed a new coat. And he could get a couple of textbooks to prepare for his courses.

But something pulled at him.

Through the night, his joy about the money evolved into questions, which evolved into concerns, which evolved into worry.

Something about this ain't right. Why would a guy do that?

In the morning, Clifton searched the guy's Madison Avenue address, which he still had on his phone from the delivery.

His concern deepened.

The guy's building came up in recent news stories, with headlines about search warrants executed in the investigation of the boy missing from Central Park, Gabriel Corado.

Clifton found news footage of police hauling off items from Newslead's headquarters, then from the Madison Avenue condo of Efrem Zyller, the head of the news division. There were formal, corporate-looking head-and-shoulders photos of Zyller.

That's him, that's the guy.

Clifton remembered how the dude seemed pretty stressed about the phone.

Guess he would be, with the NYPD and the FBI up in his face.

Again, Clifton thought of the money, how his family could use it. Still, something didn't feel right. Sure, at first, getting that kinda bank felt good, but now it felt dangerous.

Clifton looked at his phone.

What if it comes back on me? What if the guy using my phone implicated me, or made me some sort of accessory?

Clifton got up, got dressed, grabbed an apple and the scrambled-egg sandwich his mother had made for him, and then left his parents' place in the eastern section of Brooklyn for the long ride to the Upper West Side.

I gotta protect myself.

The train rocked, yawed, then the brakes scraped as it decelerated into his station. Clifton stepped onto the platform and hustled up the stairs to the street. He was stopped at the red light before crossing to the 86th Street entrance to Central Park.

Where the whole thing with the kid had started.

Waiting, Clifton checked his phone.

As part of the deal, he'd deleted the number the condo guy called. But with a few taps and swipes, Clinton knew how to resurrect it from his trash.

It was there, alright. The number, the time, duration.

Good.

Now he had a green light.

Pocketing his phone, he continued walking along the 86th Street transverse cutting across the park.

In a few minutes, he'd reach the NYPD's Central Park Precinct, where he would report everything about his delivery, and the call that was made on his phone.

64

THE FAINT JINGLE in the hall grew louder.

Escorted by two officers, Trayman Herman Shrike had been placed in enhanced restraints: handcuffed wrists linked to a waist chain.

When he arrived, the officers seated him in a chair that was bolted to the floor, at a table that was bolted to the floor. Leg irons were used to secure his ankles to an anchor in the floor.

The barren, cinder block room smelled of industrial cleaner.

Shrike's cuffs clattered on the table when he rested his hands on it and stared at the detectives sitting across from him.

"I'm Detective Lonza, this is Detective Grimes." They held open their NYPD badges with photo IDs. "Thank you for agreeing to talk to us. Our conversation is being recorded for investigative purposes."

Lonza indicated her phone on the table in active recording mode and Shrike gave a slight nod.

"As a pretrial detainee in Miranda custody, you're free not to cooperate with our inquiry about events that took place outside this institution."

Shrike nodded.

"You're under no duress, or obligation, to speak to us and can end this interview at any time. Do you understand?"

"I understand."

"How do you wish to be addressed?"

"Trayman is fine."

"Trayman," Lonza said, "are you aware that five days ago, a six-year-old boy, Gabriel Corado, got separated from his sister in Central Park, in what we're investigating as a possible abduction?"

"Two other detectives came here to question me about it. And we see the TV news in here, so I'm aware."

"You're awaiting trial on charges that two years ago you intended to kill the boy's mother, Corina Corado."

Shrike said nothing.

"Vincent Tarone, your relative, who has a relationship with the missing boy's sister, has visited you twice since the boy vanished."

Shrike's nostrils flared. "Is that simpleton working for you?"

"What?"

"Is he some sort of police plant? Did you send him here to screw up my case?"

Lonza looked at Grimes, then back at Shrike.

"No."

Shrike clamped his jaw tight, deciding whether or not to believe them.

Lonza continued: "Do you know who might be responsible for the boy's disappearance?"

"You think I had something to do with it?"

Lonza and Grimes didn't respond.

"I'm in here," Shrike said. "They don't let me out to go to Central Park."

"Trayman," Lonza said, "Vincent said you told him you know what happened to Gabriel Corado."

Shrike leaned back in his chair, raised his chin and jutted it out.

"Yes, I know what happened."

"What do you know?" Grimes said.

"The truth, and so much more."

"Are you involved in his disappearance?" Lonza asked.

"Look around. This is a jail."

"Trayman," Lonza said. "Do you possess knowledge of the boy's case? Have you directed, or been in contact with, someone who is involved?"

Shrike remained silent.

Looking hard at Shrike, Grimes said, "He knows nothing."

Shrike's jaw muscles tensed and he began to grin. "I know more than you, Ace. I know what happened."

"Enlighten us," Lonza said.

"Look at all the news stories," Shrike said. "Look at what Corina Corado is. Go back to when she talked to the Storm people. They had it right. She's the Queen of Lies. Her life is a lie. What's happening to her is right and just. It's destined because she spews fake news. She's a demon in human form sent to destroy us! She's one of the lizard people!"

"How do you know this?"

"How do you not know it?" Shrike said. "I sense you might be fake law enforcement with no jurisdiction over me, that's what I'm sensing."

Lonza let a long moment pass.

"Trayman, how do you know what you know?"

"It's channeled to me. I receive messages."

"Who sends you messages?" Lonza asked.

"They're sent to me from the cosmos because I am the glorious sword. One edge of the blade is truth, the other is light."

Shrike closed his eyes and tilted his head skyward.

"I am the sword of truth and light."

Lonza and Grimes looked at him for a long, silent moment.

Shrike slowly lowered his head, opened his eyes wide, smiled, then spoke. "Oh my. Something big is about to happen."

65

"SIXTY SECONDS."

The floor director cued the guests who were seated at the Newslead Now Network studio desk, ready to go live for the midday news program.

Corina Corado turned to Charlotte, patting her hand, then turned to Robert and squeezed his knee.

Someone out there knows. Someone saw something.

Corina took stock of the cameras, the crew. This was the studio and the desk where she'd been working in the moments before police called her about Gabriel's disappearance five days ago.

Five days.

She glanced at the show's anchor, Lynn Litton, her colleague, seated across the desk, prepping. Touching her earpiece and talking to the producer, Litton made a few edits to her script.

Corina looked at the teleprompter, then other monitors where Gabriel's face appeared. She remained in control and glimpsed herself in a monitor. She'd declined full makeup before accepting a little concealer.

Still, she looked raw.

They had received dozens of interview requests, and Corina had wrestled with whether to go to another network, or with Newslead. Outside of the detectives, her lawyer and Robert, no one knew the details about Corina's issues with Efrem Zyller. To go to a competitor might be construed as publicly pointing a finger at her employer. But Corina couldn't stomach going with Newslead because Efrem Zyller might appear in the studio. It was only after Gil Dixon assured her that Efrem would not be in the building that she agreed. Efrem was nowhere in sight when they'd arrived, but neither was Gil. She didn't see him now as she scanned the studio crew.

"Ten seconds."

The floor director gave the timing cue, counting down before pointing to Lynn Litton.

"A missing child is every parent's worst nightmare," she began. "And that nightmare became a reality when six-year-old Gabriel Corado vanished from Central Park five days ago.

"Joining us now are his mother, our Newslead colleague Corina Corado, Gabriel's father, Robert Tanner, and Gabriel's big sister, Charlotte. Thank you for being with us today."

Each family member said their thanks.

"Our hearts go out to you," Litton said, "at what has to be a profoundly anguishing time for you."

"Thank you," Robert said.

"Now," Litton said, "to give viewers some background, your family lives near the park, and Charlotte was walking Gabriel home from his school, Tillmon Parker Rose in the Upper West Side, when you got separated, correct?"

"Yes." Charlotte's voice quivered. "Gabriel was flying the airplane he'd made in his class. He chased after it near the Bridle Path on the west side."

The last photo taken of Gabriel, holding his plane, appeared on the screen.

Charlotte brushed her tears.

"Since then," Litton said, "there've been many developments. Let's take a moment to go over them." Footage rolled for the next few minutes as Litton related key aspects of the case, including reports of an arrest at Penn Station following a failed extortion attempt by foreign nationals, underscoring its magnitude and complexity before turning to the family again. "With all of this, are police close to finding Gabriel?"

"We don't know," Robert said. "They don't reveal every detail of their work to us."

"The investigation has certainly been exhaustive," Litton said. "As it's been reported, warrants were executed in this building and at the home of Efrem Zyller, head of our news division. Those warrants remain sealed. Do you have any thoughts on these actions?"

Robert said, "There are rumors and speculation."

Corina added: "I think they're being thorough in pursuing all possibilities."

"Including someone here who may be involved?" Litton said.

"Until we find Gabriel," Corina said, "how can they rule anything out? Before a case is solved, everyone is a suspect. It's a basic tenet of police investigations."

"Do you have any ideas as to what exactly happened?" Litton asked.

"All I can tell you is that a million scenarios torment me every second," Corina said.

"It could be anyone for any reason," Robert said.

"Corina, as you've pointed out, journalists often receive disturbing, hate-filled messages. You've been a target of serious threats in the past. Have police found any possible link between your threat history and Gabriel's disappearance?"

"We know they're looking at everything," Corina said. "And we have to be careful what we say so we don't inadvertently aid whoever is behind this."

"Certainly," Litton said.

"We're thankful for the support we've received," Robert said. "The cards, the letters, the kind messages. We're thankful for all those who've volunteered to search, and the police."

"Corina, the person, or persons, responsible could be watching. What would you say to them?"

She took a moment.

"I would say—" the camera moved in on her "—Gabriel's our little boy. Please, I'm begging you, let him come home. Please."

The camera continued moving closer.

"It's been five days and nights since I last hugged and kissed Gabriel and told him how much we love him. And, Gabriel, if you're seeing this, honey…"

The camera pulled in tighter on her.

"…know that we love you and we're doing all we can to bring you home."

Corina brushed at a tear.

"We should also mention that there is a significant reward for information," Litton said.

"Yes," Robert said. "It's now well over one hundred thousand dollars. We're asking anyone who knows anything about what's happened to Gabriel to come forward."

"Someone saw something," Corina said.

Robert took Corina's hand. "We've been told," he said, "that, other than his presumed abduction, no evidence has been found to suggest he's been harmed."

"There's hope," Litton said.

"We'll never give up hope," Corina said.

"Thank you," Litton said. "We'll be back after this break."

Litton moved to give the family her sincere thanks, then she pulled back to focus on what was suddenly coming through her earpiece.

"Pardon me." Litton turned to the floor director, who was signaling that they were still live. "We're not breaking away just yet. I've been informed that we have new information on the case."

Corina tensed at what it could be.

"Okay." Litton nodded. "The ReLOX Broadcasting Network is again raising questions about Corina's reporting in Central America, and Gabriel's adoption."

Corina saw the floor director signaling again.

"If you watch the monitors," Litton said, "we'll play this breaking news clip from ReLOX for your reaction."

A ReLOX anchor was reading while footage played over his shoulder. *"…has uncovered new evidence that throws into question Corina Corado's account of her activities in Nicaragua, where she allegedly rescued a baby from the arms of his mother, who was dying in the mudslides. We have obtained security images taken at a professional building near the stricken region at the time Corado had been reporting on the disaster there. It builds on earlier photos reported by the* World Sun Express.*"*

The footage, recorded in the building's lobby, showed Corina passing a business folder, along with cash, to a man, while the woman with him handed a baby to her. Corina held the baby, tenderly pressing her cheek to its head, and swaying with it in her arms before the footage ended.

"What's critical about this footage," the ReLOX anchor said, *"is that one of the offices in the building is a regional office of the Nicaraguan government's family ministry, which helps process adoptions. We also note that US Immigration provides instant access online to the required form to request to classify an orphan as an immediate relative. This could expedite the process so a US citizen could bring a child into the country, provided no Nicaraguan relatives of the orphaned child object. And US privacy laws protect all information concerning the process from being disclosed, keeping us from knowing the truth as we continue to pursue it."*

The ReLOX report ended, and the camera switched back to Newslead anchor, Lynn Litton.

"We emphasize, Newslead has not yet verified this report," Litton said. "Corina, we still must ask: What is your response to the ReLOX footage and the network's allegation?"

Stunned into silence, she stared at the screen, her thoughts spinning wildly, shooting her back to Nicaragua.

...the woman encased in the mud...holding her baby...imploring me to save her baby...

Waiting for Corina's answer, those few seconds seemed an eternity when Robert took control of the situation.

"We can't speak to anything about the authenticity of things like this. We don't know the context, or if it's been manipulated," he said. "So much gets twisted into conspiracies and entwined with threats and abusive rhetoric. Our focus is finding Gabriel."

"Thank you," Litton said, turning to the camera. "We'll be back."

As theme music played them out and the floor director signaled that they were off the air, Corina looked beyond the cameras, into the studio. While the bright lights silhouetted everyone on the periphery, she spotted a lone figure watching.

She was certain it was Efrem Zyller.

66

CORINA SAGGED INTO her sofa.

Staring at her living room floor, she tried to convince herself Gabriel was safe in his room, that the last five days were nothing but a nightmare.

But I'm not dreaming.

It had been minutes since they'd arrived home from Newslead.

We went to appeal for Gabriel and we were hit with more conspiracies. Was Efrem Zyller lurking in the studio the whole time?

Her phone was buzzing with messages as Robert appeared before her.

"Would you like some water?"

She accepted the glass he offered.

"Newslead was a disaster," she said.

"We had to do it." Charlotte sat nearby. "We have to do everything we can, Mom."

"That's right," Robert said. "We're keeping Gabriel in the public eye, to generate tips and leads—you know how it works."

"But it only brought more accusations," Corina said.

"They're always going to be there."

Corina's phone continued vibrating with interview requests; it hadn't let up since they'd left the studio. But no updates from Lonza and Grimes.

"Look." Robert held his phone out to show Corina some recent social media posts:

My heart goes out to Gabriel's family.

I'm praying they find that little boy.

Never give up hope.

"That's just a few of them. Most people aren't buying into the conspiracies," he said.

"But some are, Dad." Charlotte turned her phone toward Corina and Robert, showing them posts she'd found.

The Queen of Lies faked the whole thing.

Now her whole family is lying.

What did they do with that sweet, little Gabriel?

Lock them up!

Wynne Varden nailed this from the get-go and he's doing it now on ReLOX.

Corina grabbed the remote, turned on their TV and found the ReLOX Network, where a news panel discussion was in progress. The show had inset still images of Corina passing cash to two people, then holding a baby in the lobby of a Nicaraguan building. Discussing the case was Wynne Varden, who appeared in a quarter frame.

"...the outstanding reporting by ReLOX forces us to raise serious questions about what's really going on with Gabriel Corado's so-called abduction."

"What do you think is at play here, Wynne?" the anchor asked.

"Who really knows? This latest information we've uncovered from Nicaragua is damning. Maybe Corina Corado stole a child from a dying woman, then paid people off to adopt him illegally."

"What?" Corina shouted at the TV.

"Is this an orchestrated inside job?" Wynne Varden said. *"Is Newslead trying to cover something up with those sealed warrants?"*

"Police sealed those warrants, Varden, and you know that!" Corina yelled.

Varden went on: *"Has the whole thing been staged to garner sympathy for Corado, whose job was in question? Is it a pathetic attempt to grab ratings? For all we know, Gabriel's having a great time with a friend or a nanny at Disney World."*

Corina hurled the remote at Wynne Varden, sending it bouncing off the frame.

"Corina." Robert held her and whispered, "Maybe it's time we told everyone the truth about how Gabriel came to us, about his mother?"

"No, we can't do that. *I can't do that.* We swore we would never do that," she said, then rushed down the hall, closing the door to Gabriel's room behind her.

In the living room, Robert cursed at the TV before finding the remote and switching it off, accepting that Corina needed to be alone.

"Isn't there anything we can do to stop his lies?" he asked out loud, knowing there was nothing.

Robert began pacing, leaving the room and searching his phone for a number, intent on calling ReLOX.

Now alone in the living room, Charlotte clenched her eyes shut, anguished her family was again being torn to pieces. Burning with guilt, her fingers moved rapidly as she texted Vince Tarone.

YOU PROMISED TO HELP ME!

Seconds ticked by before he responded.

I tried today. I really tried. Something went wrong. I'm sorry.

OMG! What happened?

I can't say. But it would be wise if we didn't talk.

No! Vince PLEASE!!!!

Minutes went by with no response.

Charlotte dropped her phone in her lap.

* * *

As the afternoon slipped away, Corina remained in Gabriel's room, consumed by a firestorm of emotions.

She opened her laptop and played the video of Gabriel's sixth birthday.

She saw his mile-wide smile, face aglow in the dimmed light, everyone singing, the cake before him, the flames of six candles dancing in his eyes.

She reached for him, her fingertips almost touching the screen.

She was reminded how he came into their lives, their miracle. She thought of the private adoption, the details sealed.

The truth is sealed.

Then, at that moment, Corina thought of ReLOX, and it took her back to Nicaragua, to Evelin Flores dying in the mud, living just long enough to save her baby boy.

Corina held him in her arms as the helicopter thudded to the hospital, thinking how badly she ached to have a baby. Yes, that was her in the photos and footage, but the truth…

Corina, exhausted, had no idea how much time had passed before a soft knocking sounded at the door and Robert poked his head in.

"How are you doing?"

Her tears had dried stiff on her skin. She shrugged.

"Some people are here to see you. I think it would be good for you."

Nora, Marty and Gil were waiting in the living room. They'd brought more flowers, cards, balloons and stuffed toys.

Corina met them with hugs and thanks as she, Charlotte and Robert sorted the items on the table nearby.

"These are a few of the new ones sent to Newslead for you," Nora said.

"Yeah, they keep coming," Marty said. "A new wave arrived after you did the show with Lynn."

"We're sorry to come uninvited," Nora said. "We wanted to be with you after you'd finished the interview, but you left so quickly."

Corina nodded, then looked at Gil. "I didn't see you in the studio."

"I got there late, but what I saw looked good."

"Except for being slammed to respond to ReLOX," Corina said.

"Lynn was told to get your response," Gil said. "The video from Nicaragua was breaking on ReLOX."

"Who told her to do that?"

Gil and the others traded glances.

"We don't know, a call likely came in," Gil said.

"From upstairs? From Efrem? I saw him in the studio. I thought he wasn't supposed to be there."

The others looked puzzled.

"Efrem wasn't in the studio," Nora said.

"Corina," Gil said, "he was at a meeting across town. Look, everybody is praying for Gabriel. Yes, rumors are swirling, and the warrants made some people uncomfortable..."

"Oh my God! Some people are uncomfortable? Our son is missing, I'm accused of staging his disappearance, accused of stealing him from his dying mother and lying about his adoption, *and some people are uncomfortable!*"

"I didn't mean it that way. It came out wrong. I'm sorry," Gil said.

Corina seized one of the new gifts, a teddy bear, and hugged it desperately, her fingers digging into its plush fur as she gasped for air.

"Corina..." Nora touched her shoulder.

"Maybe we should go," Marty said.

Corina's fingertips hit something small, hard, circling the soft plush of the bear.

Pausing, shifting it to look, her heart skipped, and she screamed.

Around the bear's neck was a blue cord bracelet, with a Yankees' baseball and alphabet beads spelling *Gabriel.*

67

"No, NOTHING LIKE THAT," Frank O'Donohue said over the phone from Clearwater, Florida.

The retired detective had led the original Trayman Herman Shrike investigation. He was happy to provide Lonza with insights when she reached him.

"Our work was extensive, Vicky. We found that Shrike had no accomplices. He acted alone on his plan to assassinate Corado. He just bought into the conspiracies online and peddled by ReLOX, especially those featured on *The Wynne Files*."

"What about Shrike's family? Anything there?"

"We looked. Nothing. They alienated him because of his beliefs."

Taking notes, she paused a moment to gather her thoughts, then thanked O'Donohue and turned to Grimes, at his desk, winding down his own phone conversation and looking at his monitor.

"Got it. Thanks." Grimes ended his call. "Maclary says they've triple-checked Shrike. Other than lawyers, and Vince Tarone, no visitors, no calls in or out, no correspondence. Zip."

Weighing Grimes's update, Lonza said: "And Shrike tells us he receives cosmic messages, that something big is going to happen." She shook her head. "He's putting on a show for us with all this business about messages being channeled to him, about being the sword of light."

"Like Son of Sam and his BS claim about taking orders from a devil dog."

"I don't know." Lonza reached for her notebook. "There may be something in what Tarone was telling us."

"What?"

Lonza consulted her notes.

"Something about driving a customer who supported Shrike and giving her a tour—"

"Heads up—" Interrupting them, Lieutenant Weaver had stepped from his office, holding his phone. "DiMaria at the condo says the family's received the boy's bracelet. It's the real thing.

"And there's a ransom demand."

68

THE LETTER *G* had a tiny chip at the bottom.

The letter *R* was faded.

These details about Gabriel's Yankees' bracelet and the beads spelling his name had never been released.

It's his! It's Gabriel's!

Caressing the letters, Corina's heart shattered.

Was this the last thing he touched?

Her muscles went limp; gooseflesh rose on her skin.

"Set it down, please, and nobody else handle it." Tugging on blue nitrile gloves, detectives DiMaria and Alvarez took control. With Alvarez recording with his phone, DiMaria examined the bracelet and the stuffed teddy bear.

Attached to the bracelet with a blue ribbon was a small folded white card, bearing the words *For Corina* alongside a QR code. With Alvarez still recording, DiMaria requested Corina's phone—"They'll want to know you've received this"—and scanned the code. Activated, it led to a matrix of sites, then a message that warned that it would self-destruct in seconds.

> We have Gabriel. For his return you now have 24 hours to deposit 200 in cryptocurrency into the account to be accessed with a time-limited code that will be sent to you.

"Oh God!" Corina's knees buckled when DiMaria relayed the demand to her and Robert.

"Currently, that's around five million dollars," DiMaria said.

"I don't know if we can pull anything close to that in time," Robert said. "We may need loans. I'll call the banks."

"No, don't," Alvarez said. "Hang on. Do not notify anyone. There are steps we must take."

Charlotte stepped back, shaking her head, watching it all unfold in disbelief. The detectives made calls, first alerting Lieutenant Weaver, setting off a major response, with Lonza and Grimes among the first to arrive.

"We have strategic procedures for a kidnap ransom demand," Lonza told the family as a steady flow of investigators began filling the condo.

Like forces in a military operation, they came, setting up laptops, forensic gear and equipment. The air filled with crackling radios and the din of several phone conversations as detectives coordinated with other investigators across the city. The activity gave Corina a degree of assurance. Here were her archangels, her warriors in battle against the unseen forces that had stolen Gabriel.

They moved quickly, fingerprinting Nora, Marty and Gil. Then, taking statements, the detectives pressed them for details on the teddy bear, creating a timeline to establish how the toy had arrived at Newslead and ultimately ended up in Corina's hands.

Crime scene analysts worked on the stuffed toy, meticulously combing its fur for any trace evidence, processing the card for latents and DNA. Using new portable equipment, they x-rayed it to determine if any devices—a camera, tracker, or another digital item—had been implanted in the toy.

They processed the barcode on the toy's tag, aiming to determine point of distribution and sale. A call was made to the manufacturer.

Across Manhattan, more investigators had converged on Newslead, immediately conducting interviews, then studying phones, electronic records and security video to determine when the teddy bear arrived and who had brought it.

It had been ninety minutes since the QR code was scanned.

"Most crypto crime transactions can be tracked," Carter Dawson, an FBI agent, said. "But there can be challenges because the players can remain anonymous on networks that blur communication between the transaction and IP addresses."

"How do you track them then?" Corina asked.

"We follow the money," Dawson said.

Working with the head of security at the family's main bank, Dawson and the other cyber detectives arranged for Robert and Corina to first send the criminal enough coins in cryptocurrency to equal nearly $100,000.

"It should be an amount too big for them to ignore," Dawson said. "You'll send an accompanying note, saying you're pulling the total together as fast as you can. But you're unsure how the transactions work and wanted to start a flow of currency as a sign of good faith and request them to send you proof of life—a video or photos of Gabriel."

Nodding, Robert's face was taut with concentration. His keyboard clicked as he typed with Corina at his side, both of them staring at the monitor, at their accounts. Following Dawson's directions on cryptocurrency, and with the bank's help, things moved fast.

Corina's nerves pulsed through her in time with Robert's even breathing as he completed the actions required. Setting it all up, he came to the last point and was ready to press Send.

"All set," Robert said.

"Alright, good," Dawson said, then spoke to someone on his phone, saying, "Send it."

Robert tapped the key.

Corina clasped her hands together, entwined her fingers and squeezed until her knuckles whitened. She pressed them to her lips, as if in prayer.

This was hope, hanging by a digital thread to Gabriel.

69

Corina and Robert read the concern on the faces of the agents and detectives in his office, watching them striving to track the transaction on their laptops.

It had been close to half an hour since Robert had sent the bait payment. Dawson, the lead FBI agent, was on his phone, talking quietly with the FBI's Virtual Assets Unit while studying the monitor over the shoulder of an agent.

"Right," Dawson said, "using a mixer."

The agent worked on his laptop, examining his screen while relaying updates to Dawson.

"Encrypted and routed to random nodes on a dark web network," the agent said. "That's expected, but then routed to a VPN, then shotgunned through multiple servers at different locations around the world, generating new addresses. This guy's good."

"Yes, we tried that," Dawson said into his phone. "It's extremely difficult pinpointing the address."

Hope seemed to be fading.

Dawson glanced at Corina and Robert, then at Charlotte standing by the door, arms folded, fighting tears as she turned and left the room.

Dawson resumed concentrating on his phone and the monitor.

"Alright," he said. "We'll try a few other things. We're not done yet."

As the team of cyber experts worked, Corina took a shaky breath, knowing that hope was trailing with each passing second. She felt as if she were swimming underwater watching Robert with the agents and detectives, trying to pull more money together and track the transactions.

She thought of Gabriel's bracelet.

He has to be alive.

Blinking fast, her attention shifted. She didn't know why, but she was wrenched from her thoughts and felt drawn toward the empty office doorway where Charlotte had been standing just a minute earlier.

Where did she go?

70

Rising out of instinct or intuition, a new worry seized Corina, urging her to check on Charlotte.

Looking for her in the living room, Corina overheard a piece of conversation from the forensic analysts about blood on the bracelet. It sent her heart racing and she went to find Lonza.

"Did they find blood?" Corina asked.

"No," Lonza said. "But it's procedure to test for it."

Taking that in with some relief, Corina continued looking for Charlotte. Not seeing her on the sofa, or in the kitchen, she went down the hall to Charlotte's room. It was empty.

Corina texted her but received no response.

Back in the living room, she asked Lonza and Grimes if they'd seen her. No one had, leaving Corina to suspect that she'd slipped out again, unnoticed. She contacted Paulo downstairs at the security desk.

"No, ma'am. I haven't seen Charlotte pass through," he said. "I'll alert you if I do, absolutely."

Corina texted her again.

No response.

Thinking that maybe Charlotte had gone to Joan's place, maybe to get away from the intensity of the ransom operation, Corina grabbed her keys and left.

What if she ran off to see Vince Tarone again?

Waiting for the elevator, she was jolted by a new fear; that Charlotte had misunderstood the detectives discussing blood on Gabriel's bracelet. The bell chimed, and the doors opened to an older man and woman, Shelley and Joe Jacobi, who lived on the 47th floor.

"Oh, Corina!" Shelley embraced her. "We're praying so hard for your family. Charlotte's so distressed."

"Where did you see her?"

"On the elevator," Shelley said. "A minute ago."

"Was she going up or down?"

"Up," Shelley said. "She was so upset."

"We asked if we could do anything," Joe said.

"She said no," Shelley said. "The poor child."

"Thank you." Corina stepped back, allowing the door to close, and jabbed the call button.

A moment later, another elevator car arrived. Corina got in, her gut telling her that Charlotte was on the roof. Sometimes Charlotte went there alone when she was troubled.

Corina pressed the top button marked *SG*, remembering the day the real estate agent first showed it to her and Robert.

"...and I'll take you to the Sky Garden, with its rooftop swimming pool, terrace and L-shaped vegetable garden..."

Now, stepping from the elevator, Corina fished her key card from her pocket as she took the few final stairs up. Scanning her card on the key lock, she opened the door to a rush of wind, distant sirens and a magnificent view of the city in the soft glow of the early twilight. Breezes rippled the pool's surface, but no one was in it. The terrace with its bar, tables and patio chairs looked abandoned. No one was tending the small garden in the southeast corner.

Gusts tumbled across the rooftop.

Pushing hair from her eyes, Corina moved around the elevator cabin to the east side of the roof, and her stomach spasmed with such force, it weakened her knees.

Charlotte was sitting on the lip of the waist-high rooftop wall, her legs hanging down over the edge.

Corina started toward her when Charlotte saw her.

"Don't come closer! I'll do it!"

"Sweetheart, please come down from there. I know you're hurting."

"No!" She turned, looking down at the street, fifty stories below. "Gabriel's dead and it's my fault!"

"No, no, we don't know that! The police don't know that!"

"They found blood on his bracelet!"

"No, you misheard them. They just tested for it. But the ransom is a sign!"

"A sign of what?"

"Hope, honey." Corina inched closer.

Charlotte shook her head wildly. "I'm always screwing up. What's wrong with me?"

"Nothing's wrong with you."

Charlotte gazed at the sea of green, the glory of Central Park, as if imagining herself down there, where it all happened.

"You hate me for losing him, for talking with Vince and not watching Gabriel."

"No, I don't hate you."

"Don't lie, Corina!"

"I was mad at you, at your dad for being away, at myself, at things at my job, at everything. But I don't hate you for what happened. Honey, I need you, your dad needs you—and Gabriel's going to need you when we bring him home."

Corina inched closer as Charlotte shook her head and stared at the breathtaking skyline, a galaxy of twinkling lights. Traffic rumbled below.

"I'm a massive screw-up," Charlotte said. "I lost my brother. I can't be a good daughter, or big sister. Maybe I saw a woman watching us, but maybe no one was watching us. I'm so useless. It's like I'm cursed, like our whole family is cursed. People try to get my dad to break the law, people hate you, tell lies about you, they want you dead, and now they want Gabriel dead, too."

Corina was getting closer.

"The world's not perfect, honey. Life tests us every day."

Charlotte exploded in a sob, tears rolling down her face.

"It just hurts so much, Mom."

"I know, honey. I know. You want to kill this moment, not yourself."

Charlotte adjusted her position, skirting the edge as a jet roared overhead, its engines whining. Corina lunged, getting her arms around Charlotte, pulling her away from the edge, both of them crashing down safely on the solid floor.

"I got you." Corina gasped. "I won't let you go."

Corina kept her arms tight around Charlotte as she sobbed great heaving sobs.

71

SEVERAL BLOCKS FROM Corina Corado's home, working deep into the night at the Central Park Precinct, Officer Bonnie Graham was getting closer to locating a burner phone.

Every legal route had been expedited by Graham's supervisors to gain access to the phone's data through the provider.

Much earlier that day, Clifton Chase, a food delivery worker, had walked into the precinct with a phone number investigators believed could be critical to the Corado case. Graham had sat in on Chase's interview with the detectives, listening as he kept rubbing his hands on his pant legs.

"So, I deliver to a penthouse on Madison. Turns out to be the guy from the news, stuff about search warrants and that missing kid."

A detective showed Chase a photo lineup of eight different mug shots of white men in their forties, including one of Efrem Zyller.

"That's him." Chase tapped Zyller's photo. "The guy gives me a thousand to make one call on my phone. He wanted me to trash the number, but I got it. And I'm thinking later, hey, that's weird. I don't know what he's up to. Whatever it is, I don't need it coming back on me. That's why I'm here giving you the number, the cash, even the tip. I'm telling you to help you find that boy."

Sure, Chase had been nervous, but after running his name and finding nothing, the detectives had pegged him as a stand-up guy. He'd given them records and receipts confirming Zyller's order, delivery and the call Zyller had made. Moreover, Chase's information was timely because the boy's family had received a ransom demand. Some detectives from the precinct had been pulled in to work on the response. For her part, Graham had been tasked to see if Zyller's mystery number on Chase's phone—the number Zyller called—was linked to it.

Now, as she progressed, using information from the service provider, Graham was unable to determine the current location of the phone Zyller had called.

The phone could've been turned off, disabled or tossed.

Graham went deeper into the phone's location history. As she'd done with each piece of data in the Corado case, she analyzed it against the time Gabriel left school with his sister, their path of travel and the pinging of their phones, to when they got separated in the park.

What the…

Graham leaned nearer to her monitor. The data history had the phone pinging at Gabriel's school, Tillmon Parker Rose. Graham triple-checked the date and time. It aligned with the time Gabriel's sister picked him up. Additional pings followed them south and into the park.

The data showed the phone following the children south on West Drive to the spot where they got separated.

It continued pinging south on the Bridle Path—where Gabriel's phone had ceased pinging. The burner phone then exited the park on West 67th Street, where location tracking switched off.

But that was five days ago. Where's the mystery phone now, and will it lead us to the boy?

Graham moved fast, alerting supervisors to the fact that Efrem Zyller had called a burner number tied to the case. The new information was relayed to Lonza, Grimes and the investigators who were still pursuing the ransom through the night.

Then, while Graham worked on retrieving camera footage outside the park to be re-examined against the movement of the mystery phone, detectives were sent to Newslead and Zyller's condo to arrest him in connection with the abduction.

But he was not at Newslead, or his Upper East Side residence.

The NYPD issued an alert, making Zyller the most wanted person in the tristate area.

DAY 6

72

THE SIXTH DAY of Gabriel's disappearance arrived with morning light streaming into Robert Tanner's home office.

The FBI and NYPD cyber experts, who'd worked through the night, had jumped on the mystery phone number.

They needed to determine if it was linked to the cryptocurrency transaction of the ransom demand they were trying to track. Throughout the night they had used a number of tactics.

All had proved futile.

Now they launched a new effort. And this time, they got a pulsing blip.

"There it is." FBI agent Carter Dawson's eyes were fixed on a laptop monitor, on where the burner phone's number had surfaced.

"They must've let their guard down because the phone's now on," an agent said, eyes on his monitor. "Whoever's using the phone is sniffing at the bait money."

73

In a corner of Brooklyn's Greenpoint neighborhood, between a tattoo shop and a store known for pierogies and kielbasa, was a café called the Tranquility Town Coffee House.

It had open beam ceilings, brick walls and Mexican tiled floors with vivid colors. Burlap sacks of beans were stacked at one side of the counter, next to a glass case displaying pastries.

The air held an earthy, roasted aroma.

It was a popular place to meet a friend, read, work or just chill. Not long after opening that morning, nearly every table was occupied. At the front next to the window, sitting alone with her back to the wall, was a woman in her thirties.

She paid little attention to the people coming and going.

Exuding calm, she concentrated on her laptop, occasionally moving her cursor, like a surgeon performing a critical procedure, when an electronic buzzing sounded in her bag.

Curious, she reached for it.

It wasn't her personal phone, but the one she was currently using for work. She'd turned it on in case her client needed to reach her. Their last call hadn't ended well. Looking at it, she saw no caller ID.

Spam, maybe? As it vibrated, she risked answering, keeping her voice low: "Hello?"

"This is Detective Lonza, NYPD."

Disbelieving, the woman's mouth opened slightly.

"Look outside," Lonza said.

The woman saw several unmarked police vehicles, and at least half a dozen uniformed officers approaching on the sidewalk.

"Look at the tables around you," Lonza said.

People sitting near her, casually dressed women and men, began displaying badges on chains and holstered guns.

"After you put your phone down," Lonza said, "slowly place your hands behind your head and weave your fingers together. Do it now."

Swallowing hard, the woman set her phone down and raised her hands. She entwined her fingers and closed her eyes, cursing under her breath as someone lowered her arms behind her back and she was handcuffed.

Across the Hudson River, in Teterboro, New Jersey, the captain and co-pilot began preparations in the cockpit of a long-range private jet, bound for Rabat, Morocco.

The flight hostess set a crystal glass of Irish whiskey, neat, on the tray's cupholder beside Efrem Zyller, the sole passenger. Enjoying the whiskey's honeyed sweetness, he leaned back in his leather seat, glancing out the passenger door. Still open, the stairway was down.

A flash caught Zyller's eye and he paused his second sip.

His first thought attributed the lights to the airport's ground crews, then he distinguished a line of marked and unmarked police vehicles, roaring on the tarmac directly toward the jet, two of them stopping at the nose and blocking the plane.

Doors slammed and six people in FBI raid jackets boarded the sapphire-colored jet with a warrant for Zyller's arrest. The hostess and flight crew were taken into custody and placed into vehicles for questioning.

Inside the cabin, while agents searched every compartment of the aircraft, Zyller was ordered to stand, then was patted down and handcuffed.

"You have the right to remain silent…" an agent began.

Outside, Zyller saw other agents and state troopers surrounding the jet, with some directing ground crew to open the cargo door.

Upon completing Zyller's Miranda warning, the agent glanced to the other agents and cops who'd searched the aircraft. They shook their heads, indicating they'd found nothing inside the cabin. Looking at Zyller, the agent said: "Where is Gabriel Corado?"

"What is this? I've cooperated. I want my attorney."

An FBI radio crackled in the cabin with an update from the cargo bay search: "Negative." The agent turned to Zyller.

"Where is Gabriel Corado?"

"I don't know what you're talking about. I want my attorney. I'm not involved."

"You're very involved, sir. You're on a private jet bound for Morocco, a country that has no extradition agreement with the US."

"I have a villa there."

"You made a call from a delivery man's phone to a burner phone, one that we tracked to being a few feet away from Gabriel Corado before he went missing."

"I don't know what you're—"

The agent held up his phone, showing a photo of the woman arrested earlier at the Brooklyn café.

"A burner phone used by this woman, who is cooperating," the agent said.

The blood drained from Zyller's face.

"So I'll ask you again—where is Gabriel Corado?"

74

DETECTIVE LONZA PRESSED her lips together, studying the new video they'd obtained.

Recorded by the person who'd been following Gabriel, it was chilling.

Charlotte and Gabriel, with his plane, walking along Central Park West, then crossing into the park, moving south among the crowds. Charlotte and Gabriel stop, and he launches his plane. It crashes on a hilltop. He runs out of frame to get it. Charlotte is texting before she appears to turn to the camera, and the video ends. It resumes on the Bridle Path, no one at the moment using the gravel walkway twisting into dense brush—the camera spotting and stopping at an item on the ground.

Gabriel's bracelet.

The video ends, for good this time.

"This aligns with the pings on her phone used to make this video," Officer Bonnie Graham said. "It puts her in the park." Graham replayed it a fifth time for the lead investigators in the observation room at the 19th Precinct.

"This brings us closer than we've ever been," Lonza said.

"I almost can't believe it," Grimes said.

Lonza looked at the suspect through the observation room window. The video had been discovered on her laptop and phone after her arrest at the Tranquility Town Coffee House in Brooklyn. Refusing to answer questions about Gabriel Corado after she'd been read her Miranda rights, the woman told police only one thing: "I want an attorney."

Standing next to Lonza, looking at his phone, Lieutenant Weaver shook his head as he reread the updates.

Abigail Dawn Nash, thirty-four, no previous arrests, no warrants; studied computer science at MIT, criminology at John Jay; a licensed private investigator, employed with big agencies before going solo with ties to Efrem Zyller.

Checks on links to Ivan Beckke, Trayman Herman Shrike and the extortion attempt against Robert Tanner were negative so far. No evidence of Gabriel Corado had been found in Nash's Brooklyn apartment. Still, Nash was undeniably linked to Gabriel's bracelet, and the ransom demand. Additional evidence had been found on her devices.

Grimes ended a call with the FBI, who'd arrested Zyller in New Jersey before he could leave the country. After a quick discussion with Weaver, Grimes and Lonza were ready to interview Nash.

"I don't need to say it, but I will," Weaver said. "This could be our best shot to find the boy."

Abigail Nash had short hair, a spider tattoo on one inner wrist, lightning on the other and a gold double-hoop nose ring.

Her sharp eyes locked onto the detectives.

Entering the stark interview room, Lonza and Grimes sat across the table from Nash and Everett Salinger, her attorney.

"As you were informed after processing, this conversation is being recorded, you're in custody and under Miranda."

"Understood," Salinger said.

"Where's Gabriel Corado?" Grimes said.

"My client has no knowledge of his whereabouts."

"You're serious?" Grimes said.

"Your client is facing kidnapping, extortion and a number of charges that could lock her up for the rest of her life," Lonza said. "The evidence against you is solid. We have you for the crypto ransom demand, we have your video of you following Gabriel in the park and showing his bracelet."

"Here's a sampling of what else we found on your laptop." Grimes turned his tablet to show surveillance-style photos, taken in the time leading up to the abduction: Robert near his office; Corina, leaving Newslead; Charlotte window-shopping with friends and Gabriel being picked up at Tillmon. "You were stalking the family."

"Where is Gabriel?" Lonza asked.

Nash and Salinger said nothing; the only sound in the room was Salinger clicking his pen. A long moment passed, then Nash nodded to Salinger.

"My client is willing to cooperate in exchange for reduced charges."

"No," Lonza said. "No deals, no consideration until we have Gabriel home alive and safe."

"My client has no knowledge of..."

"Stop playing that record," Grimes said.

Salinger nodded to Nash.

"I was working for Efrem Zyller as a private investigator," she said.

"To do what?" Lonza asked.

"I'd been working exclusively for him for a few years. I dug deep into the lives of women who threatened to go public with sexual harassment complaints. I would follow them, family members, at their offices, their homes, wherever they went."

"To what end?" Lonza asked.

"Efrem wanted me to find whatever vulnerabilities he could use and then have me threaten them anonymously. To make it clear that their lives would be ruined if they didn't back off."

"Did it work?" Grimes asked.

Nash paused, looked off, shaking her head slowly with a subtle underpinning of disgust. "Every time.

"He hired me to work on Corina Corado. First, I discovered the old conspiracy claim that Gabriel was not her son and passed it to him. Not sure what he did with that. But what few people know, Efrem is an old friend of Wynne Varden's, so it's a possibility he pushed it over to Wynne, because he wanted to come back at Corado hard."

"What do you mean?"

"I suspect he was the one who floated the rumor Newslead was going to terminate Corado," Nash said. "As for my job, he wanted surveillance on her and her family, details, everything. That's what I was doing. I was in the park, making a recording, when I lost sight of the boy. At the time, I thought his sister had spotted me. But she didn't. I went down the Bridle Path, thinking the boy went that way. That's when I found his bracelet."

"How would you know it was his?" Lonza asked.

"In the course of surveilling people, I often use a telephoto lens to get details."

"So you found it?" Grimes said.

"Yes. I admit to everything I did, but I never took Gabriel Corado."

"Why did you demand a ransom from the family?" Lonza asked.

"I kept the bracelet thinking I could use it for the job. Then things exploded with his disappearance and Efrem panicked, to the point that he not only called off my job, but broke it off with me and refused to pay me."

"Why?"

"He was always slow to pay me. I don't know why. The guy's loaded but slow to pay for dirty work. I warned him it could come back to bite him. Some people think they're untouchable. Maybe he was nervous, distracted. I kept asking for my money. And he kept saying he'd get to it. But it pissed me off. On top of that, he hadn't paid me for the previous job. I was owed. Then, as things heated up with the boy's case, and with Efrem cutting ties with me, I knew I would never see my money. So I used the bracelet to extort the family. And if it came back to Zyller, so be it. He's a creep. I admit to what I did, but I didn't abduct Gabriel."

"Why didn't you come forward to us with the bracelet?" Grimes said. "There's a substantial reward."

Her face reddened, she repositioned herself in her seat, as if uncomfortable, then looked into her hands.

"I was eaten up with anger and greed for a bigger payday."

Taking a moment to weigh Nash's story, Lonza checked her notes.

"If what you say is true, did you see Gabriel on the Bridle Path, or anywhere in the park after he chased after his plane?"

"No."

Grimes called up a map of Central Park on his tablet and asked Nash to show them where she'd discovered Gabriel's bracelet. She pointed to the vicinity of washrooms not far from the entrance at West 67th Street and West Drive in the park.

"Did you see anything concerning Gabriel, anything unusual?" Lonza asked.

Nash shook her head. "A few people here and there, nothing more."

"Did you hear anything?" Lonza asked. "A scream, a cry for help?"

Nash began shaking her head but halted.

"Wait, there was something a little off with a woman."

"What about it?"

"She climbed into a pedicab and it rolled off."

"Was the woman alone?"

"Yes."

"What do you remember of her?" Lonza asked.

"White, medium build, thirties, forties, not sure."

"So, what was off about her?"

"She seemed to be in a hurry."

"In a hurry?"

"Yeah, that's what was off. I was thinking it was strange because she and the driver were not moving casually like tourists, but like with urgency."

"Urgency? Did you see Gabriel with her?"

"No."

"What do you recall about the pedicab driver?" Lonza asked.

"A white guy with a beard and a white ball cap."

"What about his cab?"

"Blue, bright blue, sky blue."

"Plate number or photo?"

"No nothing like that. But it did have a big yellow flower attached to the canopy."

75

A PEDICAB.

It was there all along, right in front of us.

Gritting her teeth, Lonza gave a small fist pump at the potential lead as she and Grimes moved into the observation room.

"A pedicab?" Grimes said to Weaver.

"The park precinct would've canvassed drivers," Weaver said. "I'll call them."

"Maybe something got missed," Grimes said to Lonza. "Nash's story could be BS, but we have to check it out."

Lonza was on her laptop, keyboard clicking. Checking her notes, she grappled with self-reproach at missing the pedicab angle and elation at uncovering it. But she shoved it all aside. They had work to do and they had to do it fast.

"We need to go back to those guys who canvassed pedicab drivers, horse carriage operators and vendors in the park," Lonza said.

"Yeah, we're on it," Weaver said, phone to his ear.

"I'll get on to Consumer and Worker Protection. See what they can do," Grimes said.

The mention of the agency gave Lonza pause and she pressed her palm to her forehead, to coax a vague memory.

"Harvey, do you remember, when the case broke, we were walking by the desk at the Central Park Precinct?"

"Yeah, there were people complaining, someone was— Hold on..."

"A couple was complaining about a pedicab driver overcharging them."

"Yeah."

"I think they said it was a blue one."

"Yeah, I think so, yeah."

"Try to get that complaint."

Lonza glimpsed Nash through the glass. She was being taken back to her holding cell to remain in custody for the charges she faced.

Lonza returned to searching for a specific file on her laptop. She found it in seconds: a video Bonnie Graham had sent her. It was the patchwork of footage from NYPD cameras and the commercial security network capturing Ivan Beckke's truck.

Biting her bottom lip, Lonza played it, watching footage shift from different perspectives showing Beckke's blue Ford F-150.

Lonza's stomach fluttered.

The pedicab in the footage next to Beckke's truck was blue, with a yellow sunflower affixed to the canopy.

The driver was bearded, wearing a white ball cap.

The passenger was in shade, but it was a woman, alone.

"Look at this." Lonza angled her laptop.

"We'll get RTCC to try facial recognition," Weaver said. "We need this enhanced and circulating, now."

76

THE STROBING EMERGENCY lights of the police vehicles blocking Efrem Zyller's jet on the tarmac at Teterboro underscored the gravity of the situation.

Corina watched replays of the news coverage in her living room. Charlotte was beside her, on the sofa, under her favorite quilt. After Corina had gotten her home safely from the roof last night, she comforted her.

"When we get through this," Corina had said softly to her, "we'll get you some help, someone you can talk to, okay? For now, you need to rest."

Charlotte nodded gently.

Now, rubbing Charlotte's leg tenderly, with Robert near, Corina contended with the news—her anger, fears and questions. She wanted to rush to Teterboro, to search the plane, to pound answers from Zyller.

Where is my son?

The live newscast cut to video recorded on a phone by someone on a sidewalk showing a woman in her thirties being arrested.

"...and, just in, a related development," the news anchor said. *"We're learning that an unidentified woman, seen here, has been arrested in Green-*

point, in connection with Gabriel Corado's suspected abduction. We'll bring you more details when we have them..."

Corina went to Robert's office, where agents and detectives were following up on the ransom, and questioned Carter Dawson, the lead FBI agent.

"What's happening with the arrests?"

Dawson hesitated, then said: "We think they're related to the ransom."

"But where's Gabriel? Did they find him? Is he safe?"

"People are in custody—that's all we can tell you."

Corina left, then texted Detective Lonza with questions about Gabriel. She held her phone to her chest, took a breath, then retreated to Gabriel's room.

Her fortress.

It was here she would confront the unimaginable.

He could be dead.

No, I refuse to accept it. But not knowing hurts so much. What horrors has he suffered being away from me?

Again, she surveyed the gifts from friends and strangers on Gabriel's bed, some of the balloons all but flattened now.

God, please help me stay strong.

Going online to check for news updates, Corina soon found herself reading social media posts about her family.

I'm praying for Gabriel, one post said.

Another said, *Can't fathom the pain his family is suffering.*

Then another: *I hope Gabriel is reunited with his mother.*

The next said, *Corado is fake media, who faked her son's disappearance to keep her job as the Queen of Lies.*

Disgust forced Corina to shut her eyes, until her phone vibrated.

Lonza had texted her response.

> Corina, we have no evidence he's been hurt. We're doing everything we can, as fast as we can.

Lonza's words were something. Not great, but something.

Again, Corina held her phone to her chest. Then she returned to the living room, rejoining the others who were watching the news. One of the local New York stations had a crew at the search center.

Against the backdrop of enlarged posters of Gabriel, they were interviewing volunteers for reaction to the latest developments. Corina recognized some of them, including Julie Landon and Cathy Miller.

"The fact police seem to be getting closer," Julie said, "means that we must never give up hope of finding Gabriel."

The camera shifted to Cathy.

"Absolutely," she said. "We want to see Gabriel reunited with his mother."

Drawing comfort from Julie, Cathy, and seeing all the others coming and going to help find Gabriel, touched Corina's heart. She knew where she needed to go.

77

THEY PASSED BY the carousel with its brilliantly colored hand-carved galloping horses and chariots.

"It's the oldest one in the city," Rafe Jarlow said.

At thirty-three, with legs muscled from pumping his pedicab mile after mile like pistons every day, Rafe gave his customers a smooth ride. The tour glided by the Wollman Rink, then the pond, with its serene waters, serenaded with birdsong and the soothing strain of a street musician's sax playing "New York, New York."

Rafe continued over the stone arches of the Gapstow Bridge.

"This bridge appeared in the movie, *Home Alone 2*, and a few others," Rafe said, stopping while his passengers, a man and woman from Auckland, New Zealand, took photos.

Moving along East Drive, a one-way roadway heading north, they passed by the Central Park Zoo. Rafe had just started saying that the zoo first opened in the eighteen hundreds when his jaw dropped.

A police car, lights blazing, siren yelping, was roaring the wrong way on the road, directly toward his pedicab. A second marked NYPD SUV, its lights strobing, followed by an unmarked car, came up from behind, trapping Rafe's pedicab.

His brakes creaked as he stopped.

Using their front doors as shields, two uniformed cops, guns aimed at Rafe, ordered him to get on the ground.

"On your stomach with your hands behind your head now!"

The officers from behind ordered the shocked passengers out of the seat, separating them from Rafe, who was handcuffed as police radio transmissions spilled into the air. Lonza and Grimes left their unmarked SUV, tugging on gloves, observing as the officers patted Rafe down, got his ID and confirmed it with Central.

"Where's the boy?" Grimes asked.

"What boy?" Rafe said.

The detectives went to his pedicab, bright blue with a large yellow flower attached to the canopy. The passenger compartment was wide enough for three people. They lifted the bench seat, found a shallow tray with tools and rags. They lifted the tray, examining the deeper underseat storage.

Large enough to fit a child.

Grimes seized Rafe's phone from his pocket and Lonza read Rafe his rights.

Radios crackled as more units arrived to process Rafe's phone and pedicab. Taking stock of the scene, he turned to Lonza, who'd gotten within inches of his face.

"Where's the woman? Has she got the boy?" she asked.

Shaking his head, Rafe Jarlow remained silent as Lonza and Grimes got him into the back of their car and took him to the 19th Precinct.

Along the way, Jarlow, handcuffs clinking in the back, said one thing.

"There is no boy."

78

Gabriel was here.

The instant Corina entered the search center, he was smiling at her from the life-size posters on the walls.

She wanted to reach for him.

But Robert squeezed her hand and she took a deep breath, grappling with the emotions surging inside her as she surveyed the room.

Dozens of people were busy at tables, and on laptops. Some were huddled, pointing to sections of enlarged maps on large rolling boards while talking into walkie-talkies. Flat-screen TVs were tuned to all-news networks. The activity was encouraging.

In all the time Gabriel had been missing, Corina had not yet visited the center, unlike Robert and Charlotte, who had come by in the days before to acknowledge the volunteers. She knew a few faces, but most were strangers.

"Hello." A woman sitting at the first table smiled. "If you've come to help, we'll start by getting you signed in," she said, then recognition dawned. "Oh, Corina, Robert!"

"We wanted to thank everyone," Corina said.

A few others came to them in a flurry of hugs and handshakes.

Vanessa Chang, a volunteer search organizer, announced their arrival, getting everyone's attention, and Corina spoke to the room.

"Please know how grateful we are for you pausing your lives and giving your time to help us find Gabriel. You'll never know how much it means to us. You've touched us so deeply. Thank you."

A walkie-talkie was passed to Corina, and she broadcast her thanks to those who were out searching.

The volunteers at the center had come from everywhere, Vanessa told Corina. She explained what everyone at the center was doing, how they were coordinating efforts with police to meticulously search the park.

They were putting up more posters with Gabriel's picture near the park and across the city and in the subway system. Vanessa showed Corina the interactive website they'd created, which catalogued, detailed and updated all of their actions. They had also assigned people to monitor news and social media. While many people were using their own laptops and phones, other resources had been donated by local organizations and businesses.

Moving with Vanessa from table to table, seeing and hearing all that was being done, overwhelmed Corina, and she hugged volunteers.

"Thank you, thank you so much," she said, her voice cracking. "I can never repay you for all you're doing for Gabriel, for us."

A woman approached and clasped her hand.

"Hello, Corina. Julie Landon, from Teaneck. You interviewed me when my son was missing."

"Yes, Logan. And he was located. How's he doing?"

"Good, everything is good. Corina, I'm here to help you find Gabriel, and to tell you not to give up hope."

"I saw the gift and the message you sent. It was so thoughtful. Thank you, Julie."

Then a middle-aged man with a kind face placed his hand on Corina's shoulder.

"Barry Keeler," he said. "Retired veteran. We'll keep searching until we find Gabriel. We won't give up."

His words gave Corina hope as she moved to a spot with a chair, a closed laptop, an empty ceramic mug and a snack pack of vanilla cookies.

"This is Cathy Miller's workspace. She tracks places that we've canvassed. But Julie's helping with that right now," Vanessa said. "Cathy was here today but had to leave for a doctor's appointment. I'm sure she would've wanted to see you."

"Yes, I interviewed her once. She's sent us messages of support." Corina nodded, registering the memory about Cathy's ten-year-old son, Burke, who went missing in rural Pennsylvania and had not yet been found.

"Cathy told me how you were so kind to her," Vanessa said. "And she's pouring her heart into helping."

"I'm very touched by everyone's generosity and I'm sorry I missed her."

They moved along, with Corina thanking people, and then came to another empty chair.

"Oh, Lee usually sits here. He logs updates from our teams on the subways."

"Yes, I reported on Lee's case, too."

"Lee would've liked to have been here. Sadly, he's at a funeral today."

"I'm sorry to hear that, and I'm sorry I missed him."

Corina took another breath.

She was glad that she had come to the center.

People had their own lives to live, yet they stopped them to help find Gabriel. The depth of their unselfish, unwavering humanity lifted her heart. She drew strength from the exhausting, unyielding support they were giving her and her family.

"Oh my God, they're doing it again!"

Attention shifted to the volunteer, standing in front of one of the TV screens, turning up the sound, staring at the "Breaking News" banner of the ReLOX Broadcasting Network.

A news anchor was joined at the desk by Vonn Bittner.

"The disturbing case of Corina Corado's missing son, Gabriel, continues to raise many troubling questions about Corado's activities in Central America," Bittner said. *"For years, Corado's maintained that she rescued a baby from the arms of its dying mother..."*

Again, ReLOX ran a series of photos, then Bittner said, *"We obtained security footage from a small, Nicaraguan airport."* The footage, grainy, but clear enough, rolled, showing Corina in a terminal, bag over her shoulder, towing a carry-on suitcase and holding a baby in her free arm. The footage was date- and time-stamped.

"Our question," Bittner said. *"Is this video of Corado fleeing the country six years ago with the baby she stole from its mother? We may not yet know the truth, but one by one we are connecting the dots."*

The report ended and went to a commercial for a product to soothe upset stomachs.

"I can't believe it," a volunteer said. "ReLOX is horrible."

All eyes turned to Corina, who was shaking her head while holding it between her hands. Robert, his jawline pulsing, put his arm around her just as someone called out.

"Our people in the park say there's been an arrest near the zoo and it could be related!"

Corina groaned, pushing her face into Robert's chest. Tightening his hold, Robert turned to the woman who'd alerted them.

"Tell us where, exactly."

79

"WHERE'S THE BOY?"

"The boy?" Rafe Jarlow looked at Lonza, then Grimes. "I don't know what you're talking about."

"We've got a witness who puts you in the spot where Gabriel Corado disappeared," Grimes said. "They identified you and your rig, which we're processing now, along with your apartment and your phone."

"Rafe," Lonza said, "you say you don't need a lawyer because you have nothing to hide."

"That's right." Jarlow lifted his chin. "In fact, you should be thanking me, because I'm a hero."

His handcuffs jingled when he scratched his nose.

Lonza and Grimes appraised him, sitting across from them in the interview room at the 19th: his pierced nostril, his ponytail, and his patchy beard covering his pocked face. Jarlow's record was pretty clean, except for a misdemeanor assault charge a year ago. He'd gotten into a fight with two other drivers who mocked him because Jarlow tried to explain to them that the earth is flat and there's a global conspiracy by airlines and scientists to convince everyone it's round. The charge was eventually dropped, but it was a head shaker, giving Lonza and Grimes some insight as to what they were dealing with.

Rafe Jarlow's arrest happened fast, arising from facial recognition, recanvassing of pedicab drivers in Central Park and help with pedicab licensing information from the city agency. That all led to a name and phone number, enabling them to pinpoint Rafe Jarlow's location near the zoo.

"Tell us why you're a hero," Lonza said.

"Because I helped rescue a child."

Grimes showed him Gabriel's picture. "This child?"

"No, not him. That kid's face is everywhere. He's part of some kind of publicity stunt," Jarlow said.

Lonza and Grimes let a moment of silence pass when Rafe narrowed his eyes at them, as if mentally prying the lid off a jar holding the truth.

"You arrested me because the evil husband complained, didn't he?"

"The evil husband?" Grimes said. "Who's that?"

"The woman's husband. That's what this is about," Rafe said. "It's the husband. She told me all about him and what happened. He's an evil man, a vile dude."

"We need you to fill in some blanks here. Who is 'she'?" Grimes said.

"The wife."

"Why don't you tell us about the evil husband and how you came to rescue a child," Lonza said. "It might help us understand why you're a hero, Rafe."

He scratched at his beard, to aid in his decision.

"Alright. Seems fair. And you seem okay, despite being cops. So, a few months back, I get a passenger, a woman. Says she's from Florida. She's alone and she starts to cry. I ask her what's wrong. She starts telling me about her life. I'm like a bartender, people tell me their woes. She says her husband got caught up in one of those pedophile rings, you know the one all those Satan-loving Hollywood phonies are running?"

"Go ahead," Lonza said.

"She asked me if I'd heard of these pedo rings, and I said sure have—I said, believers like us, we gotta destroy them. Then she came back to me every few days, telling me more each tour. She says her husband started abusing their daughter online for the ring, and when she challenged him on it, he beat her. She tried to press charges, but, well, the ring's got people in the courts, you know? Then he took their daughter and fled here.

"It took time, but she found them and learned that he regularly takes the girl to the park. She had a plan to rescue her and she begged me to help, offered me five hundred. But to rescue a kid from a pedophile? I said I would do it for free."

"Why not call police?" Lonza said.

"She said the ring has people in the NYPD, too. I'm not saying that includes you. But that's what she said."

"And you believed every word this stranger told you?" Lonza said.

"Every word."

"Why?" Grimes asked.

"It all made sense to me, and she was so honest."

"So, what was her rescue plan?" Grimes asked.

"She watched for them every day, ready to alert me when she made her move."

"How did it go down?" Grimes asked.

"On that day, she sent me an urgent message. She'd spotted them on the west side, near the West 72nd entrance and told me to get in the area. I stopped picking up new customers and let her know when I was close. Then she said they were walking south on West Drive and she was following, waiting for her chance. She told me to park behind the bathrooms near West 67th and wait. I'm there, almost hidden in the bushes.

"Then it happened, very fast. She came down the Bridle Path with her daughter. I maybe heard the kid kinda whimpering, and the woman was saying to the kid, 'Don't look back, it's not safe.' They came through the bushes and we got her to hide under the seat and we left. I don't think anyone was there. It was very fast, looked like a game of hide-and-seek."

"Did you see this girl?"

"No, her hoodie was up and tied tight. The woman told me to move fast before 'the bad people,' she called them, caught up to us. We got going pretty good. I got onto 59th Street, moved by Fifth

Avenue, to Park Avenue. I think she set her kid's phone to turn on in a few minutes after she shut it off and she tossed it in a truck around there somewhere. To throw the father off our trail. The kid was good at hiding and so quiet.

"The woman told me where she wanted to go and I dropped them off on Lexington, maybe around 53rd. The building had scaffolding, construction, all around. I went to the alley. They got out—I left and I never saw them again."

"Was there anyone else in the alley waiting?" Grimes said. "Or a vehicle?"

"Nope."

"Did you get a name of the woman?"

"Emma Parker."

"A picture?"

"No, but she said she lived in the Bronx and had a job waitressing."

"Where?"

Rafe shrugged.

At that moment, Lonza's and Grimes's phones vibrated with a text from the analysts. It contained their early preliminary findings on trace evidence after processing Rafe Jarlow's pedicab and residence. No trace of Gabriel Corado had been discovered so far in Jarlow's apartment in Bushwick. But, the message said, hair found in the pedicab's underseat storage was consistent with Gabriel Corado's. And fibers recovered there were consistent with the fabric of his clothes.

"Look," Rafe said. "I told you all I know. I'm glad we rescued the girl from her evil father, who should be in jail. Guess that makes me a hero, though, right?"

"Wrong," Lonza said.

80

GASPING INTO WALKIE-TALKIES, two volunteers from the search center trotted to the park with Corina and Robert.

They guided them along East Drive to where a pedicab driver had been arrested. They came to two women in their twenties, volunteer searchers, waiting near a bench. But by the time Corina and Robert arrived, there was no sign an arrest had taken place.

"It's over," Brittaney, one of the volunteers, said. "Two joggers told us that a pedicab driver was arrested, and his bike taken. There were rumors among the bystanders that it was about Gabriel, but police wouldn't say."

"Anyone see him, or a child, when this happened?" Robert asked.

"I don't think so."

"Anyone record the arrest?" Corina asked.

"We haven't found anyone who did."

Corina called Lonza, but it went to voicemail. Scanning the area, seeing nothing, she took a breath.

The weight of events continued pushing down on Corina after they returned home.

Charlotte was now asleep on the sofa, and seeing her resurrected images of her on the roof for Corina, compounding their tragedy.

We almost lost you.

Corina lowered herself. She caressed Charlotte's hair and kissed her head.

We won't let go. We'll never give up.

She thanked Joan for staying with Charlotte as Robert walked her to their door. The FBI agents and NYPD cyber experts, having chased down the ransom suspect, had left. And the two remaining on-duty detectives provided little new information.

Not knowing whether they were any closer to finding Gabriel—*if he's dead or alive*—was unbearable for Corina.

As Robert talked with the detectives, she studied her phone. Her messages to Lonza and Grimes went unanswered as she was flooded with news media requests.

What is your reaction to Efrem Zyller's arrest? Lina Lombardo with the *Daily News* asked.

Can you confirm there was a ransom demand? Helen Yee from Reuters asked.

Would you agree to an on-camera interview? Chuck Rustig, a producer at NBC news, asked.

We're seeking your response to the allegations made by the ReLOX Broadcasting Network, that you stole Gabriel, Brooke Browne, a local TV reporter, asked.

The ransom, the arrests, the conspiracies, the lies, accusations and allegations—the hunt to find Gabriel—continued spinning in a soul-crushing whirlwind, and Corina had no answers. Flailing in waves of helplessness, she refused to surrender.

She went to Gabriel's room.

Again, she took up the gifts and cards they'd received. She opened her laptop, read the heartfelt messages, reflected on the stories she'd done on families of murdered or missing children, while also embracing the support from the volunteers at the center. Most had endured their own tragedies.

Good people, all of them so kind, with their words and gifts.

How they'd found it in their hearts to give of themselves warmed Corina. She continued looking over it all, until a tiny ping of concern surfaced in her mind, like a pinprick of light flickering in a faraway corner of the night sky.

And her warmth froze.

Corina couldn't immediately determine what it was exactly, but something wasn't right, something slightly out of place that she'd overlooked when the detectives asked her to review her older stories, and threats, for possible leads.

Her keyboard clicking, she went to archived stories, hers and those done by others. Then she went to recent reports concerning the search for Gabriel.

There was Cathy Miller in the search center, in a shot behind Lee Farnley and Julie Landon while they were being interviewed by a New York City news team. In another report, Cathy, being interviewed in the search center, echoed Julie's support, saying: "We want to see Gabriel reunited with his mother."

"Gabriel reunited with his mother."

Something about that phrase. Corina blazed through older stories, here was one of conspiracy believers demonstrating in front of Newslead after her interview with the Ritzzkels. Studying it this time, Corina examined the words on their placards. **QUEEN OF LIES**, **FAKE NEWS**, **CORADO'S LIFE IS A LIE**.

Corina's mind raced.

Yes, she remembered. This was around the time the Ritzzkels started spreading the conspiracy that she had stolen a baby from the woman dying in Nicaragua.

Typing on her keyboard, she called up another old story. This one showed conspiracy believers outside the court in support of Trayman Herman Shrike, the man bent on killing her. Again, Corina looked closely at their placards.

CORADO SHOULD BE ON TRIAL.

LOCK HER UP.

QUEEN OF LIES.

Then, there it was, partially obscured, a placard. This time Corina slowed the footage, to a frame-a-second mode, until she could read the sign.

REUNITE THE BOY WITH HIS MOTHER.

Corina enlarged a paused frame of the woman holding the "Reunite" sign and her hand flew to her mouth.

It's Cathy Miller!

This is all wrong.

That phrase on the sign nearly matched: *Gabriel reunited with his mother.* Corina, turned to fumble through the stuffed toys, finding a teddy bear attached to a deflated balloon with the word *BELIEVE.* The attached message: *"Always believe, Gabriel will be reunited with his mother."*

Icy fear coiled up Corina's spine.

I interviewed Cathy when I profiled the support group in the basement of a Brooklyn church. Cathy was a brokenhearted, anguished woman, so grateful to have attention on her child's case. But was that all before she fell in with Greeters of the Rising Storm? Did her trauma consume her, leading her to believe that I stole a child and illegally adopted him? Was that pull so strong that she ended up supporting the man who wanted to kill me?

Corina then remembered the cookies at Cathy's workspace in the support center.

Vanilla crème.

Gabriel's favorite.

She groaned.

Had Cathy been so consumed that she'd taken extreme action?

Is it Cathy?

No, this can't be.

Fighting her tears and shaking her head, Corina took a breath.

Again, her fingers blurred on her keyboard, digging back in her story files, back to when she'd interviewed Cathy.

She found the card.

To assist producers, camera and sound crews, every story had an assignment card requiring all details for the story, like names, phone numbers, emails.

And addresses.

Corina had Cathy Miller's address.

81

Siren blaring as they got on the Cross Bronx Expressway, Grimes steered their SUV through traffic.

They blew by cars and trucks as Lonza scrutinized the face filling her phone.

Hedra Leanna Cowell, aged thirty-seven.

Faint lines were etched above her upper lip, and there were crow's feet around her eyes. They were dark blue, like a wild mountain river. It made her appear as if she were lost, searching urgently for something unattainable, Lonza thought.

A transmission spilled from the radio advising them that the Emergency Service Unit was on its way. Grimes tapped his fist gently on the wheel.

"It's coming together now, Vicky."

Lonza nodded but with a little less certainty, because the investigation had moved so fast to reach this crucial point. After questioning Rafe Jarlow, the detectives had used his information to invoke exigent circumstances. Warrants were accelerated, enabling police to search Jarlow's phone. Aided by his service provider, they extracted the number of the woman who'd called him around the time Gabriel Corado disappeared.

They identified the woman's carrier, which led to her name and address.

Hedra Leanna Cowell lived in the Bronx.

She came up for passing bad checks when they ran her name through NCIC to check for criminal history. They discovered she'd used several aliases, one of them being Cathy Miller. They also learned that while residing in Pennsylvania several years prior, she'd reported Burke, her ten-year-old son, missing.

Now, as Lonza, Grimes and more than a dozen units moved on the address, Lieutenant Weaver called Lonza, who'd covered her free ear to muffle the siren.

"We've got Cathy Miller listed as a volunteer at the search center," he said. "Our people went to the center and Miller was not there."

"What about her phone? Are we getting any pings?"

"None so far, still working on it."

"Volunteering at the center is smart. It would get her closer to everything."

After Weaver's call, Lonza, reviewing her information, saw that Miller had been born in Calgary, Alberta, Canada. Lonza made an urgent request for Canadian authorities to check her for any criminal history in Canada.

While waiting, she saw Corina Corado had sent her messages, but Lonza hadn't read them. This wasn't the time to answer; Lonza had to focus on their pursuit. It didn't take long before Central heard back on the Canadian query.

"Comes back clean," said the operator at Central. "No arrests, no wants, no warrants. Neither Cowell nor her Miller alias came up in the Canadian system."

Looking ahead as Grimes navigated around a FedEx truck, Lonza's thoughts shot back over the past five days, and how their investigation had been a maze, a complex path of dead ends and leads.

She opened Gabriel's photo.

Are we going to find you?

Are we too late?

82

Corina's heart beat faster.

The address brought them to a four-story brick building situated at the edge of Morris Park.

Robert paid their taxi driver and negotiated with him to wait; then he and Corina approached the entrance, taking stock of the exterior walls, laced with grime and graffiti.

"I think we should try police again," Robert said when they reached the dented metal front door.

Corina's body had tensed, as if she wanted to break the door down.

"Corina—" Robert pulled her from her thoughts. "Try Lonza one more time, just to be sure."

Nearly groaning under her breath, she called, and to her surprise, the detective answered.

"Corina, this isn't a good time—we're on to something."

"I have a name for you. Someone I interviewed, a conspiracy believer whose child is missing."

In the seconds that Lonza hesitated, Corina heard the siren as it matched the scream rising in her heart.

"Give me the name, Corina."

"Cathy Miller."

Lonza let another moment pass before she said, "We have that name."

"Cathy Miller? You have her name?"

"Yes, but I have to go."

"Wait, you can't— Where are you? What about Gabriel? Did you find him? We have an address, too. Did you arrest her? Did you find him?"

"Corina, please keep everything confidential. That's all I can say. I'm sorry, I have to go."

Corina lowered her phone, covering her mouth with her free hand as Robert searched her eyes.

"They know?" he asked.

She nodded, then gasped. "But they won't say if they found him. And there's no sign of police here. Oh, Robert. Is this the wrong address?"

"Hello, excuse me?" a voice from the building called to them.

Corina and Robert found the source. A woman behind the security bars of an open window on the second floor.

"Yes?" Robert said as they looked up.

"I heard you talking. Are you here for Cathy Miller?"

"Yes," Corina said. "Who are you?"

"Building super. Are you bill collectors?"

"No, but we need to see her."

"Sorry, Miller ain't here and she owes me rent money."

"You know where she went?"

"No idea. She kinda left in a hurry."

"Do you know if she had any children with her?"

"No, she didn't. Are you Children's Services?"

"No. We've got business with her," Robert said. "We'd like to see her apartment. Could you let us in, if we paid you a little toward the rent? In cash?"

The woman considered the offer.

"Wait there," she said.

A moment later, the metal door opened and the woman let them in. She had a taut, leathery face and was wearing cargo pants and a denim shirt. Her rolled sleeves revealed a myriad tapestry of colorful tattoos. She held out her palm and said: "Five hundred. Cash."

Between them, Corina and Robert had enough.

Eyeing Corina, she said, "You look familiar." Folding the bills, shoving them into her pocket, she added, "Do you make TV commercials?"

"Something like that."

"Huh. And what's your business with Cathy Miller?"

"It's personal at the moment." Corina's tension was brimming.

"Huh." The woman shrugged. "Whatever floats your boat is what I say. Miller's a bit of a weirdo, but this is New York."

"Why do you say that?" Robert asked.

"Always telling me about some great awakening, like she's in some cult."

"Can we see her place now?" Corina could barely contain her fear.

"It's on the third."

The stairway leading to the upper floors was poorly lit, the worn steps creaking. On the third floor, they were hit with a musty smell. The hallway was narrow, the walls scuffed.

One of the woman's pockets jingled as she fished out keys and stopped at unit #303.

"It's a two-bedroom," she said, inserting the key and opening the door.

They were welcomed by a waft of stale air.

They entered through the kitchen. Small, with the basics: a stove, refrigerator and microwave. The counter was bare. Robert opened the fridge, which held a milk jug and a pizza box. He closed it. There was a small dining area off the kitchen.

To freshen the place, the super went to a window. It was stuck, but her grunting and cursing got it open and sounds of the street flowed in.

The living room seemed barely able to contain the torn sofa and chair, facing the TV standing on the shelf. The paint on the beige walls had blistered and peeled in places. Around the corner, the bathroom—a plain tub and shower, toilet, sink and medicine cabinet.

The first bedroom had a plain double bed that was neatly made. Empty hangers in the small closet. Drawers of the dresser were open and empty. Robert lowered himself on the far side, then held up copies of the *Daily News* and *Post*, folded to stories about Gabriel.

They moved to the second bedroom.

The door was shut. The super tried it but it wouldn't budge. Gripping the knob, she thrust her shoulder into the door and it opened.

The rank air was the first thing they noticed.

A mattress, pillow and blanket were on the floor.

In the instant she surveyed the room, Corina's pulse hammered.

A long chain affixed to the leather straps of a harness, with small steel locks, was connected to a steel loop screwed into the closet's wood frame.

"Holy cow!" the super said. "I can't believe she did this. We have a no-pet policy!"

Corina spotted an opened package of vanilla cookies, near the mattress. *Gabriel's favorite.* Then she saw a small bundle of fabric heaped in the corner. She flew to it, recognizing Gabriel's blue plaid short-sleeved shirt, his tan shorts, white socks…but no shoes. No sign of any adidas Superstars.

Corina fell to her knees, pressing the clothes to her face.

"He was here! She had Gabriel here!"

83

It was a rented single-story house in a blue-collar neighborhood at a rough fringe of the Unionport section of the Bronx.

Lonza observed it through binoculars from the perimeter.

Rolling the focusing thumbwheel, she saw the warped vinyl siding, the tiny front lawn enclosed by a chain link fence. A sudden gust sent a discarded take-out bag skipping down the empty, narrow driveway.

The street was deserted, then a dark shadow flashed.

Lonza spotted heavily armed members of ESU moving in silence, taking positions near neighboring porches, parked cars and corners of the target house as they crept closer.

Police had already evacuated houses that were in the line of fire. And they'd established an outer perimeter, stopping anyone from entering the hot zone. Down the block a jogger had been turned away, while at the opposite end, a woman pushing a stroller was escorted to a safe detour.

A long moment passed before whispered transmissions were exchanged among the team and the ESU commander, who gave the green light.

A flashbang grenade shattered a window, exploding with a lightning burst and a deafening crack. The back and front doors were breached, and team members stormed in, raking their guns in every direction. Clearing every room in seconds, confirming the house was empty.

In fact, it was abandoned, a foreclosure.

The address Cathy Miller had given the search center, the one which matched her driver's license, which police considered her most recent, was in fact, an invalid address.

Her face stricken, Lonza cursed under her breath.

Grimes cursed out loud.

Several times.

Gripping her phone, Lonza alerted Lieutenant Weaver. "We struck out, here. Fake address."

"We're working on another address," he said. "Our BOLO has gone state-wide, and we're getting it on NCIC."

Lonza hung up, frustrated because she believed they were close. Her phone vibrated and rang.

It was Corina Corado again.

Lonza pursed her lips, unsure if she was up to talking to her. Then remembering their last call, that Corina had Miller's name and address, realization dawned as she answered.

Before Lonza got her phone to her ear, Corina was already shouting.

"Gabriel was here! I'm holding his clothes! Why aren't you here?"

84

Small eyes flitted from side to side from under the ball cap's brim.

The hat was covered by the tightly drawn hood of a loose-fitting hoodie as the child held the woman's hand.

They took their place in line at the counter for Aunt Ida's Burgers in the food court of Empire Skies Truck Plaza, on Interstate 81, at the southern edge of Watertown, New York.

They were among dozens of people—families, travelers and truckers—filling the court. The plaza offered an arcade, a grocery store, a twenty-four-hour diner, fast-food outlets and an open dining area with a couple of muted TVs suspended overhead.

Tess Eastman continued watching the woman and the child when they entered the food court. Tess was standing a few feet away, in line for Vegan Land O' Plenty, next to Aunt Ida's. The court was chaotic with clattering plates, the hum of conversations and the strains of "Take Me Home, Country Roads," mixed with the occasional roar outside of a big rig pulling out or wheeling in.

A few minutes earlier, after placing her order, Tess had glanced up at one of the muted TVs to an update on Gabriel Corado, the boy still missing from Central Park. It had been several days.

What a heartbreaking story, Tess thought.

While waiting, she debated eating in the court, or getting her order to go. She needed to get to Evans Mills, ten miles away, where the new Beth-Anne Bridger, Jake Gyllenhaal movie was being made. Tess had been called back to the production, where she was an assistant continuity supervisor. Her job was to make sure every aspect of every shot matched and was consistent, things like wardrobe, props, hair and makeup.

She had a professional eye for detail.

Thinking about the Corado case, Tess recalled word on the set that Beth-Anne Bridger was friends with Corina Corado, the boy's mother, who was a network journalist. People on set said the case was weighing on Beth-Anne, which had resulted in needing to reshoot more scenes than usual.

Now, moving up in line, Tess glanced again at the child and woman.

The oversized hoodie and loose-fitting jeans the child was wearing made it tough for Tess to determine whether she was seeing a boy or a girl. She estimated their age to be seven, maybe younger.

At that moment, almost as if sensing Tess staring, the child turned to look at her.

A boy, definitely a boy, Tess thought.

The woman, unaware, was turned away, talking quietly on her phone.

The boy's eyes widened slightly, imploringly, almost tearing up.

Something twigged in Tess.

My God, it can't be!

As she continued staring, an alarm sounded in the back of her mind. She was overcome with a powerful and sudden sensation to act.

Now, because I'll never have this chance again.

Tess crouched to his level, inching closer to the boy.

"Gabriel?" she whispered.

The boy reacted with a slight spasm that jerked his arm and hand.

"Hey!" The woman glared at Tess, raising her voice. "Leave my child alone!"

Heads turned.

"Stop bothering my child!"

Eyes went to Tess. Suddenly overwhelmed with a mix of panicked confusion, she backed off.

"Sorry, wrong person, I'm sorry."

"Get away from us!" Putting her arm protectively around the boy, the woman nudged him away. "Stay away from us!"

As the woman swept toward the door, the boy looked back at Tess, his eyes finding hers, beseeching her in silence before vanishing in the bustle.

85

NEARLY TROTTING, they reached their Toyota SUV in the truck plaza's parking lot.

The woman buckled the boy into a booster seat in the back. After buckling her own seat belt, she started the engine and headed out. While navigating, she turned to his frightened face.

"Don't worry, it's going to be alright."

The boy looked out the window as they passed big rigs.

"You did good back there, staying quiet with that creepy stranger." The woman, who'd called herself Cathy, signaled and the indicator clicked softly as she checked traffic in both directions. "I told you there would be dangerous situations. People would try to stop us, that we'd have to be careful. You did a good job, staying quiet like I told you."

"I'm still hungry."

"I know. I'm sorry we had to leave. We'll get some food soon. Promise."

Cathy guided their vehicle along the road, nearing the ramps for Interstate 81.

"When I think of all you've been through, all these years." Blinking back tears, Cathy found his face in the rearview mirror. "All the lies about you, about everything. I can't imagine what it's been like. I'm sorry for these past days. It's taken longer than I thought, but we're almost there, okay?"

Still not fully understanding, the boy could only nod.

"I'm going to reunite you with your mother." Cathy looked at him. "We've got people who're helping us, okay? No matter what happens, I will reunite you with your mom."

Approaching the overpass for I-81, they came to the ramp signs—one headed south toward New York City, the other north, to Canada.

Cathy switched on the SUV's turn signal and it clicked, like a heartbeat.

86

Inside the Empire Skies Truck Plaza, Tess Eastman wanted to escape the ripple of stares the woman's rebuke had caused.

Picking up her order, she searched a far section of the dining room hoping to retreat to an isolated table. At that moment, out the window, she glimpsed the woman and boy in the truck plaza's lot. They were hurrying, and they'd left their place in line without getting food.

The boy's face, his reaction to the name Gabriel, his ill-fitting clothes. Something's not right about this. What if I'm not mistaken? What if that is Gabriel Corado and I just shrugged it off?

That's when Tess heard her late grandmother's advice: it's always wise to err on the side of caution.

Leaving her food on a table, Tess rushed for the door.

Outside, she weaved around cars and trucks to follow them. But by the time she reached their section, she saw them pulling away in a white SUV.

Tess made her way between the big rigs while fumbling for her phone, managing to take several pictures before the SUV disappeared toward the interstate.

Turning back, Tess was catching her breath, trying to think of her next step, when she spotted the back end of a Dodge, dark blue with gold letters across the rear that said: STATE POLICE.

Back in the food court, scanning the tables, Tess saw a state trooper at a table and hurried over to her.

87

YELLOW CRIME SCENE tape cordoned off the brick apartment building in Morris Park, jouncing in the breeze.

Bystanders had gathered at the edge near police vehicles. Press vans arrived. News crews grabbed microphones, hefted cameras onto shoulders, as police radio transmissions crackled, underscoring the activity.

A canine team probed the building's perimeter, and cops were checking dumpsters. Detectives were interviewing the building's superintendent and other residents. Two officers were on the roof; others had started a preliminary search of a small park nearby while children watched.

After parking, Lonza and Grimes badged their way toward the front of the building. They lifted the tape and ducked under, but they were stopped from behind by two plainclothes detectives.

The first one said: "Sarducci and Kortese, with the 49th. You the leads?"

"Yeah, I'm Grimes, and this is Lonza."

"Come with us," Sarducci said.

They took them aside to where emergency vehicles and uniformed officers formed a police island of privacy, shielding Corina and Robert, who turned to Lonza and Grimes.

"Gabriel was here!" Corina was still gripping her son's socks, shirt and shorts, showing them to Lonza as she stepped forward. "She had Gabriel here!"

"I know, I know," Lonza said.

"We need Corina to let us have the items," a gloved detective with the Crime Scene Unit said. "It's evidence."

Scrutinizing the small bundle Corina was holding, Lonza said gently, "Okay, now we need you to give these things to the detective here."

Grimes's phone rang, and he turned to answer.

Corina said: "I interviewed her years ago in a support group. Her son is missing. And now, now—she sent me gifts, sent me messages. She even helped at the search center!" Corina's voice broke. "She kept Gabriel in there—chained, like an animal! Oh God, where is she? What's she going to do? You've got to find her!"

"Her name's Cathy Miller!" Robert said.

"Corina, I know this is hard—" Lonza nodded to the gloved detective "—but we're close now and working fast."

Lonza coaxed Corina to let go of Gabriel's belongings.

Through the gaps between the parked vehicles, Lonza glimpsed news cameras aimed at them as Corina slowly, tenderly, surrendered her son's clothes.

"We need a minute," Grimes, pausing from his call, said to Lonza.

Taking her aside so no one could hear, or see, he showed her his phone.

A photo of Gabriel Corado looking at the camera from the window of a white SUV filled the screen.

Lonza covered her mouth with one hand, her eyes glazed.

"Oh geez! It's him!"

"We got it from state police. It was taken about forty-five minutes ago."

"Where?"

"Truck stop, near Watertown."

Lonza's phone rang. Weaver was calling.

"Have you seen what just came in?"

"Yes, have we got the boy? Did they grab the suspect?"

"No, not yet. Listen. It appears to be Cathy Miller in a rental.

Everybody—State, FBI, locals—is jumping on this, to close in on her upstate. We want you two there to assist. Let the precinct people handle the scene there. You get to Floyd Bennett Field in Brooklyn now. Our guys will chopper you to Newburgh and the State guys will get you on a fixed wing and up to Watertown ASAP."

"Alright."

"One crucial thing, Vicky," Weaver said. "At this time State Police take the lead, so tell no one what we have. We need as much time as possible before our subject is aware we're on to her, or they go public."

"Got it," Lonza said.

"It'll leak out soon enough, but do not tell anyone."

"Alright."

Ending the call, Lonza told Grimes, then they took Sarducci and Kortese aside, out of earshot.

"We have to leave this with you," Lonza said. "We need to be somewhere."

Seeing what was happening, Corina and Robert went to Lonza and Grimes.

"What's going on?" Corina looked at Lonza, then Grimes, then Lonza again. "What's happened? Tell us!"

"We'll tell you when we can," Lonza said. "I'm sorry we have to go."

"Go where? Don't do this, Vicky, please!"

"I'm sorry. Just trust us, please, Corina. Trust us and hang on."

88

CORINA WAS OVERCOME watching Lonza and Grimes leave the scene at Morris Park.

She called after them: "Don't do this to us again!"

Robert and the other detectives held her back until Lonza and Grimes were gone. Corina then turned to Sarducci and Kortese.

"They're looking into another aspect of the investigation," Sarducci said.

"Did they find our son?" Robert asked.

"We don't have the details," Kortese said. "But could we go over your initial statement and—"

Someone on the other side of two uniformed cops called Corina's name, pulling her attention to a woman next to a TV cameraman, straining on her toes and waving. It took one second for Corina to recognize Dakota and Del, her colleagues from Newslead.

"Corina! You have to talk to Gil on the desk now!" Dakota held up her phone, glancing around so as not to reveal all she knew. "It's urgent!"

Churning with desperation, Corina glanced to Robert, who nodded. She excused herself from the detectives and went to Dakota.

"What is it?" Corina took Dakota's phone. "What is it, Gil?"

Gil couldn't restrain the excited tension in his voice. "Gabriel's been spotted, a credible sighting."

Corina's hand flew to her mouth.

"Where?"

"Watertown. This just happened. Our affiliate there is monitoring everything on their newsroom police scanners. He was seen with a woman at a truck stop south of the city. A witness got photos, gave them to a state trooper. They're saying it's him and they're launching a huge dragnet."

"It's for real?" Corina turned, tears in her eyes, nodding to Robert.

"It's real," Dixon said. "We're flying up a national crew now."

"I want to go with them!"

"We figured. We've got one seat open on the small charter jet. It's at Teterboro. Dakota and Del will get you there as quick as they can."

"I'm on my way."

Once Corina and Robert got into the Newslead SUV, Corina called Joan, who was at their condo with Charlotte. After telling Joan all she could, Corina asked about Charlotte.

"She's awake and doing well. I gave her some tea. I'll put her on so you can tell her the news."

There was the brief rustle of a phone being passed while Corina watched buildings flow by on Morris Park Avenue as they headed toward the expressway.

"Mom, I'm so sorry for everything I did."

Corina's heart wrenched at the image of Charlotte on the rooftop's edge.

"Honey, I understand. It's alright. Listen, something's happened," Corina said, hopeful the news would help her. "Gabriel's been seen upstate and it's a good sighting."

"Oh my God! Where?"

"Watertown. I'm headed there now. Would you like to help?"

"Yes! Anything! I want to help!"

"You know I keep a packed bag in my closet for breaking news?"

"Yes."

The strength in Charlotte's voice buoyed Corina and she turned to Robert, giving him an affirming, tear-filled smile.

"Okay, honey, this is what I need you to do..."

★★★

They made good time as they traveled along the Cross Bronx Expressway, the bridge over the Harlem River, and across Manhattan.

When Corina wasn't squeezing Robert's hand, she searched for breaking news out of Watertown on her phone. Finding nothing, she called the state police there directly and got through to a trooper. Identifying herself, struggling to remain calm, Corina asked about Gabriel.

She was put on hold.

They were on the George Washington Bridge over the Hudson, bound for New Jersey, when the trooper came back.

"Ma'am, I'm not at liberty to confirm anything at this time."

Hanging up, she closed her eyes and whispered a prayer for her son.

As they neared Teterboro Airport, Corina realized that not long ago, Efrem Zyller had been arrested here before he could fly to Morocco. Her issues with him, his shameful acts, burned like bile at the back of her throat.

She shoved them aside.

Arriving at the charter company's small lounge and gate, she was pleased to see Nora Bower, her Newslead producer, waiting. Then Corina's heart rose when Charlotte rushed into her arms.

"I brought your bag." Charlotte brushed her tears. "Find him, Mom."

"We're all working together to bring him home, honey."

Corina thanked Joan, who'd come with Charlotte in a cab.

"Thank goodness our building is closer to the airport than you were when you called from the Bronx. I told our driver it was urgent." Joan smiled. "Good luck, Corina."

Corina hugged Robert, like she'd done so many times when she'd jetted off to breaking news stories. His face told her that he knew she'd experienced dangerous situations around the world, but a pained fear stood in the back of his eyes. This was different.

"Keep us posted and be careful, Corina."

She gave him and Charlotte one last hug, then nodded to Nora, who'd already taken care of the paperwork for the flight. Corina shouldered her bag and trotted with Nora across the tarmac to the steps of the chartered Lear.

* * *

Inside the jet, Corina took comfort seeing Ellie Blair, a national reporter, and camera operator Reggie Reed. Like her, they'd covered wars, disasters and every kind of tragedy.

After a quick, warm greeting, seat belts were buckled, and with the crew advising a flight time of about forty-five minutes, the Lear rocketed down the runway. The ground dropped and New York's majestic skyline and vast metro area rose in the east. As they headed north, the sprawl gave way to the forests, the hills and eventually, the mountains.

When they leveled, Ellie, studying her phone, gave Corina the latest details.

"This is from our people on the ground and their sources: a woman at the Empire Skies Truck Plaza, south of Watertown, spotted the boy with a woman. When the witness got next to him, she was so certain the boy was Gabriel that she spoke his name. He reacted to it, causing the woman with him, the suspect, to take him away immediately."

Pursing her lips, Corina fought tears as Ellie continued.

"Our witness followed them into the parking lot, took pictures with her phone and alerted a state trooper who was in the food court. The pictures have not been made public. No media has seen them yet. But sources tell our local affiliate that the boy fits Gabriel's description, and the woman fits the BOLO for Cathy Miller, from the Bronx. So far, they've not located the vehicle, a white Toyota SUV, but they're setting up a massive dragnet to search for it. And it's possible we'll see everything in an AMBER soon."

Corina touched Ellie's arm, thanking her, then leaned back to absorb the information.

Soon, the Lear started its descent.

Corina's pulse vibrated as she tried to think clearly and push through her nightmare, begging heaven to keep Gabriel alive. The sun was sinking when they touched down. Corina closed her eyes and thought of Gabriel.

I'm coming for you, sweetheart. I'm coming.

89

DETAILED MAPS OF WATERTOWN, Jefferson County and the Thousand Islands region covered the corkboards in the meeting room of the Pamelia town hall.

The room, last used for a county quilting fair, was now the command center in the search for Gabriel Corado and Cathy Miller.

The small town of Pamelia bordered Watertown, and the hall, a blue building, sat next door to the state police barracks, near Interstate 81.

The large screen at the front of the room came to life with images of Gabriel Corado, Miller and the vehicle.

"We'll get things moving." Kyle Warner, a New York State Police investigator with the Special Victims Unit, began the latest briefing. "These photos are from our witness and security footage from Empire. We got a partial plate, and photos of Miller and the boy. We've used the images and information to issue an AMBER Alert that went out thirty minutes ago."

"Anything so far?" a detective with Watertown City Police asked.

"Not yet," Warner said, "but here's where we're at."

He outlined how, so far, roadblocks on the interstate and secondary roads had yielded no sign of the white Toyota SUV. Units equipped with plate readers hadn't seen any positive results so far.

"We've got state police air support, drones, fixed wing and helicopter."

Camera footage from roads, parks and private security, where available, was being checked. Watertown City Police were covering the city. Jefferson County Sheriff's Office, with additional state police, covered the rural areas. Alerts also went out to police in Vermont, New Hampshire, Pennsylvania and New Jersey.

"And with the border twenty-five miles away, we've got more help."

Warner said the US Border Patrol was monitoring all crossings at the bridges across the Thousand Islands. Canadian authorities—like the Canada Border Services Agency, the Ontario Provincial Police and the Royal Canadian Mounted Police—were on alert.

"We've got people on the water and in the air covering the region and the border. These guys routinely track smugglers and traffickers moving both ways across the border."

Warner then nodded to Lonza and Grimes, who were seated with the group.

"The lead investigators with the NYPD just got in—Detective Vicky Lonza and Harvey Grimes. They'll provide background on the case."

Lonza said: "Hedra Leanna Cowell, aka Cathy Miller, aged thirty-seven, from the Bronx. We'll refer to her as Miller, for now. On an immediate front, we've been unable to track her phone. We suspect she got rid of it and what we see in the truck stop footage is a burner she picked up. Our people, along with the FBI, are attempting to track any laptop, tablet or gaming system she may have.

"The Bronx rental agency uses a GPS system to track its vehicles. However, the one in Miller's SUV was accidentally disabled during its last service."

Lonza then related more background on the case, the various tentacles—the conspiracies, extortions, threats and deceptions. She concluded with details on how Miller likely carried out the abduction in Central Park, the conditions in which she kept Gabriel and how she'd inserted herself into the search.

"Miller was born in Calgary, Canada, as Hedra Leanna Cowell," Lonza said. "We're checking with the RCMP for relatives, or connections, or communication, in Canada."

"Excuse me," a Jefferson County deputy said, "is there any link between Miller and the attempt to kill Corado a few years ago?"

"That was investigated at the outset," Lonza said. "And it's being looked at again now."

Trayman Herman Shrike was in Rikers Island. The FBI in California were again investigating the Ritzzkels, but had found no connection. And nothing had been found so far in searches for any social media posts tied to Miller.

"Still, we know that the group's networks can be challenging to track on the dark web. They can go deep, go silent, and they have supporters around the world," Lonza said. "We aren't ruling anything out."

The investigators debated several theories, holding that, given that Miller was headed north out of New York City, she could continue north or head in any direction on back roads. She might also try to disappear in Watertown. One thing was clear: with the AMBER Alert, the dragnet and everyone looking for Miller and Gabriel, it was only a matter of time before they were found.

"We're losing the light," Warner said, wrapping up the briefing, "but our operation will not relent. We're going full bore all night."

As the meeting broke up, Lonza remained seated, staring at the monitor and the faces of Miller and Gabriel, knowing that this was the most dangerous time in a pursuit. Because when the noose tightened, when police were closing in, suspects grew increasingly fearful and desperate.

Sometimes to the point of ending lives.

90

THEIR PLANE LANDED at Watertown Airport and they were met by Wade McLure, a producer with Newslead's Watertown affiliate.

"All of us here hope they find your son, Ms. Corado," he said.

"Thank you." Corina managed a small smile.

"We got all that New York requested," Wade said, helping load their things into the Ford Explorer with the station's logo. "We got scanners, walkie-talkies, batteries, chargers, water and food. We've booked you into a motel near the command center. You've got this vehicle, and me as your guide, for as long as you need."

"Thanks," Nora said. "What's the latest?"

"They issued an AMBER not long ago. It's got a lot of good photos, including footage from the truck stop's security cameras."

"Yeah, we got it, too," Ellie said.

"Police are checking everything along the interstate," Wade said. "Secondary roads across the county, along the shores of the St. Lawrence, the Thousand Islands and the bridges to Canada."

"Sounds intense," Reggie said.

"It's the biggest dragnet we've ever seen. More police and media are arriving from Canada, too," Wade said. "We've got three of our news crews on it, and we've hired freelance news teams, including a couple with boats to cover us in the islands and the border," Wade said, closing the tailgate and getting behind the wheel. "Where do you want to go?"

Corina said, "The command center."

The motor roared as Wade drove from the airport, the police scanner and a news radio bleating transmissions. As they moved east, Corina again looked at Gabriel's face on her phone in the AMBER Alert. She looked at Cathy Miller and her SUV, then raised her head, searching for answers.

Corina's pulse ticked up each time she spotted a white SUV. She used the binoculars Wade provided to examine the make, model and driver. Each time her heart sped up, and each time it was not Miller. As they headed north on I-81, Reggie tilted his head to look up at the police helicopter above them. Soon the lanes of traffic slowed to a crawl and police lights flashed ahead.

"A choke point," Wade said. "They're watching for the white Toyota and stopping anyone fitting the description."

When Wade reached the checkpoint, a state trooper eyed the Ford and the occupants before recognizing Wade, then Corina.

Touching the brim of her hat, the trooper waved them through.

They had only gone a few yards when Nora said, "Pull over."

Ellie and Reggie collected gear and got out. After a quick setup, Ellie, holding a microphone, stood beside lines of traffic, and police checking vehicles as her background. As Reggie shot her, and the helicopter overhead, Ellie described this part of the search. After she'd finished her bridge stand-up, they continued driving.

Darkness was falling when they got to the Pamelia town hall. Most police had left the center.

Ellie and Nora found Kyle Warner, a New York State Police investigator who'd agreed to an on-camera interview. They did it inside the command center with the maps, where the monitor showed Gabriel and Cathy Miller's faces alongside an image of the Toyota. As Warner updated them, Corina saw Lonza and Grimes huddled with other cops and went to them.

Recognizing her, Grimes turned.

Keeping her voice steady, Corina asked, "Where are they?"

"You've seen the new images from the truck plaza that we put into the AMBER Alert?" Lonza said. "They're only a few hours old. We believe they're near."

Corina weighed everything.

Taking stock of the exhaustion and anguish etched into Corina's face, Lonza touched her shoulder.

"We're close now, Corina."

Corina nodded before rejoining the news team.

They went to their motel nearby, hefting gear and luggage to the second level where their rooms were side by side. They crowded into Ellie's room, where Ellie worked with Nora and Reggie, putting a story together, drawing on their work and footage Wade got from locals and freelancers, and sending it to New York. Then they went back to the command center to do a live stand-up with Lynn Litton, who sat on the Newslead anchor desk in New York.

Corina joined Ellie briefly, live on camera, to take a few questions from Lynn Litton, starting out with why she was in Watertown.

"I'm here to help find Gabriel. We all believe he's close."

"We understand that Cathy Miller, aka Hedra Leanna Cowell, is the suspect and that you once interviewed her. She also volunteered to help search for Gabriel. We've uncovered footage showing her supporting conspiracies and attacks directed at you. Corina, what are your thoughts about her at this time?"

"She's troubled. She needs people to understand what she's going through, and for that to happen, I ask her to release Gabriel unharmed."

Looking down at her written copy, Lynn Litton said, "You may know that Efrem Zyller, the head of Newslead's news division, was formally arraigned today on several charges."

Corina blinked and gave a slight nod.

"What is your reaction, Corina?"

"I have none. I'm focused on getting my son back."

"I understand," Litton said. "One last question, if Gabriel is seeing this now, what would you tell him, Corina?"

"I'm here, and I'm going to bring you home, honey."

When they returned to the motel, Reggie ordered some food. Corina declined to eat as they studied news reports.

They landed on the ReLOX Network and a late-night replay of the most recent episode of *The Wynne Files*.

"How much longer is this fakery going to continue?" Wynne Varden stared into the camera. *"We've presented our information."*

A montage of images appeared showing Corina in various locations with the baby she'd rescued in Nicaragua.

"It's clear what she did in Central America. And now, Efrem Zyller has been—" Varden used air quotes *"—'arrested.' Nice twist, we get it. But when is Corina Corado going to end this staged charade with actors? Like Cathy Miller, aka Hedra Leanna Cowell, the 'suspect' who fled to upstate New York. For crying out loud, we all know she was a volunteer searcher. And what many people don't know is that Corado is besties with Oscar-winner Beth-Anne Bridger, who, coincidentally, is making a movie nearby in Evans Mills. I have to ask, are Corado's Hollywood friends helping her stage this thing?"*

Nora switched the channel.

"That is disgusting," Ellie said.

"Let's go out and search," Corina said.

"We wouldn't see anything," Wade said. "We should get some sleep and go out at first light. We've got night shift people in our newsroom listening to scanners, and I've brought ours inside here. We won't miss anything." He nodded to the scanner crackling on the desk.

The group studied maps of the region, working deep into the night. It was after 3:00 a.m. when Corina went to her room. Unable to sleep, raking her hand over her face, she thought of Gabriel's mother.

Her name was Trinity. She was a runaway, addicted to drugs. A shy, quiet girl. Got pregnant. Didn't know the father. She was seventeen and living on the street before finding the courage to get help at free clinics. She'd cleaned up and secretly reached out to a lawyer friend of her family, a dysfunctional but powerful family who'd disowned her. The lawyer knew Robert and Corina, knew of their desire for a baby, and a private adoption was arranged after the baby's birth. The only things that Trinity asked for, begged for, was that her identity never be revealed as the biological mother; and that she had to cut off her connection to the baby completely. All records were sealed. All details were protected. Corina and Robert arranged to pay for Trinity to go to college and cover her living costs, but eventually they lost touch with her. Corina would never forget the fear, anguish, love and hope in Trinity's face as she told her and Robert, *"Take my baby. Give him a good life."*

Yes, Corina thought, *Gabriel is our miracle.*

91

THE MOONLIGHT REACHED through the spaces between the weathered boards of the old barn, glinting in Gabriel's eyes.

Looking at the night sky from under the thick blankets in the hay of the loft, he was warm enough. The cool air smelled like the zoo and horse poop of the carriages at the park. In the darkness, Gabriel heard pigeons cooing, then an owl hooted.

The ham and cheese sandwich, chips and apple pie the old man with white hair had given him at the big house they drove to were really good. The man got him wool socks, a big shirt and a sweater. "Used to be my grandson's. It should do the job tonight," he said.

But before the old man had fed them, he made sure they first parked the car in the stall in the barn, which was far back, past some trees. In the barn, Cathy and the man covered the car with a sheet and walled it in with bales of hay so nobody could see it. Giving them blankets and pillows, the man said they would be safe tonight in the loft.

Now, Gabriel looked at Cathy, who had taken him from Central Park and brought him all this way to here, wherever this place was. Sitting near him in the loft, her face glowing in the light of her phone, Cathy sketched in her notebook.

In the distance, he heard the thudding of a helicopter, but he couldn't see it through the gaps in the barn's walls.

Gabriel was still confused and scared about everything.

After taking him from the park, Cathy said she was working to get him back to his family, back to his mom. It was dangerous, Cathy said, people were trying to stop them. But she would protect him and they had friends along the way to help them.

But if Cathy was trying to help him, how come he didn't know her?

It was all weird and so scary that sometimes Gabriel cried.

Some of the confusing part came because he remembered, when he was young, some bad people did something to his mom, and that meant his family had to be guarded by security people.

Then it stopped, like, for a long time.

But a few days ago, in the park, going home from school with Charlotte and flying his plane, Cathy rushed right over to him, surprising him.

"Gabriel Corado, your mom and dad sent me because bad people are coming to get you!" she said, almost whispering. "Your family sent me! Come with me now!"

He didn't know her, but she knew his name, and he remembered about being guarded. He knew his mom was a reporter on TV and knew lots of people. So did his dad. And New York was so big. And if his mom and dad had sent her, it must've been true about the bad people.

"Walk with me now, Gabriel," the woman said, taking his hand, looking around as they moved away down a gravel path. "Act normal, they're close to us. I'll protect you."

"What about Charlotte and my plane?"

"She'll get it. A friend's coming for her, too. Keep quiet and act normal."

He didn't see anyone along the path, which went through a real foresty part of the park. Some branches scraped his arm and he thought he lost his baseball bracelet, which made him sad.

Then he took his phone from his pocket.

"I'll call my mom."

"No," the woman said, looking around. "They'll track you and find you. This is serious, sweetie. Better give me your phone, Gabriel, and your code, to be safe."

The woman said the people helping her to save him had it all arranged. She took out a hoodie from her backpack and put it on him fast, tying the hood tight, to be in disguise so the bad people wouldn't find him, she said.

But he was scared.

They came to a bike cab and she got him to hide under the seat, cramped and bumping in the dark for a long time. Then he remembered getting into a car and under a blanket before coming to an apartment, where she told him her name was Cathy. And that other friends of her mom had rescued Charlotte and were protecting her in another place. Cathy kept him in a room and said she needed to put him in the safety harness to keep him safe.

"This is to protect you, so the bad people can't steal you while we wait for instructions to take you back to your family."

Cathy let him go to the bathroom, take baths and brush his teeth. She brought clean clothes, and his favorite foods: pizza, tacos, vanilla cookies. He couldn't watch TV, but she got him some computer games. He got so lonely he just cried and kept asking Cathy when he could go home.

"It won't be long," Cathy kept telling him. Then one day she got a car and they drove and drove with her telling him, "We need to be more careful because the bad people will be everywhere."

Now here they were hiding in a barn, near a forest.

Cathy's phone vibrated with a message. He saw her reading it by the glow of her screen, then she smiled and began typing her response.

It didn't matter to Gabriel.

His yearning to go home had him crying, again, softly.

Cathy lowered her phone and brushed at his tears.

"Go to sleep," she whispered. "I just got the message I was waiting for from the people helping us. It'll be over soon. I promise."

DAY 7

92

Leaving the long driveway, deputy Noel Thorpe and his partner headed to the next rural property.

"Crossing off the Stackleton place." Thorpe tapped at his computer monitor above the console. "Bilkerson's next. You good?"

A happy yip came through the dividing screen from the back where Mason, a Belgian Malinois, panted.

Thorpe sipped coffee from his mug, looking at the rising sun in the coral sky. He'd been assigned to investigate the region at the northern edge of Jefferson County. He traveled down the paved road before coming to a dense wood, bordered by a fence with "Keep Out" signs declaring it private property. A few weatherworn political signs dangled.

A shame how Asa Bilkerson had let his farm go after cancer took Clara, his wife, Thorpe thought, passing through the open gate. The lane was rutted, shoulders overgrown with wild grass and weeds, the tall trees casting long shadows.

The farmhouse was not like Thorpe remembered.

Shingles were missing from the roof, the blistered paint exposing a gray weathered wood. Thorpe stopped his vehicle, shifted the transmission into Park, logged his location into his computer, then got out.

"I'll be right back."

Mason yipped an okay.

The neglect reminded Thorpe of how fleeting life was as he reached the side door and knocked. It seemed like two full minutes before he heard movement, then sounds of someone approaching the door before it opened. A man with mussed white hair and stubble, wearing frayed suspenders over a red flannel shirt holding up green farmer pants, stared at Thorpe.

"Hi, Asa," Thorpe said. "Sorry to trouble you so early, but you heard about a possible kidnapping suspect in the area?"

Bilkerson lifted his wrinkled hand to his chin.

"Might've."

"My partner and I." Thorpe turned so Bilkerson could see Mason, tail wagging with eagerness in the back seat. "Well, we're requesting your cooperation to let us have a look in the house and on your property."

"You want to search my home?"

"You can say yes, that would be good. We'd be in and out quick. You also have the right to say no. But I have to tell you, Asa, that will raise a flag and we'd get people here with a warrant, a whole big thing."

Bilkerson muttered about government, sovereign citizens and rights.

"What's that?" Thorpe said.

"Ain't nobody here but me. Let's get it over with."

Thorpe and his partner got to work in the house. Snout poking everywhere, Mason searched the kitchen, living room, dining room, bedrooms and bathroom. The place reeked of loneliness, despair and the odor of joint-pain cream. Thorpe kept a careful eye on Mason, noting his reactions, but made small talk about sports and the weather while he eyed everything. On their way in, Thorpe noticed a number of used plates and glasses in the sink—a lot for someone alone. But he raised the issue casually when he and Mason were on their way out.

"So, what did you do last night, Asa?"

"Watched the game on TV, went to bed."

"Nobody visit?"

Bilkerson shook his head.

"We're done here," Thorpe said as they stepped outside. "Thank you for cooperating. We'll head down to the barn now."

"Ain't nothing there."

"It's my job. You're welcome to join us."

"I will, seein' it's my property." Bilkerson adjusted his suspenders and walked with them.

Along the stretch to the barn, there was a sense of isolation and silence, the only sound a distant creaking from the windmill beyond the house. The earthen path was also overgrown with wildflowers and grass. Yet it appeared flattened in places, as if someone had recently driven over it. In exposed patches, Thorpe saw tire tracks in the mud.

Fresh ones.

In the back of his mind, a warning light was blinking.

Something doesn't feel right.

He watched Mason, snout working, tail wagging.

Hinges cried out for oil when they opened the rickety barn doors. Dust mites swirled in the foul air and light between the gaps. Mason went directly to a wall of stacked bales in front of a stall.

"What's in there, Asa?"

Bilkerson rubbed his chin without answering.

Mason yipped as Thorpe began removing the bales, exposing a khaki-colored tarp covering a vehicle. Mason barked. Thorpe removed the tarp, revealing a white Toyota SUV with a plate sequence matching the suspect's vehicle. Mason yipped again. Thorpe's expression hardened.

"Put your hands behind your back, turn around."

Bilkerson considered the order without moving, eyeing Thorpe's hand hovering over his holstered gun, then the old man slowly turned in surrender. Thorpe handcuffed him in seconds, read him his rights, then reached for his portable radio.

He called in his unit number and location, then said, "Got the vehicle here."

His call set the multiagency response in motion.

"You helping them, Asa?" Thorpe said as he let Mason go through the car, which was unlocked. "Where are they?"

Bilkerson remained silent. Thorpe looked at the ladder to the loft. He put Bilkerson in a sitting position on the barn floor, with Mason barking at him while guarding him.

No time to wait for backup.

Thorpe readied his sidearm and began climbing the ladder to the loft.

93

CORINA'S EYES HAD closed and she dreamed someone was saying her name.

A hand clasped her shoulder.

"Corina, we have to go!"

Snapping to consciousness, she saw Wade standing near, a yawping scanner in his hand. It took a second for Corina to register that she was atop her bed, still dressed. The first light of the rising sun was brightening her motel room.

"They found the car!" Wade held up the scanner. "On a farm at the northern edge of the county!"

Corina sat up. "Did they find Gabriel?"

"Don't know. Get ready—we have to go now!"

Minutes later, Corina, Nora, Ellie and Reggie piled into the Ford. Wade, at the wheel, sped north on the interstate. He'd alerted all of the local affiliate news crews, and the freelancers, to head to the farm.

"I know the place—it's on the shore about twenty-five minutes away!"

The police scanner continued crackling with staccato transmissions. Corina and the others knew that this was not the time to call police for directions or confirmation. You did not want them to know you were locked onto the unfolding action, giving them a chance to keep you back.

Wade slowed as they came to an interstate checkpoint and the pulsating lights of a state patrol car. They lowered the volume on their radios and Nora slipped on a headset so they wouldn't miss anything.

A state trooper got out and waved them to his stop.

"Where're you headed?"

"Just getting early shots," Wade told the trooper.

"Where?"

"At the edge of town."

The trooper took a cursory look at the media people.

"The edge of town?"

"Yeah, we might do a stand-up for the early show. Anything going on?"

"No, not around here. Alright. Go ahead. But stick close to town."

"Thanks."

They still had several miles to go, Wade said, continuing along the interstate at a normal rate until they no longer saw the trooper. Then Wade accelerated. They pushed up the volume on the radios, everyone listening intently as transmissions faded in and out through static bursts.

"...they were here in the barn loft..."

Corina's heart lifted, and she felt Wade increase his speed.

"...best I can tell...they left on foot not long ago..."

They could hear a dog barking in the background.

"...negative...can't pursue...have an arrest...request air support...affirm... will send canine to track..."

The SUV sliced through the northern countryside of Jefferson County with Corina wishing it could go faster.

94

CRESTING A HILL, stopping to catch her breath, Cathy adjusted her grip on Gabriel's hand.

Below them, the grassy land swept down to meet the St. Lawrence River and the islands.

Cathy glanced back at how far they'd trekked from Asa's barn, through an overrun apple orchard to the hill. Turning back, assessing the distance to the river, she knew they were closer now, and help was waiting on the Canadian side.

She studied her notes and sketches one more time.

They began descending.

Navigating through the grass and groves, she was encouraged each time she spotted a landmark, like the twisted tree trunk, assuring her she was moving in the right direction. They got down to the shore, coming to a pyramid-shaped boulder, then patches of tall grass. She began trotting with Gabriel toward a marsh.

"Yes, this is right," she said aloud.

Water splashed above Cathy's knees as she entered the river's edge, pushing aside tall stands of cattails. Butterflies flitted as she grabbed at the camouflage netting, pulling it away from the boat.

"Here it is! Just like they promised!"

It was a fifteen-foot fiberglass boat with a fifteen-horsepower outboard motor. Inside, a pair of orange lifejackets, wooden oars. The scraped hull was solid.

Grunting, Cathy glided the boat out of the bulrushes and reeds, then she hefted Gabriel into it before she climbed in, causing it to dip. It rocked and bobbed as she put Gabriel in his lifejacket.

She looked into his sober face; his eyes filled with tears.

"It's going to be okay, don't worry," she said, securing his straps.

Exhaling then smiling at him, Cathy, maintaining her balance, moved to the back of the boat. Remembering her days as a summer camp counselor, and consulting her notes, she began the process of starting the motor.

She first checked the fuel line connection. It looked fine, and the gas tank was full. That was good. She checked the switch. Then, squeezing the primer bulb in the line, the pungent odor of gas wafted up as the bulb hardened. She shifted the tiller to start, turned the choke, then reached for the starter cord handle but hesitated when she heard a faint barking.

Looking up through the trees to the hilltop, Cathy could see a dog, alone facing the river, looking in her direction.

Asa didn't have a dog. Could it be searchers? Police?

Cathy didn't know and she had no time to find out. She pulled the starter cord, the motor rumbling to life. She turned off the choke and put the motor in gear. The water roiled into a bubbling froth as she eased the boat from the shore.

It was less than a quarter of a mile to Canada.

95

Sirens wailed.

Reggie turned to the road behind them.

"They're coming up to us hard."

Having caught the flashing lights in his mirrors, Wade pulled over. A state police unit blasted past them, followed by a Jefferson County deputy's SUV.

"They're heading to Asa Bilkerson's place, where they found the car," said Wade, who'd been monitoring all transmissions during the drive. "We interviewed him for a story last election on fringe groups. After his wife died, he fell in with some conspiracy believers with extreme views, worrying his neighbors."

Through the police scanner's static, they heard a dispatch from air support: *"—small craft, departing now, two aboard, one possibly a child—"*

"It's them!" Corina said.

Wade got on his walkie-talkie to alert the freelancers in the area who were on the water. "If it's Bilkerson's place," Ellie said, "wouldn't they have it sealed?"

"That's right. But there's an old boat launch close by that isn't on his property. Hardly anyone but local fishermen use it."

More approaching sirens howled as Wade slowed, this time exiting the paved road for a field dotted with trees and overgrown grass.

"This is the way, hang on!"

Once they were off-road, the SUV, now in all-wheel drive, began bouncing along a barely visible cow path that led directly to a hill.

Reggie pressed his palm on the ceiling to steady himself, the others clutching armrests and handles. The grass brushed the doors, and at times the undercarriage thudded against the hidden earthen ridges. A torrent of radio transmissions blasting, Wade drove as fast as the terrain allowed, reaching the top of the hill quickly.

A moment later, a freelancer's voice came through Wade's walkie-talkie.

"We see you, Wade!"

Below, a motorboat slowed as it made its way toward the shore and old boat launch. The Ford teetered and swayed as Wade maneuvered down the slope.

Two people—a man, and a woman, who was driving—sat in the waiting boat, its motor idling. It was a large power boat—it looked new, Corina thought just as a fixed-wing plane passed by overhead.

"Mark Hickey," the man said, jumping out to help get everyone and the gear aboard as the boat's scanners and radios blurted transmissions.

"Riley Sanchez," the woman at the wheel said. "They spotted the woman and the boy's boat not far east of us! We have to hustle!"

After they hurried into the boat, Wade shouted introductions, including the fact that Riley's family owned a marina and the boat. They all turned to the horizon when the tin-splutter of a loudspeaker came from a boat far off.

"This area is restricted by the New York State Police! Repeat, the area is restricted! Stay ashore!"

"Just go!" Nora said.

Riley pushed the throttle forward. The big inboard grumbled like controlled thunder, the boat's twin props thrusting, lifting the bow, and within seconds the craft was cutting across the surface at top speed.

96

WELCOMING THE WATER misting her skin, Cathy raised her face and briefly closed her eyes.

A baptism of sorts, she thought, a celebration.

Because I'm really doing it.

As the boat's motor thrummed, powering them across the river, her thoughts pulled her through time. In the years following her tragedy, Cathy had been lost, searching for answers. She'd found them online, with the believers, with those who understood and knew the truth.

About everything.

How everything was controlled by global forces, led by a hierarchy of demons in human form whose goal was to enslave the world. How the believers had to fight back. And that's how she came to the truth about people like Corina Corado, the Queen of Lies. Cathy learned that Corina had stolen Gabriel from his mother in Nicaragua, and used her power and connections to fool the world into believing that he was her child.

Yes, she had met Corina a few years ago when she'd done a story about Cathy's support group. But Corina's reports did absolutely nothing to help Cathy find her missing son. And it was at that time

Cathy came to regard Corina with contempt: contempt for her fame, her high-paying job, her perfect life with her perfect family. The way she acted like she was better than everyone else.

Then, when Cathy gradually formed a better understanding of the believers who'd claimed Corado was a liar, Cathy had seen how Corado tried in vain to battle the Ritzzkels. She'd seen how these actions prompted believer-warrior, Herman Shrike, to attempt the most courageous action. It had inspired Cathy to do what she had to do, to give her life a purpose.

She had to rescue Gabriel.

Her mission had not been an easy one. After Shrike's valiant attempt had failed, she'd studied the Newslead building, learning Corado's patterns, hiring drivers to follow her car, learning where she lived. Cathy watched Corado's family and absorbed their details and routines, waiting for the right place and the right time, enlisting the help of a pedicab driver to prepare.

The right time came.

And I struck, like a terrible, swift sword.

It had all gone well. But Cathy had to wait a few days for everything to fall into place for the next phase in Canada. It didn't matter what Corado said in front of the TV cameras and the fake media.

The believers knew the truth.

And *The Wynne Files* and ReLOX were reporting it, further assuring Cathy that what she was doing was right and just.

During the days Cathy had to wait before moving Gabriel, she pretended to stand with Corado. To make her support seem genuine, she sent her a gift and messages. She joined the search group, getting close, learning a little about the investigation, until the time came to leave.

It had all gone smoothly.

Now, with the outboard motor droning, Cathy gazed at the passing islands. They were nearer to Canada now, so close to the Canadian believers and their network that reached to Central America. That network would return Gabriel to his mother. Cathy's heart swelled and she shouted to him.

"I can finally tell you the whole truth, Gabriel! Your mother never died! People were paid off so you could be stolen from her! We're going to reunite you!"

But worry crinkled Gabriel's face as Cathy smiled at him. He didn't understand.

Cathy's smile faded at the odor of gas.

It was intensifying.

Puzzled, she inspected the fuel tank and the linkages. Gas dripped from the motor along the fuel line to the full gas tank. The leaking formed rainbow-colored puddles under the tank and the motor. Following the shiny line up to the motor's cover, Cathy thought maybe a fuel hose clamp had loosened and gas was seeping, dripping all over the hot motor, the spark plug, when—

The shock wave forced out gas and air faster than the speed of sound, followed by a deafening blast.

97

THE BRILLIANT FIREBALL filled the lenses of the trooper's binoculars in the state police plane overhead.

"The boat just blew!" the trooper said to the pilot, reporting the explosion and location on his radio.

The blast could also be seen from a second plane farther back, chartered out of Watertown by the FBI, who'd been joined by the NYPD detectives.

"Did you see that, Vicky?" Grimes said.

Lonza saw it, and she thought only of Gabriel Corado.

On the water below, sirens whooping, engines roaring, state police and border patrol boats were cutting through the water toward the flames.

Far ahead, Riley Sanchez's power boat neared the spot.

Commands were repeated through a bullhorn. "This area is restricted by the New York State Police! Shut off your motor now!"

Riley pulled back on the throttle because they'd reached the scene. Slowing, easing closer.

Reggie and Mark, their cameras aimed, working to keep them steady, had been recording the pursuit and now the aftermath as Ellie and Nora called out for survivors.

Staring in horror at the burning hull, Corina's face was ashen. Flames licked from the boat's half-sunken skeleton. Acrid smoke curled to the sky. Oars bobbed on the surface, the twisted remnants of the boat's bench seat, an orange life jacket, *a small shoe.*

A white adidas Superstar.

Corina's shriek was ear-piercing.

Her pulse throbbing, she saw no sign of life in the debris.

But when Riley shut the engine off, Corina gasped. They all heard a splashing, coughing, then a flash of orange on the other side of the burning wreckage.

A child struggling in the water.

"Gabriel!"

Corina jumped into the water, her arms and legs pumping, her mind racing, a million thoughts blurring—the flaming wreckage, her parents' deaths; Trinity's words: *Take my baby. Give him a good life;* horrors around the world, a dying mother's arms holding up her child, *Salva a mi hijo. Por favor.* Glimpsing Gabriel's hands reaching skyward, she took his hands, arms, and pulled his trembling body to her.

"I've got you! Mommy's got you!"

At that instant, a force from below seized Corina's leg in a steely grip, pulling her and Gabriel under.

In the struggle beneath the surface, through the air bubbles, Corina met Cathy's face, her eyes bulging, her skin burned to ribbons of flesh peeled and waving in the water, exposing her white teeth and part of her skull as she pulled them…

…down…down…down.

98

GABRIEL WAS SITTING in his hospital bed, refusing to let go of his mother's hand while he ate the vanilla crème cookies the nurses had given him.

Corina, at his side, stroked his hair, the scrapes and cuts on their faces and arms marking their battle to survive. Their adrenaline, still pulsing, underscored their trauma.

Watching over them now, from the foot of Gabriel's bed, Doctor Fatima Banerjee blinked rapidly. Long after she'd assessed them, she continued marveling at what they'd endured.

"Letting him go to the surface while you fended off your attacker was the best thing to do."

Keeping her eyes on Gabriel, Corina nodded.

"Remarkably," Banerjee said, "his injuries are relatively minor—a mild concussion, some shock and dehydration. All of his vitals are good. Fortunately, sitting at the front of the boat, he was catapulted by the explosion."

"And the woman?"

"She suffered the full impact, with third-degree burns to most of her body. We did all we could, but she did not survive."

Corina closed her eyes for a moment, at the loss of a troubled life, but also, for the end of her nightmare.

Banerjee touched Corina's shoulder.

"I think being here with you is the best medicine for him. And you've got some visitors waiting."

Not long after the doctor left, Lonza and Grimes entered, with Corina telling Gabriel who they were. Grimes had more cookies for Gabriel.

"Word is you like these, buddy."

Gabriel nodded as Corina smiled and set them aside with the others.

Looking at Gabriel, Lonza said: "You're a very brave boy and you've got an awesome mother."

Without saying a word, Gabriel burrowed his head into Corina's chest.

Lonza smiled at them and opened her notebook.

"We wanted to give you an update," she said. "The FBI's pulling things together. From Bilkerson, we got names of others in the network in the US, Canada and abroad. The RCMP is charging a number of people who were planning to somehow 'repatriate' Gabriel with whoever they believed was his biological mother in Central America."

Corina shook her head.

"The details," Lonza said, "are still being investigated. We've also learned that most of those involved were conspiracy believers and sovereign citizens."

Lonza closed her notebook, thoughts of her own children fluttering through her. "You'll never know how happy I am with the way this ended." Lonza's voice wavered. "You give us all hope, you know."

Corina reached for her hand.

"Vicky, Harvey. Thank you, and thanks to all the investigators. You were relentless, pursuing everything, and with me in your face the whole time. Thank you."

Gabriel looked at the detectives, his eyes shining.

"We were just doing our job," Grimes said.

"And so were you," Lonza said.

After they left, Corina picked up her phone, a water-resistant model, which had been vibrating with requests from news media. She ignored them. She was looking for word from home when Gabriel's face lit up.

Charlotte and Robert entered.

"Charlie! Dad!"

Charlotte rushed to her little brother, wrapping her arms around him.

No words were needed. They realized how close they'd come to losing everything, and they were grateful to be a family again.

They hugged tight for the longest time.

Like they never wanted to let go.

EPILOGUE

WITHIN DAYS OF the family's return to Manhattan, Lonza and Grimes visited with a gift-wrapped package.

"This is for Gabriel from the NYPD," Lonza said. "It belongs to you."

Gabriel tore at the paper, then opened the box.

"Whoa!"

It was the model plane he'd made in school and flown only once in the park. Gabriel beamed. It was in perfect condition.

"Thank you!"

Over coffee, the detectives updated Robert and Corina on Cathy.

"The investigation in Canada has so far determined that she never had a child."

"What?" Corina said.

"It's believed that after she had a serious fall, she was told she could never have children. She had therapy off and on, and came to imagine she had a child, a son, who she called Burke. She imagined a life for them. Then she moved to the US."

Thinking back to Cathy being interviewed at the support group, how she'd shown Corina a picture of her child, one that must have been fake, Corina was now at a loss for words over the revelation. For the longest time, she grappled with sadness for Cathy's troubled and tragic life.

★ ★ ★

A few days later, Corina and Robert invited delivery driver Clifton Chase and assistant continuity supervisor Tess Eastman out for dinner. During the meal, they told Clifton and Tess that, after discussions with police, they would be splitting the reward, which had reached $200,000: Clifton for setting in motion events that pointed to Cathy; and Tess for alerting the police after spotting Gabriel with Cathy at the truck stop.

The family then held a party at the search center, where they thanked all of the volunteers.

Not long after, Corina walked Gabriel to his school, Tillmon Parker Rose, where his class held a welcome-back celebration for him. As Corina's heart filled, watching her son's smile as he was surrounded by friends, she received a call from Javier Santos, with the Globo Prensa Agency in Mexico City. She stepped into the hall to answer.

"Congratulations on locating your son," Santos said.

"Thank you, Javier."

Santos then told her how soon after Gabriel's case broke, his agency partnered with a Mexican TV network. They assigned several reporters to investigate the claims made by *The Wynne Files* and ReLOX that she had stolen the baby from Evelin Flores and raised him as Gabriel.

"We confirmed all the images, from that time, broadcast by ReLOX, actually showed you rescuing the baby, transporting him to hospital. Other images were confirmed to show you helping the family with documentation at government offices, providing them some cash to help them, then holding him at the small airport before you left. We discovered that ReLOX manipulated some of those images.

"Our team located Octavio, the boy you rescued. He's living with his relatives in a village not far from Sébaco. Independent DNA tests were conducted to confirm his identity, removing any chance of validity to the claims," Santos said. "Today we'll send our reports to all US networks, the *New York Times*, the *Washington Post*, AP, Reuters, *The Wynne Files* and ReLOX."

Corina's tears blurred while watching the short clip Santos sent her of the boy, Octavio Carlos Salgado, a six-year-old with a beautiful smile.

Consequently, following this call, *The Wynne Files* and ReLOX ceased reporting their claims, or anything about Corina and her family.

But that may have been related to the fact Corina and her family had launched a lawsuit against them for the malicious fabrications that fueled the violent attacks against them. Corina also took legal action against Efrem Zyller, a move that prompted other women to do the same. Zyller was also facing criminal charges for conspiring to extort Corina. The fact a now-disgraced news media titan was facing a reckoning kept his name and face in the news for months.

Corina's goal was to donate any settlement to charities and non-profits aimed at helping children in war-torn regions, and areas of the world hard-hit with natural disasters. A portion would also go to Octavio and his family.

For Robert, the attempt to pressure him to produce a fraudulent report on the supertall condo generated investigations by local, state and federal officials. This resulted in several actions, which led to court-ordered extensive repairs being made.

One afternoon, weeks after the kidnapping, just as things seemed to be returning to normal, Vince Tarone showed up at the family's condo. He wanted to apologize for his relative in Rikers, and for his own part in Gabriel's disappearance.

"Not just for talking to Charlotte when it happened, but I think, like long before that, I had Cathy Miller as a fare and showed her where you live."

Corina and Robert accepted his apology. Then he told them how Charlotte had looked up to him, treated him with respect, made him feel important. How, maybe because of his dad's sudden death, he felt he had to be the man of the house, and wanted to protect Charlotte in some way.

"I think it'd be wise for me not to see her anymore," he said. "I'll call her and tell her that we need to go our separate ways, but with no hard feelings, you know?"

And weeks later, Corina was stunned when she got an email with one word in the subject line: Trinity.

You don't know me, the message began.

I was Trinity's friend in rehab. In her final years of college, she relapsed, dropped out, lived on the streets and got really sick. When she saw the news about Gabriel missing, she started telling me her story about giving him up. It broke her heart but she said it was best for him. Trinity died a couple days after learning you'd been reunited. It gave her some happiness in her last moments. Just thought you should know.

A friend

The anonymous message tore at Corina's heart. She showed it to Robert, who pushed back tears. They wrote back seeking more information.

But their email bounced back.

After taking off several weeks to be with her family and recover, Corina returned to Newslead. Her first step was to make a tearful televised thank-you to her family, her friends, colleagues, police, volunteers and viewers for their support.

"And to everyone out there who is hurting, or struggling, my heartfelt words are to never stop fighting, to never give up. Never let go. Our ordeal nearly broke us, but in the end, it brought us closer together."

Corina touched her palm to her heart.

"My love to you all."

That weekend, Corina's family strolled together through Central Park.

Entering from the Upper West Side, near the Dakota at West 72nd Street, they blended in with the flow of walkers, joggers, cyclists, pedicabs and tourists. The traffic noise gave way to the soft trilling of birdsong and the clip-clop of a horse-drawn carriage along West Drive.

Walking along the pathway, they came to a rolling grassy section and stopped as Gabriel raised his plane. He twirled its plastic propeller, twisting the rubber band that stretched along the bottom. Holding it up, he counted to three then released it while thrusting the plane toward the hill. With a soft whirr it soared, climbing beautifully, turning and gliding before disappearing over the crest of the slope.

This time, his mom, dad and sister went with him to retrieve it.

Together, as a family.

★ ★ ★ ★ ★

ACKNOWLEDGMENTS & A PERSONAL NOTE

BRINGING *SOMEONE SAW SOMETHING* to you took a lot of work, and there are a lot of people I need to thank.

Some key individuals who helped me shall remain anonymous. I'm so thankful to two former news colleagues, one with a major TV news network, another with a major newspaper, both based in New York City. They were more than familiar with the pressures, challenges and threats facing journalists professionally and personally every day. Both were generous with their time, helping me with real behind-the-scenes insights.

I also want to thank the New York City Police Department, particularly the officers I visited at the Central Park Precinct. They guided me on investigative matters. For any errors, blame me because I took creative liberties with procedure, jurisdiction, the law and technology. As well, my apologies for taking license with geography, in Central Park and elsewhere. Bear in mind, this is an imagined story, one that blurs reality. Still, as a former journalist with a basic understanding of police work, I did my best to keep it as real as possible at every turn.

In bringing this story to you, I also benefited from the hard work and support of so many other people.

My thanks to my wife, Barbara, and to Wendy Dudley, for their invaluable help improving the tale.

Thanks to Laura and Michael.

Thanks to fellow author James L'Etoile, who so graciously provided a key piece of advice.

My thanks to the super-brilliant Amy Moore-Benson and the team at Meridian Artists; to the extraordinary Lorella Belli and the outstanding team at LBLA in London; to the talented Leah Mol; and to the incredible editorial, marketing, sales and PR teams at Harlequin, MIRA Books and HarperCollins.

It seems like the idea for this story and its evolution into the book you hold in your hands came so long ago. While the bulk of the tale was drafted at my desk at home, the story never left me. In the months it took to complete, parts of it were written in New York City, Toronto, Halifax and Minneapolis, on trains, in airports and hotels.

This brings me to what I believe is the most critical part of the entire enterprise: you, the reader. Those of you familiar with my stories are aware that this aspect has become something of a credo for me, one that bears repeating with each book.

Thank you for your time, for without you, the story remains an untold tale. Thank you for setting your life on pause and taking the journey. I deeply appreciate my audience around the world and those who've been with me since the beginning who keep in touch. Thank you all for your kind words. I hope you enjoyed the ride and will check out my earlier books while watching for new ones.

Feel free to send me a note. I enjoy hearing from you. I have been known to participate in book club discussions of my books via Zoom. While it may take some time, I try to respond to all messages.

Rick Mofina

www.RickMofina.com
www.Instagram.com/RickMofina
www.Twitter.com/RickMofina
www.Facebook.com/RickMofina